PENGUIN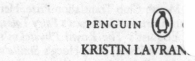

KRISTIN LAVRAN...

I: THE WREATH

SIGRID UNDSET (1882–1949) was born in Denmark, the eldest daughter of a Norwegian father and a Danish mother, and moved with her family to Oslo two years later. She published her first novel, *Fru Marta Oulie (Mrs. Marta Oulie)* in 1907 and her second, *Den lykkelige alder (The Happy Age)*, in 1908. The following year she published her first work set in the Middle Ages, *Fortællingen om Viga-Ljot og Vigdis* (later translated into English under the title *Gunnar's Daughter* and now available in Penguin Classics). More novels and stories followed, including *Jenny* (1911, first translated 1920), *Fattige skaebner(Fates of the Poor*, 1912), *Vaaren (Spring*, 1914), *Splinten av troldspeilet* (translated in part as *Images in a Mirror*, 1917), and *De kloge jomfruer (The Wise Virgins*, 1918). In 1920 Undset published the first volume of *Kristin Lavransdatter*, the medieval trilogy that would become her most famous work. *Kransen (The Wreath)* was followed by *Husfrue (The Wife)* in 1921 and *Korset (The Cross)* in 1922. Beginning in 1925 she published the four-volume *Olav Audunssøn i Hestviken* (translated into English under the title *The Master of Hestviken)*, also set in the Middle Ages. In 1928 Sigrid Undset won the Nobel Prize in Literature. During the 1930s she published several more novels, notably the autobiographical *Elleve aar* (translated as *The Longest Years*, 1934). She was also a prolific essayist on subjects ranging from Scandinavian history and literature to the Catholic Church (to which she became a convert in 1924) and politics. During the Nazi occupation of Norway, Undset lived as a refugee in New York City. She returned home in 1945 and lived in Lillehammer until her death in 1949.

TIINA NUNNALLY has translated all three volumes of *Kristin Lavransdatter* for Penguin Classics. She won the PEN/Book-of-the-Month Club Translation Prize for the third volume, *The Cross*. Her translations of the first and second volumes, *The Wreath* and *The Wife*, were finalists for the PEN Center USA West Translation Award, and *The Wife* was also a finalist for the PEN/Book-of-the-Month Club Translation Prize. Her other translations include Hans Christian Andersen's *Fairy Tales*, Undset's *Jenny*, Per Olov Enquist's *The Royal Physician's Visit* (Independent Foreign Fiction Prize); Peter Høeg's *Smilla's Sense of Snow* (Lewis Galantière Prize given by the American Translators Association); Jens Peter Jacobsen's *Niels Lyhne* (PEN Center USA West Translation Award); and Tove Ditlevsen's *Early Spring* (American-Scandinavian Foundation Translation Prize). Also the author of three novels, *Maija*, *Runemaker*, and *Fate of Ravens*, Nunnally holds an M.A. in Scandinavian Studies from the University of Wisconsin-Madison. She lives in Albuquerque, New Mexico.

To access Great Books Foundation Discussion Guides online, visit our Web site at www.penguin.com or the foundation Web site at www.greatbooks.org.

KRISTIN LAVRANSDATTER

I: THE WREATH

SIGRID UNDSET

TRANSLATED,
WITH AN INTRODUCTION AND NOTES,
BY TIINA NUNNALLY

PENGUIN BOOKS

PENGUIN BOOKS

Published by the Penguin Group

Penguin Group (USA) Inc., 375 Hudson Street, New York, New York 10014, U.S.A.
Penguin Group (Canada), 90 Eglinton Avenue East, Suite 700, Toronto, Ontario,
  Canada M4P 2Y3 (a division of Pearson Penguin Canada Inc.)
Penguin Books Ltd, 80 Strand, London WC2R 0RL, England
Penguin Ireland, 25 St Stephen's Green, Dublin 2, Ireland
  (a division of Penguin Books Ltd)
Penguin Group (Australia), 250 Camberwell Road, Camberwell, Victoria 3124,
  Australia (a division of Pearson Australia Group Pty Ltd)
Penguin Books India Pvt Ltd, 11 Community Centre, Panchsheel Park,
  New Delhi – 110 017, India
Penguin Group (NZ), 67 Apollo Drive, Rosedale, North Shore 0632,
  New Zealand (a division of Pearson New Zealand Ltd)
Penguin Books (South Africa) (Pty) Ltd, 24 Sturdee Avenue, Rosebank,
  Johannesburg 2196, South Africa

Penguin Books Ltd, Registered Offices: 80 Strand, London WC2R 0RL, England

First published in Penguin Books 1997

Originally published in Norwegian as *Kransen* by
H. Aschehoug & Company, Oslo, 1920.

LIBRARY OF CONGRESS CATALOGING-IN-PUBLICATION DATA
Undset, Sigrid, 1882–1949.
    [Kransen. English]
    The wreath / Sigrid Undset ; translated with an
introduction and notes by Tiina Nunnally.
        p.   cm. — (Penguin twentieth-century classics)
(Kristin Lavransdatter ; 1)
    ISBN 978-0-14-118041-0
    I. Nunnally, Tiina, 1952–   II. Title.   III. Series.
IV. Series: Undset, Sigrid, 1882–1949.   Kristin
Lavransdatter (Penguin Books). English ; 1.
PT8950.U5K6513   1997
839.8'2372—dc21   97-18912

Printed in the United States of America
Set in Sabon
Map by Virginia Norey

TRANSLATOR'S
ACKNOWLEDGMENTS

I am grateful to many people for their support of this translation. Special thanks go to Kristin Brudevoll and the Norwegian Literature Abroad office in Oslo for years of steadfast friendship and assistance. Thanks also to Sverre Mørkhagen for answering many of my questions in his excellent companion work, *Kristins verden*, which explains the historical background of Undset's novel. I am most grateful to Candace Robb for reading the manuscript with such care and offering me her expertise on many aspects of the medieval period. I would like to thank Christine Ingebritsen and Katherine Hanson for their sound advice and encouragement. And I am deeply indebted to Steven T. Murray for his linguistic fine-tuning of the translation and for his gift of hearing the music of the words, in both Norwegian and English. Finally, I thank my editor, Caroline White, for her fine collaboration, and Penguin Books for deciding that the time was ripe for a new English translation of Sigrid Undset's epic novel.

CONTENTS

INTRODUCTION

> If you peel away the layer of ideas and conceptions that
> are particular to your own time period, then you can step
> right into the Middle Ages and see life from the medieval
> point of view—and it will coincide with your own view.
> And if you try to reproduce precisely what you have seen,
> the narrative form will follow automatically. Then you will
> write as a contemporary. It is only possible to write novels
> from your own time.
>
> —Sigrid Undset

Sigrid Undset clearly perceived the Middle Ages as her "own time."
It was a period of Norwegian history that largely mirrored her own
worldview, combining a strong sense of loyalty to family and community with a foundation in the teachings of the Catholic Church.
She set her most famous works in the Middle Ages, immersing
herself in the legal, religious, and historical writings of the time to
create astoundingly authentic and compelling portraits of Norwegian life. And yet she was very nearly dissuaded from writing any
kind of historical novel at all.

Undset's interest in the past was solidly established during her
childhood. She was born in Denmark in 1882, the eldest daughter
of Ingvald Undset, a respected Norwegian archaeologist from
Trondheim who had written an influential book on the Iron Age.
Sigrid's mother was Charlotte Gyth Undset, an educated woman
from a distinguished Danish family in Kalundborg, who assisted
her husband in his work by acting as his secretary and illustrator.
When Sigrid was two, her family moved to Oslo, where her father
took a position with the antiquities department at the university.

Sigrid spent her early years surrounded by the artifacts and
books of her father's profession. She was allowed to handle and
examine ancient swords, jewelry, and other relics belonging to the
museum where he worked. Her father also took her to visit the

cathedral in Trondheim (formerly Nidaros, the center of ecclesiastical power in Norway during the Middle Ages), which had in-
spired his own choice of occupation. Most important of all, Sigrid
was introduced to the dramatic and stirring tales of the Icelandic
sagas. When she was ten she discovered *Njal's Saga*, which decades
later she would recall as the "most important turning point in my
life."

In 1893, Ingvald Undset's precarious health finally failed, and
Sigrid's beloved father died at the age of forty. His widow was left
with three young daughters to support on an annual state pension
of 800 kroner, a small sum even at that time. To make ends meet,
the family moved to a smaller apartment, and Charlotte Undset
was forced to sell some of their furniture, as well as her husband's
large collection of books and antiquities. Years later, Sigrid, by
then a famous author with a steady income from her writing,
searched for and bought back as many of her father's books as she
could find. And she would one day pay the greatest tribute to her
father by incarnating him in one of her noblest characters, Lavrans
Bjørgulfsøn.

In spite of the family's difficult circumstances, Charlotte Undset
decided not to seek refuge with her relatives in Denmark; she knew
that her husband wanted his children to grow up Norwegian. This
proved to be a momentous decision for her eldest daughter. The
tumultuous history and rugged, mountainous terrain of Norway—
quite different from the flat, rolling landscape of Denmark—would
play an important role in Sigrid Undset's writing.

Sigrid and her sisters were offered free tuition at the highly re-
garded and politically liberal school run by Ragna Nielsen, one of
the founders of the Norwegian Women's Union and a staunch sup-
porter of the suffragist movement. In spite of the high quality of
instruction and her own obvious intellectual abilities, Sigrid found
school dull, and she ended her formal education when she passed
the middle-level exam. She then struggled through a secretarial
training program. At the age of seventeen she went to work for
the Wisbech Electrical Company, a subsidiary of a German firm,
the Allgemeine Elektrizitäts Gesellschaft. She worked nine-hour
days for a starting salary of 30 kroner a month and stayed in that
job for ten years.

It was at this time that Sigrid Undset first realized she wanted to be a serious writer. She had written puppet plays and little stories for her sisters, but she had a talent for drawing and she had always dreamed of being a painter, not a writer. Now she put her sketchbook aside as she read Chaucer and Shakespeare, Keats and Shelley, the sagas, and legends of the saints. She studied Latin and Greek late into the night. In a letter to her Swedish pen pal Dea (Andrea Hedberg), Sigrid wrote that she had discovered in herself an "artist's temperament," which she found somewhat unsettling:

> There's nothing I have greater contempt for than "artiness," and especially for those useless creatures who possess the type of artistic temperament that produces nothing, who are artists for their own sakes, which means that they possess only the "introspective" characteristics of the artistic temperament: egotism, a lack of ability and desire to work, a lack of interest in and love for others, as well as a wild imagination, so they dream away their time . . . [But] I can no longer rein in my desire to dream, nor do I have any wish to do so. I spend all of my spare time wandering along the country roads and playing with my fantasies, scraps of made-up novels, images from my dreams, and memories of landscapes from past summers.

In 1900 she began work on a story set in 1340 about Svend Trøst and Agnete, historical figures she first encountered in the work of the Danish author Bernhard Severin Ingemann. Two years later, she had abandoned this story but was writing another, set in the late 14th century in Kalundborg.

In 1904 Sigrid Undset took her completed manuscript to Gyldendal Publishing Company in Copenhagen, and a month later she received the fateful reply from editor Peter Nansen: "Don't attempt any more historical novels. You have no talent for it. But you might try writing something modern. You never know."

This assessment was a crushing blow to the young writer, but it also provoked the stubborn side of her nature. She accepted his words as a challenge; she did not give up. Continuing with her tedious secretarial duties at the electrical company, Sigrid Undset used her free hours to work on a "modern" novel about marital infidelity, entitled *Fru Marta Oulie*, which she finished in 1906. This time she submitted her manuscript to the Norwegian publishing house of H. Aschehoug & Co. Their reader advised against publication because there were already plenty of such "everyday" stories in print. Sigrid's sister then sent the manuscript to the well-known Norwegian playwright Gunnar Heiberg, who responded enthusiastically. With his intercession, Undset's novel was finally published—by Aschehoug—to good reviews, and it sold unexpectedly well. The career of a new author was launched.

To celebrate the publication of her daughter's first novel, Charlotte Undset gave Sigrid a volume of poetry by the great nineteenth-century Danish writer Steen Steensen Blicher inscribed with the admonition: "You as a writer must always look up to Blicher as your mentor, be as incorruptibly honest as he is, look life fearlessly in the eye, see it as it is, and truthfully tell what you see."

In 1908, Undset's second book appeared: *Den lykkelige alder* (*The Happy Age*), which included two stories about young office workers like herself. This book met with even greater success and won the author a solid place in contemporary Norwegian literature. She could finally quit her job at the electrical company and turn her full attention to writing.

Then, five years after editor Nansen had proclaimed her unsuitable as an author of historical works, Undset published the short novel *Fortællingen om Viga-Ljot og Vigdis* (translated into English under the title *Gunnar's Daughter*). With this sagalike narrative she returned to the period that compelled her most: the Middle Ages. And yet it would be another decade before she was able to make full use of her detailed knowledge of the era in a passionate story of love, loyalty, and betrayal: *Kransen* (*The Wreath*), the first volume of *Kristin Lavransdatter*. Before Sigrid Undset could even begin work on her epic masterpiece, her life underwent dramatic changes.

In 1909, while traveling in Italy on a grant, she met and fell in love with Anders Castus Svarstad, a Norwegian painter thirteen years her senior. Coincidentally, as a nineteen-year-old office worker, Sigrid had bought one of his paintings from a gallery in Oslo. Svarstad was a married man with three children, and it would take him more than two years to disentangle himself from his first wife and get a divorce. In June 1912, Anders Svarstad and Sigrid Undset were finally married at the Norwegian consulate in Antwerp, Belgium.

Over the next ten years, the marriage began to founder. The couple had three children of their own, and Sigrid was determined to look after her stepchildren as well. But the combined incomes of a painter and a writer were not enough to support such a large family, and Svarstad spent most of his time in his Oslo studio, leaving the household concerns to his wife. It also soon became clear that their daughter, Maren Charlotte (called Mosse), suffered from severe mental retardation. Sigrid tried valiantly to hold the marriage together, but in the end she had to admit defeat. The financial and psychological strain became too much, and she eventually moved to Lillehammer with her daughter and two sons. Over the years, her husband and stepchildren were frequent visitors to her home, which she named Bjerkebæk, but they would never live together as a family again. When Undset converted to Catholicism in 1924, the marriage was annulled, on the grounds that the Church did not recognize Svarstad's divorce from his first wife.

As one of Undset's biographers, Borghild Krane, surmises, "Perhaps this marriage illustrates the difficulties that arise when two people marry who both have such a strong and imperative need for artistic development that for each of them it becomes an activity so essential to life that it cannot be stopped—even if it takes them away from each other."

During all the years of her marital struggles, Sigrid Undset continued to write, maintaining the habit she had adopted during her office days of staying up late into the night. She wrote book reviews and newspaper articles. She also published two more modern novels, as well as a collection of essays on feminist issues—a concern which would claim her lifelong interest, although her written positions were often in direct contradiction to her own life choices. In 1915 she published *Fortællinger om Kong Arthur og ridderne av det runde bord (Tales of King Arthur and the Knights of the Round Table)*. She immersed herself in the works of Shakespeare, Thackeray, Thomas More, and Dickens. She continued her studies of the lives of the saints and started writing essays on religious topics. The growing income from her books allowed Undset to hire two women to help her with the children and household. And at last she began work on a story that she had been thinking about for a long time, the life story of a willful young woman named Kristin Lavransdatter.

The early fourteenth century, which Sigrid Undset chose for her narrative, was a time of transition in Norway, when the Church and the Crown were solidifying their power. It was a time with few major historical figures, which allowed Undset more freedom to create her own. It was also a time of relative calm in Norway—a period between wars and before the onset of the Black Death in 1349, which would wipe out at least half the population of the country (and which plays a significant part in the third volume of Undset's story).

By this time the Catholic Church had become firmly established in Norway, and it played an increasingly powerful role in daily life. Like the majority of her peers, Sigrid Undset had been brought up Lutheran, although she received little formal religious instruction from her parents. And yet from a young age she had been drawn to the teachings of the Catholic Church, both intellectually and spiritually. In *Kristin Lavransdatter* she was able to explore her religious ideas and examine how the Catholic faith directly affected the lives of ordinary individuals.

In the early fourteenth century the entire population of Norway numbered less than 500,000 and the country was almost completely rural, with few outside influences reaching the villages in remote mountain valleys. Daily life revolved not only around religious rituals and obligations, but around the family and extended kin group. The rules for leading a good life were clearly delineated and solidly entrenched. Those who strayed or disobeyed were outlawed or exiled from the community. To lose the approval of the Church and your kinsmen was the worst imaginable fate; to be cast out was a punishment just short of death.

This was the society that Undset chose for her story of an intelligent but headstrong young woman, properly brought up and fully aware of the expectations of her parents and kinsmen, a young woman well versed in the strictures of the Church. And yet

Kristin decides to defy both her parents and her priest for the sake of passion and love. She listens to her heart rather than to all those around her. Kristin's act of rebellion might be viewed as foolhardy or courageous, but in either case, she has to suffer the consequences of her actions. She must learn to take responsibility for her own fate.

Sigrid Undset later explained that Kristin's greatest sin is not the fact that she succumbs to her sexual desires and yields to the amorous demands of her impetuous suitor before they are properly married. Of much greater import is Kristin's decision to thwart her father's wishes, to deny the traditions of her ancestors, and to defy the Church; her worst sin is that of pride. The scholar Marlene Ciklamini notes that "in medieval times the most egregious sin was *superbia*, or pride, setting oneself up as the arbiter of things human and divine, or, to express it another way, loving oneself more than God." Kristin's constant struggle to integrate a sense of spiritual humility into her strong and passionate nature underlies much of the dramatic tension in all three volumes of the novel.

The Wreath was published in the fall of 1920, and the critics gave it their highest praise. Gunnar Heiberg, whose intervention had prompted the publication of Undset's first novel, compared *The Wreath* to the works of Homer, saying it demonstrated the same "power, clarity, and depth."

The novel quickly won acclaim in other countries as well. When it first appeared in English, the *Times* of London called Undset "a creator of characters on the grand scale." *The New York Times* pronounced the novel "a well-written, well-constructed, strong and dramatic romance, founded upon those emotions and impulses which belong not to any especial time or country, but to all humanity." And the critic Edwin Bjorkman wrote in *The New York Times Book Review* that Undset's "supreme achievement is in the appealing humanity and fallibility of her characters."

A second volume, *Husfrue* (*The Wife*), followed in 1921, and the final volume, *Korset* (*The Cross*), was published in 1922.

The success of her epic trilogy brought Sigrid Undset further financial security, for which she was grateful. In addition to receiving income from book royalties, she was awarded a lifetime annual author's stipend from the Norwegian government. Success also brought fame, however, and all the intrusions this entailed. Undset had always been an exceedingly private person who zealously sheltered her children and personal life from the public eye. She had little patience for journalists and seldom gave interviews. But she could also be extremely warmhearted and generous; she responded to all the letters sent to her, and she often sent money to the steady stream of desperate people begging for help from the famous author.

With the publication of Undset's second great medieval work in 1925 and 1927—a tetralogy entitled *Olav Audunssøn* (published in English as *The Master of Hestviken*)—her status as one of Norway's greatest writers was confirmed, and her place in world literature was unquestionably assured.

In 1928, Sigrid Undset was awarded the highest honor for her work, the Nobel Prize for Literature. It was given to her principally for "her powerful pictures of Northern life in medieval times." At the age of forty-six she was one of the youngest recipients, and she was only the third woman to be honored with the prize.

At the time of the award, *Kristin Lavransdatter* had been translated into many languages and was widely known around the world. In Germany alone, there were 250,000 copies in print.

According to all accounts, Undset took the news of her award with admirable calm, although she did buy herself an elegant new dress for the occasion. At the award ceremony in Stockholm, Pär Hallström, author and member of the Swedish Academy, gave the presentation speech. He praised Undset's early novels, in which she depicted modern women "sympathetically but with merciless truthfulness . . . and conveyed the evolution of their destinies with the most implacable logic." He then paid tribute to her brilliant recreation of medieval life in *Kristin Lavransdatter* and *The Master of Hestviken*, and to her profound insight into the "complex relations between men and women." Sigrid Undset graciously expressed her thanks for the honor but declined to make a speech, explaining that she was a writer, not a speaker.

The prize was then worth 156,000 kroner, and Undset gave it all away. Part of the money went to the scholarship fund of the Norwegian Writers Union, but the bulk of the award was divided up to establish two foundations. The first would provide support to Norwegian families with mentally retarded children who needed financial assistance to care for their children at home. This was something that Undset had dreamed of doing for many years, and the stipend was named the Maren Charlotte Undset Svarstad Grant, in honor of her daughter. The other foundation was established to provide financial aid to needy Catholic children in Norway who wanted to attend parochial schools.

Eleven years later, when the Soviets invaded Finland, Undset would sell her gold Nobel medallion for 25,000 kroner and give the money to the relief effort for Finnish children.

During the 1930s, Sigrid Undset's life was a whirlwind of literary activity. As a world-famous author, she was much in demand. She served two terms as president of the Norwegian Writers Union and attended an endless number of meetings and functions associated with this role. She continued to write articles and reviews, and she published four more novels, several collections of essays, and an autobiographical novel based on her childhood entitled *Elleve aar* (translated into English as *The Longest Years*).

At the same time, she continued to care for her daughter and manage the household in Lillehammer with the help of her longtime housekeeper. At Bjerkebæk, Undset always gained some measure of peace by escaping the demands of everyday life to work in her garden. Ever since she was a child, Undset had been an avid botanist. As an eighteen-year-old she described in a letter her love of nature as "that hypnotic immersion in the corolla of a rose when you have stared at it for so long that all outlines are erased and you become dizzy with crimson." She said that she longed to "disappear into nature so that you cease to feel or think, but with all your senses you greedily draw in the light and colors, the rustling of leaves and the trickling of underground streams, the sun and the shifting shadows—that is happiness, nirvana."

Undset's love of nature so permeated her world view that it became synonymous with the truth she sought to portray in her novels, the truth that her mother had enjoined her to write about. In a speech given during the 1940s she explained what she meant by a "true novel":

We often see the word "novel" defined as the opposite of
"facts." And of course those kinds of novels do exist. But even
those types of novels do not necessarily have to be the opposite
of "truth." Facts may be true, but they are not truths—just as
wooden crates or fence posts or doors or furniture are not
"wood" in the same way that a forest is, since it consists of
the living and growing material from which these things are
made. . . . The true novel, if you understand what I mean by
that term, must also make use of facts, but above all it must
be concerned with the truth that lies behind them—the wild
mountains that are the source of the "tame" cobblestones of
the pavement or the artistically hewn stones in a work of
sculpture; the living forest which provides timber for the saw-
mills and pulp for the billions of tons of paper which we use and
misuse. Then these facts will be of secondary importance to the
author . . . they are not original; they originate from something
else.

Sigrid Undset had a remarkable ability to see beyond the
"facts," to portray the lives of her characters in realistic fashion
and yet with great psychological insight. She herself said that "to
be a writer is to be able to live lives that are not one's own." In
Kristin Lavransdatter, the meticulously researched details of
medieval life provide a rich backdrop for the narrative. But for
modern readers, the power of the novel lies not so much in the
authenticity of detail as in the author's deep understanding of the
passions and torments of the human heart.

The last years of Undset's life were a testament to the courage
and strength of her own heart. In 1939, she lost both her mother
(who had been a vital presence in her life) and her daughter. Then
on April 20, 1940, the Germans began to advance north through
Norway, and Sigrid Undset had to flee, with barely enough time
to pack a suitcase.

Undset had long been an outspoken critic of Nazism, and her
books had been banned in Germany. She had offered aid to refu-
gees from Central Europe, and she had even taken in three Finnish
children, orphaned by the war. The Norwegian government feared

that she might be forced to use her considerable reputation for Nazi propaganda purposes. She was advised to leave the country at once.

After an arduous journey over the mountains and by sea, Undset finally reached Stockholm on May 11, and there she received the devastating news that her eldest son, Anders, had fallen in battle at Gausdal two weeks before. At the end of July she and her younger son, Hans, left Sweden and traveled overland through Russia and Siberia to Japan, where they boarded a ship for San Francisco.

For the next five years Sigrid Undset lived in a small apartment in Brooklyn, New York. During her years of exile she often traveled around the United States on long lecture tours, speaking about the current situation in Norway, as well as literary topics. She became friends with Willa Cather and Marjorie Kinnan Rawlings. She was a tireless promoter of Nordic literature and wrote countless articles for newspapers and magazines. She also published essays and children's stories in English.

By the time Undset finally returned to Norway in 1945, the long years of the war had taken a heavy toll on both her energy and her health. She had endured great personal losses, and her home in Lillehammer would never be the same. The Germans had occupied Bjerkebæk for several years, and what they didn't steal they chopped up for firewood, including her father's desk, at which she had written *Kristin Lavransdatter* and all her other novels. Although Undset continued to write and to plan literary projects, her artistic zeal and physical strength were spent.

In 1947, Sigrid Undset was awarded Norway's highest honor, the Grand Cross of the Order of Saint Olav. She was the first woman of nonroyal blood ever to be recognized in this manner. The honor was given for her "distinguished literary work and for her service to her country." Two years later, on June 10, 1949, she died.

Sigrid Undset's great gift as a writer might best be described in her own appraisal of Charlotte Brontë, whom she much admired:

[Her] sense of self is grounded in her awareness that her art is bitterly true, that her talent is merely the courage to look hon-

estly into her own heart. [She] wished to depict life and reality
the way they are—life and reality as they existed in her own
heart, in the limitless possibilities of her heart, in her dreams and
yearnings, in the mirages of hunger and thirst—and in all the
tiny gray-pebble days over which life flows.

Tiina Nunnally

Seattle
February 1997

SUGGESTIONS FOR

FURTHER READING

The following reference works were used as a basis for the Introduction and may provide the reader with additional information about the author's life and work. Unfortunately, there are few sources in English.

Bayerschmidt, Carl F. *Sigrid Undset*. New York: Twayne Publishers, 1970.

Blindheim, Charlotte. *Moster Sigrid: Et familieportrett av Sigrid Undset*. Oslo: H. Aschehoug & Co., 1982.

Ciklamini, Marlene. "Sigrid Undset," in *European Writers: The Twentieth Century*, vol. 9, ed. by George Stade. New York: Charles Scribner's Sons, 1989.

Daniloff, Jan Fr., ed. *Sigrid Undset: Artikler og essays om litteratur*. Oslo: H. Aschehoug & Co., 1986.

Krane, Borghild. *Sigrid Undset: Liv og meninger*. Oslo: Gyldendal Norsk Forlag, 1970.

Pulsiano, Phillip, ed. *Medieval Scandinavia: An Encyclopedia*. New York: Garland Publishing Co., 1993.

Wasson, Tyler, ed. *Nobel Prize Winners: An H. W. Wilson Biographical Dictionary*. New York: H. W. Wilson Co., 1987.

Winsnes, A. H., ed. *Sigrid Undset: Artikler og taler fra krigstiden*. Oslo: H. Aschehoug & Co., 1952.

Ørjasæter, Tordis. *Menneskenes hjerter: Sigrid Undset—en livshistorie*. Oslo: H. Aschehoug & Co., 1993.

A NOTE ON
THE TRANSLATION

This translation is based on the first edition of *Kransen*, which was published in Norwegian in 1920. I have retained the original spelling of Norwegian names, which means that the letter *v* is often used instead of *f* (as in Olav) and *aa* is used instead of *å* (as in Jørundgaard). The occasional use of the letter ö instead of ø in proper names is intentional—the former is used in Swedish names, the latter in Norwegian. The original Norwegian text contains thousands of dashes, which tend to impede rather than enhance the reading. In most cases I have chosen to replace the dashes with commas or semicolons, or, occasionally, to create separate sentences. I have also decided to keep the Norwegian masculine title "Herr" and the feminine title "Fru" rather than to translate them into the somewhat misleading English titles of "Sir" and "Lady." Only those men who are clearly identified in the story as knights are given "Sir" as their title. It should be noted that Norwegian surnames were derived from the father's given name, followed by either "-datter" or "-søn," depending on the gender of the child. For example, Kristin's mother is named Ragnfrid Ivarsdatter, while her mother's brother is named Trond Ivarsøn. They are also referred to as Gjeslings, since they are descendants of the Gjesling lineage.

Every attempt has been made to reproduce in English the clear style, natural dialogue, and passionate flow of the original Norwegian edition without imposing any unnecessary convolutions or archaisms.

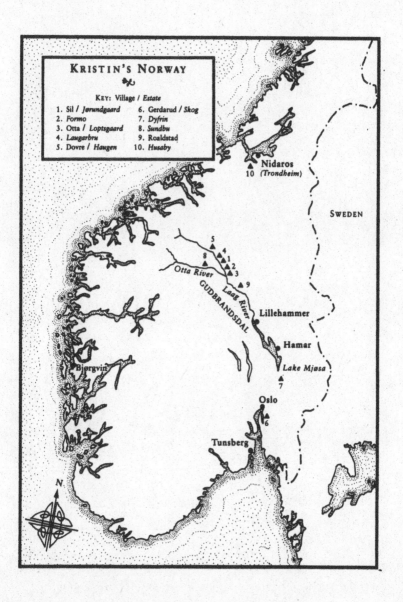

KRISTIN'S NORWAY

KEY: Village / Estate

1. Sil / Jørundgaard   6. Gerdarud / Skog
2. Formo   7. Dyfrin
3. Otta / Loptsgaard   8. Sundbu
4. Laugarbru   9. Roaldstad
5. Dovre / Haugen   10. Husaby

Nidaros
10 (Trondheim)

SWEDEN

5
4   1
8   2
Otta River   3
                9
Laag River
GUDBRANDSDAL   Lillehammer

Hamar
Lake Mjøsa
7

Bjørgvin

Oslo
6

Tunsberg

N

PART I

JØRUNDGAARD

CHAPTER 1

WHEN THE EARTHLY GOODS of Ivar Gjesling the Younger of Sundbu were divided up in the year 1306, his property at Sil was given to his daughter Ragnfrid and her husband Lavrans Bjørgulfsøn. Before that time they had lived at Skog, Lavrans's manor in Follo near Oslo, but now they moved to Jørundgaard, high on the open slope at Sil.

Lavrans belonged to a lineage that here in Norway was known as the sons of Lagmand. It originated in Sweden with a certain Laurentius Östgötelagman, who abducted the Earl of Bjelbo's sister, the maiden Bengta, from Vreta cloister and fled to Norway with her. Herr Laurentius served King Haakon the Old, and was much favored by him; the king bestowed on him the manor Skog. But after he had been in this country for eight years, he died of a lingering disease, and his widow, a daughter of the house of the Folkungs whom the people of Norway called a king's daughter, returned home to be reconciled with her kinsmen. She later married a rich man in another country. She and Herr Laurentius had had no children, and so Laurentius's brother Ketil inherited Skog. He was the grandfather of Lavrans Bjørgulfsøn.

Lavrans was married at a young age; he was only twenty-eight at the time he arrived at Sil, and three years younger than his wife. As a youth he had been one of the king's retainers and had benefited from a good upbringing; but after his marriage he lived quietly on his own estate, for Ragnfrid was rather moody and melancholy and did not thrive among people in the south. After she had had the misfortune to lose three small sons in the cradle, she became quite reclusive. Lavrans moved to Gudbrandsdal largely so that his wife might be closer to her kinsmen and friends. They had one child still living when they arrived there, a little maiden named Kristin.

3

But after they had settled in at Jørundgaard, they lived for the
most part just as quietly and kept much to themselves; Ragnfrid
did not seem overly fond of her kinsmen, since she only saw them
as often as she had to for the sake of propriety. This was partially
due to the fact that Lavrans and Ragnfrid were particularly pious
and God-fearing people, who faithfully went to church and were
glad to house God's servants and people traveling on church business or pilgrims journeying up the valley to Nidaros.¹ And they
showed the greatest respect to their parish priest, who was their
closest neighbor and lived at Romundgaard. But the other people
in the valley felt that God's kingdom had cost them dearly enough
in tithes, goods, and money already, so they thought it unnecessary
to attend to fasts and prayers so strictly or to take in priests and
monks unless there was a need for them.

Otherwise the people of Jørundgaard were greatly respected and
also well liked, especially Lavrans, because he was known as a
strong and courageous man, but a peaceful soul, honest and calm,
humble in conduct but courtly in bearing, a remarkably capable
farmer, and a great hunter. He hunted wolves and bears with particular ferocity, and all types of vermin. In only a few years he had
acquired a good deal of land, but he was a kind and helpful master
to his tenants.

Ragnfrid was seen so seldom that people soon stopped talking
about her altogether. When she first returned home to Gudbrandsdal, many were surprised, since they remembered her from the time
when she lived at Sundbu. She had never been beautiful, but in
those days she seemed gracious and happy; now she had lost her
looks so utterly that one might think she was ten years older than
her husband instead of three. People thought she took the deaths
of her children unreasonably hard, because in other ways she was
far better off than most women—she had great wealth and position and she got on well with her husband, as far as anyone could
tell. Lavrans did not take up with other women, he always asked
for her advice in all matters, and he never said an unkind word to
her, whether he was sober or drunk. And she was not so old that
she couldn't have many more children, if God would grant her
that.

They had some difficulty finding young people to serve at

Jørundgaard because the mistress was of such a mournful spirit and because they observed all of the fasts so strictly. But the servants lived well on the manor, and angry or chastising words were seldom heard. Both Lavrans and Ragnfrid took the lead in all work. The master also had a lively spirit in his own way, and he might join in a dance or start up singing when the young people frolicked on the church green on sleepless vigil nights.² But it was mostly older people who took employment at Jørundgaard; they found it to their liking and stayed for a long time.

One day when the child Kristin was seven years old, she was going to accompany her father up to their mountain pastures.

It was a beautiful morning in early summer. Kristin was standing in the loft where they slept in the summertime. She saw the sun shining outside, and she heard her father and his men talking down in the courtyard.³ She was so excited that she couldn't stand still while her mother dressed her; she jumped and leaped after she was helped into every garment. She had never before been up to the mountains, only across the gorge to Vaage, when she was allowed to go along to visit her mother's kinsmen at Sundbu, and into the nearby woods with her mother and the servants when they went out to pick berries, which Ragnfrid put in her weak ale. She also made a sour mash out of cowberries and cranberries, which she ate on bread instead of butter during Lent.

Ragnfrid coiled up Kristin's long golden hair and fastened it under her old blue cap. Then she kissed her daughter on the cheek, and Kristin ran down to her father. Lavrans was already sitting in the saddle; he lifted her up behind him, where he had folded his cape like a pillow on the horse's loin. There Kristin was allowed to sit astride and hold on to his belt. Then they called farewell to her mother, but she had come running down from the gallery with Kristin's hooded cloak; she handed it to Lavrans and told him to take good care of the child.

The sun was shining but it had rained hard during the night so the streams were splashing and singing everywhere on the hillsides, and wisps of fog drifted below the mountain slopes. But above the crests, white fair-weather clouds climbed into the blue sky, and Lavrans and his men said it was going to be a hot day later on.

Lavrans had four men with him, and they were all well armed because at that time there were all kinds of strange people in the mountains—although it seemed unlikely they would encounter any such people because there were so many in their group, and they were only going a short way into the mountains. Kristin liked all of the servants. Three of them were somewhat older men, but the fourth, Arne Gyrdsøn of Finsbrekken, was a half-grown boy and Kristin's best friend. He rode right behind Lavrans because he was supposed to tell her about everything they saw along the way as they passed.

They rode between the buildings of Romundgaard and exchanged greetings with Eirik the priest. He was standing outside scolding his daughter⁴—she ran the house for him—about a skein of newly dyed yarn that she had left hanging outdoors the day before; now it had been ruined by the rain.

On the hill across from the parsonage stood the church; it was not large but graceful, beautiful, well kept, and freshly tarred. Near the cross outside the cemetery gate, Lavrans and his men removed their hats and bowed their heads. Then Kristin's father turned around in his saddle, and he and Kristin waved to her mother. They could see her out on the green in front of the farm buildings back home; she waved to them with a corner of her linen veil.

Kristin was used to playing almost every day up here on the church hill and in the cemetery; but today she was going to travel so far that the child thought the familiar sight of her home and village⁵ looked completely new and strange. The clusters of buildings at Jørundgaard, in both the inner and outer courtyards, seemed to have grown smaller and grayer down there on the lowlands. The glittering river wound its way past into the distance, and the valley spread out before her, with wide green pastures and marshes at the bottom and farms with fields and meadows up along the hillsides beneath the precipitous gray mountains.

Kristin knew that Loptsgaard lay far below the place where the mountains joined and closed off the valley. That was where Sigurd and Jon lived, two old men with white beards; they always teased her and played with her whenever they came to Jørundgaard. She liked Jon because he carved the prettiest animals out of wood for her, and he had once given her a gold ring. But the last time he visited them, on Whitsunday, he had brought her a knight that was so beautifully carved and so exquisitely painted that Kristin thought she had never received a more marvelous gift. She insisted on taking the knight to bed with her every single night, but in the morning when she woke up he would be standing on the step in front of the bed where she slept with her parents. Her father told her that the knight got up at the first crow of the cock, but Kristin knew that her mother took him away after she fell asleep. She had heard her mother say that he would be so hard and uncomfortable if they rolled on top of him during the night.

Kristin was afraid of Sigurd of Loptsgaard, and she didn't like it when he took her on his knee, because he was in the habit of saying that when she grew up, he would sleep in her arms. He had outlived two wives and said he would no doubt outlive the third as well; so Kristin could be the fourth. But when she started to cry, Lavrans would laugh and say that he didn't think Margit was about to give up the ghost anytime soon, but if things did go badly and Sigurd came courting, he would be refused—Kristin needn't worry about that.

A large boulder lay near the road, about the distance of an arrow shot north of the church, and around it there was a dense grove of birch and aspen. That's where they played church, and Tomas, the youngest grandson of Eirik the priest, would stand up and say mass like his grandfather, sprinkling holy water and performing baptisms when there was rainwater in the hollows of the rock. But one day the previous fall, things had gone awry. First Tomas had married Kristin and Arne—Arne was still so young that he sometimes stayed behind with the children and played with them when he could. Then Arne caught a piglet that was wandering about and they carried it off to be baptized. Tomas anointed it with mud, dipped it into a hole filled with water and, mimicking his grandfather, said the mass in Latin and scolded them for their scanty offerings. That made the children laugh because they had heard the grown-ups talking about Eirik's excessive greed. And the more they laughed, the more inventive Tomas became. Then he said that this child had been conceived during Lent, and they would have to atone before the priest and the church for their sin. The older boys laughed so hard that they howled, but Kristin was

so filled with shame that she was almost in tears as she stood there
with the piglet in her arms. And while this was going on, they were
unlucky enough that Eirik himself came riding past, on his way
home after visiting a sick parishioner. When he saw what the children were up to, he leaped from his horse and handed the holy
vessel abruptly to Bentein, his oldest grandson, who was with him.
Bentein almost dropped the silver dove containing the Holy Host
on the ground. The priest rushed in among the children and
thrashed as many as he could grab. Kristin dropped the piglet, and
it ran down the road squealing as it dragged the christening gown
behind, making the priest's horses rear up in terror. The priest also
slapped Kristin, who fell, and then he kicked her so hard that her
hip hurt for days afterward. When Lavrans heard of this, he felt
that Eirik had been too harsh toward Kristin, since she was so
young. He said that he would speak to the priest about it, but
Ragnfrid begged him not to do so, because the child had received
no more than she deserved by taking part in such a blasphemous
game. So Lavrans said nothing more about the matter, but he gave
Arne the worst beating he had ever received.

That's why, as they rode past the boulder, Arne plucked at Kristin's sleeve. He didn't dare say anything because of Lavrans, so he
grimaced, smiled, and slapped his backside. But Kristin bowed her
head in shame.

The road headed into dense forest. They rode in the shadow of
Hammer Ridge; the valley grew narrow and dark, and the roar of
the Laag River was stronger and rougher. When they caught a
glimpse of the river, it was flowing icy-green with white froth between steep walls of stone. The mountain was black with forest
on both sides of the valley; it was dark and close and rank in the
gorge, and the cold wind came in gusts. They rode over the foot-
bridge across Rost Creek, and soon they saw the bridge over the
river down in the valley. In a pool just below the bridge there lived
a river sprite.[6] Arne wanted to tell Kristin about it, but Lavrans
sternly forbade the boy to speak of such things out there in the
forest. And when they reached the bridge, he jumped down from
his horse and led it across by the bridle as he held his other arm
around the child's waist.

On the other side of the river a bridle path led straight up into the heights, so the men got down from their horses and walked, but Lavrans lifted Kristin forward into his saddle so she could hold on to the saddlebow, and then she was allowed to ride Guldsvein alone.

More gray crests and distant blue peaks striped with snow rose up beyond the mountainsides as they climbed higher, and now Kristin could glimpse through the trees the village north of the gorge. Arne pointed and told her the names of the farms that they could see.

High up on the grassy slope they came to a small hut. They stopped near the split-rail fence. Lavrans shouted and his voice echoed again and again among the cliffs. Two men came running down from the small patch of pasture. They were the sons of the house. They were skillful tar-burners,[7] and Lavrans wanted to hire them to do some tar distilling for him. Their mother followed with a large basin of cold cellar milk, for it was a hot day, as the men had expected it would be.

"I see you have your daughter with you," she said after she had greeted them. "I thought I'd have a look at her. You must take off her cap. They say she has such fair hair."

Lavrans did as the woman asked, and Kristin's hair fell over her shoulders all the way to the saddle. It was thick and golden, like ripe wheat.

Isrid, the woman, touched her hair and said, "Now I see that the rumors did not exaggerate about your little maiden. She's a lily, and she looks like the child of a knight. Gentle eyes she has as well—she takes after you and not the Gjeslings. May God grant you joy from her, Lavrans Bjørgulfsøn! And look how you ride Guldsvein, sitting as straight as a king's courtier," she teased, holding the basin as Kristin drank.

The child blushed with pleasure, for she knew that her father was considered the most handsome of men far and wide, and he looked like a knight as he stood there among his servants, even though he was dressed more like a peasant, as was his custom at home. He was wearing a short tunic, quite wide, made of green-dyed homespun and open at the neck so his shirt was visible. He had on hose and shoes of undyed leather, and on his head he wore an old-fashioned wide-brimmed woolen hat. His only jewelry was

a polished silver buckle on his belt and a little filigree brooch at
the neck of his shirt. Part of a gold chain was also visible around
his neck. Lavrans always wore this chain, and from it hung a gold
cross, set with large rock crystals. The cross could be opened, and
inside was a scrap of shroud and hair from the Holy Fru Elin of
Skøvde, for the sons of Lagmand traced their lineage from one of
the daughters of that blessed woman. Whenever Lavrans was in
the forest or at work, he would put the cross inside his shirt against
his bare chest, so as not to lose it.

And yet in his rough homespun clothing he looked more high-
born than many a knight or king's retainer dressed in banquet
attire. He was a handsome figure, tall, broad-shouldered, and
narrow-hipped. His head was small and set attractively on his
neck, and he had pleasing, somewhat narrow facial features—suit-
ably full cheeks, a nicely rounded chin, and a well-shaped mouth.
His coloring was fair, with a fresh complexion, gray eyes, and
thick, straight, silky-gold hair.

He stood there talking to Isrid about her affairs, and he also
asked about Tordis, Isrid's kinswoman who was looking after
Jørundgaard's mountain pastures that summer. Tordis had recently
given birth, and Isrid was waiting for the chance to find safe pas-
sage through the forest so she could carry Tordis's little boy down
from the mountains to have him baptized. Lavrans said that she
could come along with them; he was going to return the next evening, and it would be safer and more reassuring for her to have so
many men to accompany her and the heathen child.

Isrid thanked him. "If the truth be told, this is exactly what I've
been waiting for. We all know, we poor folks who live up here in
the hills, that you will do us a favor if you can whenever you come
this way." She ran off to gather up her bundle and a cloak.

The fact of the matter was that Lavrans enjoyed being among
these humble people who lived in clearings and on leaseholdings
high up at the edge of the village. With them he was always happy
and full of banter. He talked to them about the movements of the
forest animals, about the reindeer on the high plateaus, and about
all the uncanny goings-on that occur in such places. He assisted
them in word and deed and offered a helping hand; he saw to their

sick cattle, helped them at the forge and with their carpentry work. On occasion he even applied his own powerful strength when they had to break up the worst rocks or roots. That's why these people always joyfully welcomed Lavrans Bjørgulfsøn and Guldsvein, the huge red stallion he rode. The horse was a beautiful animal with a glossy coat, white mane and tail, and shining eyes—known in the villages for his strength and fierceness. But toward Lavrans he was as gentle as a lamb. And Lavrans often said that he was as fond of the horse as of a younger brother.

The first thing Lavrans wanted to attend to was the beacon at Heimhaugen. During those difficult times of unrest a hundred years earlier or more, the landowners along the valleys had erected beacons in certain places on the mountainsides, much like the wood stacked in warning bonfires at the ports for warships along the coast. But these beacons in the valleys were not under military authority; the farmer guilds kept them in good repair, and the members took turns taking care of them.

When they came to the first mountain pasture, Lavrans released all the horses except the pack horse into the fenced meadow, and then they set off on a steep pathway upward. Before long there was a great distance between trees. Huge pines stood dead and white, like bones, next to marshy patches of land—and now Kristin saw bare gray mountain domes appearing in the sky all around. They climbed over long stretches of scree, and in places a creek ran across the path so that her father had to carry her. The wind was brisk and fresh up there, and the heath was black with berries, but Lavrans said that they had no time to stop and pick them. Arne leaped here and there, plucking off berries for her, and telling her which pastures they could see below in the forest—for there was forest over all of Høvringsvang at that time.

Now they were just below the last bare, rounded crest, and they could see the enormous heap of wood towering against the sky and the caretaker's hut in the shelter of a sheer cliff.

As they came over the ridge, the wind rushed toward them and whipped through their clothes—it seemed to Kristin that something alive which dwelled up there had come forward to greet them. The wind gusted and blew as she and Arne walked across the expanse of moss. The children sat down on the very end of a ledge, and Kristin stared with big eyes—never had she imagined that the world was so huge or so vast.

There were forest-clad mountain slopes below her in all directions; her valley was no more than a hollow between the enormous mountains, and the neighboring valleys were even smaller hollows; there were many of them, and yet there were fewer valleys than there were mountains. On all sides gray domes, golden-flamed with lichen, loomed above the carpet of forest; and far off in the distance, toward the horizon, stood blue peaks with white glints of snow, seeming to merge with the grayish-blue and dazzling white summer clouds. But to the northeast, close by—just beyond the pasture woods—stood a cluster of magnificent stone-blue mountains with streaks of new snow on their slopes. Kristin guessed that they belonged to the Raanekamp, the Boar Range, which she had heard about, for they truly did look like a group of mighty boars walking away with their backs turned to the village. And yet Arne said that it was half a day's ride to reach them.

Kristin had thought that if she came up over the crest of her home mountains, she would be able to look down on another village like their own, with farms and houses, and she had such a strange feeling when she saw what a great distance there was between places where people lived. She saw the little yellow and green flecks on the floor of the valley and the tiny glades with dots of houses in the mountain forests; she started to count them, but by the time she had reached three dozen, she could no longer keep track. And yet the marks of settlement were like nothing in that wilderness.

She knew that wolves and bears reigned in the forest, and under every rock lived trolls and goblins and elves, and she was suddenly afraid, for no one knew how many there were, but there were certainly many more of them than of Christian people. Then she called loudly for her father, but he didn't hear her because of the wind—he and his men were rolling great boulders down the rock face to use as supports for the timbers of the beacon.

But Isrid came over to the children and showed Kristin where the mountain Vaage Vestfjeld lay. And Arne pointed out Graafjeld, where the people of the villages captured reindeer in trenches and where the king's hawk hunters⁸ lived in stone huts. That was the sort of work that Arne wanted to do himself someday—but he also wanted to learn to train birds for the hunt—and he lifted his arms overhead, as if he were flinging a hawk into the air.

Isrid shook her head.

"It's a loathsome life, Arne Gyrdsøn. It would be a great sorrow for your mother if you became a hawk hunter, my boy. No man can make a living doing that unless he keeps company with the worst kind of people, and with those who are even worse."

Lavrans had come over to them and caught the last remark.

"Yes," he said, "there's probably more than one household out there that pays neither taxes nor tithes."

"I imagine you've seen one thing and another, haven't you, Lavrans?" Isrid hinted. "You who have journeyed so deep into the mountains."

"Ah, well," Lavrans said reluctantly, "that could be—but I don't think I should speak of such things. We must not begrudge those who have exhausted their peace in the village whatever peace they may find on the mountain, that's what I think. And yet I've seen yellow pastures and beautiful hay meadows in places where few people know that any valleys exist. And I've seen herds of cattle and flocks of sheep, but I don't know whether they belonged to people or to the others."

"That's right," said Isrid. "Bears and wolves are blamed for the loss of cattle up here in the mountain pastures, but there are much worse robbers on the slopes."

"You call them worse?" said Lavrans thoughtfully, stroking his daughter's cap. "In the mountains south of the Raanekamp I once saw three little boys, the oldest about Kristin's age, and they had blond hair and tunics made of hides. They bared their teeth at me like young wolves before they ran away and hid. It's not so surprising that the poor man they belonged to should be tempted to take a cow or two for himself."

"Well, wolves and bears all have young ones too," said Isrid peevishly. "And you don't choose to spare them, Lavrans. Neither the full-grown ones nor their young. And yet they have never been taught laws or Christianity, as have these evil-doers that you wish so well."

"Do you think I wish them well because I wish for them something slightly better than the worst?" said Lavrans with a faint smile. "But come along now, let's see what kind of food packets Ragnfrid has given us for today." He took Kristin's hand and led her away. He bent down to her and said softly, "I was thinking of your three baby brothers, little Kristin."

They peeked into the caretaker's hut, but it was stuffy and smelled of mold. Kristin took a quick look around, but there were only earthen benches along the walls, a hearthstone in the middle of the floor, barrels of tar, and bundles of resinous pine sticks and birchbark. Lavrans thought they should eat outdoors, and a little farther down a birch-covered slope they found a lovely green plateau.

They unloaded the pack horse and stretched out on the grass. And there was plenty of good food in Ragnfrid's bag—soft bread and thin *lefse*,[9] butter and cheese, pork and wind-dried reindeer meat, lard, boiled beef brisket, two large kegs of German ale, and a small jug of mead. They wasted no time in cutting up the meat and passing it around, while Halvdan, the oldest of the men, made a fire; it was more comforting to have heat than to be without it in the forest.

Isrid and Arne pulled up heather and gathered birch twigs and tossed them into the flames; the fire crackled as it tore the fresh foliage from the branches so that little white charred specks flew high up into the red mane of the blaze. Thick dark smoke swirled up toward the clear sky. Kristin sat and watched; the fire seemed happy to be outside and free to play. It was different; not like when it was confined to the hearth back home and had to slave to cook the food and light up the room for them.

She sat there leaning against her father, with one arm over his knee. He gave her as much as she wanted to eat from all the best portions and offered her all the ale she could drink, along with frequent sips of the mead.

"She'll be so tipsy she won't be able to walk down to the pasture," said Halvdan with a laugh, but Lavrans stroked her plump cheeks.

"There are enough of us here to carry her. It will do her good. Drink up, Arne. God's gifts will do you good, not harm, all you who are still growing. The ale will give you sweet red blood and make you sleep well. It won't arouse rage or foolishness."

And the men drank long and hard too. Isrid did not stint herself either, and soon their voices and the roar and hiss of the fire became a distant sound in Kristin's ears; she felt her head grow heavy. She also noticed that they tried to entice Lavrans to tell them about the strange things he had witnessed on his hunting expeditions. But he would say very little, and she thought this so comforting and reassuring. And she had eaten so much.

Her father was holding a chunk of soft barley bread. He shaped little pieces with his fingers so they looked like horses, and he broke off tiny scraps of meat and set them astride the bread horses. Then he made them ride down his thigh and into Kristin's mouth. Before long she was so tired that she could neither yawn nor chew—and then she toppled over onto the ground and fell asleep.

When she woke up, she was lying in the warmth and darkness of her father's arms—he had wrapped his cape around both of them. Kristin sat up, wiped the sweat from her face, and untied her cap so the air could dry her damp hair.

It must have been late in the day, for the sunshine was a gleaming yellow and the shadows had lengthened and now fell toward the southeast. There was no longer even a breath of wind, and mosquitoes and flies were buzzing and humming around the sleeping group of people. Kristin sat quite still, scratching the mosquito bites on her hands, and looked around. The mountain dome above them shone white with moss and gold from the lichen in the sunshine, and the beacon of weather-beaten timbers towered against the sky like the skeleton of some weird beast.

She started to feel uneasy—it was so odd to see all of them asleep in the bright, bare light of day. Whenever she woke up at home in the night, she would be lying snugly in the dark with her mother on one side and the tapestry that hung over the timbered wall on the other. Then she would know that the door and smoke vent of the room had been closed against the night and the weather outside; and she could hear the small noises of the sleeping people who lay safe and sound among the furs and pillows. But all of these bodies lying twisted and turned on the slope around the small

mound of white and black ashes might just as well have been dead;
some of them lay on their stomachs and some on their backs with
their knees pulled up, and the sounds they uttered frightened Kristin. Her father was snoring heavily, but when Halvdan drew in a
breath, a squeak and a whistle came from his nose. And Arne was
lying on his side with his face hidden in his arm and his glossy
light-brown hair spread out on the heath. He lay so still that Kristin was afraid he might be dead. She had to bend over and touch
him; then he stirred a bit in his sleep.

Suddenly it occurred to Kristin that they might have slept a
whole night and that it was now the next day. Then she grew so
alarmed that she shook her father, but he merely grunted and kept
on sleeping. Kristin felt heavy-headed herself, but she didn't dare
lie down to sleep. So she crept over to the fire and poked at it with
a stick—there were still some embers glowing. She added some
heather and small twigs, which she found close at hand, but she
didn't want to venture outside the circle of sleepers to find bigger
branches.

Suddenly there was a thundering and crashing from the field
nearby; Kristin's heart sank and she grew cold with fear. Then she
saw a red body through the trees, and Guldsvein emerged from the
alpine birches and stood there, looking at her with his clear, bright
eyes. She was so relieved that she jumped up and ran toward the
stallion. The brown horse that Arne had ridden was there too,
along with the pack horse. Then Kristin felt quite safe; she went
over and patted all three of them on the flank, but Guldsvein
bowed his head so she could reach up to stroke his cheeks and tug
on his golden-white forelock. He snuffled his soft muzzle in her
hands.

The horses ambled down the birch-covered slope, grazing, and
Kristin walked along with them, for she didn't think there was any
danger if she kept close to Guldsvein—he had chased off bears
before, after all. The blueberries grew so thick there, and the child
was thirsty and had a bad taste in her mouth. She had no desire
for any ale just then, but the sweet, juicy berries were as good as
wine. Over in the scree she saw raspberries too; then she took
Guldsvein by the mane and asked him nicely to come with her,
and the stallion obediently followed the little girl. As she moved

farther and farther down the slope, he would come to her whenever she called him, and the other horses followed Guldsvein.

Kristin heard a stream trickling and gurgling somewhere nearby. She walked toward the sound until she found it, and then she lay down on a slab of rock and washed her sweaty, mosquito-bitten face and hands. Beneath the rock slab the water stood motionless in a deep black pool; on the other side a sheer rock face rose up behind several slender birch trees and willow thickets. It made the finest mirror, and Kristin leaned over and looked at herself in the water. She wanted to see if what Isrid had said was true, that she resembled her father.

She smiled and nodded and bent forward until her hair met the blond hair framing the round young face with the big eyes that she saw in the water.

All around grew such a profusion of the finest pink tufts of flowers called valerian; they were much redder and more beautiful here next to the mountain stream than back home near the river. Then Kristin picked some blossoms and carefully bound them together with blades of grass until she had the loveliest, pinkest, and most tightly woven wreath. The child pressed it down on her hair and ran over to the pool to see how she looked, now that she was adorned like a grown-up maiden about to go off to a dance.

She bent over the water and saw her own dark image rise up from the depths and become clearer as it came closer. Then she saw in the mirror of the stream that someone was standing among the birches on the other side and leaning toward her. Abruptly she straightened up into a kneeling position and looked across the water. At first she thought she saw only the rock face and the trees clustered at its base. But suddenly she discerned a face among the leaves—there was a woman over there, with a pale face and flowing, flaxen hair. Her big light-gray eyes and her flaring, pale-pink nostrils reminded Kristin of Guldsvein's. She was wearing something shiny and leaf-green, and branches and twigs hid her figure up to her full breasts, which were covered with brooches and gleaming necklaces.

Kristin stared at the vision. Then the woman raised her hand and showed her a wreath of golden flowers and beckoned to her with it.

Behind her, Kristin heard Guldsvein whinny loudly with fear. She turned her head. The stallion reared up, gave a resounding shriek, and then whirled around and set off up the hillside, making the ground thunder. The other horses followed. They rushed straight up the scree, so that rocks plummeted down with a crash, and branches and roots snapped and cracked.

Then Kristin screamed as loud as she could. "Father!" she shrieked. "Father!" She sprang to her feet and ran up the slope after the horses, not daring to look back over her shoulder. She clambered up the scree, tripped on the hem of her dress, and slid down, then climbed up again, scrabbling onward with bleeding hands, crawling on scraped and bruised knees, calling to Guldsvein in between her shouts to her father—while the sweat poured out of her whole body, running like water into her eyes, and her heart pounded as if it would hammer a hole through her chest; sobs of terror rose in her throat.

"Oh, Father, Father!"

Then she heard his voice somewhere above her. She saw him coming in great leaps down the slope of the scree—the bright, sun-white scree. Alpine birches and aspens stood motionless along the slope, their leaves glittering with little glints of silver. The mountain meadow was so quiet and so bright, but her father came bounding toward her, calling her name, and Kristin sank down, realizing that now she was saved.

"Sancta Maria!" Lavrans knelt down next to his daughter and pulled her to him. He was pale and there was a strange look to his mouth that frightened Kristin even more; not until she saw his face did she realize the extent of her peril.

"Child, child . . ." He lifted up her bloody hands, looked at them, noticed the wreath on her bare head, and touched it. "What's this? How did you get here, little Kristin?"

"I followed Guldsvein," she sobbed against his chest. "I was so afraid because you were all asleep, but then Guldsvein came. And then there was someone who waved to me from down by the stream. . . ."

"Who waved? Was it a man?"

"No, it was a woman. She beckoned to me with a wreath of gold—I think it was a dwarf maiden, Father."

"Jesus Christus," said Lavrans softly, making the sign of the cross over the child and himself.

He helped her up the slope until they came to the grassy hillside; then he lifted her up and carried her. She clung to his neck and sobbed; she couldn't stop, no matter how much he hushed her.

Soon they reached the men and Isrid, who clasped her hands together when she heard what had happened.

"Oh, that must have been the elf maiden—I tell you, she must have wanted to lure this pretty child into the mountain."

"Be quiet," said Lavrans harshly. "We shouldn't have talked about such things the way we did here in the forest. You never know who's under the stones, listening to every word."

He pulled out the golden chain with the reliquary cross from inside his shirt and hung it around Kristin's neck, placing it against her bare skin.

"All of you must guard your tongues well," he told them. "For Ragnfrid must never hear that the child was exposed to such danger."

Then they caught the horses that had run into the woods and walked briskly down to the pasture enclosure where the other horses had been left. Everyone mounted their horses, and they rode over to the Jørundgaard pasture; it was not far off.

The sun was about to go down when they arrived. The cattle were in the pen, and Tordis and the herdsmen were doing the milking. Inside the hut, porridge had been prepared for them, for the pasture folk had seen them up at the beacon earlier in the day and they were expected.

Not until then did Kristin stop her weeping. She sat on her father's lap and ate porridge and thick cream from his spoon.

The next day Lavrans was to ride out to a lake farther up the mountain; that's where some of his herdsmen had taken the oxen. Kristin was supposed to have gone with him, but now he told her to stay at the hut. "And you, Tordis and Isrid, must see to it that the door is kept locked and the smoke vent closed until we come back, both for Kristin's sake and for the sake of the little unbaptized child in the cradle."

Tordis was so frightened that she didn't dare stay up there any longer with the baby; she had not yet been to church herself since giving birth. She wanted to leave at once and stay down in the village. Lavrans said he thought this reasonable; she could travel with them down the mountain the next evening. He thought he could get an older widow who was a servant at Jørundgaard to come up here in her place.

Tordis had spread sweet, fresh meadow grass under the hides on the bench; it smelled so strong and good, and Kristin was almost asleep as her father said the Lord's Prayer and *Ave Maria* over her.

"It's going to be a long time before I take you with me to the mountains again," said Lavrans, patting her cheek.

Kristin woke up with a start.

"Father, won't you let me go with you to the south in the fall, as you promised?"

"We'll have to see about that," said Lavrans, and then Kristin fell at once into a sweet sleep between the sheepskins.

EVERY SUMMER Lavrans Bjørgulfsøn would ride off to the south to see to his estate at Follo. These journeys of her father were like yearly mileposts in Kristin's life: those long weeks of his absence and then the great joy when he returned home with wonderful gifts—cloth from abroad for her bridal chest, figs, raisins, and gingerbread from Oslo—and many strange things to tell her.

But this year Kristin noticed that there was something out of the ordinary about her father's trip. It was postponed again and again. The old men from Loptsgaard came riding over unexpectedly and sat at the table with her father and mother, talking about inheritances and allodial property,[1] repurchasing rights, and the difficulties of running a manor from a distance; and about the episcopal seat and the king's castle in Oslo, which took so many of the workers away from the farms in the neighboring areas. The old men had no time to play with Kristin, and she was sent out to the cookhouse to the maids. Her uncle, Trond Ivarsøn of Sundbu, also came to visit them more often than usual—but he had never been in the habit of teasing or playing with Kristin.

Gradually she began to understand what it was all about. Ever since he had come to Sil, her father had sought to acquire land there in the village, and now Sir Andres Gudmundsøn had offered to exchange Formo, which was his mother's ancestral estate, for Skog, which lay closer to him, since he was one of the king's retainers and seldom came to the valley. Lavrans was loath to part with Skog, which was his ancestral farm; it had come into his family as a gift from the king. And yet the exchange would be advantageous to him in many ways. But Lavrans's brother, Aasmund Bjørgulfsøn, was also interested in acquiring Skog—he was now living in Hadeland, where he had a manor that he had obtained through marriage—and it was uncertain whether Aasmund would relinquish his ancestral property rights.

But one day Lavrans told Ragnfrid that this year he wanted to take Kristin along with him to Skog. She should at least see the estate where she had been born and the home of his forefathers if it was going to pass out of their possession. Ragnfrid thought this a reasonable request, even though she was a little uneasy about sending so young a child on such a long journey when she was not going along herself.

During the first days after Kristin had seen the elf maiden, she was so fearful that she kept close to her mother; she was even frightened by the mere sight of any of the servants who had been up on the mountain that day and who knew what had happened to her. She was glad that her father had forbidden anyone to mention it.

But after some time had passed, she thought that she would have liked to talk about it. In her own mind she told someone about it—she wasn't sure who—and the strange thing was that the more time that passed, the better she seemed to remember it, and the clearer her memory was of the fair woman.

But the strangest thing of all was that every time she thought about the elf maiden, she would feel such a yearning to travel to Skog, and she grew more and more afraid that her father would refuse to take her.

Finally one morning she woke up in the loft above the storeroom and saw that Old Gunhild and her mother were sitting on the doorstep looking through Lavrans's bundle of squirrel skins. Gunhild was a widow who went from farm to farm, sewing furs into capes and other garments. Kristin gathered from their conversation that now she was the one who was to have a new cloak, lined with squirrel skins and trimmed with marten. Then she realized that she was going to accompany her father, and she jumped out of bed with a cry of joy.

Her mother came over to her and caressed her cheek.

"Are you so happy then, my daughter, to be going so far away from me?"

                              *   *   *

Ragnfrid said the same thing on the morning of their departure from Jørundgaard. They were up before dawn; it was dark outside, and a thick mist was drifting between the buildings when Kristin peeked out the door at the weather. It billowed like gray smoke around the lanterns and in front of the open doorways. Servants ran back and forth from the stables to the storehouses, and the women came from the cookhouse with steaming pots of porridge and trenchers of boiled meat and pork. They would have a good meal of hearty food before they set off in the cold of the morning.

Indoors the leather bags with their traveling goods were opened up again, and forgotten items were placed inside. Ragnfrid reminded her husband of all the things he was supposed to tend to for her, and she talked about kinsmen and acquaintances who lived along the way—he must give a certain person her greetings, and he must not forget to ask after someone else she mentioned.

Kristin ran in and out, saying goodbye many times to everyone in the house, unable to sit still anywhere.

"Are you so happy then, Kristin, to be going so far away from me, and for such a long time?" asked her mother. Kristin felt both sad and crestfallen, and she wished that her mother had not said such a thing. But she replied as best she could.

"No, dear Mother, but I'm happy to be going with my father."

"Yes, I suppose you are," said Ragnfrid with a sigh. Then she kissed the child and fussed with the maiden's clothes a bit.

At last they sat in the saddles, everyone who was to accompany them on the journey. Kristin was riding Morvin, the horse that had once been her father's. He was old, wise, and steady. Ragnfrid handed the silver goblet with one last fortifying drink to her husband, placed a hand on her daughter's knee, and told her to remember everything that she had impressed upon her.

Then they rode out of the courtyard into the gray dawn. The fog hovered as white as milk over the village. But in a while it began to disperse and then the sun seeped through. Dripping with dew and green with the second crop of hay, the pastures shimmered in the white haze, along with pale stubble-fields and yellow trees and mountain ash with glittering red berries. The blue of the mountainsides was dimly visible, rising up out of the mist and steam. Then the fog broke and drifted in wisps among the grassy slopes, and they rode down through the valley in the most glorious sunshine—Kristin foremost in the group, at her father's side.

They arrived in Hamar on a dark and rainy evening. Kristin was sitting in front on her father's saddle, for she was so tired that everything swam before her eyes—the lake gleaming palely off to the right, the dark trees dripping moisture on them as they rode underneath, and the somber black clusters of buildings in the colorless, wet fields along the road.

She had stopped counting the days. It seemed to her that she had been on this long journey forever. They had visited family and friends who lived along the valley. She had gotten to know children on the large manors, she had played in unfamiliar houses and barns and courtyards, and she had worn her red dress with the silk sleeves many times. They had rested along the side of the road in the daytime when it was good weather. Arne had gathered nuts for her, and after their meals she had been allowed to sleep on top of the leather bags containing their clothes. At one estate they had been given silk-covered pillows in their beds. On another night they had slept in a roadside hostel, and whenever Kristin woke up she could hear a woman weeping softly and full of despair in one of the other beds. But every night she had slept snugly against her father's broad, warm back.

Kristin woke up with a start. She didn't know where she was, but the odd ringing and droning sound she had heard in her dreams continued. She was lying alone in a bed, and in the room where it stood, a fire was burning in the hearth.

She called to her father, and he rose from the hearth where he was sitting and came over to her, accompanied by a heavyset woman.

"Where are we?" she asked.

Lavrans laughed and said, "We're in Hamar now, and this is Margret, Shoemaker Fartein's wife. You must greet her nicely, for you were asleep when we arrived. But now Margret will help you get dressed."

"Is it morning?" asked Kristin. "I thought you would be coming to bed now. Can't you help me instead?" she begged, but Lavrans replied rather sternly that she should thank Margret for her willingness to help.

"And look at the present she has for you!"

It was a pair of red shoes with silk straps. The woman smiled at Kristin's joyful face and then helped her put on her shift and stockings in bed so that she wouldn't have to step barefoot onto the dirt floor.

"What's making that sound?" asked Kristin. "Like a church bell, but so many of them."

"Those are our bells," laughed Margret. "Haven't you heard about the great cathedral here in town? That's where you're going now. That's where the big bell is ringing. And bells are ringing at the cloister and the Church of the Cross too."

Margret spread a thick layer of butter on Kristin's bread and put honey in her milk so that the food would be more filling—she had so little time to eat.

Outside it was still dark and frost had set in. The mist was so cold that it bit into her skin. The footpaths made by people and cattle and horses were as hard as cast iron, so that Kristin's feet hurt in her thin new shoes. In one place, she stepped through the ice into a rut in the middle of the narrow street, which made her legs wet and cold. Then Lavrans lifted her up on his back and carried her.

She peered into the darkness, but there was little she could see of the town—she glimpsed the black gables of houses and trees outlined against the gray sky. Then they reached a small meadow that glittered with rime, and on the other side of the meadow she could make out a pale gray building as huge as a mountain. There were large stone buildings surrounding it, and here and there light shone through peepholes in the wall. The bells, which had been silent for a while, started ringing again, and now the sound was so powerful that it made icy shivers run down her spine.

It was like entering the mountain, thought Kristin as they stepped inside the vestibule of the church; they were met by darkness and cold. They went through a doorway, and there they en-

countered the chill smell of old incense and candles. Kristin was in
a dark and vast room with a high ceiling. Her eyes couldn't pen-
etrate the darkness, neither overhead nor to the sides, but a light
was burning on an altar far in front of them. A priest was standing
there, and the echo of his voice crept oddly around the room, like
puffs of air and whispers. Lavrans crossed himself and his child
with holy water, and then walked forward. Even though he stepped
cautiously, his spurs rang loudly against the stone floor. They
passed giant pillars, and looking between the pillars was like peer-
ing into coal-black holes.

Up front near the altar Lavrans knelt down, and Kristin knelt
at his side. Her eyes began adjusting to the dark. Gold and silver
gleamed from altars between the pillars, but on the altar before
them, candles were glowing in gilded candlesticks, and the holy
vessels shone, as did the great, magnificent paintings behind. Kristin again thought of the mountain—this is the way she had imagined it must be inside, so much splendor, but perhaps even more
light. And the dwarf maiden's face appeared before her. But then
she raised her eyes and saw above the painting the figure of Christ
himself, huge and stern, lifted high up on the cross. She was frightened. He didn't look gentle and sad, as he did back home in their
own warm, brown-timbered church, where he hung heavily from
his arms, his feet and hands pierced through, and his blood-
spattered head bowed beneath the crown of thorns. Here he stood
on a step, his arms rigidly outstretched and his head erect; his hair
was gleaming gold and adorned with a golden crown; his face was
lifted upward, with a harsh expression.

Then Kristin tried to follow the priest's words as he prayed and
sang, but his speech was so rapid and indistinct. At home she was
able to distinguish each word, for Sira Eirik had the clearest voice,
and he had taught her what the holy words meant in Norwegian
so that she could better keep her thoughts on God when she was
in church.

But she couldn't do that here, for she was constantly noticing
things in the dark. There were windows high up on the wall, and
they began to grow lighter with the day. And near the place where
they were kneeling, a strange gallowslike structure of wood had
been raised; beyond it lay light-colored blocks of stone, and

troughs and tools lay there too. Then she could hear that people had arrived and were padding around in there. Her eyes fell once more on the stern Lord Jesus on the wall, and she tried to keep her thoughts on the service. The icy cold of the stone floor made her legs stiff all the way up to her hips, and her knees ached. Finally everything began to swirl around her, because she was so tired.

Then her father stood up. The service was over. The priest came forward to greet her father. While they talked, Kristin sat down on a step because she saw the altar boy do the same. He yawned, and that made her yawn too. When he noticed that she was looking at him, he stuck his tongue in his cheek and crossed his eyes at her. Then he pulled out a pouch from under his clothing and dumped out the contents onto the stone floor: fish hooks, lumps of lead, leather straps, and a pair of dice; and the whole time he made faces at Kristin. She was quite astonished.

Then the priest and Lavrans looked at the children. The priest laughed and told the boy that he should go off to school, but Lavrans frowned and took Kristin by the hand.

It was starting to get lighter inside the church. Sleepily, Kristin clung to Lavrans's hand while he and the priest walked under the wooden scaffold, talking about Bishop Ingjald's construction work.

They wandered through the entire church, and at last they came out into the vestibule. From there a stone stairway led up into the west tower. Kristin trudged wearily up the stairs. The priest opened a door to a beautiful side chapel, but then Lavrans told Kristin to sit down outside on the steps and wait while he went in to make his confession. Afterward she could come in to kiss the shrine of Saint Thomas.

At that moment an old monk wearing an ash-brown cowl came out of the chapel. He paused for a minute, smiled at the child, and pulled out some sacking and homespun rags that had been stuffed into a hole in the wall. He spread them out on the landing.

"Sit down here; then you won't be so cold," he said, and continued on down the stairs in his bare feet.

Kristin was asleep when Father Martein, as the priest was called, came out to get her. From the church rose the loveliest song, and

inside the chapel, candles burned on the altar. The priest gestured
for Kristin to kneel beside her father, and then he took down a
little golden reliquary that stood above the altar. He whispered to
her that inside was a fragment of Saint Thomas of Canterbury's
bloody clothing, and he pointed to the holy image, so that Kristin
could press her lips to the feet.

Lovely tones were still streaming from the church as they went
downstairs. Father Martein told them that the organist was prac-
ticing while the schoolboys sang. But they had no time to listen, for Lavrans was hungry; he had fasted before confession. Now
they would go over to the guest quarters at the canons' house[2]
to eat.

Outside, the morning sun gleamed gold on the steep shores of
distant Lake Mjøsa, so that all of the faded leafy groves looked
like golden dust in the dark blue forests. The lake was rippled with
little white specks of dancing foam. The wind blew cold and fresh,
making the multicolored leaves float down onto the frost-covered
hill.

A group of horsemen appeared between the bishop's citadel and
the house belonging to the Brothers of the Holy Cross. Lavrans
stepped aside and bowed with his hand to his breast as he nearly
swept the ground with his hat; then Kristin realized that the horse-
man in the fur cape had to be the bishop himself, and she sank in
a curtsey almost to the ground.

The bishop reined in his horse and greeted them in return, beck-
oning Lavrans to approach, and he spoke with him for a moment.

Then Lavrans came back to the priest and the child and said,
"I have been invited to dine at the bishop's citadel. Do you think,
Father Martein, that one of the canons' servants could accompany
this little maiden home to Shoemaker Fartein's house and tell my
men that Halvdan should meet me here with Guldsvein at the hour
of midafternoon prayers?"

The priest replied that this could easily be arranged. Then the
barefoot monk who had spoken to Kristin in the tower stairway
stepped forward and greeted them.

"There's a man over in our guest house who has business with
the shoemaker anyway; he can take your message, Lavrans Bjørgulfsøn. And then your daughter can either go with him or stay at

the cloister until you return. I'll see to it that she's given food over there."

Lavrans thanked him and said, "It's a shame that you should be troubled with this child, Brother Edvin."

"Brother Edvin gathers up all the children he can," said Father Martein with a laugh. "Then he has someone to preach to."

"Yes, I don't dare offer you learned gentlemen here in Hamar my sermons," said the monk, smiling, and without taking offense. "I'm only good at talking to children and farmers, but that's no reason to tie a muzzle on the ox that threshes."

Kristin gave her father an imploring look; she thought there was nothing she would like better than to go with Brother Edvin. So Lavrans thanked him, and as her father and the priest followed the bishop's entourage, Kristin put her hand in the monk's and they walked down toward the monastery, which was a cluster of wooden houses and a light-colored stone church all the way down near the water.

Brother Edvin gave her hand a little squeeze, and when they glanced at each other, they both had to laugh. The monk was tall and gaunt but quite stoop-shouldered. The child thought he looked like an old crane because his head was small, with a narrow, shiny, smooth pate above a bushy white fringe of hair, and perched on a long, thin, wrinkled neck. His nose was also as big and sharp as a beak. But there was something about him that made Kristin feel at ease and happy just by looking up into his long, furrowed face. His old watery-blue eyes were red-rimmed, and his eyelids were like thin brown membranes with thousands of wrinkles radiating from them. His hollow cheeks, with their reddish web of veins, were crisscrossed with wrinkles that ran down to his small, thin-lipped mouth. But it looked as if Brother Edvin had become so wrinkled simply from smiling at people. Kristin thought she had never seen anyone who looked so cheerful or so kind. He seemed to carry within him a luminous and secret joy, and she was able to share it whenever he spoke.

They walked along the fence of an apple orchard where a few yellow and red fruits still hung on the trees. Two friars wearing black-and-white robes were raking withered beanstalks in the garden.

The monastery was not much different from any other farm, and the guest house into which the monk escorted Kristin closely resembled a humble farmhouse, although there were many beds. In one of the beds lay an old man, and at the hearth sat a woman wrapping an infant in swaddling clothes; two older children, a boy and a girl, stood near her.

They complained, both the man and the woman, because they had not yet received their lunch. "But they don't want to bring food to us twice, so here we sit and starve while you run around in town, Brother Edvin."

"Don't be so angry, Steinulv," said the monk. "Come over here, Kristin, and say hello. Look at this pretty maiden who is going to stay here today and eat with us."

He told Kristin that Steinulv had fallen ill on his way home from a meeting, and he had been allowed to stay in the cloister's guest house instead of the hospice because a kinswoman who was living at the hospice was so mean that he couldn't stand to be there.

"But I can tell they're getting tired of having me here," said the old man. "When you leave, Brother Edvin, no one will have time to take care of me, and then they'll probably make me go back to the hospice."

"Oh, you'll be well long before I'm done with my work at the church," said Brother Edvin. "Then your son will come to get you." He took a kettle of hot water from the hearth and let Kristin hold it as he attended to Steinulv. Then the old man grew more tractable, and a moment later a monk came in, bringing food and drink for them.

Brother Edvin said a prayer over the food and then sat down next to Steinulv on the edge of the bed so he could help the old man eat. Kristin sat down near the woman and fed the little boy, who was so small that he couldn't reach the porridge bowl, and who spilled whenever he tried to dip into the bowl of ale. The woman was from Hadeland and had come with her husband and children to visit her brother who was a monk at the cloister. But he was out wandering among the villages, and she complained bitterly about having to sit there wasting time.

Brother Edvin spoke gently to the woman. She must not say that she was throwing her time away when she was here in the bishop's Hamar. Here were all the splendid churches, and all day long the monks and canons celebrated mass and chanted the offices of the day. And the town was so beautiful, even lovelier than Oslo itself, although it was somewhat smaller. But here, nearly every farm had a garden. "You should have seen it when I arrived in the springtime," the monk said. "The whole town was white with flowers. And since then the sweetbriar roses have bloomed . . ."

"Well, what good does that do me?" said the woman peevishly. "And it seems to me that there are more holy places here than holiness."

The monk chuckled and shook his head. Then he rummaged around in his straw pallet and pulled out a big pile of apples and pears, which he shared among the children. Kristin had never tasted such luscious fruit. The juice ran out of her mouth with every bite she took.

Then Brother Edvin had to go off to church, and he said that Kristin could come along. They cut across the cloister courtyard, and through a little side door they entered the church's choir.

Construction was still going on at this church too, and scaffolding had been set up at the juncture of the nave and the transept. Brother Edvin told Kristin that Bishop Ingjald was having the choir renovated and decorated. The bishop was immensely wealthy, and he used all of his riches to adorn the churches of the town. He was an excellent bishop and a good man. The friars of Olav's cloister were also good men: celibate, learned, and humble. It was a poor monastery, but they had received Brother Edvin kindly. His home was at the Minorite[3] cloister in Oslo, but he had been given permission to beg for alms here in the Hamar diocese.

"Come over here," he said, leading Kristin to the foot of the scaffolding. He climbed up a ladder and rearranged several planks high above. Then he went back down and helped the child to ascend.

On the gray stone wall above her, Kristin saw strange, flickering specks of light, red as blood and yellow as ale, blue and brown and green. She wanted to look behind her, but the monk whispered, "Don't turn around." When they stood together high up on the planks, he gently turned her around, and Kristin saw a sight so glorious that it almost took her breath away.

Directly opposite her, on the south wall of the nave, stood a picture that glowed as if it had been made from nothing but glittering gemstones. The multicolored specks of light on the wall came from rays emanating from the picture itself; she and the monk were standing in the midst of its radiance. Her hands were red, as if she had dipped them in wine; the monk's face seemed to be completely gilded, and from his dark cowl the colors of the picture were dimly reflected. She gave him a questioning glance, but he merely nodded and smiled.

It was like standing at a great distance and looking into heaven. Behind a lattice of black lines she began to distinguish, little by little, the Lord Jesus himself, wearing the costliest red cloak; the Virgin Mary in robes as blue as the sky; and the holy men and maidens in gleaming yellow and green and violet attire. They stood beneath the arches and pillars of illuminated houses surrounded by intertwining branches and twigs with extraordinary, bright leaves.

The monk pulled her a little farther out toward the edge of the scaffold.

"Stand here," he whispered. "Then the light will fall on you from Christ's own cloak."

From the church below the faint smell of incense and the odor of cold stone drifted up toward them. It was gloomy down below, but rays of sunlight were entering diagonally through a series of windows on the south wall of the nave. Kristin began to see that the heavenly picture must be some sort of windowpane,⁴ for it filled that type of opening in the wall. The others were empty or closed off with panes of horn in wooden frames. A bird appeared, perched on the windowsill, chirped briefly, and then flew away. Outside the wall of the choir the sound of metal on stone could be heard. Otherwise everything was quiet; only the wind came in small gusts, sighed a little between the church walls, and then died away.

"Well, well," said Brother Edvin with a sigh. "No one can make things like this in Norway. They may paint with glass in Nidaros, but not like this. But in the lands to the south, Kristin, in the great cathedrals, there they have picture panes as big as the portals of this church."

Kristin thought about the pictures in the church back home. The altars of Saint Olav and Saint Thomas of Canterbury had paintings on the front panels and the tabernacles behind. But those pictures seemed dull to her and without radiance as she thought about them now.

They climbed down the ladder and went up into the choir. There stood the altar, naked and bare, and on its stone top were stacked up small boxes and cups made of metal and wood and ceramic; odd little knives, pieces of iron, and pens and brushes lay next to them. Then Brother Edvin told Kristin that these were his tools. He was skilled in the craft of painting pictures and carving tabernacles, and he had made the exquisite paintings that stood nearby on the choir chairs. They were intended for the front panels of the altars here in the friars' church.

Kristin was allowed to watch as he mixed colored powders and stirred them in little ceramic cups, and she helped him carry the things over to a bench next to the wall. As the monk went from one painting to the next, sketching fine red lines in the fair hair of the holy men and women so curls and waves were made visible, Kristin followed close on his heels, watching him and asking questions. And the monk explained what he had painted.

In one of the paintings Christ sat on a golden chair, and Saint Nikulaus and Saint Clement stood near him under a canopy. On either side was depicted the life of Saint Nikulaus. In one place he was an infant sitting on his mother's knee; he had turned away from the breast she offered him, for he was so holy, even in his cradle, that he refused to nurse more than once on Fridays. Next to this was a picture of him placing the money bags at the door of the house where three maidens lived who were so poor that they couldn't find husbands. Kristin saw how he cured the child of the Roman knight, and she saw the knight sail off in a boat with the false golden chalice in his hands. The knight had promised the holy bishop a golden chalice, which had been in his family for a thousand years, as payment for returning the child to good health. But then he tried to betray Saint Nikulaus by giving him a false golden chalice instead. That's why the boy fell into the sea with the real golden chalice in his hand. But Saint Nikulaus carried the child unharmed beneath the water, and he emerged onto shore as his father stood in Saint Nikulaus's church, offering the false goblet. All of this was shown in the picture, painted with gold and the most beautiful of colors.

In another painting the Virgin Mary sat with the Christ child on her knee. He had put one hand up under his mother's chin, and he was holding an apple in the other. With them stood Saint Sunniva and Saint Kristina. They were leaning gracefully from the hips, their faces a lovely pink and white, and they had golden hair and wore golden crowns.

Brother Edvin gripped his right wrist with his left hand as he painted leaves and roses in their crowns.

"It seems to me that the dragon is awfully small," said Kristin, looking at the image of the saint who was her namesake. "It doesn't look as if it could swallow up the maiden."

"And it couldn't, either," said Brother Edvin. "It was no bigger than that. Dragons and all other creatures that serve the Devil only seem big as long as we harbor fear within ourselves. But if a person seeks God with such earnestness and desire that he enters into His power, then the power of the Devil at once suffers such a great defeat that his instruments become small and impotent. Dragons and evil spirits shrink until they are no bigger than goblins and cats and crows. As you can see, the whole mountain that Saint Sunniva was trapped inside is so small that it will fit on the skirt of her cloak."

"But weren't they inside the caves?" asked Kristin. "Saint Sunniva and the Selje men? Isn't that true?"

The monk squinted at her and smiled again.

"It's both true and not true. It seemed to be true for the people who found the holy bodies. And it seemed true to Sunniva and the Selje men, because they were humble and believed that the world is stronger than all sinful people. They did not imagine that they might be stronger than the world because they did not love it. But if they had only known, they could have taken all the mountains and flung them out into the sea like tiny pebbles. No one and nothing can harm us, child, except what we fear and love."

"But what if a person doesn't fear and love God?" asked Kristin in horror.

The monk put his hand on her golden hair, gently tilted her

head back, and looked into her face. His eyes were blue and open wide.

"There is no one, Kristin, who does not love and fear God. But it's because our hearts are divided between love for God and fear of the Devil, and love for this world and this flesh, that we are miserable in life and death. For if a man knew no yearning for God and God's being, then he would thrive in Hell, and we alone would not understand that he had found his heart's desire. Then the fire would not burn him if he did not long for coolness, and he would not feel the pain of the serpent's bite if he did not long for peace."

Kristin looked up into his face; she understood nothing of what he said.

Brother Edvin continued, "It was because of God's mercy toward us that He saw how our hearts were split, and He came down to live among us, in order to taste, in fleshly form, the temptations of the Devil when he entices us with power and glory, and the menace of the world when it offers us blows and contempt and the wounds of sharp nails in our hands and feet. In this manner He showed us the way and allowed us to see His love."

The monk looked down into the child's strained and somber face. Then he laughed a little and said in an entirely different tone of voice, "Do you know who was the first one to realize that Our Lord had allowed Himself to be born? It was the rooster. He saw the star and then he said—and all the animals could speak Latin back then—he cried, 'Christus natus est!' "

Brother Edvin crowed out the last words, sounding so much like a rooster that Kristin ended up howling with laughter. And it felt so good to laugh, because all the strange things that he had just been talking about had settled upon her like a burden of solemnity.

The monk laughed too.

"It's true. Then when the ox heard about it, he began to bellow, 'Ubi, ubi, ubi?'

"But the goat bleated and said, 'Betlem, Betlem, Betlem.'

"And the sheep was so filled with longing to see Our Lady and her Son that he baa'd at once, 'Eamus, eamus!'

"And the newborn calf lying in the straw got up and stood on his own legs. 'Volo, volo, volo!' he said.

"Haven't you heard this before? No, I should have known. I realize that he's a clever priest, that Sira Eirik who lives up there with you, and well educated, but he probably doesn't know about this because it's not something you learn unless you journey to Paris. . . ."

"Have you been to Paris then?" asked the child.

"God bless you, little Kristin, I've been to Paris and traveled elsewhere in the world as well, and yet you mustn't think me any better for it, because I fear the Devil and love and desire this world like a fool. But I hold on to the cross with all my strength—one must cling to it like a kitten hanging on to a plank when it falls into the sea.

"And what about you, Kristin? How would you like to offer up those lovely curls of yours and serve Our Lady like these brides that I've painted here?"

"There are no other children at home besides me," replied Kristin. "So I will probably marry, I would think. Mother has already filled chests and trunks with my dowry."

"Yes, I see," said Brother Edvin, stroking her forehead. "That's the way folk dispatch their children these days. To God they give the daughters that are lame and blind and ugly and infirm; or if they think He has given them too many children, they let Him take some of them back. And yet they wonder why the men and maidens who live in the cloisters are not all holy people. . . ."

Brother Edvin took Kristin into the sacristy and showed her the monastery's books, which were displayed on stands. They contained the most beautiful pictures. But when one of the monks came in, Brother Edvin said he was merely looking for a donkey's head to copy.

Afterward he shook his head at himself. "There you see my fear, Kristin. But they're so nervous about their books here in this house. If I had the proper faith and love, I wouldn't stand here and lie to Brother Aasulv. But then I could just as well take these old leather gloves and hang them up on that ray of sunshine over there."

Kristin went with the monk over to the guest house and had something to eat, but otherwise she sat in the church all day long, watching him work and talking to him. And not until Lavrans came back to get Kristin did either she or the monk remember the message that should have been sent to the shoemaker.

Kristin remembered those days she spent in Hamar better than anything else she experienced on that long journey. Oslo was no doubt larger than Hamar, but since she had already seen a town, it did not seem so extraordinary to her. Nor did she think Skog was as beautiful as Jørundgaard, even though the buildings were finer. She was glad she wasn't going to live there. The manor was set on a hill, and below lay Botn Fjord, gray and melancholy with black forests, while on the opposite shore and beyond the buildings the sky reached all the way down to the tops of the trees. There were no towering or steep mountainsides like those back home to lift the sky high overhead or to soften and frame the view so that the world was neither too big nor too small.

The journey home was cold; it was almost Advent, and when they had traveled a short distance into the valley, they came upon snow. They had to borrow sleighs and ride for most of the way.

The exchange of estates was handled in such a manner that Lavrans turned over Skog to his brother Aasmund but retained the right of repurchase for himself and his descendants.

CHAPTER 3

IN THE SPRING after Kristin's long journey, Ragnfrid gave birth to a daughter. Both parents had no doubt wished that the child would be a boy, but this did not trouble them for long, and they developed the deepest love for little Ulvhild. She was an exceedingly pretty child, healthy, good-natured, happy, and serene. Ragnfrid loved this new child so much that she continued to nurse her even after she turned two. For that reason Ragnfrid followed Sira Eirik's advice and refrained from participating in her usual strict fasts and devout rituals for as long as she had the child at her breast. Because of this and because of her joy for Ulvhild, Ragnfrid blossomed; and Lavrans thought he had never seen his wife look so happy and beautiful and approachable in all the years of their marriage.

Kristin also felt it was a great joy that they had been given her little infant sister. She had never thought about the fact that her mother's somber disposition had made life at home so subdued. She thought things were as they should be: her mother disciplined or admonished her, while her father teased and played with her. Now her mother was gentler toward her and gave her more freedom; she caressed her more often too, so Kristin didn't notice that her mother also had less time to spend with her. She loved Ulvhild, as everyone did, and was pleased when she was allowed to carry her sister or rock her cradle. And later on the little one was even more fun; as she began to crawl and walk and talk, Kristin could play with her.

In this manner the people of Jørundgaard enjoyed three good years. Good fortune was also with them in many ways, and Lavrans did a great deal of construction and made improvements on the estate. The buildings and stables had been old and small when he came to Jørundgaard, since the Gjeslings had leased out the farm for several generations.

Then came Whitsuntide of the third year. At that time Ragnfrid's brother Trond Ivarsøn of Sundbu and his wife Gudrid and
their three small sons were visiting. One morning the grown-ups
were sitting up on the loft gallery talking, while the children
played in the courtyard. There Lavrans had started building a new
house, and the children were climbing up onto the timbers that
had been brought by wagon. One of the Gjesling boys had hit
Ulvhild and made her cry, so Trond went down and scolded his
son as he picked Ulvhild up in his arms. She was the prettiest and
most amenable child that one could imagine, and her uncle had
great affection for her, although he was not usually very fond of
children.

At that moment a man came walking across the courtyard from
the barnyard leading a huge black ox, but the ox was mean and
intractable, and it tore away from the man. Trond leaped up on
top of the pile of timbers, chasing the older children ahead of him,
but he was carrying Ulvhild in one arm and he had his youngest
son by the hand. A log suddenly rolled beneath his feet, and
Ulvhild fell from his grasp and down the hill. The log slid after her
and then rolled until it came to rest on the child's back.

Lavrans dashed down from the gallery at once. He came racing
over and tried to lift the log. Suddenly the ox charged toward him.
He grabbed for its horns but he was knocked off his feet; then he
managed to seize hold of its nostrils, pulled himself halfway up,
and held on to the ox until Trond recovered from his confusion,
and the men who came running from the house threw harnesses
over the animal.

Ragnfrid was on her knees, trying to raise the log. Lavrans lifted
it enough so that she could pull the child out and place her on her
lap. The little girl whimpered terribly when they touched her, but
Ragnfrid sobbed loudly, "She's alive, thank God, she's alive."

It was a great miracle that Ulvhild had not been crushed; the
log had fallen in such a way that it had come to rest with one end
lying on top of a rock in the grass. When Lavrans straightened up,
blood ran from his mouth, and his clothes had been ripped to
shreds across his chest from the ox's horns.

Tordis came running with a sheet made from hides; carefully
she and Ragnfrid lifted the child onto it, but she sounded as if she

was suffering intolerable pain at even the slightest touch. Ragnfrid and Tordis carried her into the winter house.

Kristin stood pale and rigid on the pile of timbers; the little boys clung to her, crying. All the servants of the farm had now gathered in the courtyard, the women weeping and wailing. Lavrans ordered them to saddle Guldsvein and one more horse. But when Arne brought the horses, Lavrans fell to the ground when he tried to mount. Then he ordered Arne to ride over to the priest while Halvdan would travel south to bring back a wise woman who lived near the place where the rivers converged.

Kristin saw that her father's face was grayish white; he had bled so much that his light-blue clothing was completely covered with reddish-brown spots. Suddenly he straightened up, tore an axe out of the hands of one of the men, and strode over to where several servants were still holding on to the ox. He struck the beast between the horns with the blade of the axe so that the ox sank to its knees, but Lavrans kept on hammering away until blood and brains were spattered everywhere. Then he was seized by a coughing fit and fell backward onto the ground. Trond and one of the men had to carry him inside.

Kristin thought her father was dead; she screamed loudly and ran after him as she called to him with all her heart.

Inside the winter house Ulvhild had been placed on her parents' bed. All of the pillows had been thrown to the floor so that the child could lie flat. It looked as if she had already been laid out on the straw of her deathbed. But she was moaning loudly and incessantly, and her mother was leaning over her, stroking and patting her, wild with grief because there was nothing she could do.

Lavrans was lying on the other bed. He got up and staggered across the floor to console his wife.

Then she sprang up and screamed, "Don't touch me! Don't touch me! Jesus, Jesus, I am so worthless that you should strike me dead—will there never be an end to the misfortune I bring upon you?"

"You haven't . . . my dear wife, this is not something you have brought upon us," said Lavrans, placing a hand on her shoulder. She shuddered at his touch and her pale gray eyes glistened in her gaunt, sallow face.

"No doubt she means that *I* am the one who caused this," said Trond Ivarsøn harshly.

His sister shot him a look of hatred and replied, "Trond knows what I mean."

Kristin ran to her parents but they both pushed her aside. And Tordis, who came over with a kettle of hot water, took her gently by the shoulders and said, "Go over to our house, Kristin. You're in the way here."

Tordis wanted to attend to Lavrans, who was sitting on the step of the bed, but he told her that he was not gravely wounded.

"But can't you ease Ulvhild's pain a little? God help us, her moans could arouse pity from the stone inside the mountain."

"We don't dare touch her until the priest arrives, or Ingegjerd, the wise woman," said Tordis.

Arne came in just then and reported that Sira Eirik was not at home.

Ragnfrid stood there for a moment, wringing her hands. Then she said, "Send word to Fru Aashild at Haugen. Nothing else matters, if only Ulvhild can be saved."

No one paid any attention to Kristin. She crept up onto the bench behind the headboard of the bed, tucked up her legs, and rested her head on her knees.

Now she felt as if her heart were being crushed between hard fists. Fru Aashild was going to be summoned! Her mother had never wanted them to send for Fru Aashild, not even when she herself was near death when she gave birth to Ulvhild, nor when Kristin was so ill with fever. People said she was a witch; the bishop of Oslo and the canons of the cathedral had sat in judgment on her. She would have been executed or burned at the stake if she hadn't been of such high birth that she was like a sister to Queen Ingebjørg. But people said that she had poisoned her first husband, and that she had won her present husband, Herr Bjørn, through witchcraft. He was young enough to be her son. She did have children, but they never came to visit their mother. So those two high-born people, Bjørn and Aashild, sat on their small farm in Dovre, having lost all their riches. None of the gentry in the valley would have anything to do with them, but secretly people sought out Fru Aashild's advice. Poor folk even went to her openly with their troubles and ills; they said she was kind, but they were also afraid of her.

Kristin thought that her mother, who was otherwise constantly praying, should have called on God and the Virgin Mary instead. She tried to pray herself—especially to Saint Olav,[1] for she knew that he was kind and he had helped so many who suffered from illness and wounds and broken bones. But she couldn't collect her thoughts.

Her parents were now alone in the room. Lavrans was lying on the bed again and Ragnfrid sat leaning over the injured child, occasionally wiping Ulvhild's forehead and hands with a damp cloth and moistening her lips with wine.

A long time passed. Tordis looked in on them now and then; she wanted so desperately to help, but each time Ragnfrid sent her away. Kristin wept soundlessly and prayed in silence, but every once in a while she would think about the witch, and she waited tensely to see her enter the room.

Suddenly Ragnfrid broke the silence. "Are you asleep, Lavrans?"

"No," replied her husband. "I'm listening to Ulvhild. God will help His innocent lamb, my wife—we mustn't doubt that. But it's hard to lie here and wait."

"God hates me for my sins," said Ragnfrid in despair. "My children are in peace where they are—I don't dare doubt that. And now Ulvhild's time has come too. But He has cast me out, for my heart is a viper's nest of sin and sorrow."

Just then the door opened. Sira Eirik stepped inside, straightening up his enormous body as he stood in the doorway, and pronounced in his deep, clear voice, "God help those in this house!"

The priest placed the box containing his medical things[2] on the step of the bed, went over to the hearth, and poured warm water over his hands. Then he pulled out his cross, raised it to all four corners of the room, and murmured something in Latin. After that he opened the smoke vent so that light could stream into the room. Then he went over and looked at Ulvhild.

Kristin was afraid that he would discover her and chase her away—usually very little escaped Sira Eirik's eye. But he didn't look around. The priest took a vial out of his box, poured something onto a tuft of finely carded wool, and placed it over Ulvhild's nose and mouth.

"Soon her suffering will lessen," said the priest. He went over to Lavrans and attended to him as he asked them to tell him how the accident had occurred. Lavrans had two broken ribs and he had received a wound to his lungs, but the priest didn't think he was in danger.

"What about Ulvhild?" asked her father sorrowfully.

"I'll tell you after I have examined her," replied the priest. "But you must go up to the loft and rest; we need quiet here and more room for those who will take care of her." He put Lavrans's arm around his shoulder, lifted up the man, and helped him out. Kristin would have preferred to go with her father, but she didn't dare show herself.

When Sira Eirik returned, he didn't speak to Ragnfrid but cut the clothes off Ulvhild, who was now whimpering less and seemed to be half asleep. Cautiously he ran his hands over the child's body and limbs.

"Are things so bad for my child, Eirik, that you don't know what to do? Is that why you have nothing to say?" asked Ragnfrid in a subdued voice.

The priest replied softly, "It looks as if her back is badly injured, Ragnfrid. I don't know anything else to do except to let God and Saint Olav prevail. There's not much I can do here."

The mother said vehemently, "Then we must pray. You know that Lavrans and I will give everything you ask for, sparing nothing, if you can convince God to allow Ulvhild to live."

"I think it would be a miracle," said the priest, "if she were to live and regain her health."

"But aren't you always talking about miracles both day and night? Don't you think a miracle could happen for my child?" she said in the same tone of voice.

"It's true that miracles do occur," said the priest, "but God does not grant everyone's prayers—we do not know His mysterious ways. And don't you think it would be worse for this pretty little maiden to grow up crippled and lame?"

Ragnfrid shook her head and cried softly, "I have lost so many, priest, I cannot lose her too."

"I'll do everything I can," replied the priest, "and pray with all my might. But you must try, Ragnfrid, to bear whatever fate God visits upon you."

The mother murmured softly, "Never have I loved any of my children as I have loved this one. If she too is taken from me, I think my heart will break."

"God help you, Ragnfrid Ivarsdatter," said Sira Eirik, shaking his head. "You want nothing more from all your prayers and fasting than to force your will on God. Does it surprise you, then, that it has accomplished so little good?"

Ragnfrid gave the priest a stubborn look and said, "I have sent for Fru Aashild."

"Well, you may know her, but I do not," said the priest.

"I will not live without Ulvhild," said Ragnfrid in the same voice as before. "If God won't help her, then I will seek the aid of Fru Aashild, or offer myself up to the Devil if he will help!"

The priest looked as if he wanted to make a sharp retort, but he restrained himself. He leaned down and touched the injured girl's limbs again.

"Her hands and feet are cold," he said. "We must put some kegs of hot water next to her—and then you must not touch her again until Fru Aashild arrives."

Kristin soundlessly slipped down onto the bench and pretended to sleep. Her heart was pounding with fear. She had not understood much of the conversation between Sira Eirik and her mother, but it had frightened her greatly, and she knew it wasn't meant for her ears.

Her mother stood up to get the kegs; then she broke down, sobbing. "Pray for us, nevertheless, Sira Eirik!"

A little while later her mother came back with Tordis. The priest and the women bustled around Ulvhild, and then Kristin was discovered and sent away.

The light dazzled Kristin as she stood in the courtyard. She thought that most of the day had passed while she sat in the dark winter house, but the buildings were light gray and the grass was shimmering, as glossy as silk in the white midday sun. Beyond the golden lattice of the alder thicket, with its tiny new leaves, the river glinted. It filled the air with its cheerful, monotonous roar, for it flowed strongly down a flat, rocky riverbed near Jørundgaard. The mountainsides rose up in a clear blue haze, and the streams leaped down the slopes through melting snow. The sweet, strong spring outside made Kristin weep with sorrow at the helplessness she felt all around her.

No one was in the courtyard, but she heard people talking in the servants' room. Fresh earth had been spread over the spot where her father had killed the ox. She didn't know what to do with herself; then she crept behind the wall of the new building, which had been raised to a height of a couple of logs. Inside were Ulvhild's and her playthings; she gathered them up and put them into a hole between the lowest log and the foundation. Lately Ulvhild had wanted all of Kristin's toys, and that had made her unhappy at times. She thought now that if her sister got well, she would give her everything she owned. And that thought comforted her a little.

Kristin thought about the monk at Hamar—he at least was convinced that miracles could happen for everyone. But Sira Eirik was not as sure of it, nor were her parents, and they were the ones she was most accustomed to listening to. It fell like a terrible burden upon her when she realized for the first time that people could have such different opinions about so many things. And not just evil, godless people disagreeing with good people, but also good people such as Brother Edvin and Sira Eirik—or her mother and father. She suddenly realized that they too thought differently about many things.

Tordis found Kristin asleep there in the corner late in the day, and she took her indoors. The child hadn't eaten a thing since morning. Tordis kept vigil with Ragnfrid over Ulvhild that night, and Kristin lay in her bed with Jon, Tordis's husband, and Eivind and Orm, her little boys. The smell of their bodies, the man's snoring, and the even breathing of the two children made Kristin quietly weep. Only the night before she had lain in bed, as she had every night of her life, with her own father and mother and little Ulvhild. It was like thinking about a nest that had been torn apart and scattered, and she herself had been flung from the shelter and wings that had always warmed her. At last she cried herself to sleep, alone and miserable among all those strangers.

On the following morning when Kristin got up, she learned that her uncle and his entire entourage had left Jørundgaard—in anger. Trond had called his sister a crazy, demented woman and her husband a spineless fool who had never learned to rein in his wife. Kristin grew flushed with rage, but she was also ashamed. She realized that a grave impropriety had taken place when her mother had driven her closest kinsmen from the manor. And for the first time it occurred to Kristin that there was something about her mother that was not as it should be—that she was different from other women.

As she stood and pondered this, a maidservant came up to her and asked her to go up to the loft to her father.

But when she stepped into the loft room Kristin forgot all about tending to him, for across from the open doorway, with the light shining directly in her face, sat a small woman, whom she realized must be the witch—although Kristin had not expected her to look like that.

She seemed as small as a child, and delicate, for she was sitting in the big high-backed chair that had been brought up to the room. A table had also been placed in front of her, covered with Ragnfrid's finest embroidered linen cloth. Pork and fowl were set forth on silver platters, there was wine in a bowl of curly birchwood, and she had Lavrans's own silver goblet to drink from. She had finished eating and was wiping her small, slender hands on one of Ragnfrid's best towels. Ragnfrid herself stood in front of her, holding a brass basin of water.

Fru Aashild let the towel drop into her lap, smiled at the child, and said in a lovely, clear voice, "Come over here to me!" And to Kristin's mother she said, "You have beautiful children, Ragnfrid."

Her face was full of wrinkles but pure white and pink like a child's, and her skin looked as if it were just as soft and fine to the touch. Her lips were as red and fresh as a young woman's, and her big hazel eyes gleamed. An elegant white linen wimple framed her face and was fastened tightly under her chin with a gold brooch; over it she wore a veil of soft, dark-blue wool, which fell loosely over her shoulders and onto her dark, well-fitting clothes. She sat as erect as a candle, and Kristin sensed rather than thought that she had never seen such a beautiful or noble woman as this old witch whom the gentry of the village refused to have anything to do with.

Fru Aashild held Kristin's hand in her own soft old hands; she spoke to her kindly and with humor, but Kristin could not find a word to reply.

Fru Aashild said to Ragnfrid with a little laugh, "Do you think she's afraid of me?"

"No, no," Kristin almost shouted.

Fru Aashild laughed even more and said, "She has wise eyes, this daughter of yours, and good strong hands. And she's not accustomed to slothfulness either, I can see. You're going to need someone who can help you care for Ulvhild when I'm not here. So you can let Kristin assist me while I'm at the manor. She's old enough for that, isn't she? Eleven years old?"

Then Fru Aashild left, and Kristin was about to follow her. But Lavrans called to her from his bed. He was lying flat on his back with pillows stuffed under his knees; Fru Aashild had ordered him to lie in this manner so that the injury to his chest would heal faster.

"You're going to get well soon, aren't you, Father?" asked Kristin, using the formal means of address. Lavrans looked up at her. Never before had she addressed him in that manner.

Then he said somberly, "I'm not in danger, but it's much more serious for your sister."

"I know," said Kristin with a sigh.

Then she stood next to his bed for a while. Her father did not speak again, and Kristin could find nothing more to say. And when Lavrans told her some time later to go downstairs to her mother and Fru Aashild, Kristin hurried out and rushed across the courtyard to the winter house.

FRU AASHILD stayed at Jørundgaard for most of the summer, which meant that people came there to seek her advice. Kristin heard Sira Eirik speak jeeringly of this, and it dawned on her that her parents did not much care for it either. But she pushed aside all thoughts of these things, nor did she pay any heed to what her own opinion of Fru Aashild might be; she was her constant companion and never tired of listening to and watching the woman.

Ulvhild still lay stretched out flat on her back in the big bed. Her small face was white to the very edge of her lips, and she had dark circles under her eyes. Her lovely blond hair smelled sharply of sweat because it hadn't been washed in such a long time; it had turned dark and had lost its sheen and curl so that it looked like old, windblown hay. She looked tired and tormented and patient, and she would smile, feeble and wan, whenever Kristin sat by her on the bed to talk and to show her all the lovely presents she had received from her parents and their friends and kinsmen far and wide. There were dolls, toy birds and cattle, a little board game, jewelry, velvet caps, and colorful ribbons. Kristin had put it all in a box for her. Ulvhild would look at everything with her somber eyes, sigh, and then let the treasures fall from her weary hands.

But whenever Fru Aashild came over to her, Ulvhild's face would light up with joy. Eagerly she drank the refreshing and sleep-inducing brews that Fru Aashild prepared for her. She never complained when the woman tended to her, and she would lie still, listening happily, whenever Fru Aashild played Lavrans's harp and sang—she knew so many ballads that were unfamiliar to the people there in the valley.

Often she would sing for Kristin when Ulvhild had fallen asleep. And sometimes she spoke of her youth, when she lived in the south

48

of the country and frequented the courts of King Magnus and King Eirik and their queens.

Once, as they were sitting there and Fru Aashild was telling stories, Kristin blurted out what she had thought about so often.

"It seems strange to me that you're always so happy, when you've been used to—" she broke off, blushing.

Fru Aashild looked down at the child, smiling.

"You mean because now I'm separated from all those things?" She laughed quietly and then she said, "I've had my glory days, Kristin, but I'm not foolish enough to complain because I have to be content with sour, watered-down milk now that I've drunk up all my wine and ale. Good days can last a long time if one tends to things with care and caution; all sensible people know that. That's why I think that sensible people have to be satisfied with the good days—for the grandest of days are costly indeed. They call a man a fool who fritters away his father's inheritance in order to enjoy himself in his youth. Everyone is entitled to his own opinion about that. But I call him a true idiot and fool only if he regrets his actions afterward, and he is twice the fool and the greatest buffoon of all if he expects to see his drinking companions again once the inheritance is gone.

"Is something wrong with Ulvhild?" Fru Aashild asked gently, turning to Ragnfrid, who had given a start from her place near the child's bed.

"No, she's sleeping quietly," said the mother as she came over to Fru Aashild and Kristin, who were sitting near the hearth. With her hand on the smoke vent pole, Ragnfrid stood and looked down into the woman's face.

"Kristin doesn't understand all this," she said.

"No," replied Fru Aashild. "But she also learned her prayers before she understood them. At those times when one needs either prayers or advice, one usually has no mind to learn or to understand."

Ragnfrid raised her black eyebrows thoughtfully. When she did that, her light, deep-set eyes looked like lakes beneath a black forest meadow. That's what Kristin used to think when she was small, or perhaps she had heard someone say that. Fru Aashild looked at

her with that little half smile of hers. Ragnfrid sat down at the
edge of the hearth, picked up a twig, and poked at the embers.

"But the person who has wasted his inheritance on the most
wretched of goods—and then later sees a treasure he would give
his life to own—don't you think that he would deplore his own
stupidity?"

"No bargain is without some loss, Ragnfrid," said Fru Aashild.
"And whoever wishes to give his life must take the risk and see
what he can win."

Ragnfrid jerked the burning twig from the fire, blew out the
flame, and curled her hand around the glowing end so that a blood-
red light shone between her fingers.

"Oh, it's all nothing but words, words, words, Fru Aashild."

"There is very little worth paying for so dearly, Ragnfrid," said
the other woman, "as with one's own life."

"Yes, there is," said Kristin's mother fervently. "My husband,"
she whispered almost inaudibly.

"Ragnfrid," said Fru Aashild quietly, "many a maiden has had
the same thought when she was tempted to bind a man to her and
gave up her maidenhood to do so. But haven't you read about men
and maidens who gave God all they owned, and entered cloisters
or stood naked in the wilderness and then regretted it afterward?
They're called fools in the holy books. And it would certainly be
a sin to think that God was the one who had deceived them in
their bargain."

Ragnfrid sat quite still for a moment. Then Fru Aashild said,
"Come along with me, Kristin. It's time to go out and collect the
dew that we'll use to wash Ulvhild in the morning."

Outside, the courtyard was white and black in the moonlight.
Ragnfrid accompanied them through the farmyard down to the
gate near the cabbage garden. Kristin saw the thin silhouette of
her mother leaning against the fence nearby. The child shook dew
from the large, ice-cold cabbage leaves and from the folds of the
lady's-mantle into her father's silver goblet.

Fru Aashild walked silently at Kristin's side. She was there only
to protect her, for it was not wise to let a child go out alone on

such a night. But the dew would have more power if it was collected by an innocent maiden.

When they came back to the gate, Ragnfrid was gone. Kristin was shaking with cold as she put the icy silver goblet into Fru Aashild's hands. In her wet shoes she ran over to the loft where she slept with her father. She had her foot on the first step when Ragnfrid emerged from the shadows beneath the gallery of the loft. In her hands she held a bowl of steaming liquid.

"I've warmed up some ale for you, daughter," said Ragnfrid.

Kristin thanked her gratefully and put her lips to the rim. Then her mother asked, "Kristin, those prayers and other things that Fru Aashild is teaching you—is there anything sinful or ungodly about them?"

"I can't believe that," replied the child. "They all mention Jesus and the Virgin Mary and the names of the saints."

"What has she been teaching you?" asked her mother again.

"Oh, about herbs, and how to ward off bleeding and warts and strained eyes—and moths in clothing and mice in the storehouse. And which herbs to pick in sunlight and which ones have power in the rain. But I mustn't tell the prayers to anyone else, or they will lose their power," she said quickly.

Her mother took the empty bowl and set it on the steps. Suddenly she threw her arms around her daughter, pulled her close, and kissed her. Kristin noticed that her mother's cheeks were hot and wet.

"May God and Our Lady guard and protect you against all evil—we have only you now, your father and I; you're the only one that misfortune has not touched. My dear, my dear—never forget that you are your father's dearest joy."

Ragnfrid went back to the winter house, undressed, and crawled into bed with Ulvhild. She put her arm around the child and pressed her face close to the little one's so that she could feel the warmth of Ulvhild's body and smell the sharp odor of sweat from the child's damp hair. Ulvhild slept soundly and securely as always after Fru Aashild's evening potion. There was a soothing scent from the Virgin Mary grass spread under the sheet. And yet Ragnfrid lay there for a long time, unable to sleep, and stared up at the

little scrap of light in the roof where the moon shone on the horn
pane of the smoke vent.

Fru Aashild lay in the other bed, but Ragnfrid never knew
whether she was asleep or awake. Fru Aashild never mentioned
that they had known each other in the past, and that frightened
Ragnfrid quite badly. She thought she had never felt so bitterly sad
or in such an agony of fear as she did now, even though she knew
that Lavrans would regain his full health—and that Ulvhild would
survive.

Fru Aashild seemed to enjoy talking to Kristin, and for each day
that passed, the maiden became better friends with her.

One day when they had gone out to pick herbs, they sat down
next to the river in a little grassy clearing at the foot of a scree.
They could look down at the courtyard of Formo and see Arne
Gyrdsøn's red shirt. He had ridden over with them and was going
to look after their horses while they were up in the mountain
meadow gathering herbs.

As they sat there, Kristin told Fru Aashild about her encounter
with the dwarf maiden. She hadn't thought about the incident for
many years, but now it suddenly came back to her. And as she
spoke, the strange thought occurred to her that there was some
resemblance between Fru Aashild and the dwarf woman—even
though she realized full well that they did not look at all alike.

But when she had finished telling the story, Fru Aashild sat in
silence for a moment and gazed out across the valley.

Finally she said, "It was wise of you to flee, since you were only
a child back then. But haven't you ever heard of people who took
the gold the dwarf offered them, and then trapped the troll in a
rock afterward?"

"I've heard of such stories," said Kristin, "but I would never
dare do that myself. And I don't think it's the right thing to do."

"It's good when you don't dare do something that doesn't seem
right," said Fru Aashild with a little laugh. "But it's not so good
if you think something isn't right because you don't dare do it."
Then she added abruptly, "You've grown up a great deal this summer. I wonder if you realize how lovely you've become."

"Yes, I know," said Kristin. "They say I look like my father."

Fru Aashild laughed softly.

"Yes, it would be best if you took after Lavrans, both in temperament and appearance. And yet it would be a shame if they married you to someone up here in the valley. Farming customs and the ways of smallholders should not be disdained, but these gentry up here all think they're so grand that their equals are not to be found in all of Norway. I'm sure they wonder how I can manage to live and prosper even though they've closed their doors to me. But they're lazy and arrogant and refuse to learn new ways—and then they blame everything on the old enmity with the monarchy in the time of King Sverre.[1] It's all a lie—your ancestor reconciled with King Sverre and accepted gifts from him. But if your mother's brother wanted to serve the king and join his retinue, then he would have to cleanse himself, both inside and out, which is not something Trond is willing to do. But you, Kristin, you ought to marry a man who is both chivalrous and courtly. . . ."

Kristin sat staring down at the Formo courtyard, at Arne's red back. She hadn't been aware of it herself, but whenever Fru Aashild talked about the world she had frequented in the past, Kristin always pictured the knights and counts in Arne's image. Before, when she was a child, she had always envisioned them in her father's image.

"My nephew, Erlend Nikulaussøn of Husaby—now he would have been a suitable bridegroom for you. He has grown up to be so handsome, that boy. My sister Magnhild came to visit me last year when she was on her way through the valley, and she brought her son along with her. Well, you won't be able to marry him, of course, but I would have gladly spread the blanket over the two of you in the wedding bed. His hair is as dark as yours is fair, and he has beautiful eyes. But if I know my brother-in-law, he has already set his sights on a better match for Erlend than you would be."

"Does that mean I'm not a good match, then?" asked Kristin with surprise. She was never offended by anything Fru Aashild said, but she felt embarrassed and chagrined that Fru Aashild might be somehow better than her own family.

"Yes, of course you're a good match," said Fru Aashild. "And

yet you couldn't expect to become part of my lineage. Your an-
cestor here in Norway was an outlaw and a foreigner, and the
Gjeslings have sat moldering away on their estates for such a long
time that almost no one remembers them outside of this valley.
But my sister and I married the nephews of Queen Margret
Skulesdatter."

Kristin didn't even think to object that it was not her ancestor
but his brother who had come to Norway as an outlaw. She sat
and gazed out over the dark mountain slopes across the valley, and
she remembered that day, many years ago, when she went up onto
the ridge and saw how many mountains there were between her
own village and the rest of the world. Then Fru Aashild said they
ought to head home, and she asked Kristin to call for Arne. Kristin
put her hands up to her mouth and shouted and then waved her
kerchief until she saw the red speck down in the courtyard turn
and wave back.

Some time later Fru Aashild returned home, but during the fall and
the first part of winter she often came to Jørundgaard to spend a
few days with Ulvhild. The child was now taken out of bed in the
daytime, and they tried to get her to stand on her own, but her
legs crumpled beneath her whenever she tried it. She was fretful,
pale, and tired, and the laced garment that Fru Aashild had made
for her from horsehide and slender willow branches plagued her
terribly; all she wanted to do was lie in her mother's lap. Ragnfrid
was constantly holding her injured daughter, so Tordis was now
in charge of all the housekeeping. At her mother's request, Kristin
accompanied Tordis, to help and to learn.

Kristin sometimes longed for Fru Aashild, who occasionally
would talk to her a great deal, but at other times Kristin would
wait in vain for a word beyond the casual greeting as Fru Aashild
came and went.

Instead, Fru Aashild would sit with the grown-ups and talk.
That was always what happened when she brought her husband
along with her, for now Bjørn Gunnarsøn also came to Jørundgaard. One day in the fall, Lavrans had ridden over to Haugen to
take Fru Aashild payment for her doctoring: the best silver pitcher
and matching platter they owned. He had stayed the night and

afterward had high praise for their farm. He said it was beautiful and well tended, and not as small as people claimed. Inside the buildings everything looked prosperous, and the customs of the house were as courtly as those of the gentry in the south of the country. What Lavrans thought of Bjørn he didn't say, but he always received the man courteously when Bjørn accompanied his wife to Jørundgaard. On the other hand, Lavrans was exceedingly fond of Fru Aashild, and he believed that most of what people said about her was a lie. He also said that twenty years earlier she would hardly have required witchcraft to bind a man to her—she was sixty now but still looked young, and she had a most appealing and charming manner.

Kristin noticed that her mother was not happy about all this. It's true that Ragnfrid never said much about Fru Aashild, but one time she compared Bjørn to the flattened yellow grass that can be found under large rocks, and Kristin thought this an apt description. Bjørn had an oddly faded appearance—he was quite fat, pale, and sluggish, and slightly bald—even though he was not much older than Lavrans. And yet it was still apparent that he had once been an extremely handsome man. Kristin never exchanged a single word with him. He said little, preferring to stay in one spot, wherever he happened to be seated, from the moment he stepped in the door until it was time for bed. He drank an enormous amount but it seemed to have little effect on him. He ate almost nothing, and occasionally he would stare at someone in the room, stony-faced and pensive, with his strange, pale eyes.

They had not seen their kinsmen from Sundbu since the accident occurred, but Lavrans had been over to Vaage several times. Sira Eirik, on the other hand, came to Jørundgaard as often as before, and there he frequently met Fru Aashild. They had become good friends. People thought this a generous attitude on the part of the priest, since he himself was a very capable doctor. This was also probably one of the reasons why people on the large estates had not sought Fru Aashild's advice, at least not openly, because they considered the priest to be competent enough. It was not easy for them to know how to act toward two people who in some ways had been cast out of their own circles. Sira Eirik himself said that they caused no one any harm, and as for Fru Aashild's witchcraft, he was not her parish priest. It could be that the woman knew more than was good for the health of her soul—and yet one should not forget that ignorant people often spoke of witchcraft as soon as a woman showed herself to be wiser than the councilmen. For her part, Fru Aashild spoke highly of the priest and diligently went to church if she happened to be at Jørundgaard on a holy day.

Christmas was a sad time that year. Ulvhild was still unable to stand on her own. And they neither saw nor heard from their kinsmen at Sundbu. Kristin noticed that people in the village were talking about the rift and that her father took it to heart. But her mother didn't care, and Kristin thought this was callous of her.

One evening toward the end of the holidays, Sira Sigurd, Trond Gjesling's house priest, arrived in a big sleigh, and his primary mission was to invite them all to visit Sundbu.

Sira Sigurd was not well liked in the surrounding villages, for he was the one who actually managed Trond's properties for him—or at least he was the one who was blamed whenever Trond acted harshly or unjustly, and Trond tended to plague his tenants somewhat. The priest was exceedingly clever at writing and figuring; he knew the law and was a skilled doctor, although not as skilled as he thought. But judging by his behavior, no one would think him a clever man; he often said foolish things. Ragnfrid and Lavrans had never liked him, but the Sundbu people, as was reasonable, set great store by their priest, and both they and he were greatly disappointed that he had not been called on to tend to Ulvhild.

On the day that Sira Sigurd came to Jørundgaard—unfortunately for him—Fru Aashild and Herr Bjørn were already there, as were Sira Eirik, Arne's parents Gyrd and Inga of Finsbrekken, Old Jon from Loptsgaard, and a friar from Hamar, Brother Aasgaut.

While Ragnfrid had the tables set once more with food for the guests and Lavrans pored over the boxes of sealed letters that the priest had brought, Sira Sigurd asked to see Ulvhild. She had already been put to bed for the night and was sleeping, but Sira Sigurd woke her up, examined her back and limbs, and asked her

questions—at first kindly enough, but with increasing impatience
as Ulvhild grew frightened. Sigurd was a small man, practically a
dwarf, but he had a big, flame-red face. When he tried to lift her
onto the floor to test her legs, Ulvhild began to scream. Then Fru
Aashild stood up, went over to the bed, and covered her with the
blanket, saying that the child was sleepy—she wouldn't have been
able to stand up even if her legs were healthy.

The priest began to protest vehemently; he was also considered
a capable doctor. But Fru Aashild took his hand, led him over to
the high seat[2] at the table, and started talking about what she had
done for Ulvhild as she asked his opinion on everything. Then he
grew more amenable, and he ate and drank of Ragnfrid's good
repast.

But when the ale and wine began to go to his head, Sira Sigurd
was once again in a foul mood, quarrelsome and bad tempered.
He was quite aware that no one in the room liked him. First he
turned to Gyrd, who was the envoy of the Bishop of Hamar at
Vaage and Sil. There had been numerous disputes between the
bishopric and Trond Ivarsøn. Gyrd didn't say much, but Inga was
a hot-tempered woman, and then Brother Aasgaut joined in the
discussion.

He said, "You shouldn't forget, Sira Sigurd, that our worthy
Father Ingjald is your prelate too; we know all about you in Hamar. You revel in all that is good at Sundbu, and give little thought
to the fact that you are dedicated to other work than acting as
Trond's eye-servant, helping him do everything that is unjust so
that he endangers his own soul and diminishes the power of the
Church. Haven't you ever heard about what happens to those disobedient and unfaithful priests who contravene their own spiritual
fathers and superiors? Don't you know about the time when the
angels led Saint Thomas of Canterbury to the gates of Hell and let
him peek inside? He was greatly surprised not to see any of those
who had opposed him as you oppose your bishop. He was just
about to praise God's mercy, for the holy man wished all sinners
to be saved, when the angel asked the Devil to lift his tail. With a
tremendous roar and a horrid stench of sulfur, out spewed all the
priests and learned men who had betrayed the interests of the
Church. And then he saw where all of them had ended up."

"You're lying, monk," said the priest. "I've heard that story too, but it was friars, not priests, who were spewed out of the Devil's behind like wasps from a wasp's nest."

Old Jon laughed louder than all the servants and cried, "No doubt it was both, I'll bet it was. . . ."

"Then the Devil must have a very wide tail," said Bjørn Gunnarsøn.

And Fru Aashild smiled and said, "Yes, haven't you heard it said that everything bad has a long rump dragging behind?"

"You be quiet, Fru Aashild," shouted Sira Sigurd. "You shouldn't talk about the long rump that bad people drag behind them. Here you sit as if you were the mistress of the house instead of Ragnfrid. But it's odd that you haven't been able to cure her child—don't you have any more of that powerful water you used to use? The water that could make a dismembered sheep whole again in the soup pot and turn a woman into a maiden in the bridal bed? I know all about that wedding here in the village when you prepared the bath for the despoiled bride. . . ."

Sira Eirik jumped up, grabbed the other priest by the shoulder and flank, and threw him right across the table so that pitchers and cups toppled and food and drink spilled onto the table-cloths and floor. Sira Sigurd landed flat on his back, his clothing torn.

Eirik leaped over the table and was about to strike him again, bellowing over the din, "Shut your filthy trap, you damned priest!"

Lavrans tried to separate them, but Ragnfrid stood at the table, as white as a corpse, wringing her hands. Then Fru Aashild ran over and helped Sira Sigurd to his feet and wiped the blood from his face.

She handed him a goblet of mead as she said, "You shouldn't be so stern, Sira Eirik, that you can't stand to hear a joke late in the evening after so many drinks. Now sit down, and I'll tell you about that wedding. It wasn't here in this valley at all, and it's my misfortune that I was not the one who knew about that water. If I had been able to brew it, we wouldn't be sitting up there on that little farm. Then I'd be a rich woman with property out in the big villages somewhere—near the town and cloisters and bishops and canons," she said, smiling at the three clergymen.

"But someone must have known the art in the old days, because this was in the time of King Inge, as far as I know, and the bridegroom was Peter Lodinsøn of Bratteland. But I won't say which of his three wives was the bride, since there are living descendants from all three. Well, this bride probably had good reason to wish for that water, and she managed to get it too. She prepared a bath for herself out in the shed, but before she managed to bathe, in came the woman who was to be her mother-in-law. She was muddy and dirty from the ride to the wedding manor, so she took off her clothes and stepped into the tub. She was an old woman, and she had had nine children by Lodin. But on that night both Lodin and Peter had a different kind of pleasure than they had counted on."

Everyone in the room laughed heartily, and both Gyrd and Jon called to Fru Aashild to tell more such ribald tales.

But she refused. "Here sit two priests and Brother Aasgaut and young boys and maidservants. We should stop now before the talk grows indecent and vulgar; remember that these are the holy days."

The men protested, but the women agreed with Fru Aashild. No one noticed that Ragnfrid had left the room. A little later Kristin, who had been sitting at the far end of the women's bench among the maidservants, stood up to go to bed. She was sleeping in Tordis's house because there were so many guests at the farm.

It was biting cold, and the northern lights were flaring and flickering above the domed mountains to the north. The snow creaked under Kristin's feet as she ran across the courtyard, shivering, with her arms crossed over her breast.

Then she noticed that in the shadows beneath the old loft someone was pacing vigorously back and forth in the snow, throwing out her arms, wringing her hands, and moaning loudly. Kristin recognized her mother. Frightened, she ran over to her and asked her if she was ill.

"No, no," said Ragnfrid fiercely. "I just had to get out. Go to bed now, child."

Kristin turned around when her mother softly called her name.

"Go into the house and lie down in bed with your father and Ulvhild—hold her in your arms so that he doesn't crush her by mistake. He sleeps so heavily when he's drunk. I'll go up and sleep here in the old loft tonight."

"Jesus, Mother," said Kristin. "You'll freeze to death if you sleep there—and all alone. What will Father say if you don't come to bed tonight?"

"He won't notice," replied her mother. "He was almost asleep when I left, and tomorrow he'll get up late. Go and do as I say."

"You'll be so cold," whimpered Kristin, but her mother pushed her away, somewhat more gently, and then shut herself inside the loft.

It was just as cold inside as out, and pitch dark. Ragnfrid fumbled her way over to the bed, tore the shawl from her head, took off her shoes, and crawled under the furs. They chilled her to the bone; it was like sinking into a snow drift. She pulled the covers over her head, tucked up her legs, and put her hands into the bodice of her clothing. And she lay there in that way, weeping—alternately crying quite softly, with streaming tears, and then screaming and gnashing her teeth in between her sobs. Finally she had warmed up the bed enough that she began to feel drowsy, and then she cried herself to sleep.

CHAPTER 5

IN THE SPRINGTIME of Kristin's fifteenth year, Lavrans Bjørgulfsøn and Sir Andres Gudmundsøn of Dyfrin agreed to meet at Holledis *ting*.[1] There they decided that Andres's second son, Simon, should be betrothed to Kristin Lavransdatter and that he would be given Formo, the property which Andres had inherited from his mother. The men sealed the agreement with a handshake, but no document was drawn up about it because Andres first had to arrange for the inheritance of his other children. And no betrothal ale was drunk either, but Sir Andres and Simon accompanied Lavrans back to Jørundgaard to see the bride, and Lavrans gave a great banquet.

Lavrans had finished building the new house—two stories tall, with brick fireplaces in both the main room and the loft. It was richly and beautifully decorated with wood carvings and fine furniture. He had also renovated the old loft and expanded the other buildings, so that he could now live in a manner befitting a squire. By this time, he possessed great wealth, for he had been fortunate in his undertakings, and he was a wise and thoughtful master. He was especially known for breeding the finest horses and the best cattle of all types. And now that he had arranged things so that his daughter would acquire Formo through marriage with a man of the Dyfrin lineage, people said that he had successfully achieved his goal of becoming the foremost landowner in the village. Lavrans and Ragnfrid were also very pleased, as were Sir Andres and Simon.

Kristin was a little disappointed when she first saw Simon Andressøn, for she had heard such high praise of his handsome appearance and noble manner that there was no limit to what she had expected of her bridegroom.

Simon was indeed handsome, but he was rather heavyset for a man of only twenty; he had a short neck, and his face was as round and shiny as the moon. His hair was quite beautiful, brown and curly, and his eyes were gray and clear, but they seemed slightly pinched because his eyelids were puffy. His nose was too small and his mouth was also small and pouting, but not ugly. And in spite of his stoutness he was light-footed and quick and agile in all his movements, and he was an able sportsman. He was rather impetuous and rash in his speech, but Lavrans felt that he nevertheless showed both good sense and wisdom when he spoke to older men.

Ragnfrid soon came to like him, and Ulvhild developed at once the greatest affection for him; he was also particularly kind and loving toward the little maiden who was ill. And after Kristin had grown accustomed to his round face and his way of speaking, she was entirely satisfied with her betrothed and pleased that her father had arranged the marriage for her.

Fru Aashild was invited to the banquet. Ever since the people of Jørundgaard had taken up with her, the gentry of the nearest villages had once again begun to remember her high birth, and they paid less attention to her strange reputation; so now Fru Aashild was often in the company of others.

After she had seen Simon, she said, "He's a good match, Kristin. This Simon will do well in the world—you'll be spared many types of sorrow, and he'll be a kind man to live with. But he seems to me rather too fat and cheerful. If things were the same in Norway today as they were in the past and as they are in other countries, where people are no sterner toward sinners than God is Himself, then I would suggest you find yourself a friend who is thin and melancholy—someone you could sit and talk to. Then I would say that you could fare no better than with Simon."

Kristin blushed even though she didn't fully understand what Fru Aashild meant. But as time passed and her dowry chests were filled and she listened to the constant talk of her marriage and what she would take to her new home, she began to yearn for the matter to be bound with a formal betrothal and for Simon to come north. After a while she began to think about him a great deal, and she looked forward to seeing him again.

Kristin was now grown-up, and she was exceedingly beautiful. She most resembled her father. She was tall and small-waisted, with slender, elegant limbs, but she was also buxom and shapely. Her face was rather short and round; her forehead low and broad and as white as milk; her eyes large, gray, and gentle under finely etched brows. Her mouth was a little too big, but her full lips were a fresh red, and her chin was round like an apple and nicely shaped. She had lovely thick, long hair, but it was rather dark now, more brown than gold, and quite straight. Lavrans liked nothing better than to hear Sira Eirik boast about Kristin. The priest had watched the maiden grow up, had taught her reading and writing, and was very fond of her. But Lavrans was not particularly pleased to hear the priest occasionally compare his daughter to a flawless and glossy-coated young mare.

Yet everyone said that if the accident had not befallen Ulvhild, she would have been many times more beautiful than her sister. She had the prettiest and sweetest face, white and pink like roses and lilies, with white-gold, silky-soft hair that flowed and curled around her slender neck and thin shoulders. Her eyes resembled those of the Gjesling family: they were deep-set beneath straight black brows, and they were as clear as water and grayish blue, but her gaze was gentle, not sharp. The child's voice was also so clear and lovely that it was a joy to listen to her whether she spoke or sang. She had an agile talent for book learning and for playing all types of stringed instruments and board games, but she took little interest in needlework because her back would quickly tire.

It seemed unlikely that this pretty child would ever regain the full health of her body, although she improved somewhat after her parents took her to Nidaros to the shrine of Saint Olav. Lavrans and Ragnfrid went there on foot, without a single servant or maid to accompany them, and they carried the child on a litter between them for the entire journey. After that, Ulvhild was so much better that she could walk with a crutch. But it was not likely that she would ever be well enough to marry, and so, when the time came, she would probably be sent to a convent with all the possessions that she would inherit.

They never talked about it, and Ulvhild was not aware that she was any different from other children. She was very fond of finery and beautiful clothes, and her parents didn't have the heart to re-fuse her anything; Ragnfrid stitched and sewed for her and adorned her like a royal child. Once some peddlers came through the village and stayed the night at Laugarbru, where Ulvhild was allowed to examine their wares. They had some amber-yellow silk, and she was set on having a shift made from it. Lavrans normally never traded with the kind of people who traveled through the villages, illegally selling goods from the town, but this time he bought the entire bolt at once. He also gave Kristin cloth for her bridal shift, which she worked on during the summer. Before that she had never owned shifts made of anything but wool, except for a linen shift for her finest gown. But Ulvhild was given a shift made of silk to wear to banquets and a Sunday shift of linen with a bodice of silk.

Lavrans Bjørgulfsøn now owned Laugarbru as well, which was tended by Tordis and Jon. Lavrans and Ragnfrid's youngest daughter Ramborg lived with them there; Tordis had been her wetnurse. Ragnfrid would hardly even look at the child during the first days after her birth because she said that she brought her children bad luck. And yet she loved the little maiden dearly and was constantly sending gifts to her and to Tordis. Later on she would often go over to Laugarbru to visit Ramborg, but she preferred to arrive after the child was asleep, and then she would sit with her. Lavrans and the two older daughters often went to Laugarbru to play with the little one; she was a strong and healthy child, though not as pretty as her sisters.

That summer was the last one that Arne Gyrdsøn spent at Jørund-gaard. The bishop had promised Gyrd to help the boy make his way in the world, and in the fall Arne was to leave for Hamar.

Kristin had undoubtedly noticed that Arne was fond of her, but in many ways her feelings were quite childish, so she didn't give it much thought and behaved toward him as she always had, ever since they were children. She sought out his company as often as she could and always took his hand when they danced at home or on the church hill. The fact that her mother didn't approve of this, she found rather amusing. But she never spoke to Arne about Simon or about her betrothal, for she noticed that he grew dispir-ited whenever it was mentioned.

Arne was good with his hands and he wanted to make Kristin a sewing chest to remember him by. He had carved an elegant and beautiful box and frame, and now he was working in the smithy to make iron bands and a lock for it. On a fine evening with fair weather late in the summer, Kristin went over to talk to him. She took along one of her father's shirts to mend, sat down on the stone doorstep, and began to sew as she chatted with the young man inside the smithy. Ulvhild was with her too, hopping around on her crutch and eating raspberries that were growing among the stones piled up on the ground.

After a while Arne came over to the smithy door to cool off. He wanted to sit down next to Kristin, but she moved away a bit and asked him to take care not to get soot on the sewing that she was holding on her lap.

"So that's how things have become between us?" said Arne. "You don't dare let me sit with you because you're afraid that the farm boy will get you dirty?"

Kristin looked at him in surprise and then said, "You know quite well what I meant. But take off your apron, wash the coal from your hands, and sit down here with me and rest a while." And she made room for him.

But Arne lay down in the grass in front of her.

Then Kristin continued, "Now don't be angry, dear Arne. Do you think I would be so ungrateful for the lovely present that you're making for me, or that I would ever forget that you've always been my best friend here at home?"

"Have I been?" he asked.

"You know you have," said Kristin. "And I'll never forget you. But you, who are about to go out into the world—maybe you'll acquire wealth and honor before you know it. You'll probably forget me long before I forget you."

"You'll never forget me," said Arne and smiled. "But I'll forget you before you forget me—you're such a child, Kristin."

"You're not very old yourself," she replied.

"I'm just as old as Simon Darre," he said. "And we can bear helmets and shields just as well as the Dyfrin people, but my parents have not had fortune on their side."

He had wiped off his hands on some tufts of grass. Now he took hold of Kristin's ankle and pressed his cheek against her foot, which was sticking out from the hem of her dress. She tried to pull her foot away, but Arne said, "Your mother is at Laugarbru, and Lavrans rode off from the farm—and from the buildings no one can see us sitting here. Just this once you must let me talk about what's on my mind."

Kristin replied, "We've always known, both you and I, that it would be futile for us to fall in love with each other."

"Can I put my head in your lap?" asked Arne, and when she didn't reply, he did it anyway, wrapping his arm around her waist. With the other hand he tugged on her braids.

"How will you like it," he asked after a moment, "when Simon lies in your lap like this and plays with your hair?"

Kristin didn't answer. She felt as if a weight suddenly fell upon her—Arne's words and Arne's head on her knees—it seemed to her as if a door were opening into a room with many dark corridors leading into more darkness. Unhappy and heartsick, she hesitated, refusing to look inside.

"Married people don't do things like this," she said abruptly and briskly, as if with relief. She tried to imagine Simon's plump, round face looking up at her with the same gaze in his eyes as Arne now had; she heard his voice—and she couldn't help laughing.

"I don't think Simon would ever lie down on the ground to play with my shoes!"

"No, because he can play with you in his own bed," said Arne. His voice made Kristin feel suddenly sick and helpless.

She tried to push his head off her lap, but he pressed it harder against her knees and said gently, "But I would play with your shoes and your hair and your fingers and follow you in and out all day long, Kristin, if you would be my wife and sleep in my arms every night."

He pulled himself halfway up, put his hands on her shoulders, and looked into her eyes.

"It's not proper for you to talk to me this way," said Kristin quietly and shyly.

"No, it's not," said Arne. He got to his feet and stood in front of her. "But tell me one thing—wouldn't you rather it had been me?"

"Oh, I would rather . . ." She sat in silence for a moment. "I would rather not have any man at all—not even . . ."

Arne didn't move. He said, "Would you rather go into a convent then, as they've planned for Ulvhild, and be a maiden all your days?"

Kristin wrung her hands in her lap. She felt a strange, sweet trembling inside her—and with a sudden shudder she realized how sad it was for her little sister. And her eyes filled with tears of sorrow for Ulvhild's sake.

"Kristin," said Arne gently.

At that moment Ulvhild screamed loudly. Her crutch had lodged between some stones and she had fallen. Arne and Kristin ran over to her, and Arne lifted her into her sister's arms. She had cut her mouth and was bleeding badly.

Kristin sat down with her in the doorway to the smithy, and Arne brought water in a wooden bowl. Together they began to wash Ulvhild's face. She had also scraped the skin on her knees. Kristin bent tenderly over the small, thin legs.

Ulvhild's wailing soon stopped and she whimpered softly, the way children do who are used to suffering pain. Kristin pressed Ulvhild's head against her breast and rocked her gently.

Then the bell up in Olav's church began ringing for vespers.

Arne spoke to Kristin, but she sat there as if she neither heard nor sensed what he said as she bent over her sister. Then he grew frightened and asked her whether she thought the injuries were serious. Kristin shook her head but refused to look at him.

A little later she stood up and started walking toward the farm, carrying Ulvhild in her arms. Arne followed, silent and confused. Kristin looked so preoccupied that her face was completely rigid. As she walked, the bell continued to toll across the meadows and valley; it was still ringing as she went into the house.

She placed Ulvhild on the bed which the sisters had shared ever since Kristin had grown too old to sleep with her parents. Then she took off her own shoes and lay down next to the little one. She lay there and listened for the bell long after it had stopped ringing and the child was asleep.

It had occurred to her, as the bell began to peal, while she sat with Ulvhild's little bloodied face in her hands, that perhaps this was an omen for her. If she would take her sister's place—if she would promise herself to the service of God and the Virgin

Mary—then maybe God would grant the child renewed vigor and good health.

Kristin remembered Brother Edvin saying that these days parents offered to God only the crippled and lame children or those for whom they could not arrange good marriages. She knew her parents were pious people, and yet she had never heard them say anything except that she would marry. But when they realized that Ulvhild would be ill all her days, they at once proposed that she should enter a convent.

But Kristin didn't want to do it; she resisted the idea that God would perform a miracle for Ulvhild if she became a nun. She clung to Sira Eirik's words that so few miracles occurred nowadays. And yet she had the feeling this evening that it was as Brother Edvin had said—that if someone had enough faith, then he could indeed work miracles. But she did not want that kind of faith; she did not love God and His Mother and the saints in that way. She would never love them in that way. She loved the world and longed for the world.

Kristin pressed her lips to Ulvhild's soft, silky hair. The child slept soundly, but the elder sister sat up, restless, and then lay down again. Her heart was bleeding with sorrow and shame, but she knew that she could not believe in miracles because she was unwilling to give up her inheritance of health and beauty and love.

Then she tried to console herself with the thought that her parents would never give her permission to do such a thing. Nor would they ever believe that it would do any good. She was already betrothed, after all, and they would undoubtedly be loath to lose Simon, whom they liked so much. She felt betrayed because they seemed to find this son-in-law so splendid. She suddenly thought with displeasure of Simon's round, red face and his small, laughing eyes, of his leaping gait—it occurred to her all of a sudden that he bounced like a ball—and of his teasing manner of speaking, which made her feel awkward and stupid. And it was not such a splendid thing, either, to be given to him and then move only as far as Formo. And yet she would rather have him than be sent to a convent. But what about the world beyond the mountains? The king's castle, and the counts and the knights that Fru Aashild had talked about, a handsome man with melancholy eyes who would follow her in and out and never grow tired. . . . She remembered Arne on that summer day long ago when he lay on his side and slept with his shiny brown hair spread out on the heath—she had loved him as if he were her own brother back then. It wasn't proper for him to speak to her the way he had today, when he knew they could never have each other.

Word was sent from Laugarbru that her mother would stay there overnight. Kristin got up to undress and get ready for bed. She began to unlace her dress, but then she put her shoes back on, wrapped her cloak around her, and went out.

The night sky, bright and green, stretched above the mountain crests. It was almost time for the moon to rise, and at the spot where it waited below the ridge, small clouds drifted past, gleaming like silver underneath; the sky grew lighter and lighter, like metal gathering dew.

Kristin ran between the fences, across the road, and up the hill toward the church. It was asleep, black and locked, but she went over to the cross that stood nearby—a memorial to the time when Saint Olav once rested there as he was fleeing from his enemies.

Kristin knelt down on the stone and placed her folded hands on the base. "Holy Cross, the strongest of masts, the fairest of trees, the bridge for those who are ill to the fair shores of health . . ."

As she spoke the words of the prayer, she felt her yearning gradually spread like rings on water. The various thoughts that were making her uneasy were smoothed out, her mind grew calmer, more tender, and a gentle sorrow, empty of all thought, replaced her troubles.

She stayed there on her knees, aware of all the sounds of the night. The wind was sighing so oddly, the river was roaring beyond the groves on the other side of the church, and the stream was flowing nearby, right across the road—and everywhere, both close at hand and far away in the dark, her eyes and her ears caught hints of tiny rivulets of running and dripping water. The river flashed white down in the village. The moon glided up over a small gap in the mountains; stones and leaves wet with dew shimmered faintly, and the newly tarred timbers of the bell tower near the cemetery gate shone dull and dark. Then the moon vanished again where the ridge of the mountain rose higher. Many more gleaming white clouds appeared in the sky.

She heard a horse approaching at a slow pace higher up the road, and the sound of men's voices, speaking evenly and softly. Kristin was not afraid of people so close to home where she knew everyone; she felt quite safe.

Her father's dogs came rushing toward her, turned around and bounded back to the grove, then turned again and raced back to her; then her father called a greeting as he emerged from among the birches. He was leading Guldsvein by the bridle; a bunch of birds dangled in front of the saddle, and Lavrans was carrying a hooded hawk on his left hand. He was in the company of a tall, hunchbacked man in monk's clothing, and before Kristin had even seen his face, she knew it was Brother Edvin. She went to greet them, and she couldn't have been more surprised than if she had dreamed it. She merely smiled when Lavrans asked her whether she recognized their guest.

Lavrans had met the monk up by Rost Bridge. Then he had persuaded him to come home with him and stay the night at the farm. But Brother Edvin insisted on being allowed to sleep in the cowshed: "For I've picked up so many lice that you can't have me lying in your good beds."

And no matter how much Lavrans begged and implored, the monk was adamant; at first he even wanted them to bring his food out into the courtyard. But finally they coaxed him inside the house, and Kristin put wood in the fireplace in the corner and set candles on the table, while a maid brought in food and drink.

The monk sat down on the beggar's bench near the door, but he would only take cold porridge and water for his evening meal. And he refused to accept Lavrans's offer to prepare a bath for him and to have his clothes washed.

Brother Edvin scratched and rubbed himself and his gaunt old face beamed with glee.

"No, no," he said. "The lice bite better at my proud hide than any scourges or the guardian's words. I spent this summer under an overhang up on the mountain. They had given me permission to go into the wilderness to fast and pray, and there I sat, thinking

that I was as pure as a holy hermit, and the poor people over in
Setna valley brought food up to me and thought they beheld a
pious monk, living a pure life. 'Brother Edvin,' they said, 'if there
were more monks like you, then we would soon mend our ways,
but when we see priests and bishops and monks shoving and fighting like piglets at the trough . . .' Well, I told them that was not a
Christian way to talk—but I liked hearing it all the same, and I
sang and prayed so my voice resounded in the mountains. Now it
will be to my benefit to feel how the lice are biting and fighting on
my skin and to hear the good housewives, who want to keep their
houses clean and neat, shouting that the filthy monkhide can just
as well sleep in the barn during the summer. I'm heading north to
Nidaros now, to celebrate Saint Olav's Day, and it will do me good
to see that people aren't so keen to come near me."

Ulvhild woke up. Then Lavrans went over and lifted her up in
his cape.

"Here is the child I told you about, dear Father. Place your
hands on her and pray to God for her, the way you prayed for the
boy up north in Meldal—we heard he regained his health."

The monk gently put his hand under Ulvhild's chin and looked
into her eyes. Then he lifted one of her hands and kissed it.

"You should pray instead, you and your wife, Lavrans Bjørgulfsøn, that you will not be tempted to bend God's will with this
child. Our Lord Jesus himself has set these small feet on a path so
that she can walk safely toward the house of peace—I can see in
your eyes, blessed Ulvhild, that you have your intercessors in that
other house."

"I heard that the boy in Meldal got well," said Lavrans quietly.

"He was the only child of a poor widow, and there was no one
to feed or clothe him when the mother passed away, except the
village. And yet the woman only asked that God give her a fearless
heart so that she might have faith that He would let happen whatever was best for the boy. I did nothing more than pray alongside her."

"It's not easy for Ragnfrid and me to be content with that,"
said Lavrans gloomily. "Especially since she's so pretty and so
good."

"Have you seen the child they have over in Lidstad, in the south of the valley?" asked the monk. "Would you rather your daughter were like that?"

Lavrans shuddered and pressed the child close.

"Don't you think," Brother Edvin went on, "that in God's eyes we are all like children for whom He has reason to grieve, crippled as we are by sin? And yet we don't think that things are the worst in the world for us."

He walked over to the painting of the Virgin Mary on the wall, and everyone knelt down as he said the evening prayer. They felt that Brother Edvin had offered them great comfort.

But after he had left the house to find his sleeping place, Astrid, who was in charge of all the maids, vigorously swept the floor everywhere the monk had stood and hastily threw the sweepings into the fire.

The next morning Kristin got up early, put some milk porridge and wheat cakes into a lovely red-flecked bowl made from birch roots—for she knew that the monk never touched meat—and took the food out to him. No one else in the house was awake yet.

Brother Edvin was standing on the ramp to the cowshed, ready to leave, with his staff and bag in hand. With a smile he thanked Kristin for her trouble and sat down in the grass and ate, while Kristin sat at his feet.

Her little white dog came running over to them, making the tiny bells on his collar ring. Kristin pulled the dog onto her lap, and Brother Edvin snapped his fingers, tossing little bits of wheat cake into the dog's mouth, as he praised the animal.

"It's the same breed that Queen Eufemia brought over to Norway," he said. "Everything is so splendid here at Jørundgaard now."

Kristin blushed with pleasure. She knew the dog was particularly fine, and she was proud to own him. No one else in the village had a pet dog. But she hadn't known that he was of the same type as the queen's pet dogs.

"Simon Andressøn sent him to me," she said, hugging the dog as he licked her face. "His name is Kortelin."

She had planned to speak to the monk about her uneasiness and ask for his advice. But now she had no wish to spend any more time on her thoughts of the night before. Brother Edvin believed that God would do what was best for Ulvhild. And it was generous of Simon to send her such a gift even before their betrothal had been formally acknowledged. She refused to think about Arne— he had behaved badly toward her, she thought.

Brother Edvin picked up his staff and bag and asked Kristin to give his greetings to the others; he wouldn't wait for everyone to wake up, but would set off while the day was cool. She walked with him up past the church and a short way into the grove.

When they parted, he offered her God's peace and blessed her.

"Give me a few words, as you did for Ulvhild, dear Father," begged Kristin as she stood with her hand in his.

The monk poked his bare foot, knotty with rheumatism, in the wet grass.

"Then I would impress upon your heart, my daughter, that you should pay close attention to the way God tends to the welfare of the people here in the valley. Little rain falls, but He has given you water from the mountains, and the dew refreshes the meadows and fields each night. Thank God for the good gifts He has given you, and don't complain if you think you are lacking something else that you think would be beneficial. You have beautiful golden hair, so do not fret because it isn't curly. Haven't you heard about the woman who sat and wept because she had only a little scrap of pork to give to her seven hungry children for Christmas dinner? Saint Olav came riding past at that very moment. Then he stretched out his hand over the meat and prayed to God to feed the poor urchins. But when the woman saw that a slaughtered pig lay on the table, she began to cry because she didn't have enough bowls and pots."

Kristin ran off toward home, and Kortelin danced around at her feet as he nipped at her clothing and barked, making all his tiny silver bells ring.

CHAPTER 6

ARNE WAS HOME at Finsbrekken for the last time before he left for Hamar. His mother and sisters were outfitting him with clothes.

The day before he was supposed to ride south he went to Jørundgaard to say farewell. There he asked Kristin in a whisper whether she would meet him on the road south of Laugarbru on the following evening.

"I would like us to be alone, just the two of us, the last time we meet," he said. "Do you think that's too much to ask? We who have grown up together as brother and sister?" he added when Kristin hesitated a moment before replying.

Then she promised to come if she could slip away from home.

The next morning it snowed, but later in the day it began to rain and soon the roads and fields were nothing but gray mud. Wisps of fog hovered and drifted along the mountain ridges, occasionally dropping down and twining into white mist at the foot of the mountains, but then the weather closed in again.

Sira Eirik came over to help Lavrans put together several boxes of letters. They went into the hearth house because it was more comfortable there in that kind of weather than in the larger house where the fireplace filled the room with smoke. Ragnfrid was at Laugarbru, where Ramborg was recuperating from an illness and fever she had suffered earlier that fall.

So it was not difficult for Kristin to slip away from the farm unnoticed; she didn't dare take a horse, so she went on foot. The road was a morass of slushy snow and withered leaves; the air smelled mournfully raw and dead and moldy, and now and then a gust of wind would blow the rain right into her face. Kristin pulled her hood up over her head and held her cloak closed with both hands as she walked briskly onward. She was a little ap-

prehensive—the clamor of the river sounded so muffled in the oppressive air, and the clouds were black and ragged, drifting above
the mountain crests. Occasionally she would stop and listen behind
her, thinking that she might hear Arne.

After a while she became aware of a horse's hooves on the sod-
den road, and then she stopped, for she had reached a rather desolate spot and thought it would be a suitable place for them to say
goodbye to each other undisturbed. A moment later she saw the
rider appear behind her, and Arne jumped down from his horse,
leading it forward as he walked toward her.

"It was good of you to come," he said, "in this awful weather."

"It's worse for you, who will have to ride such a long way. But
why are you leaving so late in the evening?"

"Jon has invited me to stay at Loptsgaard tonight," said Arne.
"And I thought it would be easier for you to come here at this
time of day."

They stood in silence for a moment. Kristin thought she had
never before realized how handsome Arne was. He wore a shiny
steel helmet, and under it a brown woolen hood that framed his
face and spread out over his shoulders; underneath, his thin
face looked so bright and fair. His leather breastplate was old,
flecked with rust, and scratched from the coat of mail that had
been worn over it—Arne's father had given it to him—but it fit
snugly on his slender, lithe, and strong body. He wore a sword
at his side and carried a spear in his hand; his other weapons
hung from his saddle. He was a full-grown man and looked imposing.

Kristin put her hand on his shoulder and said, "Do you remember, Arne, that you once asked me whether I thought you were as
splendid a fellow as Simon Andressøn? I want to tell you something
now, before we part. You seem to me as much his superior in fair
appearance and bearing as he is held above you in birth and wealth
by people who value such things most."

"Why are you telling me this?" asked Arne breathlessly.

"Because Brother Edvin impressed on my heart that we should
thank God for His good gifts and not be like the woman who wept
because she had no bowls when Saint Olav multiplied the meat for

her. So you shouldn't fret over the fact that He hasn't given you as much wealth as He has physical gifts. . . ."

"Is that what you meant?" said Arne. And when Kristin didn't reply he went on, "I was wondering whether you meant that you would rather have been married to me than to that other man."

"I probably would, at that," she said quietly. "For I know you much better."

Arne threw his arms around her so tight that he lifted her feet off the ground. He kissed her face many times, but then he set her down.

"God help us, Kristin. You're such a child!"

She stood there with her head bowed, but she kept her hands on his shoulders. He gripped her wrists and held them tight.

"I see now that you don't realize, my sweet, how my heart aches because I am going to lose you. Kristin, we've grown up together like two apples on a branch. I loved you before I began to realize that one day someone else would come and tear you away from me. As certain as God had to die for us all, I don't know how I can ever be happy again in this world after today."

Kristin wept bitterly and lifted her face so that he could kiss her.

"Don't talk like that, my Arne," she begged, patting his arm.

"Kristin," said Arne in a muted voice, taking her in his arms again. "Couldn't you consider asking your father . . . Lavrans is such a good man, he would never force you against your will. Couldn't you ask him to wait a few years? No one knows how my fortune may change—we're both so young."

"I must do what those at home want me to do," she sobbed.

Then tears overcame Arne too.

"You have no idea, Kristin, how much I love you." He hid his face on her shoulder. "If you did, and if you loved me too, then you would go to Lavrans and beg him sweetly—"

"I can't do that," sobbed the maiden. "I don't think I could ever love a man so dearly that I would go against my parents' will for his sake." She slipped her hands under Arne's hood and heavy steel helmet to find his face. "You mustn't cry like that, Arne, my dearest friend."

"I want you to have this," he said after a moment, giving her a small brooch. "And think of me now and then, for I will never forget you, or my sorrow."

It was almost completely dark by the time Kristin and Arne had said their last farewells. She stood and gazed after him when he finally rode away. A yellow light shone through the clouds, and the light was reflected in their footsteps, where they had walked and stood in the slush of the road; it looked so cold and bleak, she thought. She pulled out the linen cloth covering her bodice and wiped her tear-streaked face; then she turned around and set off for home.

She was wet and cold and she walked fast. After a while she heard someone approaching on the road behind her. She was a little frightened; it was possible that strangers might be traveling on this main road, even on an evening like this, and she had a lonely stretch ahead of her. Steep black scree rose up on one side, but on the other there was a sharp drop-off, covered with pine woods all the way down to the pale, leaden river at the bottom of the valley. So she was relieved when the person behind her called her name; she stopped and waited.

The person who approached was a tall, thin man wearing a dark surcoat with lighter colored sleeves. When he came closer, Kristin saw that he was dressed as a priest and carried an empty knapsack on his back. She now recognized Bentein Prestesøn, as they called him—Sira Eirik's grandson. She noticed at once that he was quite drunk.

"Well, one departs and the other arrives," he said and laughed after they had greeted each other. "I met Arne from Brekken just now—and I see that you're walking along and crying. So how about giving me a little smile because I've come back home? The two of us have also been friends since childhood, haven't we?"

"It's a poor bargain to have you come back to the valley in his stead," said Kristin crossly. She had never liked Bentein. "Quite a few people will say the same, I'm afraid. And your grandfather was so happy that you were getting on so well down south in Oslo."

"Oh, yes," said Bentein with a snicker and a sneer. "So you think I was getting on well, do you? Like a pig in a wheat field, that's how it was for me, Kristin—and the end result was the same. I was chased off with a shout and a long stick. Well, well. He doesn't have much joy from his offspring, my grandfather. Why are you walking so fast?"

"I'm freezing," said Kristin curtly.

"No more than I am," said the priest. "The only clothing I have to wear is what you see. I had to sell my cape for food and ale in Lillehammer. But you must still have warmth in your body from saying farewell to Arne. I think you should let me come under your furs with you." And he seized hold of her cloak, threw it around his shoulders, and wrapped his wet arm around her waist.

Kristin was so startled by his boldness that it took a moment for her to regain her senses—then she tried to tear herself away, but he was holding on to her cloak and it was fastened with a sturdy silver clasp. Bentein put his arms around her again and tried to kiss her, shoving his mouth close to her chin. She tried to strike him, but he was gripping her upper arms.

"I think you've lost your mind," she seethed as she struggled against him. "How dare you manhandle me as if I were a . . . You're going to regret this bitterly tomorrow, you miserable wretch."

"Oh, tomorrow you won't be so stupid," said Bentein, tripping her with his leg so that she fell to her knees in the mud of the road. Then he pressed his hand over her mouth.

And yet Kristin still did not think to scream. Now she finally realized what he intended to do to her, but rage overcame her with such fury and violence that she hardly felt any fear. She snarled like an animal in battle and fought against this man who was holding her down so that the ice-cold snow water soaked through her clothing and reached her burning hot flesh.

"Tomorrow you'll know enough to keep quiet," said Bentein. "And if it can't be concealed, you can always blame Arne; people will sooner believe that. . . ."

He had put a finger in her mouth, so she bit him with all her might, and Bentein screamed and loosened his grip. As quick as lightning Kristin pulled one hand free and shoved it into his face, pressing her thumb as hard as she could into his eye. He bellowed

and got up on one knee. She wriggled free like a cat, pushed the
priest so that he fell onto his back, and then ran off down the road
as the mud spurted up behind her with every step.

She ran and ran without looking back. She heard Bentein coming after her, and she raced off with her heart pounding in her
throat, as she moaned softly and peered ahead—would she never
reach Laugarbru? At last Kristin came to the part of the road where
it passed through the fields. She saw buildings clustered on the
hillside, and suddenly realized that she didn't dare go to her
mother—not the way she looked, covered with mud and withered
leaves from head to toe, her clothing torn.

She could feel Bentein coming closer. She bent down and picked
up two big rocks, and when he was near enough she threw them;
one of them struck him so hard that it knocked him down. Then
she started running again and didn't stop until she stood on the
bridge.

Trembling, she stood there holding on to the railing; everything
went black and she was afraid that she would sink into uncon-
sciousness—but then she thought about Bentein. What if he came
and found her like that? Shaking with shame and bitterness, she
kept on going, but her legs could hardly bear her, and now she
felt how her face stung from the scratches of his fingernails, and
she had hurt both her back and her arms. Tears came, hot as fire.

She wished Bentein would be dead from the rock she had
thrown; she wished she had gone back and put an end to him, that
she had taken out her knife, but she noticed that she must have
lost it.

Then she realized again that she dared not be seen like this at
home; it occurred to her that she could go to Romundgaard. She
would complain to Sira Eirik.

But the priest had not yet returned from Jørundgaard. In the
cookhouse she found Gunhild, Bentein's mother. The woman was
alone, and then Kristin told her how her son had behaved toward
her. But she didn't mention that she had gone out to meet Arne.
When she realized that Gunhild thought she had been at Laugarbru, she didn't dissuade her.

Gunhild said very little but cried a great deal as she washed

Kristin's clothing and mended the worst rips. And the young girl
was so distressed that she didn't notice the glances Gunhild cast at
her in secret.

As Kristin was leaving, Gunhild put on her own cloak and followed her out the door, but then headed toward the stable. Kristin
asked her where she was going.

"Surely I should be allowed to ride over and tend to my son,"
said the woman, "to see if you've killed him with that rock or
what's happened to him."

Kristin had nothing to say in reply, so she simply told Gunhild
to make sure that Bentein left the village as soon as possible; she
never wanted to lay eyes on him again. "Or I'll speak of this to
Lavrans, and then you can well imagine what will happen."

Bentein headed south hardly more than a week later; he carried
letters to the Bishop of Hamar from Sira Eirik, asking the bishop
if he could find some occupation for Bentein or give him some
assistance.

CHAPTER 7

ONE DAY during the Christmas season, Simon Andressøn arrived at Jørundgaard on horseback, quite unexpected. He apologized for coming in this manner, uninvited and alone, without kinsmen, but Sir Andres was in Sweden on business for the king. He himself had been at home at Dyfrin for some time, but there he had only the company of his younger sisters and his mother, who was ill in bed, and the days had grown so dreary for him; he suddenly felt such an urge to come and see them.

Ragnfrid and Lavrans thanked him warmly for making the long journey at the height of winter. The more they saw of Simon, the more they liked him. He was well acquainted with everything that had been agreed upon between Andres and Lavrans, and it was now decided that the betrothal ale for the young couple would be celebrated before the beginning of Lent, if Sir Andres returned home before then—otherwise, at Easter.

Kristin was quiet and shy when she was with her betrothed; she found little to talk about with him. One evening when everyone had been sitting and drinking, Simon asked her to go outside with him to get some fresh air. As they stood on the gallery in front of the loft room, he put his arm around her waist and kissed her. After that, he did it often whenever they were alone. She wasn't pleased by this, but she allowed him to do it because she knew there was no escape from the betrothal. Now she thought of her marriage as something she had to do, but not something that she looked forward to. And yet she liked Simon well enough, especially when he was talking to the others and did not touch her or speak to her.

She had been so unhappy the entire autumn. It did no good to tell herself that Bentein had done her no harm; she felt herself defiled just the same.

81

Nothing could be as it had been before, now that a man had dared to do such a thing to her. She lay awake at night, burning with shame, and she couldn't stop thinking about it. She remembered Bentein's body against hers when she fought with him, and his hot ale-breath. She was forced to think about what might have happened, and she was reminded, as a shudder rippled through her flesh, of what he had said: that if it could not be concealed, then Arne would be blamed. Images raced through her head of everything that would have followed if she had ended up in such misfortune and then people had found out about her meeting with Arne. And what if her mother and father had believed such a thing of Arne? And Arne himself . . . She saw him as he had looked on that last evening, and she felt as if she were sinking down before him in shame simply because she *might* have dragged him down along with her into sorrow and disgrace. And her dreams were so vile. She had heard about the desires and temptations of the flesh in church and in the Holy Scriptures, but it had meant nothing to her. Now it had become clear that she herself and everyone else had a sinful, fleshly body encompassing the soul, biting into it with harsh bands.

Then she imagined how she might have killed Bentein or blinded him. That was the only consolation she could find—to indulge in dreams of revenge against that hideous dark figure who was always haunting her thoughts. But it never helped for long; she would lie next to Ulvhild at night and weep about everything that had been visited upon her by violence. In her mind, Bentein had managed to breach her maidenhood all the same.

On the first workday after the Christmas season, all the women of Jørundgaard were busy in the cookhouse. Ragnfrid and Kristin had also spent most of the day there. Late in the evening, while some of the women were cleaning up after the baking and others were preparing the evening meal, the milkmaid came rushing in, screaming as she threw up her hands.

"Jesus, Jesus—has anyone ever heard more dreadful news! They're carrying Arne Gyrdsøn home in a sleigh—God help Gyrd and Inga in their misery."

In came a man who lived in a house a short way down the road, and with him was Halvdan. They were the ones who had met the funeral procession.

The women crowded around them. On the very outskirts of the circle stood Kristin, pale and trembling. Halvdan, Lavrans's own servant who had known Arne since he was a boy, sobbed loudly as he spoke.

It was Bentein Prestesøn who had killed Arne. On New Year's Eve the bishop's men were sitting in the men's house drinking, when Bentein came in. He had become a scribe for a priest, a Corpus Christi prebendary.[1] At first the men didn't want to let Bentein in, but he reminded Arne that they were from the same village. So Arne allowed him to sit with him, and they both began to drink. But then they came to blows, and Arne fought so fiercely that Bentein seized a knife from the table and stabbed Arne in the throat and then several times in the chest. Arne died almost at once.

The bishop took this misfortune greatly to heart; he personally saw to it that the body was properly tended to, and he had his own men accompany it on the long journey home. He had Bentein thrown in irons and excommunicated from the Church, and if he had not already been hanged, then he soon would be.

Halvdan had to tell the story several times as more people crowded into the room. Lavrans and Simon also came over to the cookhouse when they noticed all the noise and commotion in the courtyard. Lavrans was much distressed; he ordered his horse to be saddled, for he wanted to ride over to Brekken at once. As he was about to leave, his eyes fell on Kristin's white face.

"Perhaps you would like to go with me?" he asked. Kristin hesitated for a moment, shuddering, but then she nodded, for she didn't dare utter a word.

"Isn't it too cold for her?" said Ragnfrid. "Tomorrow they will hold the wake, and then we'll all go."

Lavrans looked at his wife; he also glanced at Simon's face, and then he went over and put his arm around Kristin's shoulder.

"You must remember that she's his foster sister," he said. "Perhaps she would like to help Inga attend to the body."

And even though Kristin's heart was gripped with fear and despair, she felt a warm surge of gratitude toward her father for his words.

Then Ragnfrid wanted them to eat the evening porridge before they left, if Kristin would be going along. She also wanted to send gifts to Inga—a new linen sheet, candles, and freshly baked bread. She asked them to tell Inga that she would come to help them prepare for the burial.

Little was eaten but much was said in the room while the food stood on the table. One person reminded the other about the trials that God had visited upon Gyrd and Inga. Their farm had been destroyed by a rock slide and flood, and many of their older children had died, so all of Arne's siblings were still quite young. But fortune had been with them for several years now, ever since the bishop had appointed Gyrd of Finsbrekken as his envoy, and the children they had been blessed to keep were good-looking and full of promise. But Inga had loved Arne more dearly than all the rest.

People felt sorry for Sira Eirik too. The priest was loved and respected, and the people in the village were proud of him; he was well educated and capable, and in all his years with the Church he had not missed a single holy day or mass or service that he was obliged to observe. In his youth he had been a soldier under Count Alv of Tornberg, but he had brought trouble on himself by killing a man of exceedingly high birth, and so he had turned to the Bishop of Oslo. When the bishop realized how quick Eirik was to acquire book learning, he had accepted him into the priesthood. And if not for the fact that he still had enemies because of that killing in the past, Sira Eirik would probably never have stayed at that little church. It's true that he was quite avaricious, both for his own purse and for his church. But the church was, after all, quite attractively furnished with vessels and draperies and books, and he did have those children—but he had never had anything but trouble and sorrow from his family. In the countryside people thought it unreasonable to expect priests to live like monks, since they had to have women servants on their farms and might well be in need of a woman to look after things for them when they had to make such long and arduous journeys through the parish in all kinds of weather. People also remembered that it was not so long ago that priests in Norway had been married men. So no one blamed Sira Eirik for having three children by the housekeeper who was with him when he was young. On this evening, however, they said that it looked as if God wanted to punish Eirik for taking a mistress, since his children and grandchildren had caused him so much grief. And some people said that there was good reason for priests not to have wives or children—for enmity and indignation were bound to arise between the priest and the people of Finsbrekken. Until now they had been the best of friends.

Simon Andressøn was quite familiar with Bentein's conduct in Oslo, and he told the others about it. Bentein had become a scribe for the provost of the Maria Church and was considered a clever fellow. And there were plenty of women who were quite fond of him; he had those eyes and a quick tongue. Some thought him a handsome man—mostly women who felt they had been cheated by their husbands, or young maidens who enjoyed having men act freely toward them. Simon laughed; they knew what he meant, didn't they? Well, Bentein was so shrewd that he didn't get too close to those kinds of women; with them he exchanged only words, and he won a reputation for leading a pure life.

It so happened that King Haakon, who was a pious and decent man himself, wanted his men to maintain disciplined and proper behavior—at least the younger men. The others he had little control over. But the king's priest always heard about whatever pranks the young men managed to sneak out and take part in—drunken feasts, gambling, ale-drinking, and the like. And then the rascals had to confess and repent, and they received harsh punishment; yes, two or three of the wildest boys were even sent away. But at last it came to light that it was that fox, Bentein *secretarius*, who had been secretly frequenting all of the ale houses and establishments that were even worse; he had actually listened to the confessions of whores and had given them absolution.

Kristin was sitting next to her mother. She tried to eat so that no one would notice how things stood with her, but her hand shook so badly that she spilled some of the porridge with every spoonful, and her tongue felt so thick and dry in her mouth that she could hardly swallow the bread. But when Simon began to talk about Bentein she had to give up all pretense of eating. She gripped the edge of the bench with her hands; terror and loathing took such a hold on her that she felt dizzy and filled with nausea. He was the one who had tried to . . . Bentein and Arne, Bentein and Arne . . . Sick with impatience she waited for the others to finish. She longed to see Arne, Arne's handsome face, to fall to her knees and grieve, forgetting everything else.

When Ragnfrid helped Kristin into her outer garments, she kissed her daughter on the cheek. Kristin was unaccustomed to receiving any kind of caress from her mother, and it felt so good. She rested her head on Ragnfrid's shoulder for a moment, but she could not cry.

When she came out to the courtyard, she saw that there were more people coming with them—Halvdan, Jon of Laugarbru, and Simon and his servant. She felt unreasonably anguished that the two strangers would be going along.

It was a biting cold night; the snow creaked underfoot, and the stars glittered, as dense as frost, in the black sky. After they had gone a short distance, they heard howls and shouts and furious hoofbeats south of the meadows. A little farther along the road the whole pack of riders came storming up behind them and then raced on past. The sound of ringing metal and vapor from the steaming, frost-covered bodies of the horses rose up before Lavrans and his party as they moved out of the way into the snow. Halvdan shouted at the wild throng—it was the youths from the farms south of the village. They were still celebrating Christmas and were out trying their horses. Those who were too drunk to take notice raced on ahead, thundering and bellowing as they hammered on their shields. But a few of them understood the news that Halvdan had yelled after them; they dropped away from the group, fell silent, and joined Lavrans's party as they whispered to the men in the back of the procession.

They continued on until they could see Finsbrekken on the slope alongside the Sil River. There was a light between the buildings; in the middle of the courtyard the servants had set pine torches in a mound of snow, and the firelight gleamed red across the white hillock, but the dark houses looked as if they were streaked with clotted blood. One of Arne's little sisters was standing outside, stamping her feet, with her arms crossed under her cloak. Kristin kissed the tear-stained face of the freezing child. Her heart was as heavy as stone, and she felt as if there was lead in her limbs as she climbed the stairs to the loft where they had laid him out.

The sound of hymns and the radiance of many lighted candles filled the doorway. In the center of the loft stood the coffin Arne had been brought home in, covered with a sheet. Boards had been placed over trestles and the coffin had been lifted on top. At its head stood a young priest with a book in his hands, singing. All around him people were kneeling with their faces hidden in their thick capes.

Lavrans lit his candle from one of the candles in the room, set it firmly on the board of the bier, and knelt down. Kristin was about to do the same, but she couldn't get her candle to stand; then Simon stepped over to help her. As long as the priest prayed, everyone remained on their knees, repeating his words in a whisper, so that the steam hovered around their mouths. It was ice-cold in the loft.

When the priest closed his book, the people rose; many had already gathered in the death chamber. Lavrans went over to Inga. She was staring at Kristin and seemed not to hear Lavrans's words; she stood there with the gifts he had given her, holding them as if unaware that she had anything in her hands.

"So you have come too, Kristin," she said in an odd, strained tone of voice. "Perhaps you would like to see my son, the way he has come back to me?"

She moved a few candles aside, grabbed Kristin's arm with a trembling hand, and with the other she tore the cloth from the dead man's face.

It was grayish-yellow like mud, and his lips were the color of lead; they were slightly parted so that the even, narrow, bone-white teeth seemed to offer a mocking smile. Beneath the long eyelashes could be seen a glimpse of his glazed eyes, and there were several bluish-black spots high on his cheeks that were either bruises from the fight or the marks of a corpse.

"Perhaps you would like to kiss him?" asked Inga in the same tone of voice, and Kristin obediently leaned forward and pressed her lips to the dead man's cheek. It was clammy, as if from dew, and she thought she could faintly smell the stench of the corpse; he had no doubt begun to thaw out in the heat from all the candles.

Kristin remained leaning there, with her hands on the bier, for she did not have the strength to stand up. Inga pulled aside more of the shroud so the gash from the knife wound across his collarbone was visible.

Then she turned to the people and said in a quavering voice, "I see that it's a lie, what people say, that a dead man's wounds will bleed if he's touched by the one who caused his death. He's colder now, my boy, and not as handsome as when you last met him down on the road. You don't care to kiss him now, I see—but I've heard that you didn't refuse his lips back then."

"Inga," said Lavrans, stepping forward, "have you lost your senses? What are you saying?"

"Oh, you're all so grand over there at Jørundgaard—you were much too rich a man, Lavrans Bjørgulfsøn, for my son to dare court your daughter with honor. And no doubt Kristin thought she was too good for him too. But she wasn't too good to run after him on the road at night and dally with him in the thickets on the evening he left. Ask her yourself and we'll see if she dares to deny it, as Arne lies here dead—she who has brought this upon us with her loose ways. . . ."

Lavrans did not ask the question; instead he turned to Gyrd.

"You must rein in your wife—she has taken leave of her senses."

But Kristin raised her pale face and looked around in despair.

"I did go out to meet Arne on that last evening, because he asked me to do so. But nothing happened between us that was not proper." And as she seemed to pull herself together and fully realize what was implied, she shouted loudly, "I don't know what you mean, Inga. Are you defaming Arne as he lies here? Never did he try to entice or seduce me."

But Inga laughed loudly.

"Arne? No, not Arne. But Bentein didn't let you play with him that way. Ask Gunhild, Lavrans, who washed the filth off your daughter's back, and ask any man who was in the men's quarters at the bishop's citadel on New Year's Eve when Bentein ridiculed Arne for having let her go and then was made her fool. She let

Bentein come under her fur as she walked home, and she tried to play the same game with him—"

Lavrans gripped Inga by the shoulder and pressed his hand against her mouth.

"Get her out of here, Gyrd. It's shameful that you should talk this way before the body of this good boy. But even if all of your children lay here dead, I would not stand and listen to your lies about mine. And you, Gyrd, will have to answer for what this demented woman is saying."

Gyrd took hold of his wife to lead her away, but he said to Lavrans, "It's true that Arne and Bentein were talking about Kristin when my son lost his life. It's understandable that you may not have heard it, but there has been talk here in the village this fall. . . ."

Simon slammed his sword into the nearest clothes chest.

"No, good folks, now you will have to find something other than my betrothed to talk about in this death chamber. Priest, can't you harness these people so that everything proceeds according to custom?"

The priest—Kristin now saw that he was the youngest son from Ulvsvold who had been home for Christmas—opened his book and took up his position next to the bier. But Lavrans shouted that those who had spoken of his daughter, whoever they might be, would have to eat their words.

And then Inga screamed, "Go ahead and take my life, Lavrans, just as she has taken all my solace and joy—and celebrate her marriage to this son of a knight, and yet everyone will know that she was married to Bentein on the road. Here—" And she threw the sheet that Lavrans had given her across the bier to Kristin. "I don't need Ragnfrid's linen to wrap around Arne for burial. Make yourself a kerchief out of it, or keep it to swaddle your wayside bastard—and go over to help Gunhild mourn for the hanged man."

Lavrans, Gyrd, and the priest all seized hold of Inga. Simon tried to lift up Kristin, who was lying across the bier. But she vehemently shook off his hand, and then, still on her knees, she straightened up and shouted loudly, "May God my Savior help me, that is a lie!"

She put out her hand and held it over the nearest candle on the bier.

It looked as if the flame wavered and moved aside. Kristin felt everyone's eyes upon her—for a very long time, it seemed. Then she suddenly noticed a searing pain in her palm, and with a piercing shriek she collapsed onto the floor.

She thought she had fainted, but she could feel Simon and the priest lifting her up. Inga screamed something. She saw her father's horrified face and heard the priest shout that no one should consider it a true trial—this was not the way to ask God to bear witness—and then Simon carried Kristin out of the loft and down the stairs. Simon's servant ran to the stable and a moment later Kristin, still only half conscious, was sitting on the front of Simon's saddle, wrapped in his cape, as he rode down toward the village as fast as his horse could carry them.

They had almost reached Jørundgaard when Lavrans overtook them. The rest of their entourage came thundering along the road far behind.

"Say nothing to your mother," said Simon as he set Kristin down next to the door. "We've heard far too much senseless talk tonight; it's no wonder that you fainted in the end."

Ragnfrid was lying awake when they came in and she asked how things had gone at the vigil. Simon spoke for all of them. Yes, there were many candles and many people. Yes, a priest was there—Tormod of Ulvsvold. Of Sira Eirik, he heard that he had ridden south to Hamar that very evening, so they would avoid any difficulty at the burial.

"We must have a mass said for the boy," said Ragnfrid. "May God give Inga strength. She has been sorely tried, that good, capable woman."

Lavrans fell in with the tone that Simon had set, and in a little while Simon said that now they must all go to bed—"For Kristin is both tired and sad."

Some time later, when Ragnfrid had fallen asleep, Lavrans threw on some clothes and went over to sit on the edge of the bed where his daughters were sleeping. In the dark he found Kristin's hand, and then he said gently, "Now you must tell me, child, what is true and what is a lie in all this talk that Inga is spouting."

Sobbing, Kristin told him of everything that had happened on the evening that Arne left for Hamar. Lavrans said little. Then Kristin crawled forward on the bed and threw her arms around his neck, whimpering softly.

"I am to blame for Arne's death—it's true what Inga said. . . ."

"Arne himself asked you to come and meet him," said Lavrans, pulling the covers up around his daughter's bare shoulders. "It was thoughtless of me to allow the two of you to spend so much time together, but I thought the boy had better sense. I won't blame the two of you; I can see that these things are heavy for you to bear. And yet I never imagined that any of my daughters would fall into ill repute here in our village. It will be painful for your mother when she hears this news. But you went to Gunhild instead of coming to me—that was so unwise that I can't understand how you could act so foolishly."

"I don't want to stay here in the village any longer," wept Kristin. "I don't dare look a single person in the eye. And all the sorrow I have caused those at Romundgaard and at Finsbrekken . . ."

"Yes," said Lavrans, "they will have to make sure, both Gyrd and Sira Eirik, that these lies about you are put in the ground along with Arne. Otherwise it is Simon Andressøn who can best defend you in this matter." And he patted her in the dark. "Don't you think he handled things well and with good sense?"

"Father," Kristin begged, fearful and fervent, as she clung to him, "send me to the cloister, Father. Yes, listen to me—I've thought about this for a long time. Maybe Ulvhild will get well if I go in her place. Do you remember the shoes that I sewed for her this autumn, the ones with pearls on them? I pricked my fingers so badly, I bled from the sharp gold thread. I sat and sewed those shoes because I thought it was wrong that I didn't love my sister enough to become a nun and help her. Arne asked me about that once. If I had said yes back then, none of this would have happened."

Lavrans shook his head.

"Lie down now," he told her. "You don't know what you're saying, my poor child. Now you must try to sleep."

But Kristin lay there, feeling the pain in her burned hand; bitterness and despair over her fate raged in her heart. Things could not have gone worse for her if she had been the most sinful of women; everyone would believe . . . No, she couldn't, she couldn't stand to stay here in the village. Horror after horror appeared before her. When her mother found out about this . . . And now there was blood between them and their parish priest, hostility among all those around her who had been friends her whole life. But the most extreme and oppressive fears seized her whenever she thought of Simon—the way he had picked her up and carried her off and spoken for her at home and acted as if she were his property. Her father and mother had yielded to him as if she already belonged more to him than to them.

Then she remembered Arne's face, cold and hideous. She remembered that she had seen an open grave waiting for a body the last time she came out of church. The chopped-up lumps of earth lay on the snow, hard and cold and gray as iron—that was where she had brought Arne.

Suddenly she thought about a summer night many years before. She was standing on the loft gallery at Finsbrekken, the same loft where she had been struck down this evening. Arne was playing ball with some boys down in the courtyard, and the ball came sailing up to her on the gallery. She held it behind her back and refused to give it up when Arne came to retrieve it. Then he tried to take it from her by force, and they had fought over it on the gallery, then inside the loft among the chests. The leather sacks full of clothes that were hanging there knocked them on the head when they ran into them during the chase. They had fought and tumbled over that ball.

And now she finally seemed to realize that he was dead and gone, and that she would never see his brave, handsome face or feel his warm hands again. She had been so childish and heartless that it had never occurred to her how he would feel about losing her. She wept in despair and thought she deserved her own unhappiness. But then she started thinking again about everything that still awaited her, and she wept because she thought the punishment that would befall her was too severe.

Simon was the one who told Ragnfrid about what had happened at the vigil at Brekken the night before. He made no more of the matter than was necessary. But Kristin was so dazed from grief and a sleepless night that she felt a purely unreasonable bitterness toward him, because he could speak of it as if it were not so terrible after all. She also felt a great displeasure at the way her parents let Simon act as if he were the master of the house.

"So you don't think anything of it, Simon?" asked Ragnfrid anxiously.

"No," replied Simon. "And I don't think anyone else will either; they know you and her and they know this Bentein. But there's not much to talk about in this remote village; it's perfectly reasonable for people to help themselves to this juicy tidbit. Now we'll have to teach them that Kristin's reputation is too rich a diet for the peasants around here. But it's too bad that she was so frightened by his coarseness that she didn't come to you at once, or go to Sira Eirik himself. I think that whorehouse priest would have gladly testified that he had meant no more than some innocent teasing if you had spoken to him, Lavrans."

Both parents agreed that Simon was right. But Kristin gave a shriek and stamped her foot.

"But he knocked me to the ground. I hardly know what he did to me. I was out of my senses; I no longer remember a thing. For all I know, it might be as Inga says. I haven't been well or happy for a single day since. . . ."

Ragnfrid gave a cry and pressed her hands together; Lavrans leaped to his feet. Even Simon's face changed expression; he gave Kristin a sharp look, went over to her, and put his hand under her chin. Then he laughed.

"God bless you, Kristin. You would have remembered it if he had done you any harm. It's no wonder she's been feeling melancholy and unwell since that unlucky evening when she was given such a fright—she who has never met with anything but kindness and goodwill before," he said to the others. "Anyone can see from her eyes, which bear no ill intent and would rather believe in good than evil, that she is a maiden and not a woman."

Kristin looked up into the small, steady eyes of her betrothed. She raised her arms halfway up; she wanted to place them around his neck.

Then Simon went on. "You mustn't think, Kristin, that you won't forget all about this. I don't intend for us to settle at Formo right away and never allow you to leave this valley. 'No one has the same color of hair or temperament in the rain as in the sun,' said old King Sverre when they accused his 'Birch-Leg' followers[2] of growing arrogant with success."

Lavrans and Ragnfrid smiled. It amused them to hear the young man speak as if he were a wise old bishop.

Simon continued. "It would not be proper for me to admonish you, the man who is to be my father-in-law, but perhaps I might say this much: we were dealt with more strictly, my siblings and I. We were not allowed to move so freely among the servants as I see it is Kristin's custom. My mother used to say that if you play with the cottager's children, in the long run you'll end up with lice in your hair; and there is some truth to that."

Lavrans and Ragnfrid said nothing to this. But Kristin turned away, and the desire she had felt for a moment to put her arms around Simon Darre's neck had vanished completely.

Around midday Lavrans and Simon put on their skis and went off to tend to several traps up on the ridge. Outdoors it was now beautiful weather, sunny and not nearly as bitter cold. Both men were relieved to slip away from all the sorrow and tears at home, so they skied a great distance, all the way up to the bare rock.

They lay in the sun under a steep cliff and drank and ate. Then Lavrans talked a little about Arne; he had been very fond of the boy. Simon joined in, praising the dead man, and said that he didn't find it strange that Kristin should grieve for her foster brother. Then Lavrans mentioned that perhaps they should not pressure her so much, but give her a little more time to regain her composure before they celebrated the betrothal ale. She had said that she would like to go to a cloister for a while.

Simon sat up suddenly and gave a long whistle.

"You don't care for the idea?" asked Lavrans.

"Oh, yes, yes," replied the other man hastily. "This seems to be the best counsel, dear father-in-law. Send her to the sisters in Oslo for a year; then she'll learn how people talk about each other out in the world. I happen to know a little about several of the maidens who are there," he said and laughed. "They wouldn't lie down and die of grief over two mad boys tearing each other apart for their sake. Not that I would want such a maiden for my wife, but I don't think it would do Kristin any harm to meet some new people."

Lavrans put the rest of the food in the knapsack and said, without looking at the young man, "You are fond of Kristin, I think."

Simon laughed a little but did not look at Lavrans.

"You must know that I have great affection for her—and for you, as well," Simon said brusquely, and then he stood up and put on his skis. "I have never met any maiden I would rather marry."

Right before Easter, while it was still possible to drive a sleigh down the valley and across Lake Mjøsa, Kristin made her second journey to the south. Simon came to escort her to the cloister. So this time she traveled with her father and her betrothed, sitting in the sleigh, wrapped in furs. And accompanying them were servants and sleighs full of her chests of clothing and gifts of food and furs for the abbess and the sisters of Nonneseter.

PART II

THE WREATH

CHAPTER 1

EARLY ONE SUNDAY morning at the end of April, Aasmund Bjørg-ulfsøn's church boat glided past the point on the island of Hovedø as the bells rang in the cloister church, and bells from the town chimed their reply out across the bay, sounding louder, then fainter as the wind carried the notes.

The sky was clear and pale blue, with light fluted clouds drifting across it, and the sun was glinting restlessly on the rippling water. It seemed quite springlike along the shore; the fields were almost bare of snow, and there were bluish shadows and a yellowish sheen on the leafy thickets. But snow was visible in the spruce forest atop the ridges framing the settlements of Aker, and to the west, on the distant blue mountains beyond the fjord, many streaks of white still gleamed.

Kristin was standing in the bow of the boat with her father and Gyrid, Aasmund's wife. She turned her gaze toward the town, with all of its light-colored churches and stone buildings rising up above the multitudes of grayish-brown wooden houses and the bare crowns of the trees. The wind ruffled the edges of her cloak and tousled her hair beneath her hood.

They had let the livestock out to pasture at Skog the day before, and Kristin had suddenly felt such a homesickness for Jørundgaard. It would be a long time before they could let out the cattle back home. She felt a tender and sympathetic longing for the winter-gaunt cattle in the dark stalls; they would have to wait and endure for many days yet. She missed everyone so—her mother, Ulvhild, who had slept in her arms every night for all these years, little Ramborg. She longed for all the people back home and for the horses and dogs; for Kortelin, whom Ulvhild would take care of while she was gone; and for her father's hawks, sitting on their perches with hoods over their heads. Next to them hung the gloves made of horsehide, which had to be worn when handling them, and the ivory sticks used to scratch them.

All the terrible events of the winter now seemed so far away, and she only remembered her home as it had been before. They had also told her that no one in the village thought ill of her. Nor did Sira Eirik; he was angry and aggrieved by what Bentein had done. Bentein had escaped from Hamar, and it was said that he had run off to Sweden. So things had not been as unpleasant between her family and the people of the neighboring farm as Kristin had feared.

On their way south they had stayed at Simon's home, and she had met his mother and siblings; Sir Andres was still in Sweden. She had not felt at ease there, and her dislike of the family at Dyfrin was all the greater because she knew of no reasonable explanation for it. During the entire journey she had told herself that they had no reason to be haughty or to consider themselves better than her ancestors—no one had ever heard of Reidar Darre, the Birch-Leg, until King Sverre found the widow of the baron at Dyfrin for him to wed.

But they turned out not to be haughty at all, and Simon even spoke of his ancestor one evening. "I have now found out for certain that he was supposed to have been a comb maker—so you will truly be joining a royal lineage, Kristin," he said.

"Guard your tongue, my boy," said his mother, but they all laughed.

Kristin felt so oddly distressed when she thought of her father. He laughed a great deal whenever Simon gave him the least reason to do so. The thought occurred to her that perhaps her father would have liked to laugh more often in his life. But she didn't like it that he was so fond of Simon.

During Easter they were all at Skog. Kristin noticed that her Uncle Aasmund was a stern master toward his tenants and servants. She met a few people who asked after her mother and who spoke affectionately of Lavrans; they had enjoyed better days when he was living there. Aasmund's mother, who was Lavrans's step-mother, lived on the farm in her own house. She was not particularly old, but she was sickly and feeble. Lavrans seldom spoke of

her at home. Once when Kristin asked her father whether he had
had a quarrelsome stepmother, he had replied, "She has never done
much for me, good or bad."

Kristin reached for her father's hand, and he squeezed hers in
return.

"I know you'll be happy with the worthy sisters, my daughter.
There you'll have other things to think about than yearning for us
back home."

They sailed so close to the town that the smell of tar and salt fish
drifted out to them from the docks. Gyrid pointed out the churches
and farms and roads that stretched upward from the water's edge.
Kristin recognized nothing from the last time she had been there
except for the ponderous towers of Halvard's Cathedral. They
sailed west, around the entire town, and then put in at the nuns'
dock.

Kristin walked between her father and her uncle past a cluster
of warehouses and then reached the road, which led uphill past
the fields. Gyrid followed after them, escorted by Simon. The servants stayed behind to help several men from the cloister load the
trunks onto a cart.

The convent Nonneseter and all of Leiran lay inside the town's
boundaries, but there were only a few houses clustered here and
there along the road. The larks were chirping overhead in the pale
blue sky, and tiny yellow Michaelmas daisies teemed on the sallow
dirt hills, but along the fences the roots of the grass were green.

As they went through the gate and entered the colonnade, all
the nuns came walking toward them in a procession from church,
with music and song streaming after them from the open doorway.

Kristin stared uneasily at the many black-clad women with
white wimples framing their faces. She sank into a curtsey, and the
men bowed with their hats pressed to their chests. Following the
nuns came a group of young maidens—some of them were
children—wearing dresses of undyed homespun, with black-and-
white belts made of twisted cord around their waists. Their hair
was pulled back from their faces and braided tightly with the same
kind of black-and-white cord. Kristin unconsciously put on a

haughty expression for the young maidens because she felt shy, and she was afraid that they would think she looked unrefined and foolish.

The convent was so magnificent that she was completely overwhelmed. All the buildings surrounding the inner courtyard were made of gray stone. On the north side the long wall of the church loomed above the other buildings; it had a two-tiered roof and a tower at the west end. The surface of the courtyard was paved with flagstones, and the entire area was enclosed by a covered arcade supported by stately pillars. In the center of the square stood a stone statue of *Mater Misericordiae*, spreading her cloak over a group of kneeling people.

A lay sister came forward and asked them to follow her to the parlatory, the abbess's reception room. Abbess Groa Guttormsdatter was a tall, stout old woman. She would have been good-looking if she hadn't had so many stubbly hairs around her mouth. Her voice was deep and made her sound like a man. But she had a pleasant manner, and she reminded Lavrans that she had known his parents, and then asked after his wife and their other children. At last she turned kindly to Kristin.

"I have heard good things of you, and you seem to be clever and well brought up, so I do not think you will give us any reason for displeasure. I have heard that you are promised to that noble and good man, Simon Andressøn, whom I see before me. We think it wise of your father and your betrothed to send you here to the Virgin Mary's house for a time, so that you can learn to obey and to serve before you are charged with giving orders and commands. I want to impress on you now that you should learn to find joy in prayer and the divine services so that in all your actions you will be in the habit of remembering your Creator, the Lord's gentle Mother, and all the saints who have given us the best examples of strength, rectitude, fidelity, and all the virtues that you ought to demonstrate if you are to manage property and servants and raise children. You will also learn in this house that one must pay close attention to time, because here each hour has a specific purpose and chore. Many young maidens and wives are much too fond of lying in bed late in the morning, and of lingering at the table in the evening, carrying on useless conversation. But you do not look as if you were that kind. Yet you can learn a great deal from this year that will benefit you both here and in that other home."

Kristin curtseyed and kissed her hand. Then Fru Groa told Kristin to follow an exceptionally fat old nun, whom she called Sister Potentia, over to the nuns' refectory. She invited the men and Fru Gyrid to dine with her in a different room.

The refectory was a beautiful hall. It had a stone floor and arched windows with glass panes. A doorway led into another room, and Kristin could see that this room too must have glass windowpanes, because the sun was shining inside.

The sisters had already sat down and were waiting for the food. The older nuns were sitting on a stone bench covered with cushions along the wall under the windows. The younger sisters and the bareheaded maidens wearing light homespun dresses sat on a wooden bench in front of the table. Tables had also been set in the adjoining room, which was intended for the most distinguished of the corrodians[1] and the lay servants; there were several old men among them. These people did not wear cloister garb, but they did wear dark and dignified attire.

Sister Potentia showed Kristin to a place on the outer bench while she herself went over to a seat near the abbess's place of honor at the head of the table, which would remain empty today.

Everyone rose, both in the main hall and in the adjoining room, as the sisters said the blessing. Then a young, pretty nun came forward and stepped up to a lectern which had been placed in the doorway between the rooms. And while two of the lay sisters in the main hall and two of the youngest nuns in the other room brought in the food and drink, the nun read in a loud and lovely voice—without pausing or hesitating at a single word—the story of Saint Theodora and Saint Didymus.

From the very first moment, Kristin thought most about showing good table manners, for she noticed that all the sisters and young maidens had such elegant comportment and ate so properly, as if they were at the most magnificent banquet. There was an abundance of the best food and drink, but everyone took only modest portions, using only the tips of their fingers to help themselves from the platters. No one spilled any soup on the tablecloth or on their clothes, and everyone cut up the meat into such tiny pieces that they hardly sullied their lips; they ate so carefully that not a sound could be heard.

Kristin was sweating with fear that she wouldn't be able to act as refined as the others. She also felt uncomfortable in her brightly colored attire among all the women dressed in black and white. She imagined that they were all staring at her. Then, as she was about to eat a piece of fatty mutton breast and was holding it with two fingers pressed against the bone while in her right hand she held the knife, trying to cut easily and neatly, the whole thing slipped away from her. The bread and the meat leaped onto the tablecloth as the knife fell with a clatter to the floor.

The sound was deafening in that quiet room. Kristin blushed red as blood and was about to bend down to pick up the knife, but a lay sister wearing sandals came over, soundlessly, and gathered up the things. But Kristin could eat nothing more. She also noticed that she had cut her finger, and she was afraid of bleeding on the tablecloth, so she sat there with her hand wrapped up in a fold of her dress, thinking that now she was making spots on the lovely light-blue gown that she had been given for her journey to Oslo. And she didn't dare raise her eyes from her lap.

After a while she started to listen more closely to what the nun was reading. When the chieftain could not sway the maiden Theodora's steadfast will—she would neither make sacrifices to false gods nor let herself be married—he ordered her to be taken to a brothel. Furthermore, he exhorted her along the way to think of her freeborn ancestors and her honorable parents, upon whom an everlasting shame would now fall, and he promised that she would be allowed to live in peace and remain a maiden if she would agree to serve a pagan goddess, whom they called Diana.

Theodora replied, unafraid, "Chastity is like a lamp, but love for God is the flame. If I were to serve the devil-woman whom you call Diana, then my chastity would be worth no more than a rusty lamp without fire or oil. You call me freeborn, but we are all born thralls, since our first parents sold us to the Devil. Christ has redeemed me, and I am obliged to serve him, so I cannot marry his enemies. He will protect his dove, but if he would cause you to break my body, which is the temple of his Holy Spirit, then it shall not be reckoned to my shame, as long as I do not consent to betray his property in enemy hands."

Kristin's heart began to pound, because this reminded her in a certain way of her encounter with Bentein. It struck her that perhaps this was her sin, that she had not for a moment thought of God or prayed for His help. Then Sister Cecilia read about Saint Didymus. He was a Christian knight, but he had kept his Christianity secret from all except a few friends. He went to the house where the maiden was confined. He gave money to the woman who owned the house, and then he was allowed to go to Theodora. She fled to a corner like a frightened rabbit, but Didymus greeted her as a sister and the bride of his Lord and said that he had come to save her. Then he talked to her for a while, saying: "Shouldn't a brother risk his own life for his sister's honor?" And finally she did as he asked; she exchanged clothes with him and allowed herself to be strapped into his coat of mail. He pulled the helmet down over her eyes and drew the cape closed under her chin, and then he told her to go out with her face hidden, like a youth who was ashamed to be in such a place.

Kristin thought about Arne and had the greatest difficulty in holding back her sobs. She stared straight ahead, with tear-filled eyes, as the nun read the end of the story—how Didymus was led off to the gallows and Theodora came rushing down from the mountains, threw herself at the executioner's feet, and begged to be allowed to die in his place. Then those two pious people argued about who would be the first to win the crown, and they were both beheaded on the same day. It was the twenty-eighth day of April in the year A.D. 304, in Antioch, as Saint Ambrosius has written of it.

When they rose from the table, Sister Potentia came over and patted Kristin kindly on the cheek. "Yes, I can imagine that you are longing for your mother." Then Kristin's tears began to fall. But the nun pretended not to notice, and she led Kristin to the dormitory where she was going to live.

It was in one of the stone buildings along the colonnade, a

beautiful room with glass windowpanes and an enormous fireplace at the far end. Along one wall stood six beds and along the other were all of the maidens' chests.

Kristin wished she would be allowed to sleep with one of the little girls, but Sister Potentia called to a plump, fair-haired, fully grown maiden.

"This is Ingebjørg Filippusdatter, who will be your bedmate. The two of you should get acquainted." And then she left.

Ingebjørg took Kristin's hand at once and began to talk. She was not very tall and much too fat, especially in her face; her eyes were tiny because her cheeks were so fat. But her complexion was pure, pink and white, and her hair was yellow like gold and so curly that her thick braids twisted and turned like ropes, and little locks were constantly slipping out from under her headband.

She immediately began asking Kristin about all sorts of things but never waited for an answer. Instead, she talked about herself and reeled off all her ancestors in all the branches; they were grand and enormously wealthy people. Ingebjørg was also betrothed, to a rich and powerful man, Einar Einarssøn of Aganæs—but he was much too old and had twice been widowed. It was her greatest sorrow, she said. But Kristin couldn't see that she was taking it particularly hard. Then Ingebjørg talked a little about Simon Darre—it was strange how carefully she had studied him during that brief moment when they passed each other in the arcade. Then Ingebjørg wanted to look in Kristin's chest, but first she opened her own and showed Kristin all of her gowns. As they were rummaging in the chests, Sister Cecilia came in. She reproached them and told them that was not a proper activity on a Sunday. And then Kristin felt downhearted again. She had never been reprimanded by anyone except her own mother, and it felt odd to be scolded by strangers.

Ingebjørg was completely unperturbed.

That night, after they had gone to bed, Ingebjørg lay there talking, right up until Kristin fell asleep. Two elderly lay sisters slept in a corner of the room. They were supposed to see to it that the maidens did not remove their shifts at night—for it was against the rules for the girls to undress completely—and that they got up in time for matins at the church. But otherwise they didn't concern

THE WREATH 107

themselves with keeping order in the dormitory, and they pretended not to notice when the maidens lay in bed talking or eating treats they had hidden in their chests.

When Kristin awoke the next morning, Ingebjørg was already in the middle of a long story, and Kristin wondered whether she had been talking all night.

CHAPTER 2

THE FOREIGN MERCHANTS who spent the summer trading in Oslo arrived in the city in the spring, around Holy Cross Day, which was ten days before the Vigil of Saint Halvard. For that celebration, people came in throngs from all the villages from Lake Mjøsa to the Swedish border, so the town was teeming with people during the first weeks of May. It was best to buy goods from the foreigners during that time, before they had sold too many of their wares.

Sister Potentia was in charge of the shopping at Nonneseter, and on the day before the Vigil of Saint Halvard she had promised Ingebjørg and Kristin that they could go along with her into town. But around noon some of Sister Potentia's kinsmen came to the convent to visit her; she would not be able to go out that day. Then Ingebjørg managed to beg permission for them to go alone, although this was against the rules. As an escort, an old farmer who received a corrody from the cloister was sent along with them. His name was Haakon.

By this time, Kristin had been at Nonneseter for three weeks, and in all that time she had not once set foot outside the convent's courtyards and gardens. She was astonished to see how springlike it had become outside. The small groves of leafy trees out in the fields were shiny green, and the wood anemones were growing as thick as a carpet beneath the lustrous tree trunks. Bright fair-weather clouds came sailing above the islands in the fjord, and the water looked fresh and blue, rippled by small gusts of spring wind.

Ingebjørg skipped along, snapping off clusters of leaves from the trees and smelling them, turning to stare at the people they passed, but Haakon reproached her. Was that the proper way for a noble maiden to act, and one who was wearing convent attire, at that? The maidens had to take each other by the hand and walk along behind him, quietly and decorously; but Ingebjørg let her

108

eyes wander and her mouth chatter all the same, since Haakon was slightly deaf. Kristin now wore the garb of a young sister: an un-dyed, pale-gray homespun dress, a woolen belt and headband, and a simple dark-blue cloak with the hood pulled forward so that her braided hair was completely hidden. Haakon strode along in front of them with a big brass-knobbed stick in his hand. He was dressed in a long black coat, with an *Agnus Dei* made of lead hanging on his chest and a picture of Saint Christopher on his hat. His white hair and beard were so well-brushed that they glinted like silver in the sun.

The upper part of the town, from the nuns' creek and down toward the bishop's citadel, was a quiet neighborhood. There were no market stalls or hostelries, only farms belonging mostly to gen-try from the outlying villages. The buildings faced the street with dark and windowless timbered gables. But on this day, the lane was already crowded up there, and servants were hanging over the farm fences, talking to the people walking past.

As they came out near the bishop's citadel, they joined a great throng at the marketplace in front of Halvard's Cathedral and Olav's cloister. Booths had been set up on the grassy slope and there were strolling players who were making trained dogs jump through barrel hoops. But Haakon wouldn't let the maidens stop to watch, nor would he allow Kristin to enter the church; he said it would be more fun for her to see it on the great festival day itself.

On the road in front of Clement's Church, Haakon took them both by the hand, for here the crowd was even bigger, with people coming in from the wharves or from the lanes between the town-yards.[1] The girls were going to Miklegaard, where the shoemakers worked. Ingebjørg thought the dresses that Kristin had brought from home were pretty and nice, but she said that the footwear Kristin had with her from the village could not be worn on fine occasions. And when Kristin saw the foreign-made shoes, of which Ingebjørg had many pairs, she thought she could not rest until she had bought some for herself.

Miklegaard was one of the largest townyards in Oslo. It ex-tended all the way from the wharves up toward Shoemaker Lane, with more than forty buildings surrounding two big courtyards.

Now booths with homespun canopies had also been set up in the courtyards, and above the tents towered a statue of Saint Crispin. There was a great crush of people shopping. Women were running back and forth to the cookhouses with pots and buckets, children were getting tangled up in people's feet, horses were being led in and out of the stables, and servants were carrying loads in and out of the storage sheds. Up on the galleries of the lofts where the finest wares were sold, the shoemakers and hawkers in the booths called to the maidens below, dangling toward them small, colorful, gold-stitched shoes.

But Ingebjørg headed for the loft where Shoemaker Didrek had his workshop; he was German but had a Norwegian wife and owned a building in Miklegaard.

The old man was conducting business with a gentleman wearing a traveling cape and a sword at his belt, but Ingebjørg stepped forward boldly, bowed, and said, "Good sir, won't you allow us to speak with Didrek first? We must be back home at our convent before vespers, and you perhaps have more time?"

The gentleman greeted her and stepped aside. Didrek gave Ingebjørg a poke with his elbow and asked her with a laugh whether they were dancing so much at the cloister that she had already worn out all the shoes she had bought the year before. Ingebjørg gave him a poke back and said that they were hardly used at all, good heavens, but here was another maiden—and she pulled Kristin over to him. Then Didrek and his apprentice brought a chest out to the gallery, and he started taking out the shoes, each pair more beautiful than the last. Kristin sat down on a box and he tried the shoes on her feet. There were white shoes, and brown and red and green and blue shoes; shoes with painted heels made of wood, and shoes with no heels at all; shoes with buckles, shoes with silken ties, and shoes made from two or three different colored leathers. Kristin almost thought she liked them all. But they were so expensive that she was shocked—not a single pair cost less than a cow back home. Her father had given her a purse with one mark of silver counted out in coins when he left; this was to be her spending money, and Kristin had thought it a great sum. But she could see that Ingebjørg didn't think she could buy much with it at all.

Ingebjørg also had to try on shoes, just for fun. It didn't cost anything, said Didrek with a laugh. She bought a pair of leaf-green shoes with red heels, but she had to take them on credit; Didrek knew her, after all, as well as her family.

But Kristin could see that Didrek did not much care for this, and he was also dismayed because the tall gentleman in the traveling cape had left the loft; they had spent a long time trying on shoes. So Kristin chose a pair of shoes without heels made of thin, blue-violet leather; they were stitched with silver and rose-colored stones. But she didn't like the green silk straps. Then Didrek said that he could change them, and he took them along to a room at the back of the loft. There he had boxes of silk ribbons and small silver buckles—things which shoemakers were actually not allowed to sell, and many of the ribbons were too wide and the buckles too big for shoes anyway.

Both Kristin and Ingebjørg had to buy a few of these odds and ends, and by the time they had drunk a little sweet wine with Didrek and he had wrapped up their purchases in a homespun cloth, it had grown quite late, and Kristin's purse had grown much lighter.

When they came out onto East Lane again, the sun was quite gold, and the dust from all the traffic in the town hung like a faint haze over the street. It was so warm and lovely, and people were arriving from Eikaberg with great armfuls of new foliage to decorate their houses for the holiday. Then Ingebjørg decided that they should walk out toward Gjeita Bridge. On market days there was always so much entertainment going on in the paddocks along the river, with jugglers and fiddlers. Ingebjørg had even heard that a whole ship full of foreign animals had arrived, and they were being displayed in cages down on the shore.

Haakon had had some German beer at Miklegaard and was now quite amenable and in good spirits, so when the maidens took him by the arm and begged so nicely, he relented, and the three of them walked over toward Eikaberg.

On the other side of the river there were only a few small farms scattered across the green slopes between the river and the steep incline. They went past the Minorites' cloister, and Kristin's heart shrank with shame, for she suddenly remembered that she had

wanted to offer most of her silver for Arne's soul. But she had not
wanted to speak of this to the priest at Nonneseter; she was afraid
of being questioned. She had thought that perhaps she could go
out to visit the barefoot friars in the pastures to see whether
Brother Edvin had returned—she would have liked so much to
meet him. But she didn't know how properly to approach one of
the monks or to broach the topic. And now she had so little money
left that she didn't know whether she could afford a mass; maybe
she would have to settle for offering a thick wax candle.

Suddenly they heard a terrible roar from countless voices out at
the paddock on the shore—it was as if a storm were passing over
the swarm of people gathered down there. And then the whole
crowd came rushing up toward them, shrieking and hollering. Everyone was running in wild terror, and several people screamed to
Haakon and the maidens that the leopards were loose.

They raced back toward the bridge, and they heard people
shouting to each other that a cage had tipped over and two leopards had escaped; someone also mentioned a snake. The closer they
came to the bridge, the greater the crowd. A baby fell from a woman's arms right in front of them, and Haakon stood over the little
one to protect him. A moment later Kristin and Ingebjørg caught
a glimpse of the old man far off to one side, holding the child in
his arms, and then they lost sight of him.

At the narrow bridge the mob surged forward so fiercely that
the maidens were forced out into a field. They saw people running
along the riverbank; young men jumped into the water and began
to swim, but the older people leaped into the moored boats, which
became instantly overloaded.

Kristin tried to make Ingebjørg listen to her; she screamed that
they should run over to the Minorites' cloister. The gray-cowled
monks had come rushing over and were trying to gather the terrified people. Kristin was not as frightened as her friend, and they
saw nothing of the wild animals, but Ingebjørg had completely lost
her head. The swarms of people surged forward again, and then
were driven back from the bridge because a large crowd of men
who had gone to the nearest farms to arm themselves was now
headed back, some on horseback, some running. When Ingebjørg
was almost trampled by a horse, she gave a shriek and took off up

the hill toward the forest. Kristin had never imagined that
Ingebjørg could run so fast—she was reminded of a hunted boar
—and she ran after her so that they wouldn't become separated.

They were deep inside the forest before Kristin managed to stop
Ingebjørg on a small pathway which seemed to lead down toward
the road to Trælaborg. They paused for a moment to catch their
breath. Ingebjørg was sniffling and crying, and she said she didn't
dare go back alone through the town and all the way out to the
convent.

Kristin didn't think it a good idea either, with so much commotion in the streets; she thought they should find a house where
they might hire a boy to accompany them home. Ingebjørg recalled
a bridle path to Trælaborg farther down near the shore, and she
was certain that along the path were several houses. So they followed the path downhill.

Distressed as they both were, it seemed to them that they walked
for a long time before they finally saw a farm in the middle of a
field. In the courtyard they found a group of men sitting at a table
beneath some ash trees, drinking. A woman went back and forth,
bringing pitchers out to them. She gave the two maidens in convent
attire a surprised and annoyed look, and none of the men seemed
to want to accompany them when Kristin explained their need.
But finally two young fellows stood up and said they would escort
the girls to Nonneseter if Kristin would pay them an *ørtug*.[2]

She could tell from their speech that they weren't Norwegian,
but they seemed to be decent men. She thought their demand
shamefully exorbitant, but Ingebjørg was scared out of her wits
and she didn't think they should walk home alone so late in the
day, so she agreed.

No sooner had they come out onto the forest path than the men
drew aside and began talking to each other. Kristin was upset by
this, but she didn't want to show her apprehension, so she spoke
to them calmly, told them about the leopards, and asked them
where they were from. She also looked around, pretending that at
any minute she expected to meet the servants who had been es-
corting them; she talked about them as if they were a large group.
Gradually the men said less and less, and she understood very little
of their language anyway.

After a while Kristin noticed that they were not headed the way she had come with Ingebjørg; the path led in a different direction, more to the north, and she thought they had already gone much too far. Deep inside her, terror was smoldering, but she dared not let it slip into her thoughts. She felt oddly strengthened having Ingebjørg along; the girl was so foolish that Kristin realized she would have to handle things for both of them. Under her cloak she pulled out the reliquary cross that her father had given her, clasped her hand around it, and prayed with all her heart that they might meet up with someone soon, as she tried to gather her courage and pretend that nothing was wrong.

A moment later she saw that the path led out onto a road, and at that spot there was a clearing. The bay and the town lay far below them. The men had led them astray, either willfully or because they were not familiar with the paths. They were high up on the slope and far north of Gjeita Bridge, which Kristin could see. The road they had reached seemed to lead in that direction.

Then she stopped, took out her purse, and began to count out the ten *penninger* into her hand.

"Now, good sirs," she said, "we no longer need your escort. We know the way from here. We give you thanks for your trouble, and here is your payment, as we agreed. God be with you, good friends."

The men looked at each other for a moment, quite foolishly, so that Kristin was almost about to smile. But then one of them said with an ugly leer that the road down to the bridge was a desolate one; it would not be advisable for them to go alone.

"No one would be so malicious or so stupid as to want to stop two maidens, especially two dressed in convent attire," replied Kristin. "We prefer to go alone," and then she handed them the money.

The man grabbed hold of her wrist, stuck his face close to hers, and said something about a "Kuss" and a "Beutel." Kristin understood that they would be allowed to go unharmed if she would give him a kiss and her purse.

She remembered Bentein's face close to hers, just like this, and for a moment fear seized her; she felt nauseated and sick. But she pressed her lips together, calling upon God and the Virgin Mary in her heart—and at that moment she heard hoofbeats on the path coming from the north.

Then she struck the man in the face with her coin purse so that he stumbled, and she shoved him in the chest so that he toppled off the path and tumbled down into the woods. The other German grabbed her from behind, tore the purse out of her hand, and tugged at the chain around her neck, breaking it. She was just about to fall, but she seized hold of the man, attempting to get her cross back. He tried to pull away; the robber had now heard someone approaching too. Ingebjørg screamed loudly, and the horsemen on the path came racing as fast as they could. They emerged from the thickets; there were three of them. Ingebjørg ran toward them, shrieking, and they jumped down from their horses. Kristin recognized the gentleman from Didrek's loft; he drew his sword, grabbed the German she was struggling with by the scruff of his neck, and struck him with the flat of the blade. His men ran after the other one, seized him, and beat him with all their might.

Kristin leaned against the rock face. Now that it was over she was shaking, but what she felt most was astonishment that her prayer had been answered so quickly. Then she noticed Ingebjørg. The girl had thrown back her hood, letting her cloak fall loosely over her shoulders, and she was arranging her thick blonde braids on her breast. Kristin burst out laughing at the sight. She sank down and had to cling to a tree because she couldn't hold herself up; it was as if she had water instead of marrow in her bones, she felt so weak. She trembled and laughed and cried.

The gentleman came over to her and cautiously placed his hand on her shoulder.

"No doubt you have been more frightened than you dared show," he said, and his voice was pleasant and kind. "But now you must get hold of yourself; you acted so bravely while the danger lasted."

Kristin could only nod. He had beautiful bright eyes, a thin, tan face, and coal-black hair that was cropped short across his forehead and behind his ears.

Ingebjørg had managed to arrange her hair properly at last; she

came over and thanked the stranger with many elegant words. He
stood there with his hand on Kristin's shoulder as he spoke to the
other maiden.

"We'll take these birds along to town so they can be thrown in
the dungeon," he said to his men who were holding the two Germans, who said they belonged to the Rostock ship. "But first we
must escort the maidens back to their convent. I'm sure you can
find some straps to tie them up with. . . ."

"Do you mean the maidens, Erlend?" asked one of the men.
They were young, strong, and well-dressed boys, and they were
both flushed after the fight.

Their master frowned and was about to give a sharp reply. But
Kristin put her hand on his sleeve.

"Let them go, kind sir!" She gave a small shudder. "My sister
and I would be most reluctant to have this matter talked about."

The stranger looked down at her, bit his lip, and nodded as he
gazed at her. Then he gave each of the prisoners a blow on the
back of the neck with the flat of his blade so that they fell forward.
"Get going," he said, giving them a kick, and they took off as fast
as they could. The gentleman turned back to the maidens and
asked them if they would like to ride.

Ingebjørg allowed herself to be lifted up into Erlend's saddle,
but it turned out that she couldn't stay in it; she slipped down
again at once. He gave Kristin a questioning look, and she told
him that she was used to riding a man's saddle.

He grasped her around the knees and lifted her up. She felt a
thrill pass through her, sweet and good, because he held her away
from himself so carefully, as if he were afraid to get too close to
her. Back home they had never paid attention if they pressed her
too close when they helped her onto her horse. She felt so strangely
honored.

The knight—as Ingebjørg called him, even though he wore silver
spurs[3]—offered the other maiden his hand, and his men leaped
onto their horses. Ingebjørg now wanted them to go north, around
the town and along the foot of the Ryen hills and the Marte outcrop, not through the streets. Her excuse was that Sir Erlend and
his men were fully armed, weren't they? The knight replied somberly that the ban against bearing weapons was not so strictly en-

forced for those who were traveling, or for all the people in town who were now hunting wild beasts. Kristin realized full well that Ingebjørg wanted to take the longest and least traveled road in order to talk more with Erlend.

"This is the second time we have delayed you this evening, sir," said Ingebjørg.

Erlend replied gravely, "It doesn't matter; I'm going no farther than to Gerdarud tonight—and it stays light all night long."

Kristin was so pleased that he neither teased nor jested but spoke to her as he would to an equal, or more than that. She thought of Simon; she had never met any other young men of the courtly class. But this man was probably somewhat older than Simon.

They made their way down into the valley below the Ryen hills and up along the stream. The path was narrow, and the young leafy bushes flicked wet, fragrant branches at Kristin. It was a little darker down there, the air was chill, and the foliage was wet with dew along the streambed.

They moved slowly, and the hooves of the horses sounded muffled against the damp, grass-covered path. Kristin swayed in the saddle; behind her she could hear Ingebjørg talking, and the stranger's dark, calm voice. He didn't say much, answering as if preoccupied—as if he were feeling the same as she was, thought Kristin. She felt so strangely drowsy, but safe and content now that all the events of the day had slipped away.

It was like waking up as they emerged from the forest, out onto the slopes below the Marte outcrop. The sun had gone down and the town and the bay lay below them in clear, pallid light. The Aker ridges were limned with bright yellow beneath the pale blue sky. Sounds carried a long way in the quiet of the evening, as if they were coming from the depths of the cool air. From somewhere along the road came the screech of a wagon wheel, and dogs barked to each other from farms on opposite sides of the town. But in the forest behind them birds chirped and sang at the top of their voices now that the sun had gone down.

Smoke drifted through the air as dry grass and leaves were burned, and in the middle of a field a bonfire flared red; the great fiery rose made the clarity of the night seem dim.

They were riding between the fences of the convent's fields when the stranger spoke to Ingebjørg again. He asked her what she thought would be best: Should he escort her to the door and ask to speak with Fru Groa, so that he could tell her how this had all come about? But Ingebjørg thought they should sneak in through the church; then they might be able to slip into the convent without being noticed. They had been gone much too long. Perhaps Sister Potentia had forgotten them because of the visit from her kinsmen.

It didn't occur to Kristin to wonder why it was so quiet in the square in front of the west entrance of the church. Usually there was a great hubbub in the evening as people from the neighboring area came to the nuns' church. And all around stood houses where many of the lay servants and corrodians lived. This was where they said farewell to Erlend. Kristin paused to pet his horse; it was black, with a handsome head and gentle eyes. She thought it looked like Morvin, the horse she had ridden back home when she was a child.

"What's the name of your horse, sir?" she asked as the animal turned his head and snuffled at the man's chest.

"Bajard," he said, looking at Kristin over the horse's neck. "You ask the name of my horse, but not mine?"

"I would indeed like to know your name, sir," she replied, with a little bow.

"Erlend Nikulaussøn is my name," he said.

"Then we must thank you, Erlend Nikulaussøn, for your good assistance tonight," replied Kristin, giving him her hand.

Suddenly her face flushed bright red; she pulled her hand halfway out of his grasp.

"Fru Aashild Gautesdatter at Dovre—is she your kinswoman?" she asked.

She saw with surprise that he too turned blood red. He let go of her hand abruptly and replied, "She is my mother's sister. It's true that I am Erlend Nikulaussøn of Husaby." He gave Kristin such a strange look that she grew even more confused, but she pulled herself together.

"I should have thanked you with better words, Erlend Nikulaussøn, but I don't know what to say to you."

Then he bowed, and she thought she should say goodbye, even

though she would have preferred to talk with him longer. At the entrance to the church she turned around, and when she saw that Erlend was still standing next to his horse, she raised her hand and waved.

Inside the convent great fear and commotion reigned. Haakon had sent a messenger home on horseback while he himself walked through the town searching for the maidens, and servants had been sent out to help him. The nuns had heard that the wild animals had supposedly killed and devoured two children in town. This turned out to be a rumor, and the leopard—there was only one—had been captured well before vespers by several men from the king's castle.

Kristin stood with her head bowed and kept silent as the abbess and Sister Potentia vented their anger on the maidens. She seemed to be asleep inside. Ingebjørg wept and spoke in their defense: they had gone out with Sister Potentia's permission, after all, with the proper escort, and they were not to blame for what had happened afterward.

But Fru Groa told them to stay in the church until the clock struck midnight and try to turn their thoughts to spiritual matters and thank God, who had saved their lives and honor. "God has clearly shown you the truth about the world," she said. "Wild beasts and the Devil's servants threaten His children every step of the way, and there is no salvation unless you cleave to Him with entreaties and prayers."

She gave each of them a lit candle and told them to go with Sister Cecilia Baardsdatter, who often sat in the church alone, praying into the night.

Kristin placed her candle on the altar of Saint Laurentius and knelt down on the prayer bench. She stared steadily into the flame as she said her *Pater noster* and *Ave Maria*. Gradually the glow of the taper seemed to envelop her, shutting out everything else surrounding her and the candle. She felt her heart open up, brimming over with gratitude and promises and love for God and His gentle Mother—she felt them so near. She had always known that they saw her, but on this night she *felt* that it was so. She saw the world as if in a vision: a dark room into which a beam of sunlight fell, with dust motes tumbling in and out, from darkness to light, and she felt that now she had finally moved into the sunbeam.

She thought she would gladly have stayed in the quiet night-dark church forever—with the few tiny specks of light like golden stars in the night, the sweet fragrance of old incense, and the warm smell of burning wax. With herself resting inside her own star.

This sense of joy seemed to vanish when Sister Cecilia silently approached and touched her shoulder. Curtseying before the altar, the three women slipped out of the small south entrance into the convent courtyard.

Ingebjørg was so sleepy that she got into bed without talking. Kristin was relieved; she was reluctant to be disturbed, now that she was thinking so clearly. And she was glad they had to keep their shifts on at night—Ingebjørg was so fat and sweated heavily.

Kristin lay awake for a long time, but the deep current of sweetness which had borne her as she knelt in the church would not return. And yet she still felt its warmth inside her; she fervently thanked God, and she sensed a feeling of strength in her spirit as she prayed for her parents and her sisters and for the soul of Arne Gyrdsøn.

Father, she thought. She felt such a longing for him, for all they had had together before Simon Darre had entered their lives. A new tenderness for Lavrans welled up inside her, as if there were a presentiment of maternal love and maternal sorrows in her love for her father that night. She was dimly aware that there was much in life that he had not received. She thought of the old black wooden church at Gerdarud, where at Eastertide she had seen the graves of her three little brothers and her grandmother—her father's own mother, Kristin Sigurdsdatter—who had died as she gave birth to him.

What could Erlend Nikulaussøn be doing at Gerdarud? She could not fathom it.

She wasn't conscious of giving any more thought to him that night, but the whole time the memory of his thin, dark face and his quiet voice had hovered somewhere in the shadows, just beyond the radiance of her soul.

When Kristin woke up the next morning, the sun was shining

in the dormitory, and Ingebjørg told her that Fru Groa herself had
sent word to the lay sisters that they should not be awakened for
matins. They had permission to go over to the cookhouse now to
have some food. Kristin felt warm with joy at the kindness of the
abbess. It was as if the whole world had been good to her.

CHAPTER 3

THE FARMERS' GUILD at Aker was dedicated to Saint Margareta, and every year began its meeting on the twentieth of July, which was Saint Margareta's Day. On that day the brothers and sisters would gather with their children, guests, and servants at Aker Church to attend mass at the Saint Margareta altar. Afterward they would go to the guild hall, which stood near Hofvin Hospice; there they would drink for five days.

But because both Aker Church and Hofvin Hospice belonged to Nonneseter, and since many of the Aker peasants were tenant farmers of the convent, the custom had arisen for the abbess and several of the eldest sisters to honor the guild by attending the celebrations on the first day. And the young maidens of the convent who were there to be educated but who were not going to enter the order were allowed to go along and dance in the evening; and for this celebration they would wear their own clothes and not their convent attire.

So there was a great commotion in the young novices' dormitory on the evening before Saint Margareta's Day. Those maidens who were to attend the banquet rummaged through their chests and laid out their finery, while the others looked on and moped. Some of the girls had set small pots on the hearth and were boiling water to make their skin soft and white. Others were brewing something that they rubbed in their hair; afterward, when they had wound strands of their hair tightly around leather straps, they would have wavy and curly tresses.

Ingebjørg took out all that she owned of finery, but she couldn't decide what to wear. Not her best leaf-green velvet dress, anyway; it was too costly and too elegant to wear to such a farmers' guild. But a thin little maiden who was not going along—Helga was her name, and she had been given to the convent as a child—pulled

Kristin aside and whispered that Ingebjørg would of course wear the green dress and her pink silk shift.

"You've always been kind to me, Kristin," said Helga. "It's most improper for me to get involved in such things, but I'm going to tell you anyway. The knight who escorted you home on that evening in the spring—I have both seen and heard that Ingebjørg has talked to him since then. They have spoken to each other in church, and he has waited for her up along the fenced road when she goes to visit Ingunn at the corrodians' house. But it's you that he asks for, and Ingebjørg has promised to bring you out there with her. I'll wager that you've never heard about this before, have you?"

"It's true that Ingebjørg has never mentioned this to me," said Kristin. She pursed her lips so the other maiden wouldn't see the smile that threatened to appear. So that's the kind of girl Ingebjørg was. "I expect she realizes that I'm not the type to run off to meetings with strange men behind house corners and fences," she said haughtily.

"Then I could have spared myself the trouble to tell you this news, since it would have been more proper for me not to mention it," said Helga, offended; and the two parted.

But all evening Kristin had to try not to smile whenever anyone looked at her.

The next day Ingebjørg dawdled for a long time, wearing only her shift. Kristin finally realized that the other maiden was not going to get dressed until she herself was done.

Kristin didn't say a word, but she laughed as she went over to her chest and took out her golden-yellow silk shift. She had never worn it before, and it felt so soft and cool as it slid over her body. It was beautifully trimmed with silver and blue and brown silk at the neck and across the part of the bodice that would be visible above the neckline of her dress. There were also matching sleeves. She pulled on her linen stockings and tied the ribbons of the dainty blue-violet shoes, which Haakon had fortunately managed to bring home on that tumultuous day. Ingebjørg looked at her.

Then Kristin laughed and said, "My father has always taught me that we should not show contempt for our inferiors, but you are no doubt so grand that you won't want to dress up for peasants and tenant farmers."

Her face as red as a berry, Ingebjørg dropped the woolen shift from her white hips and put on the pink silk one. Kristin slipped her best velvet dress over her head; it was violet-blue and cut deep across the bodice, with slit sleeves and cuffs that trailed almost to the ground. She wrapped the gilded belt around her waist and slung her gray squirrel cloak over her shoulders. Then she spread out her thick blond hair over her shoulders and placed the circlet studded with roses on her forehead.

She noticed that Helga was watching them. Then she took from her chest a large silver clasp. It was the one she had worn on her cloak the night that Bentein had confronted her on the road, and she had never wanted to wear it since. She went over to Helga and said softly, "I realize that you meant to show me kindness yesterday; you must believe I know that." And she handed the clasp to Helga.

Ingebjørg was also quite beautiful when she had finished dressing, wearing her green gown with a red silk cloak over her shoulders and her pretty, curly hair falling loose. They had been in a race to outdress each other, thought Kristin and laughed.

The morning was cool and fresh with dew when the procession wound its way from Nonneseter, heading west toward Frysja. The haying season was almost over in that area, but along the fences grew clusters of bluebells and golden Maria-grass. The barley in the fields had sprouted spikes and rippled pale silver with a sheen of faint rose. In many places where the path was narrow and led through the fields, the grain brushed against people's knees.

Haakon walked in front, carrying the convent's banner with the image of the Virgin Mary on blue silk cloth. Behind him walked the servants and corrodians, and then came Fru Groa and four old nuns on horseback, followed by the young maidens on foot; their colorful, secular feast attire shimmered and fluttered in the sun. Several corrodian women and a few armed men brought up the rear of the procession.

They sang as they walked across the bright meadows, and whenever they met others on the side roads, the people would step aside and greet them respectfully. All across the fields small groups of people were walking and riding, heading toward the church from every house and farm. In a little while they heard behind them hymns sung by deep male voices, and they saw the cloister banner from Hovedø rise up over a hill. The red silk cloth gleamed in the sun, bobbing and swaying with the footsteps of the man who was bearing it.

The mighty, sonorous voice of the bells drowned out the neighs and whinnies of the stallions as they came over the last hill to the church. Kristin had never seen so many horses at one time—a surging, restless sea of glossy equine backs surrounded the green in front of the entrance to the church. People dressed for the celebration were standing, sitting, and lying on the slope, but everyone stood up in greeting when the Maria banner from Nonneseter was carried in amongst them, and they all bowed deeply to Fru Groa.

It looked as if more people had come than the church could hold, but an open space closest to the altar had been reserved for the people from the convent. A moment later the Cistercian monks from Hovedø came in and went up to the choir, and then song resounded throughout the church from the throats of men and boys.

During the mass, when everyone had risen, Kristin caught sight of Erlend Nikulaussøn. He was tall, and his head towered above those around him. She saw his face from the side. He had a high, narrow forehead and a large, straight nose; it jutted out like a triangle from his face and was strangely thin, with fine, quivering nostrils. There was something about it that reminded Kristin of a skittish, frightened stallion. He was not as handsome as she thought she had remembered him; the lines in his face seemed to extend so long and somberly down to his soft, small, attractive mouth—oh yes, he was handsome after all.

He turned his head and saw her. She didn't know how long they continued to stare into each other's eyes. Then her only thought was for the mass to be over; she waited expectantly to see what would happen next.

As everyone began to leave the crowded church, there was a great crush. Ingebjørg pulled Kristin along with her, backward into the throng; they were easily separated from the nuns, who were

the first to leave. The girls were among the last to approach the
altar with their offering and then exit from the church.

Erlend was standing outside, right next to the door, between the
priest from Gerdarud and a stout, red-faced man wearing a magnificent blue velvet surcoat. Erlend was dressed in silk but in dark
colors—a long, brown-and-black patterned surcoat and a black
cape interwoven with little yellow falcons.

They greeted each other and walked across the slope toward the
spot where the men's horses were tethered. As they exchanged
words about the weather, the beautiful mass, and the great crowd
of people in attendance, the fat, ruddy-faced gentleman—he wore
golden spurs and his name was Sir Munan Baardsøn—offered his
hand to Ingebjørg. He seemed to find the maiden exceedingly
attractive. Erlend and Kristin fell behind; they walked along in
silence.

There was a great hubbub on the church hill as people began
to ride off. Horses jostled past each other and people shouted,
some of them angry, some of them laughing. Many of them rode
in pairs—men with their wives behind them or children in front
on the saddle—and young boys leaped up to ride with a friend.
They could already see the church banners, the nuns, and the priest
far below them.

Sir Munan rode past; Ingebjørg was sitting in front of him, in
his arms. They both shouted and waved.

Then Erlend said, "My men are both here with me. They could
take one of the horses and you could have Haftor's—if you would
prefer that?"

Kristin blushed as she replied, "We're so far behind the others
already, and I don't see your men, so . . ." Then she laughed and
Erlend smiled.

He leaped into the saddle and helped her up behind him. At
home Kristin often sat sideways behind her father after she grew
too old to sit astride the horse's loins. And yet she felt a little shy
and uncertain as she placed one of her hands over Erlend's shoulder; with the other hand she supported herself against the horse's
back. Slowly they rode down toward the bridge.

After a while Kristin felt that she ought to speak since he did not, and she said, "It was unexpected, sir, to meet you here today."

"Was it unexpected?" asked Erlend, turning his head around toward her. "Hasn't Ingebjørg Filippusdatter brought you my greeting?"

"No," said Kristin. "I haven't heard of any greeting. She has never mentioned you since that day when you came to our aid back in May," she said slyly. She wanted Ingebjørg's duplicity to come to light.

Erlend didn't turn around, but she could hear in his voice that he was smiling when he spoke again.

"And what about the little black-haired one—the novitiate—I can't remember her name. I even paid her a messenger's fee to give you my greetings."

Kristin blushed, but then she had to laugh. "Yes, I suppose I owe it to Helga to tell you that she earned her pay," she said.

Erlend moved his head slightly, and his neck came close to her hand. Kristin shifted her hand at once to a place farther out on his shoulder. Rather uneasy, she thought that perhaps she had shown greater boldness than was proper, since she had come to this feast after a man had, in a sense, arranged to meet her there.

After a moment Erlend asked, "Will you dance with me tonight, Kristin?"

"I don't know, sir," replied the maiden.

"Perhaps you think it might not be proper?" he asked. When she didn't answer, he went on. "It could be that it's not. But I thought perhaps you might not think it would do any harm if you took my hand tonight. And by the way, it has been eight years since I took part in a dance."

"Why is that, sir?" asked Kristin. "Is it because you are married?" But then it occurred to her that if he were a married man, it would not have been seemly for him to arrange this rendezvous with her. So she corrected herself and said, "Perhaps you have lost your betrothed or your wife?"

Erlend turned around abruptly and gave her a peculiar look.

"Me? Hasn't Fru Aashild . . ." After a moment he asked, "Why did you blush when you heard who I was that evening?"

Kristin blushed again but did not reply.

Then Erlend went on. "I would like to know what my aunt has told you about me."

"Nothing more than that she praised you," said Kristin hastily. "She said you were handsome and so highborn that . . . she said that compared to a lineage such as yours and hers, we were of little consequence, my ancestors and I."

"Is she still talking about such things, there, where she now resides?" said Erlend with a bitter laugh. "Well, well, if it comforts her . . . And she has said nothing else about me?"

"What else would she say?" asked Kristin. She didn't know why she felt so strange and anxious.

"Oh, she might have said . . . ," replied Erlend in a low voice, his head bowed, "she might have said that I had been excommunicated and had to pay dearly for peace and reconciliation."

Kristin said nothing for a long time. Then she said quietly, "I've heard it said that there are many men who are not masters of their fortunes. I've seen so little of the world. But I would never believe of you, Erlend, that it was for any . . . ignoble . . . matter."

"God bless you for such words, Kristin," said Erlend. He bent his head and kissed her wrist so fervently that the horse gave a start beneath them. When the animal was once again walking calmly, he said with great ardor, "Won't you dance with me tonight, Kristin? Later I'll tell you everything about my circumstances—but tonight let's be happy together."

Kristin agreed, and they rode for a while in silence.

But a short time later Erlend began asking about Fru Aashild, and Kristin told him everything she knew; she had much praise for her.

"Then all doors are not closed to Bjørn and Aashild?" asked Erlend.

Kristin replied that they were well liked and that her father and many others thought that most of what had been said of the couple was untrue.

"What did you think of my kinsman, Munan Baardsøn?" asked Erlend with a chuckle.

"I didn't pay much heed to him," said Kristin, "and it didn't seem to me that he was much worth looking at anyway."

"Didn't you know that he's her son?" asked Erlend.

"Fru Aashild's son?" said Kristin in astonishment.

"Yes, the children couldn't take their mother's fair looks, since they took everything else," said Erlend.

"I didn't even know the name of her first husband," said Kristin.

"They were two brothers who married two sisters," said Erlend. "Baard and Nikulaus Munansøn. My father was the older one; Mother was his second wife, but he had no children by his first wife. Baard, who married Aashild, wasn't a young man either, and apparently they never got on well. I was a child when it all happened, and they kept as much from me as they could. But she left the country with Herr Bjørn and married him without the counsel of her kinsmen—after Baard was dead. Then people wanted to annul their marriage. They claimed that Bjørn had slept with her while her first husband was still alive and that they conspired together to get rid of my father's brother. But they couldn't find any proof of this, and they had to let the marriage stand. But they had to give up all their possessions. Bjørn had killed their nephew too—the nephew of my mother and Aashild, I mean."

Kristin's heart was pounding. At home her parents had taken strict precautions to keep the children from hearing impure talk. But things had occurred in their village, too, that Kristin had heard about—a man who lived in concubinage with a married woman. That was adultery, one of the worst of sins. They were also to blame for the husband's violent death, and then it was a case for excommunication and banishment. Lavrans had said that no woman had to stay with her husband if he had been with another man's wife. And the lot of offspring from adultery could never be improved, even if the parents were later free to marry. A man could pass on his inheritance and name to his child by a prostitute or a wandering beggar woman, but not to his child from adultery—not even if the mother was the wife of a knight.

Kristin thought about the dislike she had always felt toward Herr Bjørn, with his pallid face and his slack, corpulent body. She couldn't understand how Fru Aashild could always be so kind and amenable toward the man who had lured her into such shame; to think that such a gracious woman could have allowed herself to be fooled by him. He was not even nice to her; he let her toil with all the work on the farm. Bjørn did nothing but drink ale. And yet Aashild was always so gentle and tender when she spoke to her husband. Kristin wondered whether her father knew about this, since he had invited Herr Bjørn into their house. Now that she thought about it, it seemed odd to her that Erlend would speak in this manner of his close kinsmen. But he probably thought that she knew about it already.

"It would please me," said Erlend after a moment, "to visit her, my Aunt Aashild, sometime—when I journey north. But is he still a handsome man, my kinsman Bjørn?"

"No," said Kristin. "He looks like a mound of hay that has lain on the ground all winter long."

"Ah yes, it must wear on a man," said Erlend with the same bitter smile. "Never have I seen a more handsome man—that was twenty years ago, and I was only a small boy back then—but I have never seen his equal."

A short time later they reached the hospice. It was an enormous and grand estate with many buildings of both stone and wood: a hospital, an almshouse, a guest inn for travelers, the chapel, and the rectory. There was a great tumult in the courtyard, for food was being prepared for the banquet in the hospice's cookhouse, and the poor and the sick guild members were also to be served the very best on that day.

The guild hall was beyond the gardens of the hospice, and people were heading that way through the herb garden, for it was quite famous. Fru Groa had brought in plants that no one in Norway had ever heard of before and, besides that, all the plants that usually grew in such gardens seemed to thrive better in hers—flowers and cooking herbs and medicinal herbs. She was the most skilled woman in all such matters, and she had even translated herbals from Salerno into the Norwegian language. Fru Groa had been particularly friendly toward Kristin ever since she noticed that the maiden knew something of the art of herbs and wanted to know more about it.

So Kristin pointed out to Erlend what plants were growing in the beds on both sides of the green lane as they walked. In the noonday sun there was a hot, spicy fragrance of dill and celery, onions and roses, southernwood and wallflowers. Beyond the shadeless, sun-baked herb garden, the rows of fruit trees looked enticingly cool; red cherries gleamed in the dark foliage, and apple trees bowed their branches, weighted down by green fruit.

Surrounding the garden was a hedge of sweetbriar. There were still some roses left—they looked no different from other hedge roses, but the petals smelled of wine and apples in the heat of the sun. People broke off twigs and pinned them to their clothing as they passed. Kristin picked several roses too, tucking them into the circlet at her temples. She held one in her hand, and after a moment Erlend took it from her, without saying a word. He carried it for a while and then stuck it into the filigree brooch on his chest. He looked self-conscious and embarrassed, and did it so clumsily that he scratched his fingers and drew blood.

In the banquet loft several wide tables had been set up: one for the men and one for the women along the walls. In the middle of the floor there were two tables where the children and the young people sat together.

At the women's table Fru Groa sat in the high seat; the nuns and most of the wives of high standing sat along the wall, and the unmarried women sat on the opposite bench, with the maidens from Nonneseter closest to the head of the table. Kristin knew that Erlend was looking at her, but she didn't dare turn her head even once, either when they were standing or after they sat down. Not until they rose and the priest began to read the names of the deceased guild brothers and sisters did she cast a hasty glance toward the men's table. She caught a glimpse of him as he stood near the wall, behind the burning candle on the table. He was looking at her.

The meal lasted a long time with all of the toasts in honor of God, the Virgin Mary, and Saint Margareta, Saint Olav, and Saint Halvard, interspersed with prayers and hymns.

Kristin could see through the open door that the sun had gone down; the sound of fiddles and songs could be heard from out on the green, and the young people had already left the tables when Fru Groa said to the young daughters that now they might go out to play for a while, if they so pleased.

* * *

Three red bonfires were burning on the green; around them moved the chains of dancers, now aglow, now in silhouette. The fiddlers were sitting on stacks of chests, bowing the strings of their instruments; they were playing and singing a different tune in each circle. There were far too many people to form only one dance. It was nearly dusk already; to the north the crest of the forested ridges stood coal-black against the yellowish green sky.

People were sitting under the gallery of the loft, drinking. Several men leaped up as soon as the six maidens from Nonneseter came down the stairs. Munan Baardsøn ran up to Ingebjørg and dashed off with her, and Kristin was seized by the wrist—it was Erlend; she already knew his touch. He gripped her hand so tightly that their rings scraped against each other and bit into their flesh.

He pulled her along to the farthest bonfire, where many children were dancing. Kristin took a twelve-year-old boy by the hand, and Erlend had a tiny, half-grown maiden on his other side.

No one was singing in their circle just then—they walked and swayed from side to side, in time with the sound of the fiddle. Then someone shouted that Sivord the Dane should sing a new ballad for them. A tall, fair man with enormous fists stepped in front of the chain of dancers and performed his song:

> They are dancing now at Munkholm
> across the white sand.
> There dances Ivar Herr Jonsøn
> taking the Queen's hand.
> Do you know Ivar Herr Jonsøn?

The fiddle players didn't know the tune; they plucked a little on the strings, and the Dane sang alone. He had a beautiful, strong voice.

> Do you remember, Danish Queen,
> that summer so clear
> when you were led out of Sweden
> and to Denmark here.

When you were led out of Sweden
and to Denmark here
with a golden crown so red
and on your cheek a tear.

With a golden crown so red
and on your cheek a tear.
Do you remember, Danish Queen,
the first man you held dear!

The fiddlers played along once more, and the dancers hummed the newly learned tune and joined in with the refrain.

And are you, Ivar Herr Jonsøn,
my very own man,
then tomorrow from the gallows
you shall surely hang!

And it was Ivar Herr Jonsøn
but he did not quail,
he sprang into the golden boat,
clad in coat of mail.

May you be granted, Danish Queen,
as many good nights
as do fill the vault of heaven
all the stars so bright.

May you be granted, Danish King,
life so fraught with cares
as the linden tree has leaves
and the hart has hairs.
Do you know Ivar Herr Jonsøn?

It was late at night, and the bonfires were mere mounds of glowing embers that grew dimmer and dimmer. Kristin and Erlend stood hand in hand beneath the trees by the garden fence. Behind them the noise of the revelers had died out; a few young boys were humming and leaping around the ember mounds, but the fiddlers had gone off to bed and most of the people had left. Here and there a woman walked around in search of her husband, toppled by ale somewhere outdoors.

"I wonder where I've left my cloak," whispered Kristin. Erlend put his arm around her waist and wrapped his cape around both of them. Walking close together, they went into the herb garden.

A remnant of the day's hot, spicy scent wafted toward them, muted and damp with the coolness of the dew. The night was quite dark, the sky hazy gray with clouds above the treetops. But they sensed that others were in the garden.

Erlend pressed the maiden to him once and asked in a whisper, "You're not afraid, are you Kristin?"

Suddenly she vaguely remembered the world outside this night —it was madness. But she was so blissfully robbed of all power. She leaned closer to the man and whispered faintly; she didn't know herself what she said.

They reached the end of the path; there was a stone fence along the edge of the woods. Erlend helped her up. As she was about to jump down to the other side, he caught her and held her in his arms for a moment before he set her down in the grass.

She stood there with her face raised and received his kiss. He placed his hands at her temples. She thought it so wonderful to feel his fingers sinking into her hair, and then she put her hands up to his face and tried to kiss him the way he had kissed her.

When he placed his hands on her bodice and stroked her breasts, she felt as if he had laid her heart bare and then seized it; gently he parted the folds of her silk shift and kissed the place in between—heat rushed to the roots of her heart.

"You I could never hurt," whispered Erlend. "Don't ever weep a single tear for my sake. I never thought a maiden could be as good as you are, my Kristin. . . ."

He pulled her down into the grass under the bushes; they sat with their backs against the stone fence. Kristin said not a word, but when he stopped caressing her, she raised her hand and touched his face.

After a moment Erlend asked, "Are you tired, dear Kristin?" And when she leaned against his chest, he wrapped his arms around her and whispered, "Sleep, Kristin, sleep here with me."

She slipped deeper and deeper into the darkness and the warmth and the joy at his chest.

When she woke up, she was lying stretched out on the grass with her cheek against the brown silk of his lap. Erlend was still sitting with his back against the stone fence; his face was gray in the gray light, but his wide-open eyes were so strangely bright and beautiful. She saw that he had wrapped his cape all around her; her feet were wonderfully warm inside the fur lining.

"Now you have slept on my lap," he said, smiling faintly. "May God reward you, Kristin. You slept as soundly as a child in her mother's arms."

"Haven't you slept, Herr Erlend?" asked Kristin, and he smiled down into her newly awakened eyes.

"Perhaps someday the night will come when you and I dare to fall asleep together—I don't know what you will think once you have considered that. I have kept vigil here in the night. There is still so much between us, more than if a naked sword had lain between you and me. Tell me, will you have affection for me after this night is over?"

"I will have affection for you, Herr Erlend," said Kristin. "I will have affection for you as long as you wish—and after that I will love no one else."

"Then may God forsake me," said Erlend slowly, "if ever a woman or maiden should come into my arms before I dare to possess you with honor and in keeping with the law. Repeat what I have said," he implored her.

Kristin said, "May God forsake me if I ever take any other man into my arms, for as long as I live on this earth."

"We must go now," said Erlend after a moment. "Before everyone wakes up."

They walked along the outside of the stone fence, through the underbrush.

"Have you given any thought to what should happen next?" asked Erlend.

"You must decide that, Erlend," replied Kristin.

"Your father," he said after a pause. "Over in Gerdarud they say that he's a kind and just man. Do you think he would be greatly opposed to breaking the agreement he has made with Andres Darre?"

"Father has so often said that he would never force any of his daughters," said Kristin. "The main concern is that our lands would fit so well together. But I'm certain that Father would not want me to lose all joy in the world for that reason." She had a sudden inkling that it might not be quite as simple as that, but she pushed it aside.

"Then maybe this will be easier than I thought last night," said Erlend. "God help me, Kristin—I can't bear to lose you. Now I will never be happy if I can't have you."

They parted among the trees, and in the dim light of dawn Kristin found the path to the guest house where everyone from Nonneseter was sleeping. All the beds were full, but she threw her cloak over some straw on the floor and lay down in her clothes.

When she woke up, it was quite late. Ingebjørg Filippusdatter was sitting on a bench nearby, mending a fur border that had torn loose from her cloak. She was full of chatter, as always.

"Were you with Erlend Nikulaussøn all night long?" she asked. "You ought to be a little more careful about that young man, Kristin. Do you think Simon Andressøn would like it if you befriended him?"

Kristin found a basin and began to wash herself. "And what about your betrothed? Do you think he would like it that you danced with Munan the Stump last night? But we have to dance with anyone who invites us on such an evening; and Fru Groa gave us permission, after all."

Ingebjørg exclaimed, "Einar Einarssøn and Sir Munan are friends, and besides, he's married and old. And he's ugly too, but amiable and courteous. Look what he gave me as a souvenir of the night." And she held out a gold buckle which Kristin had seen on Sir Munan's hat the day before. "But that Erlend—well, the ban was lifted from him this past Easter, but they say that Eline Ormsdatter has been staying at his manor at Husaby ever since. Sir Munan says that he has fled to Sira Jon at Gerdarud because he's afraid that he'll fall back into sin if he sees her again."

Kristin, her face white, went over to the other girl.

"Didn't you know that?" asked Ingebjørg. "That he lured a woman from her husband somewhere up north in Haalogaland? And that he kept her at his estate in spite of the king's warning and the archbishop's ban? They have two children together too. He had to flee to Sweden, and he has had to pay so many fines that Sir Munan says he'll end up a pauper if he doesn't mend his ways soon."

"Oh yes, you can be sure that I knew all about it," said Kristin, her face rigid. "But that's all over now."

"Yes, that's what Sir Munan said, that it's been over between them so many times before," replied Ingebjørg thoughtfully. "It won't affect you—you're going to marry Simon Darre, after all. But that Erlend Nikulaussøn is certainly a handsome man."

The company from Nonneseter was going to leave that same day, after the midafternoon prayers. Kristin had promised Erlend to meet him at the stone fence where they had sat during the night, if she could find a way to come.

He was lying on his stomach in the grass, with his head on his arms. As soon as he saw her, he leaped up and offered her both of his hands as she was about to jump down.

She took them, and they stood for a moment, hand in hand.

Then Kristin said, "Why did you tell me that story about Herr Bjørn and Fru Aashild yesterday?"

"I can see that you know," replied Erlend, abruptly letting go of her hands. "What do you think of me now, Kristin?

"I was eighteen years old back then," he continued vehemently. "It was ten years ago that the king, my kinsman, sent me on the journey to Vargøy House, and then we spent the winter at Steigen. She was married to the judge Sigurd Saksulvsøn. I felt sorry for her because he was old and unbelievably ugly. I don't know how it happened; yes, I was fond of her too. I told Sigurd to demand what he wanted in fines; I wanted to do right by him—he's a decent man in many ways—but he wanted things to proceed according to the law, and he took the case to the *ting*. I was to be branded for adultery with the woman in whose house I had been a guest, you see.

"My father got wind of it, and then King Haakon found out too. And he . . . he banished me from his court. And if you need to know the whole story: there's nothing left between Eline and me except the children, and she cares very little for them. They're at Østerdal, on a farm that I own there. I've given the farm to Orm, the boy. But she doesn't want to be with them. I suppose she expects that Sigurd can't live forever, but I don't know what she wants.

"Sigurd took her back, but she says she was treated like a dog and a slave on his farm. So she asked me to meet her in Nidaros. I was not faring much better at Husaby with my father. I sold everything I could get my hands on and fled with her to Halland; Count Jacob has been a kind friend to me. What else could I do? She was carrying my child. I knew that so many men had managed to escape unscathed from such a relationship with another man's wife—if they were rich, that is. But King Haakon is the sort of man who treats his own most sternly. We were separated from each other for a year, but then my father died, so she came back. And then other things happened. My tenants refused to pay their land rent or to speak to my envoys because I had been excommunicated. I retaliated harshly, and then a case was brought against me for robbery, but I had no money to pay my house servants. You can see that I was too young to deal sensibly with these difficulties, and my kinsmen refused to help me—except for Munan, who did as much as he dared without angering his wife.

"So now you know, Kristin, that I have compromised much, both my land and my honor. You would certainly be much better served if you stayed with Simon Andressøn."

Kristin put her arms around his neck.

"We will stand by what we swore to each other last night, Erlend—if you feel as I do."

Erlend pulled her close, kissed her, and then said, "You must also have faith that my circumstances are bound to change. Now no one in the world has power over me except you. Oh, I thought about so many things last night as you lay asleep in my lap, my fair one. The Devil cannot have so much power over a man that I would ever cause you sorrow or harm, you who are the most precious thing in my life."

CHAPTER 4

DURING THE TIME he lived at Skog, Lavrans Bjørgulfsøn had given property to Gerdarud Church for requiems to be held for the souls of his parents on the anniversaries of their deaths. His father Bjørgulf Ketilsøn's death date was the thirteenth of August, and this year Lavrans had made arrangements for his brother to bring Kristin out to his estate so that she could attend the mass.

She was afraid that something might happen to prevent her uncle from keeping his promise. She thought she had noticed that Aasmund was not particularly fond of her. But on the day before the mass was to be held, Aasmund Bjørgulfsøn arrived at the convent to get his niece. Kristin was told to dress in secular attire, but dark and simple in appearance. People had begun to remark that the sisters of Nonneseter spent a great deal of time outside the convent, and the bishop had therefore decreed that the young daughters who were not to become nuns should not wear anything resembling convent garb when they went to visit their kinsmen— then the populace would not mistake them for novices or nuns of the order.

Kristin was in a joyous mood as she rode along the road with her uncle, and Aasmund became more cheerful and friendly toward her when he noticed that the maiden was an affable companion. Otherwise, Aasmund was rather dejected; he said it seemed likely that a campaign[1] was about to be launched in the fall and that the king would sail with his army to Sweden to avenge the vile deed that had been perpetrated against his brother-in-law and his niece's husband. Kristin had heard about the murder of the Swedish dukes and thought it an act of the worst cowardice, although all such affairs of the realm seemed so distant to her. No one talked much about such things back home in the valley. But she also remembered that her father had participated in the campaign against

Duke Eirik at Ragnhildarholm and Konungahella. Aasmund explained everything that had happened between the king and the dukes. Kristin didn't understand much of what he said, but she paid close attention to what her uncle told her about the betrothals that had been agreed upon and then broken by the king's daughters. It gave her some comfort to hear that it was not the same in all places as it was back home in the villages, where an arranged betrothal was considered almost as binding as a marriage. So she gathered her courage, told her uncle about her adventures on the evening before the Vigil of Saint Halvard, and asked him whether he knew Erlend of Husaby. Aasmund gave Erlend a good report, saying that he had acted unwisely, but that his father and the king were mostly to blame. He said they had behaved as if the boy had been the horn of the Devil himself because he had landed in such a predicament. The king was much too pious, and Sir Nikulaus was angry because Erlend had wasted so much good property, so they had both thundered about adultery and the fires of hell.

"Any able-bodied young man has to have a certain amount of defiance in him," said Aasmund Bjørgulfsøn. "And the woman was exceedingly beautiful. But you have no reason to have anything to do with Erlend, so pay no heed to his affairs."

Erlend did not attend the mass as he had promised Kristin he would, and she thought more about this than about the word of God. But she felt no remorse over it. She merely had the odd feeling of being a stranger to everything to which she had previously felt herself bound.

She tried to console herself; Erlend probably thought it best that no one who had authority over her should find out about their friendship. She could understand this herself. But she had longed to see him with all her heart, and she wept when she went to bed that evening in the loft where she slept with Aasmund's small daughters.

The next day she headed up toward the woods with the youngest of her uncle's children, a little maiden six years old. When they had gone some distance, Erlend came running after them. Kristin knew who it was before she even saw him.

"I've been sitting up here on the hill looking down at the farm-yard all day long," he said. "I was sure that you'd find some chance to slip away."

"Do you think I've come out here to meet you?" said Kristin with a laugh. "And aren't you afraid to be wandering in my uncle's woods with your dogs and bow?"

"Your uncle has given me permission to hunt here for a short time," said Erlend. "And the dogs belong to Aasmund—they found me up here this morning." He patted the dogs and picked up the little girl. "You remember me, don't you, Ragndid? But you mustn't say that you've talked to me, and then I'll give you this." He took out a little bundle of raisins and handed it to the child. "I had intended it for you," he told Kristin. "Do you think this child can keep quiet?"

Both of them spoke quickly and laughed. Erlend was wearing a short, snug brown tunic, and he had a small red silk cap pressed down onto his black hair; he looked so young. He laughed and played with the child, but every once in a while he would take Kristin's hand, squeezing it so hard it hurt.

He talked about the rumors of the campaign with joy. "Then it will be easier for me to win back the friendship of the king. Everything will be easier then," he said fervently.

At last they sat down in a meadow some distance up in the woods. Erlend had the child on his lap. Kristin sat at his side. He was playing with her fingers in the grass. He put into her hand three gold rings tied together with a string.

"Later on," he whispered to her, "you shall have as many as you can fit on your fingers.

"I'll wait for you here in this field every day at this time, for as long as you are at Skog," he said as they parted. "Come when you can."

The next day Aasmund Bjørgulfsøn, along with his wife and children, left for Gyrid's ancestral estate at Hadeland. They had become alarmed by the rumors of the campaign. The people around Oslo were still filled with terror ever since Duke Eirik's devastating incursion[2] into the region some years before. Aasmund's old mother was so frightened that she decided to seek refuge at Nonneseter; she was too frail to travel with the others. So Kristin would stay at Skog with the old woman, whom she called Grandmother, until Aasmund returned from Hadeland.

Around noontime, when the servants on the farm were resting, Kristin went up to the loft where she slept. She had brought along some clothing in a leather bag, and she hummed as she changed her clothes.

Her father had given her a dress made of thick cotton fabric from the East; it was sky-blue with an intricate red flower pattern. This is what she put on. She brushed and combed out her hair, tying it back from her face with red silk ribbons. She wrapped a red silk belt tightly around her waist and slipped Erlend's rings onto her fingers, all the while wondering whether he would find her beautiful.

She had let the two dogs that had been up in the forest with Erlend sleep in the loft with her at night. Now she enticed them to come with her. She sneaked around the buildings and took the same path up through the outlying fields that she had used the day before.

The forest meadow lay empty and still in the glare of the noonday sun. There was a hot fragrance coming from the spruce trees that surrounded it on all sides. The blazing sun and the blue sky seemed strangely close and harsh against the treetops.

Kristin sat down in the shade at the edge of the clearing. She wasn't disappointed at Erlend's absence. She was sure that he would come, and she felt a peculiar joy at being allowed to sit there alone, the first to arrive.

She listened to the soft buzz of insects across the yellow, scorched grass. She plucked off several dry, spice-scented flowers that she could reach without moving more than her hand. She twirled them between her fingers and sniffed at them; with her eyes wide open she sank into a kind of trance.

She didn't move when she heard a horse approaching from the forest. The dogs growled and raised their hackles; then they bounded up across the meadow, barking and wagging their tails. Erlend jumped down from his horse at the edge of the forest and let it go with a slap on its loins. Then he ran down toward Kristin with the dogs leaping around him. He grabbed their snouts with his hands and walked toward her between the two animals, which were elk-gray and wolflike. Kristin smiled and reached out her hand without getting up.

Once, as she was looking down at his dark-brown head lying in her lap between her hands, a memory abruptly rose up before her. It stood there, clear and distant, the way a house far off on the slope of a ridge can suddenly emerge quite clearly from the dark clouds as it is struck by a ray of sunshine on a turbulent day. And her heart suddenly seemed filled with all of the tenderness that Arne Gyrdsøn had once wanted, back when she hardly even understood his words. Anxiously she drew the man to her, pressing his face against her breast, kissing him as if she were afraid that he might be taken from her. And when she looked at his head lying in her embrace, she thought it was like having a child in her arms. She hid his eyes with her hand and sprinkled little kisses over his mouth and cheek.

The sun had disappeared from the meadow. The intense color above the treetops had deepened to a dark blue, spreading over the entire sky. There were small copper-red streaks in the clouds, like smoke from a fire. Bajard came toward them, gave a loud whinny, and then stood motionless, staring. A moment later the first lightning flashed, followed at once by thunder, not far away.

Erlend stood up and took the reins of the horse. There was an old barn at the bottom of the meadow, and that's where they headed. He tethered Bajard to some planks just inside the door. In the back of the barn was a mound of hay, and there Erlend spread out his cape. They sat down with the dogs at their feet.

Soon the rain had formed a curtain in front of the doorway. The wind rushed through the forest and the rain lashed against the hillside. A moment later they had to move farther inside because of a leak in the roof.

Every time there was lightning and thunder, Erlend would whisper, "Aren't you afraid, Kristin?"

"A little," she would whisper back and then press closer to him.

They had no idea how long they sat there. The storm passed over quite quickly, and they could still hear the thunder far away, but the sun was shining outside the door in the wet grass, and fewer and fewer glittering drops were falling from the roof. The sweet smell of hay grew stronger in the barn.

"I have to go now," said Kristin.

And Erlend replied, "I suppose you do." He put his hand on her foot. "You'll get wet. You must ride, and I'll walk. Out of the forest . . ." He gave her such a strange look.

Kristin was trembling—she thought it was because her heart was pounding so hard—and her hands were clammy and cold. When he kissed the bare skin above her knee, she tried powerlessly to push him away. Erlend raised his face for a moment, and she was suddenly reminded of a man who had once been given food at the convent—he had kissed the bread they handed to him. She sank back into the hay with open arms and let Erlend do as he liked.

She was sitting bolt upright when Erlend lifted his head from his arms. Abruptly he propped himself up on his elbow.

"Don't look like that, Kristin!"

His voice etched a wild new pain into Kristin's soul. He wasn't happy—he was distressed too.

"Kristin, Kristin . . ."

And a moment later he asked, "Do you think I lured you out here to the woods because I wanted this from you, to take you by force?"

She stroked his hair but didn't look at him.

"I wouldn't call it force. No doubt you would have let me go as I came if I had asked you to," she said softly.

"I'm not sure of that," he replied, hiding his face in her lap.

"Do you think I will forsake you?" he asked fervently. "Kristin—I swear on my Christian faith—may God forsake me in my last hour if I fail to be faithful to you until I die."

She couldn't say a word; she merely caressed his hair, over and over.

"Now, surely, it must be time for me to go home," she said at last, and she felt as if she were waiting with dread for his reply.

"I suppose it is," he said gloomily. He stood up quickly, went over to his horse, and began to untie the reins.

Then Kristin stood up too—slowly, feeling faint and shattered. She didn't know what she had expected him to do—perhaps help her up onto his horse and take her along with him so that she could avoid going back to the others. Her whole body seemed to be aching with astonishment—that this was the iniquity that all the songs were about. And because Erlend had done this to her, she felt as if she had become his possession, and she couldn't imagine how she could live beyond his reach anymore. She was going to have to leave him now, but she could not conceive of doing so.

Down through the woods he walked, leading the horse and holding Kristin's hand in his, but they could think of nothing to say to each other.

When they had gone so far that they could see the buildings of Skog, he said farewell.

"Kristin, don't be sad. Before you know it the day will come when you'll be my wife."

But her heart sank as she spoke.

"Then you have to leave me?" she asked fearfully.

"As soon as you've left Skog," he said, and his voice sounded more vibrant all at once. "If there's no campaign, then I'll speak to Munan. He's been urging me for a long time to get married; I'm certain he'll accompany me and speak to your father on my behalf."

Kristin bowed her head. For every word he spoke, the time that lay before her seemed longer and more impossible to imagine—the convent, Jørundgaard—it was as if she were floating in a stream that was carrying her away from everything.

"Do you sleep alone in the loft, now that your kinsmen have gone?" asked Erlend. "If so, I'll come and talk to you tonight. Will you let me in?"

"Yes," murmured Kristin. And then they parted.

The rest of the day Kristin sat with her grandmother, and after the evening meal she helped the old woman into bed. Then she went up to the loft where she slept. There was a small window in the room, and Kristin sat down on the chest that stood beneath it; she had no desire to go to bed.

She had to wait for a long time. It was pitch dark outside when she heard the quiet footsteps on the gallery. He tapped on the door with his cape wrapped around his knuckles, and Kristin stood up, drew back the bolt, and let Erlend in.

She noticed that he was pleased when she threw her arms around his neck and pressed herself against him.

"I was afraid you'd be angry with me," he said.

Some time later he said, "You mustn't grieve over this sin. It's not a great one. God's law is not the same as the law of the land in this matter. Gunnulv, my brother, once explained it all to me. If two people agree to stand by each other for all eternity and then lie with each other, they are married before God and cannot break their vows without committing a great sin. I would tell you the word in Latin if I could remember it—I knew it once."

Kristin wondered what could have been the reason for Erlend's brother to speak of this, but she brushed aside the nagging fear that it might have been about Erlend and someone else. And she sought solace in his words.

They sat next to each other on the chest. Erlend put his arm around Kristin, and now she felt warm and secure—at his side was the only place she would ever feel safe and protected again.

From time to time Erlend would say a great deal, speaking elatedly. Then he would fall silent for long periods, simply caressing her. Without knowing it, Kristin was gathering up from all he said every little thing that might make him more attractive and dear to her, and that would lessen his blame in all she knew about him that was not good.

Erlend's father, Sir Nikulaus, was so old when his children were born that he had neither the patience nor the ability to raise them himself. Both sons had grown up in the home of Sir Baard Petersøn of Hestnæs. Erlend had no siblings other than his brother Gunnulv, who was one year younger and a priest at Christ Church. "I love him more dearly than anyone, except for you."

Kristin asked Erlend whether Gunnulv looked like him, but he laughed and said they were quite different in both temperament and appearance. Gunnulv was abroad, studying. This was the third year he had been gone, but twice he had sent letters home; the last one arrived the year before, when he was about to leave Sancta Genoveva in Paris and head for Rome. "Gunnulv will be happy when he comes home and finds me married," said Erlend.

Then he talked about the vast inheritance he had acquired from his parents. Kristin realized that he hardly knew himself how his affairs now stood. She was quite familiar with her father's land dealings, but Erlend's dealings had been of the opposite kind. He had sold and scattered, mortgaged and squandered his property, especially during the past few years as he had tried to separate from his mistress, thinking that with time his wild life would be forgotten and his kinsmen would take him back. He had believed that in the end he would be named sheriff of half of Orkdøla county, just as his father had been.

"But now I have no idea how things will finally go," he said. "Maybe I'll end up on a farm on some scruffy slope like Bjørn Gunnarsøn, and I'll have to carry out the dung on my back the way slaves used to do in the past because I own no horses."

"God help you," said Kristin, laughing. "Then I'd better come with you. I think I know more about peasant ways than you do."

"But I don't imagine that you've ever carried a dung basket," he said, laughing too.

"No, but I've seen how they spread out the muck, and I've sown grain almost every year back home. My father usually plows the closest fields himself, and then he lets me sow the first section because I'll bring him luck . . ." The memory painfully pierced her heart, and she said hastily, "And you'll need a woman to bake and brew the weak ale and wash out your only shirt and do the milking. You'll have to lease a cow or two from the nearest wealthy farmer."

"Oh, thank God I can hear you laugh a little once again," said Erlend, taking her onto his lap so that she lay in his arms like a child.

During the six nights before Aasmund Bjørgulfsøn returned home, Erlend came up to the loft to be with Kristin each evening.

On the last night he seemed just as unhappy as she was; he said many times that they would not be parted from each other a day longer than was necessary.

Finally he said in a subdued voice, "If things should go so badly that I cannot return here to Oslo before winter—and you happen to be in need of a friend's help—then you can safely turn to Sira Jon here at Gerdarud; we've been friends since childhood. And Munan Baardsøn you can also trust."

Kristin could only nod. She realized that he was talking about the same thing that had been on her mind every single day, but Erlend didn't mention it again. Then she was silent too, not wanting to show him how sick at heart she felt.

The other times he had left her as the hour grew late, but on this last night he pleaded earnestly to be allowed to lie down and sleep with her for a while.

Kristin was afraid, but Erlend said defiantly, "You should realize that if I'm discovered here in your chamber, I know how to defend myself."

She wanted so badly to keep him with her a little longer, and she was incapable of refusing him anything.

But she was worried that they might sleep too long. So for most of the night she sat up, leaning against the headboard, dozing a little now and then, not always conscious of when he was actually caressing her and when she had simply dreamed it. She kept one hand on his chest, where she could feel the beat of his heart, and turned her face toward the window so she could watch for the dawn outside.

Finally she had to wake him. She threw on some clothes and walked out onto the gallery with him. He leaped over the railing on the side of the house facing another building. Then he disappeared around the corner. Kristin went back inside and crawled into bed again; then she let herself go and wept for the first time since she had become Erlend's possession.

AT NONNESETER the days passed as they had before. Kristin spent her time in the dormitory and the church, the weaving room, the library, and the refectory. The nuns and the convent servants harvested the crops of the herb garden and orchard, Holy Cross Day arrived in the fall with its procession, and then came the time of fasting before Michaelmas. Kristin was astonished that no one seemed to notice anything different about her. But she had always been quiet in the company of strangers, and Ingebjørg Filippusdatter, who was her companion day and night, managed to talk enough for both of them.

So no one noticed that her thoughts were far away from everything around her. Erlend's mistress. She told herself this: now she was Erlend's mistress. It was as if she had dreamed it all—the evening of Saint Margareta's Day, the time in the barn, the nights in her bedchamber at Skog. Either she had dreamed all that or she was dreaming now. But one day she would have to wake up; one day it would all come out. Not for a moment did she doubt that she was carrying Erlend's child.

But she couldn't really imagine what would happen to her when this came to light—whether she would be thrown into a dark cell or be sent home. Far off in the distance she glimpsed the faint images of her father and mother. Then she would close her eyes, dizzy and sick, submerged by the imagined storm, trying to steel herself to bear the misfortune, which she thought would inevitably end with her being swept into Erlend's arms for all eternity—the only place where she now felt she had a home.

So in this sense of tension there was just as much anticipation as there was terror; there was sweetness as well as anguish. She was unhappy, but she felt that her love for Erlend was like a plant that had been sown inside her, and for every day that passed it sprouted a new and even lusher abundance of flowers, in spite of her misery. She had experienced the last night that he had slept with her as a delicate and fleeting sweetness, and a passion and joy awaited her in his embrace which she had never known before. Now she trembled at the memory; it felt to her like the hot, spicy gust from the sun-heated gardens. Wayside bastard—those were the words that Inga had flung at her. She reached out for the words and held them tight. Wayside bastard—a child that had been conceived in secret in the woods or meadows. She remembered the sunshine and the smell of the spruce trees in the glade. Every new, trickling sensation, every quickened pulse in her body she took to be the unborn child, reminding her that now she had ventured onto new paths; and no matter how difficult they might be to follow, she was certain that in the end they would lead her to Erlend.

She sat between Ingebjørg and Sister Astrid, embroidering on the great tapestry with the knights and birds beneath the twining leaves. All the while she was thinking that she would run away once her condition could no longer be concealed. She would walk along the road, dressed as a poor woman, with all the gold and silver she owned knotted into a cloth in her hand. She would pay for a roof over her head at a farm somewhere in an isolated village. She would become a servant woman, carrying water buckets on a yoke across her shoulders. She would tend to the stables, do the baking and washing, and suffer curses because she refused to name the father of her child. Then Erlend would come and find her.

Sometimes she imagined that he would come too late. Snow-white and beautiful, she would be lying in the poor peasant bed. Erlend would lower his head as he stepped through the doorway. He was wearing the long black cape he had worn when he came to her on those nights at Skog. The farm woman had led him to the room where she lay. He sank down and took her cold hands in his, his eyes desperate with grief. "Is this where you are, my only joy?" Then, bowed with sorrow, he would leave, with his infant son pressed to his breast inside the folds of his cape.

No, that's not how she wanted things to end. She didn't want to die, and Erlend must not suffer such a sorrow. But she was so despondent, and it helped to think such things.

Then all of a sudden it became chillingly clear to her—the child was not something she had merely imagined, it was something inevitable. One day she would have to answer for what she had done, and she felt as if her heart had stopped in terror.

But after some time had passed, she realized it was not as certain as she had thought that she was with child. She didn't understand why this did not make her happy. It was as if she had been lying under a warm blanket, weeping; now she had to get up and step into the cold. Another month passed, then another. Finally she was convinced—she had escaped that misfortune. Freezing and empty, she now felt more unhappy than ever, and in her heart a tiny bitterness toward Erlend was brewing. Advent was approaching and she had not heard a word, either about him or from him; she had no idea where he was.

And now she felt she could no longer endure the anguish and uncertainty; it was as if a bond between them had been broken. Now she was truly frightened. Something might happen and she would never see him again. She was separated from everything she had been bound to in the past, and the bond between them was such a fragile one. She didn't think that he would forsake her, but so many things might happen. She couldn't imagine how she would be able to stand the day-to-day uncertainty and agony of this waiting time any longer.

Sometimes she would think about her parents and sisters. She longed for them, but with the feeling that she had lost them for good.

And occasionally in church, and at other times as well, she would feel a fervent yearning to become part of it all, this community with God. It had always been part of her life, and now she stood outside with her unconfessed sin.

She told herself that this separation from her home and family and Christianity was only temporary. But Erlend would have to lead her back by the hand. When Lavrans consented to the love between her and Erlend, then she would be able to go to her father as she had before; and after she and Erlend were married, they would make confession and atone for their offense.

She began looking for evidence that other people, like herself, were not without sin. She paid more attention to gossip, and she

took note of all the little things around her which indicated that
not even the sisters in the convent were completely holy and un-
worldly. There were only small things—under Fru Groa's guidance
Nonneseter was, in the eyes of the outside world, exactly as a holy
order of nuns ought to be. The nuns were zealous in their service
to God, diligent, and attentive to the poor and the sick. Confine-
ment to the cloister was not so strictly enforced that the sisters
could not receive visits from their friends and kinsmen in the parlatory; nor were they prevented from returning these visits in the
town if the occasion so warranted. But no nun had ever brought
shame upon the order through her actions in all the years that Fru
Groa had been in charge.

Kristin had now developed an alert ear for all the small distur-
bances within the convent's walls: little complaints and jealousies
and vanities. Other than nursing, no nun would lend a hand with
the rough housework; they all wanted to be learned and skilled
women. Each one tried to outshine the other, and those sisters who
did not have talent for such refined occupations gave up and
drifted through the hours as if in a daze.

Fru Groa herself was both learned and wise. She kept a vigilant
eye on the conduct and industry of her spiritual daughters, but she
paid little heed to the welfare of their souls. She had always been
friendly and kind toward Kristin and seemed to favor her above
the other young daughters, but that was because Kristin was well
trained in book learning and needlework and was diligent and
quiet. Fru Groa never expected replies from the sisters. On the
other hand, she enjoyed talking to men. They came and went in
her parlatory: landholders and envoys associated with the convent,
predicant brothers from the bishop, and representatives from the
cloister at Hovedø, with which she was involved in a legal matter.
She had her hands full tending to the convent's large estates, the
accounts, sending out clerical garb, and taking in and then sending
off books to be copied. Not even the most ill-tempered person
could find anything improper about Fru Groa's behavior. She simply liked to talk about those things that women seldom knew anything about.

The prior, who lived in a separate building north of the church,
seemed to have no more will than the reed pen or switch of the

abbess. Sister Potentia, for the most part, ruled the house. She was primarily intent on maintaining the customs that she had observed in the distinguished German convents where she had lived during her novitiate. Her former name was Sigrid Ragnvaldsdatter, but she had changed her name when she assumed the habit of the order, as was the custom in other countries. She was also the one who had decided that the pupils who were only at Nonneseter for a short time should also wear the attire of young novices.

Sister Cecilia Baardsdatter was not like the other nuns. She walked around in silence, her eyes downcast. She always replied meekly and humbly, acted as everyone's maidservant, preferred to take on the roughest tasks, and fasted more often than was prescribed—as much as Fru Groa would allow. And in church she would kneel for hours after the evening hymn or go there long before matins.

But one evening, after she had spent the whole day at the creek washing clothes along with two lay sisters, she suddenly began to sob loudly at the supper table. She threw herself onto the stone floor, crawled on her knees among the sisters, and beat her breast. With burning cheeks and streaming tears she begged them to forgive her. She was the worst sinner of them all—she had been stone-hard with arrogance all her days. It was arrogance and not humility or gratitude for the death of Christ the Savior that had sustained her when she was tempted in the world; she had fled to the convent not because she loved a man's soul but because she had loved her own pride. She had served her sisters with arrogance, she had drunk vanity from her water goblet, and she had spread her bare bread thick with conceit while the sisters drank ale and ate butter on their bread.

From all this Kristin understood that not even Cecilia Baardsdatter was completely pure of heart. An unlit tallow candle that has hung from the ceiling and turned filthy with soot and cobwebs—that was how she compared her loveless chastity.

Fru Groa herself went over and lifted up the sobbing young woman. Sternly she said that as punishment for her outburst Cecilia would move from the sisters' dormitory into the abbess's own bed and stay there until she had recovered from this fever.

"And then, Sister Cecilia, you will sit in my chair for eight days.

We will ask your advice in spiritual matters and show you such respect because of your godly conduct that you will grow sated from the tribute of sinful people. Then you must judge whether this is worth so much struggle, and decide either to live by the rules as the rest of us do or to continue the trials that no one demands of you. Then you can contemplate whether all the things that you say you do now so that we might look up to you, henceforward you will do out of love of God and so that He might look upon you with mercy."

And so it was. Sister Cecilia lay in the abbess's room for two weeks; she had a high fever, and Fru Groa nursed the nun herself. When she had recovered, for eight days she had to sit at the abbess's side in the place of honor both in church and at home, and everyone served her. She wept the whole time, as if she were being beaten. Afterward she was much gentler and happier. She continued to live in almost the same manner as before, but she would blush like a bride if anyone looked at her, whether she was sweeping the floor or walking alone to church.

This episode with Sister Cecilia aroused in Kristin a strong yearning for peace and reconciliation with everything from which she had come to feel herself cut off. She thought about Brother Edvin, and one day she gathered her courage and asked Fru Groa for permission to visit the barefoot friars to see a friend of hers there.

She could tell that Fru Groa was not pleased; there was little friendship between the Minorites and the other cloisters of the diocese. And the abbess was no more favorably disposed when she heard who Kristin's friend was. She said that this Brother Edvin was an unreliable man of God, always roaming about the country seeking alms in other dioceses. In many places the peasantry considered him a holy man, but he didn't seem to realize that the first duty of a Franciscan monk was obedience to his superiors. He had heard the confessions of outlaws and those who had been excommunicated; he had baptized their children and sung them into their graves without asking for permission. And yet his sin was as much due to lack of understanding as it was to defiance, and he had patiently borne the reprimands which had been imposed on him because of these matters. The Church had treated him with for-

bearance because he was skilled at his craft; but even in the exe-
cution of his art he had come into conflict with others. The
bishop's master painters in Bergen refused to allow him to work
in their diocese.

Kristin was bold enough to ask where this monk with the un-
Norwegian name had come from. Fru Groa was in a mood to talk.
She said that he was born in Oslo, but his father was an English-
man, Rikard the Armormaster, who had married a farmer's daughter from the Skogheim district, and they had taken up residence in
Oslo. Two of Edvin's brothers were respected armorers in town.
But Edvin, the eldest of the armormaster's sons, had been a restless
soul all his days. He had no doubt felt an attraction for the monastic life since early childhood; he had joined the gray monks at
Hovedø as soon as he reached the proper age. They sent him to a
cloister in France to be educated; he had excellent abilities. From
there he managed to win permission to leave the Cistercian order
and enter the order of the Minorites instead. And when the brothers arbitrarily decided to build their church out in the fields to the
east, against the orders of the bishop,[1] Brother Edvin had been one
of the worst and most obstinate among them—he had even used
a hammer to strike one of the men sent by the bishop to stop the
work and had almost killed him.

It had been a long time since anyone had talked at such length
with Kristin. When Fru Groa dismissed her, the young maiden bent
down and kissed the abbess's hand, respectfully and fervently, and
tears sprang at once into her eyes. But Fru Groa, who saw that
Kristin was crying, thought it was from sorrow—and so she said
that perhaps one day she would be allowed to go out to visit
Brother Edvin after all.

And several days later Kristin was told that some of the convent's servants had to go over to the king's castle, so at the same
time they could accompany her out to the brothers in the fields.

Brother Edvin was home. Kristin had not imagined that she
would be so happy to see anyone other than Erlend. The old man
sat and stroked her hand as they talked, thanking her for coming.
No, he hadn't been to her part of the country since that night he
had stayed at Jørundgaard, but he had heard that she was to

marry, and he offered her his congratulations. Then Kristin asked him to go over to the church with her.

They had to go out of the cloister and around to the main entrance; Brother Edvin didn't dare lead her across the courtyard. He seemed in general quite timid and afraid to do anything that might offend. He had grown terribly old, thought Kristin.

And when she had placed her offering on the altar for the priest of the church and then asked Edvin to hear her confession, he grew quite frightened. He didn't dare; he had been strictly forbidden to listen to confessions.

"Perhaps you've heard about it," he said. "I didn't think that I could deny these poor souls the gifts that God has bestowed on me so freely. But I was supposed to exhort them to seek reconciliation at the proper place. . . . Well then. But you, Kristin, you will have to confess to the prior at the convent."

"There is something that I cannot confess to the prior," said Kristin.

"Do you think it would benefit you if you confess to me something that you wish to conceal from your proper confessor?" said the monk more sternly.

"If you cannot hear my confession," said Kristin, "then you can let me talk to you and ask your advice about what is on my mind."

The monk looked around. The church was empty at the moment. He sat down on a chest that stood in the corner. "You must remember that I cannot absolve you, but I will advise you and I will keep silent as if you had spoken in confession."

Kristin stood before him and said, "You see, I cannot become Simon Darre's wife."

"As to this matter, you know I cannot advise you otherwise than the prior would," said Brother Edvin. "Disobedient children bring God no joy, and your father has done his best for you—you must realize that."

"I don't know what your advice will be when you hear the rest," said Kristin. "The situation is such that Simon is too good to gnaw on the bare branch from which another man has broken off the blossom."

She looked directly at the monk. But when she met his eye and noticed how the dry, wrinkled old face suddenly changed and became filled with grief and horror, something seemed to break inside her; the tears poured out, and she tried to throw herself to her knees. But Edvin pulled her vehemently back.

"No, no, sit down here on the chest with me. I cannot hear your confession." He moved aside to make room for her.

Kristin continued to cry.

He stroked her hand and said softly, "Do you remember that morning, Kristin, when I saw you for the first time on the stairs of Hamar Cathedral? I once heard a legend, when I was abroad, about a monk who could not believe that God loved all of us wretched, sinful souls. An angel came and touched his sight so that he saw a stone at the bottom of the sea, and under the stone lived a blind, white, naked creature. And the monk stared at the creature until he began to love it because it was so small and pitiful. When I saw you sitting there, so tiny and pitiful inside that huge stone building, then I thought it was reasonable that God should love someone like you. You were lovely and pure, and yet you needed protection and help. I thought I saw the whole church, with you inside it, lying in the hand of God."

Kristin said softly, "We have bound ourselves to each other with the most solemn of oaths—and I have heard that such an agreement consecrates us before God just as much as if our parents had given us to each other."

But the monk replied with despair, "I see, Kristin, that someone has been telling you of the canonical law without fully understanding it. You could not promise yourself to this man without sinning against your parents; God placed them above you before you met him. And won't it also be a sorrow and a shame for this man's kinsmen if they learn that he has seduced the daughter of a man who has carried his shield with honor all these years? And you were also betrothed. I see that you do not think you have sinned so greatly—and yet you dare not confess this to your parish priest. And if you think you are as good as married to this man, why don't you wear the linen wimple instead of going around bareheaded among the young maidens, with whom you have so little in common now? For now your thoughts must be on other things than theirs are."

"I don't know what I'm thinking about," said Kristin wearily. "It's true that all my thoughts are with this man, whom I yearn for. If it weren't for Father and Mother, then I would gladly pin up my hair on this very day—I wouldn't care if they called me a paramour, if only I could be called his."

"Do you know whether this man's intentions are such that you might be his with honor someday?" asked Brother Edvin.

Then Kristin told him about everything that had happened between Erlend Nikulaussøn and herself. And as she talked, she seemed to have forgotten that she had ever doubted the outcome of the whole matter.

"Don't you see, Brother Edvin," she continued, "we couldn't control ourselves. God help me, if I met him here outside the church, after I leave you, I would go with him if he asked me to. And you should know that I have now seen that other people have sinned as we have. When I was back home I couldn't understand how anything could have such power over the souls of people that they would forget all fear of sin, but now I have seen so much that if one cannot rectify the sins one has committed out of desire or anger, then heaven must be a desolate place. They say that you too once struck a man in anger."

"That's true," said the monk, "and it is only through God's mercy that I am not called a murderer. That was many years ago. I was a young man back then, and I didn't think I could tolerate the injustice that the bishop wished to exercise against us poor brothers. King Haakon—he was the duke at that time—had given us the land for our building, but we were so poor that we had to do the work on our church ourselves, with the help of a few workmen who lent a hand more for their reward in heaven than for what we were able to pay them. Perhaps it was arrogance on the part of the mendicant monks that we wanted to build our church with such splendor; but we were as happy as children in the meadows, singing hymns as we chiseled and built walls and toiled. May God bless Brother Ranulv. He was a master builder, a skilled stonemason; I think God Himself had granted this man all his knowledge and skills. I was cutting altarpieces from stone back then. I had finished one of Saint Clara, with the angels leading her to the church of Saint Francis early Christmas morning. It had turned out beautifully, and we all rejoiced over it. Then those cowardly devils tore down the walls, and the stones toppled and crushed my altarpieces. I lunged at a man with a hammer; I couldn't control myself.

"Yes, I see that you're smiling, Kristin. But don't you realize how badly things stand with you now? For you would rather hear about other people's frailties than about the deeds of decent people, which might serve as an example for you."

As Kristin was about to leave, Brother Edvin said, "It's not easy to advise you. If you were to do what's right, then you would bring sorrow to your parents and shame upon your entire lineage. But you must try to win release from your promise to Simon Andressøn. Then you must wait patiently for the joy that God will send you. Do penance in your heart as best you can—and do not let this Erlend tempt you to sin more often, but ask him lovingly to seek reconciliation with your kinsmen and with God.

"I cannot absolve you of your sin," said Brother Edvin as they parted. "But I will pray for you with all my heart."

Then he placed his thin old hands on Kristin's head and said a prayer of blessing and peace for her in farewell.

CHAPTER 6

AFTERWARD Kristin could not remember everything that Brother Edvin had said to her. But she left him with a strange feeling of clarity and serene peace in her soul.

Before, she had struggled with a hollow and secret fear, trying to defy it: her sin had not been so great. Now she felt that Edvin had shown her clearly and lucidly that she had indeed sinned, that such and such were her sins, and that she would have to take them upon her shoulders and try to bear them with patience and dignity. She strove to think of Erlend without impatience, in spite of the fact that he had sent no word and she missed his caresses. She simply had to be faithful and full of kindness toward him. She thought about her parents and promised herself that she would repay all their love after they had first recovered from the sorrow that she was going to cause them by breaking with the Dyfrin people. And she thought most about Brother Edvin's advice that she should not seek solace by looking at the failings of others; she felt herself growing humble and kind, and soon realized how easy it was for her to win the friendship of others. At once she felt consoled that it was not so difficult, after all, to get along with people—and then she thought that it shouldn't be so difficult for her and Erlend either.

Up until the day when she gave Erlend her promise, she had always tried diligently to do everything that was right and good, but she had done everything at the bidding of other people. Now she felt that she had grown up from maiden to woman. This was not just because of the passionate, secret caresses she had received and given. She had not merely left her father's guardianship and subjected herself to Erlend's will. Brother Edvin had impressed on her the responsibility of answering for her own life, and for Erlend's as well, and she was willing to bear this burden with grace and dignity. So she lived among the nuns during the Christmas season; during the beautiful services and amidst the joy and peace, she no doubt felt herself unworthy, but she consoled herself with the belief that the time would soon come when she would be able to redeem herself again.

But on the day after New Year's, Sir Andres Darre arrived unexpectedly at the convent together with his wife and all five children. They were going to spend the last part of the Christmas holidays with friends and kinsmen in town, and they came to ask Kristin to join them at the place where they were staying for several days.

"I've been thinking, my daughter, said Fru Angerd, "that you probably wouldn't mind seeing some new faces by now."

The Dyfrin people were staying in a beautiful house that was part of an estate near the bishop's citadel. Sir Andres's nephew owned it. There was a large room where the servants slept and a magnificent loft room with a brick fireplace and three good beds. Sir Andres and Fru Angerd slept in one of the beds, along with their youngest son, Gudmund, who was still a child. Kristin and their two daughters, Astrid and Sigrid, slept in the second bed. And in the third slept Simon and his older brother, Gyrd Andressøn.

All of Sir Andres's children were good-looking—Simon the least so, and yet people still considered him handsome. And Kristin noticed even more than when she had been at the Dyfrin manor the year before that both his parents and his four siblings listened closely to Simon and did everything he wished. All his kinsmen loved each other heartily but agreed without rancor to place Simon foremost.

These people led a joyful and happy life, going to one of the churches each day to make their offerings, meeting to drink among friends each evening, and allowing the young to play and dance. Everyone showed Kristin the greatest kindness, and no one seemed to notice how little joy she felt.

At night, when the candles were put out in the loft and everyone had gone to bed, Simon would get up and come over to where the maidens lay. He would sit for a while on the edge of the bed, speaking mostly to his sisters, but in the dark he would sneak his hand up to Kristin's breast and let it stay there. She would lie there, sweating with indignation.

Now that her sense for such matters was so much keener, she realized there were many things that Simon was both too proud and too shy to say to her, once he noticed that she didn't want to go into such topics. And she felt a strange, bitter anger toward him because it seemed to her that he was trying to make himself seem a better man than the one who had taken her—even though he had no idea of the other man's existence.

But one evening when they had been out dancing at another estate, Astrid and Sigrid stayed behind and were going to sleep with a foster sister. Late that night, when the people from Dyfrin had gone to bed in the loft, Simon came over to Kristin's bed and climbed in; he lay on top of the furs.

Kristin pulled the covers up to her chin and crossed her arms tightly over her chest. After a moment Simon reached out his hand to touch her breasts. She felt the silk embroidery at his wrists, so she realized that he had not undressed.

"You're just as shy in the dark as in the daylight, Kristin," said Simon with a chuckle. "Surely you'll let me hold your hand, won't you?" he asked, and Kristin gave him her fingertips.

"Don't you think we might have a few things to talk about, now that we have the chance to be alone for a little while?" he said. And Kristin thought that now she would be able to speak. So she agreed. But then she could not utter a word.

"Can I come under the furs?" he asked again. "It's cold in the room." And he slipped in between the furs and the woolen blanket she had over her. He crooked one arm behind her head, but in such a way that he did not touch her. And they lay there like that for a while.

"You're not an easy person to woo, either," said Simon after a pause, and then laughed in resignation. "I promise you I won't so much as kiss you, if you don't want me to. But surely you can talk to me, can't you?"

Kristin moistened her lips with the tip of her tongue, but she still remained silent.

"It seems to me that you're lying here trembling," Simon continued. "Is it because you have something against me, Kristin?"

She didn't think that she could lie to Simon, so she said, "No," but nothing more.

Simon lay there a little longer, trying to get a conversation started. But finally he laughed again and said, "I see that you think I should be satisfied with this—that you have nothing against me—for tonight, at least, and that I should even be happy. It's strange how proud you are too. But you must give me a kiss, all the same; then I'll go and not plague you any longer."

He took his kiss, sat up, and set his feet on the floor. Kristin thought that now she would manage to tell him what had to be said—but he had already left her bed, and she could hear him getting undressed.

The next day Fru Angerd was not as friendly toward Kristin as she usually was. The young maiden realized that she must have heard something and felt that the betrothed girl had not received her son in the manner that his mother felt she should have.

Later in the afternoon Simon mentioned that he was thinking of trading for a horse that was owned by one of his friends. He asked Kristin whether she would like to go along and watch. She said yes, and they went into town together.

The weather was clear and beautiful. It had snowed a little during the night, but now the sun was shining, and it was still so cold that the snow squeaked under their feet. Kristin enjoyed getting out in the cold and walking, so when Simon had found the horse that he was thinking of, she talked to him about it in the most lively manner; she had some knowledge of horses, since she had always spent so much time with her father. And this one was a fine animal: a mouse-gray stallion with narrow black stripes along his back and a short, clipped mane. He was well built and spirited, but quite small and slight.

"He won't last long under a fully-armed man," said Kristin.

"No, but that's not what I had in mind, either," said Simon.

He led the horse out to the open area behind the farm, let him run and walk, rode the animal himself, and then had Kristin ride him too. They stayed outdoors in the white pasture for a long time.

Finally, as Kristin was feeding bread to the horse from her hand, Simon leaned against the animal with his arm over his back and said suddenly, "It seems to me, Kristin, that you and my mother have been rather cross with each other."

"I haven't meant to be cross with your mother," she said, "but I can't find much to say to Fru Angerd."

"You don't seem to find much to say to me, either," said Simon. "I won't force myself on you, Kristin, before the time comes. But things can't go on like this; I never get a chance to talk to you."

"I have never been talkative," said Kristin. "I know that myself, and I don't expect you to think it a great loss if things don't work out between us."

"You know what I think about that subject," replied Simon, looking at her.

Kristin blushed as red as blood. And she was startled to find that she was not averse to Simon Darre's wooing.

After a moment he said, "Is it Arne Gyrdsøn, Kristin, that you think you can't forget?" Kristin stared at him. Simon continued, and his voice was kind and understanding, "I won't blame you for that. You grew up as siblings, and barely a year has passed. But you can depend on this: I want only what's best for you."

Kristin's face had grown quite pale. Neither of them spoke as they walked through town in the twilight. At the end of the street, in the greenish blue sky, the crescent of the new moon hung with a bright star in its embrace.

One year, thought Kristin, and she could hardly remember when she had last given Arne a thought. It gave her a fright—maybe she was a loose, vile woman. A year since she had seen him lying on the bier in the death chamber, when she thought she would never be happy again. She whimpered silently in fear at the inconstancy of her own heart and at the transitory nature of all things. Erlend, Erlend—would he forget her? But worse yet was that she might ever forget him.

Sir Andres and his children went to the great Christmas celebration at the king's castle. Kristin saw all the finery and splendor, and they were also invited into the hall where King Haakon sat with Fru Isabel Bruce, the widow of King Eirik. Sir Andres went forward to greet the king, while his children and Kristin remained behind. She thought of everything that Fru Aashild had told her, and she remembered that the king was Erlend's close kinsman—their fathers' mothers had been sisters. And she was Erlend's wife by seduction; she had no right to stand here, especially not among these good, fine people, the children of Sir Andres.

Suddenly she saw Erlend Nikulaussøn. He had stepped forward in front of Queen Isabel and was standing there with his head bowed and his hand on his breast while she spoke a few words to him. He was wearing the brown silk surcoat that he had worn to their banquet rendezvous. Kristin stepped behind Sir Andres's daughters.

When Fru Angerd, some time later, escorted the three maidens over to the queen, Kristin could not see Erlend anywhere, but she didn't dare raise her eyes from the floor. She wondered if he was standing somewhere in the hall; she thought she could feel his eyes on her. But she also thought that everyone was staring at her, as if they could tell that she was standing there like a liar with the gold wreath on her hair, which fell loosely over her shoulders.

He was not in the hall where the young people were served dinner and where they danced after the tables had been cleared away. Kristin had to dance with Simon that evening.

Along one wall stood a built-in table, and that's where the king's servants set ale and mead and wine all night long. Once when Simon took Kristin over there and drank a toast to her, she saw that Erlend was standing quite close to her, behind Simon. He looked at her, and Kristin's hand shook as Simon gave her the goblet and she raised it to her lips. Erlend whispered fiercely to the man who was with him—a tall, heavyset, but handsome older man, who shook his head dismissively with an angry expression. In the next moment Simon led Kristin back to the dance.

She had no idea how long that dance lasted; the ballad seemed endless and every moment was tedious and painful with longing and unrest. At last it was over, and Simon escorted her over to the table for drinks again.

One of his friends approached and spoke to him, leading him away a few paces, over to a group of young men. Then Erlend stood before her.

"I have so much I want to say to you," he whispered. "I don't know what to say first. In Christ's name, Kristin, how are things with you?" he asked hastily, for he noticed that her face had turned as white as chalk.

She couldn't see him clearly; it was as if there was running water between their faces. He picked up a goblet from the table, drank from it, and handed it to Kristin. She thought it was much too heavy, or that her arm had been pulled from its socket; she couldn't manage to raise it to her lips.

"Is that how things stand—that you'll drink with your betrothed but not with me?" asked Erlend softly. But Kristin dropped the goblet and swooned forward into his arms.

When she woke up she was lying on a bench with her head in the lap of a maiden she didn't know. They had loosened her belt and the brooch on her breast. Someone was slapping her hands, and her face was wet.

She sat up. Somewhere in the circle of people around her she saw Erlend's face, pale and ill. She felt weak herself, as if all her bones had melted, and her head felt huge and hollow. But somewhere in her mind a single thought, clear and desperate, shone— she had to talk to Erlend.

Then she said to Simon Darre, who was standing close by, "It must have been too hot for me. There are so many candles burning in here, and I'm not accustomed to drinking so much wine."

"Are you all right now?" asked Simon. "You frightened everyone. Perhaps you would like me to take you home?"

"I think we should wait until your parents leave," said Kristin calmly. "But sit down here. I don't feel like dancing anymore." She patted the cushion beside her. Then she stretched out her other hand to Erlend.

"Sit down here, Erlend Nikulaussøn. I didn't have a chance to give you my full greeting. Ingebjørg was just saying lately that she thought you had forgotten all about her."

She saw that he was having a much more difficult time composing himself than she was. It cost her great effort to hold back the tender little smile that threatened to appear on her lips.

"You must thank the maiden for still remembering me," he said, stammering. "And here I was so afraid that she had forgotten *me*."

Kristin hesitated for a moment. She didn't know what message

she could bring from the flighty Ingebjørg that would be inter-
preted correctly by Erlend. Then bitterness rose up inside her for
all those months of helplessness, and she said, "Dear Erlend, did
you think that we maidens would forget the man who so magnificently defended our honor?"

She saw that he looked as if she had struck him. And she regretted it at once when Simon asked what she meant. Kristin told
him of her adventure with Ingebjørg out in the Eikaberg woods.
She noticed that Simon was not pleased. Then she asked him to
go in search of Fru Angerd, to see if they would be leaving soon.
She was tired after all. When he had gone, she turned to look at
Erlend.

"It's odd," he said in a low voice, "how resourceful you are—
I wouldn't have thought it of you."

"I've had to learn to conceal things, as you might well imagine,"
she said somberly.

Erlend breathed heavily. He was still quite pale.

"Is that it?" he whispered. "But you promised to go to my
friends if that should come about. God knows, I've thought about
you every single day, about whether the worst had happened."

"I know what you mean by the worst," replied Kristin tersely.
"You needn't worry about that. It seems worse to me that you
would not send me a word of greeting. Can't you understand that
I'm living there with the nuns like some strange bird?" She stopped
because she could feel the tears rising.

"Is that why you're with the Dyfrin people now?" he asked.
Then she grew so full of despair that she couldn't answer.

She saw Fru Angerd and Simon appear in the doorway. Erlend's hand lay on his knee, close to her own, but she could not
touch it.

"I have to talk to you," he said fiercely. "We haven't said a
word to each other of what we should have talked about."

"Come to the mass at the Maria Church after the last day of
the Christmas season," Kristin said hastily, as she stood up and
stepped forward to meet the others.

Fru Angerd was quite loving and kind toward Kristin on the
way home, and she helped the maiden into bed herself. Kristin
didn't have a chance to speak to Simon until the following day.

Then he said, "How is it that you would agree to convey messages between this Erlend and Ingebjørg Filippusdatter? You should not lend a hand in this matter, if they have some secret business between them."

"I don't think there's anything behind it," said Kristin. "She's just a chatterbox."

"I thought you would have been more sensible," said Simon, "than to venture into the woods and out onto roads alone with that magpie." But Kristin reminded him with some fervor that it was not their fault they had gone astray. Simon didn't say another word.

The next day the Dyfrin people escorted her back to the convent before setting off for home themselves.

Erlend came to vespers at the convent church every day for a week, but Kristin didn't have the chance to exchange a single word with him. She felt as if she were a hawk that sat chained to a roost with a hood pulled over its eyes. She was also unhappy about every word they had said to each other at their last meeting; that was not the way it was supposed to have been. It didn't help that she told herself it had happened so suddenly for both of them that they hardly knew what they were saying.

But one afternoon, at dusk, a beautiful woman who looked like the wife of a townsman appeared in the parlatory. She asked for Kristin Lavransdatter and said that she was the wife of a clothing merchant. Her husband had just arrived from Denmark with some fine cloaks, and Aasmund Bjørgulfsøn wished to give one of them to his niece, so the maiden was to go with her to select it herself.

Kristin was allowed to accompany the woman. She thought it unlike her uncle to want to give her a costly gift, and peculiar that he would send a stranger to get her.

At first the woman said little, replying only briefly to Kristin's questions, but when they had walked all the way into town, she suddenly said, "I don't want to fool you, lovely child that you are. I'm going to tell you how things truly stand so you can decide for yourself. It wasn't your uncle who sent me, but a man—maybe you can guess his name, and if you can't, then you shouldn't come with me. I have no husband, and I have to make a living for myself

and mine by keeping an inn and serving ale. So I can't be too afraid
of either sin or servants—but I will not let my house be used for
purposes of deceiving you within my walls."

Kristin stopped, her face flushed. She felt strangely hurt and
ashamed on Erlend's behalf.

The woman said, "I will accompany you back to the convent,
Kristin, but you must give me something for my trouble. The
knight promised me a large reward, but I was also beautiful once,
and I too was deceived. And then you can remember me in your
prayers tonight. They call me Brynhild Fluga."

Kristin took a ring from her finger and gave it to the woman.

"That was kind of you, Brynhild, but if the man is my kinsman
Erlend Nikulaussøn, then I have nothing to fear. He wants me to
reconcile him with my uncle. You will not be blamed—but thank
you for warning me."

Brynhild Fluga turned away to hide her smile.

She led Kristin through the alleys behind Clement's Church and
north toward the river. A few small, isolated farms were situated
on the bank. They walked between several fences, and there came
Erlend to meet them. He glanced around and then took off his
cape and wrapped it around Kristin, pulling the hood forward over
her face.

"What do you think of this ruse?" he asked quickly, in a low
voice. "Do you think I've done wrong? But I had to talk to you."

"It won't do much good for us to think about what's right and
what's wrong," said Kristin.

"Don't talk like that," implored Erlend. "I take the blame. Kristin, I've longed for you every day and every night," he whispered
close to her ear.

A shudder passed through her as she briefly met his glance. She
felt guilty because she had been thinking about something besides
her love for him when he looked at her in that way.

Brynhild Fluga had gone on ahead. When they reached the inn,
Erlend asked Kristin, "Do you want to go into the main room, or
should we talk upstairs in the loft?"

"As you please," replied Kristin.

"It's cold up there," said Erlend softly. "We'll have to get into
the bed." Kristin merely nodded.

The instant he had closed the door behind them, she was in his arms. He bent her this way and that like a wand, blinding her and smothering her with kisses, as he impatiently tore both cloaks off her and tossed them to the floor. Then he lifted the girl in the pale convent dress in his arms, pressing her to his shoulder, and carried her over to the bed. Frightened by his roughness and by her own sudden desire for this man, she put her arms around him and buried her face in his neck.

It was so cold in the loft that they could see their own breath like a cloud of smoke in front of the little candle standing on the table. But there were plenty of blankets and furs on the bed, covered by a great bearskin, which they pulled all the way up over their faces.

She didn't know how long she had lain like that in his arms when Erlend said, "Now we must talk about those things that have to be discussed, my Kristin. I don't dare keep you here long."

"I'll stay here the whole night if you want me to," whispered Kristin.

Erlend pressed his cheek to hers.

"Then I would not be much of a friend to you. Things are bad enough already, but I won't have people gossiping about you because of me."

Kristin didn't reply, but she felt a twinge of pain. She didn't understand how he could say such a thing, since he was the one who had brought her here to Brynhild Fluga's house. She didn't know how she knew it, but she realized that this was not a good place. And he had expected that everything would proceed just as it did, for he had a cup of mead standing inside the bed drapes.

"I've been thinking," continued Erlend, "that if there's no other alternative, then I'll have to take you away by force, to Sweden. Duchess Ingebjørg received me kindly this autumn and spoke of the kinship between us. But now I'm paying for my sins—I've fled the country before, you know—and I don't want you to be mentioned as that other one's equal."

"Take me home to Husaby with you," said Kristin quietly. "I can't bear to be separated from you and to live with the maidens in the convent. Surely both your kinsmen and mine will be reasonable enough that they'll allow us to be together and become reconciled with them."

Erlend hugged her tight and moaned, "I can't take you to Husaby, Kristin."

"Why can't you?" she asked in a whisper.

"Eline came back this fall," he said after a moment. "I can't make her leave the farm," he continued angrily, "not unless I carry her by force out to the sleigh and drive her away myself. And I don't think I could do that—she brought both of our children home with her."

Kristin felt as if she were sinking deeper and deeper. In a voice that was brittle with fear she said, "I thought you had parted from her."

"I thought so too," replied Erlend curtly. "But she apparently heard in Østerdal, where she was living, that I was thinking of marriage. You saw the man I was with at the Christmas banquet—that was my foster father, Baard Petersøn of Hestnæs. I went to him when I returned from Sweden; I visited my kinsman, Heming Alvsøn, in Saltvik too. I told them that I wanted to get married now and asked them to help me. That must be what Eline heard.

"I told her to demand whatever she wanted for herself and the children. But they don't expect Sigurd, her husband, to survive the winter, and then no one can prevent us from living together.

"I slept in the stables with Haftor and Ulv, and Eline slept in the house in my bed. I think my men had a good laugh behind my back."

Kristin couldn't say a word.

After a moment Erlend went on, "You know, on the day when our betrothal is formally celebrated, she'll have to realize that it will do her no good—that she has no power over me any longer.

"But it will be bad for the children. I hadn't seen them in a year—they're good-looking children—and there's little I can do to secure their situation. It wouldn't have helped them much even if I had been able to marry their mother."

Tears began to slide down Kristin's cheeks.

Then Erlend said, "Did you hear what I said? That I have spoken to my kinsmen? And they were pleased that I want to marry. Then I told them that it was you I wanted and no one else."

"And weren't they pleased about that?" asked Kristin at last, timidly.

"Don't you see," said Erlend gloomily, "that there was only one thing they could say? They cannot and they will not ride with me to speak with your father until this agreement between you and Simon Andressøn has been dissolved. It hasn't made things any easier for us, Kristin, that you have celebrated Christmas with the Dyfrin people."

Kristin broke down completely and began to sob quietly. She had no doubt felt that there was something unwise and ignoble about her love, and now she realized that the blame was hers.

She shivered with cold as she got out of bed a short time later and Erlend wrapped both cloaks around her. It was now completely dark outside, and Erlend accompanied her to Clement's churchyard; then Brynhild escorted her the rest of the way to Nonneseter.

CHAPTER 7

THE FOLLOWING WEEK Brynhild Fluga came with word that the cloak was now finished, and Kristin went with her and was with Erlend in the loft room as before.

When they parted he gave her a cloak, "so you have something to show at the convent," he said. It was made of blue velvet interwoven with red silk, and Erlend asked her whether she noticed that they were the same colors as the dress she had worn on that day in the forest. Kristin was surprised that she could be so happy over what he said; she felt as if he had never given her greater joy than with those words.

But now they could no longer use this excuse to meet, and it was not easy to think of something else. Erlend went to vespers at the convent church, and several times after the service Kristin went on an errand up to the corrodians' farms; they stole a few words with each other up along the fences in the dark of the winter evening.

Then Kristin thought of asking Sister Potentia for permission to visit several palsied old women, charity cases of the convent, who lived in a house out in a field some distance away. Behind the house was a shed where the women kept a cow. Kristin offered to tend to the animal for them when she visited, and then she would let Erlend come in while she worked.

She noticed with some surprise that in spite of Erlend's joy at being with her, a tiny scrap of bitterness had settled in his mind that she had been able to think up this excuse.

"It was not to your best advantage that you became acquainted with me," he said one evening. "Now you've learned to use these kinds of secret ruses."

"*You* should not be blaming me for that," replied Kristin dejectedly.

174

"It's not you that I blame," said Erlend at once, embarrassed.

"I never thought," she went on, "that it would be so easy for me to lie. But what must be done can be done."

"That's not always true," said Erlend in the same voice as before. "Do you remember this past winter, when you couldn't tell your betrothed that you wouldn't have him?"

Kristin didn't reply, but merely stroked his face.

She never felt so strongly how much she loved Erlend as when he said such things that made her feel dejected or surprised. And she was glad that she could take the blame for everything that was disgraceful or ignoble about their love. If she had had the courage to speak to Simon as she should have, then they could have progressed a long way in settling these matters. Erlend had done all that he could when he had spoken of marriage to his kinsmen. This is what she told herself whenever the days at the convent grew long and dreary. Erlend had wanted to make everything right and proper. With tender little smiles she would think about him as he looked whenever he described their wedding. She would ride to the church dressed in silk and velvet, and she would be led to the bridal bed with the tall golden crown on her hair, which would be spread out over her shoulders—her lovely, beautiful hair, he said, running her braids through his fingers.

"But for you it won't be the same as if you had never possessed me," Kristin once said thoughtfully when he had spoken of such things.

Then he had pulled her ardently to him.

"Don't you think I can remember the first time I celebrated Christmas, or the first time I saw the mountainsides turn green back home after winter? Oh, of course I'll remember the first time I had you, and every time after that. But to possess you, that's like perpetually celebrating Christmas or hunting birds on the green slopes."

Joyfully she crept closer in his arms.

Not that she for a moment believed that things would go as Erlend so confidently expected. Kristin thought that a judgment day was sure to befall them before long. It was impossible for things to continue to go so well. But she was not particularly afraid. She was much more frightened that Erlend might have to

travel north before the matter could be settled, and she would have
to stay behind, separated from him. He was over at the fortress on
Akersnes right now; Munan Baardsøn was there while the Royal
Treasurer was in Tunsberg, where the king lay deathly ill. But one
day Erlend would no doubt have to return home to see to his
property. She refused to admit that this frightened her because he
would be going home to Husaby where his mistress was waiting
for him. But she was less afraid of being caught in sin with Erlend
than of standing up alone and telling Simon, and her father as well,
what was in her heart.

And so she almost wished that some punishment would befall
her, and soon. For now she had no thoughts for anything but
Erlend. She longed for him in the daytime and she dreamed of him
at night. She felt no repentance, but she consoled herself with the
thought that the day would come when she would have to pay
dearly for everything they had taken in secret. And during those
brief evening hours when she could be together with Erlend in the
poor women's cowshed, she would throw herself into his arms so
ardently, as if she had paid with her soul to be his.

But time passed, and it looked as if Erlend was to have the good
fortune that he was counting on. Kristin noticed that no one at the
convent ever suspected her, although Ingebjørg had discovered that
she met with Erlend. But Kristin could see that the other girl never
thought it was anything more than a little amusement she was
allowing herself. That a betrothed maiden of good family would
dare to break the agreement that her kinsmen had made was something that would never occur to Ingebjørg. And for a moment fear
raced through Kristin once more; perhaps this was something completely unheard of, this situation she had landed in. And then she
wished again that she would be found out, so that it could be
brought to an end.

Easter arrived. Kristin couldn't understand what had happened
to the winter; each day that she had not seen Erlend had been as
long as a dismal year, and the long gloomy days had become linked
together into endless weeks. But now it was spring and Easter, and
it seemed to her as if they had just celebrated Christmas. She asked
Erlend not to seek her out during the holidays; and it seemed to

Kristin that he acquiesced to all her wishes. It was just as much her fault as his that they had sinned against the strictures of Lent. But she wanted them to observe the Easter holiday—even though it hurt not to see him. He might have to leave quite soon; he hadn't said anything about it, but she knew that the king was now dying, and she thought that this might cause some change in Erlend's position.

This was how matters stood for Kristin, when, a few days after Easter, she was summoned down to the parlatory to speak with her betrothed.

As soon as Simon came toward her and put out his hand, she realized that something was wrong. His face was not the same as usual; his small gray eyes weren't laughing, and they were untouched by his smile. Kristin couldn't help noticing that it suited him to be a little less jovial. And he looked quite handsome in the traveling clothes he wore: a long, blue, tight-fitting outer garment that men called a *cote-hardie*, and a brown shoulder-cape with a hood, which he had thrown back. His light brown hair was quite curly from the raw, damp air.

They sat and talked for a while. Simon had been at Formo during Lent, and he was over at Jørundgaard almost daily. They were all well there. Ulvhild was as healthy as anyone could expect. Ramborg was home now; she was charming and lively.

"The time is almost over, the year that you were supposed to spend here at Nonneseter," said Simon. "They're probably preparing everything for our betrothal feast at your home."

Kristin didn't reply as Simon continued.

"I told Lavrans that I would ride to Oslo to speak with you about it."

Kristin looked down and said quietly, "Things are such, Simon, that I would prefer to speak with you in private about this matter."

"I too have felt that this would be necessary," replied Simon Andressøn. "I was going to ask that you obtain Fru Groa's permission for us to walk in the garden together."

Kristin stood up abruptly, and slipped soundlessly out of the room. A short time later she returned, accompanied by one of the nuns with a key.

A door from the parlatory opened onto the herb garden, which lay beyond the buildings on the west side of the convent. The nun unlocked the door, and they stepped out into a fog so dense that they could see only a few steps in front of them amidst the trees. The closest trunks were black as coal; beads of moisture clung to every branch and twig. Small patches of new snow were melting on the wet soil, but beneath the bushes tiny white and yellow lilies had already sprouted flowers, and it smelled fresh and cool from the violet-grass.

Simon led her to the nearest bench. He sat down, leaning forward slightly with his elbows propped on his knees. Then he looked up at her with an odd little smile.

"I almost think I know what you want to tell me," he said. "There's another man that you like better than me?"

"That is true," replied Kristin softly.

"I think I know his name too," said Simon, his voice more harsh. "Is it Erlend Nikulaussøn of Husaby?"

After a moment Kristin said in a low voice, "So this has come to your attention?"

Simon hesitated before he answered.

"Surely you can't think me so stupid that I wouldn't notice anything when we were together at Christmastime? I couldn't say anything then, because my father and mother were present. But this is the reason that I wanted to come here alone this time. I don't know whether it's wise of me to speak of this matter, but I thought that we ought to talk of such things before we are joined in marriage.

"But as it happened, when I arrived here yesterday, I met my kinsman, Master Øistein. And he spoke of you. He said that he saw you walking across Clement's churchyard one evening, and that you were with a woman they call Brynhild Fluga. I swore a sacred oath that he must have been mistaken. And if you tell me that it's untrue, I will take you at your word."

"The priest was right," replied Kristin stubbornly. "You forswore yourself, Simon."

He sat in silence for a moment before he spoke again.

"Do you know who this Brynhild Fluga is, Kristin?" When she

shook her head, he said, "Munan Baardsøn set her up in a house here in town after he was married—she sells wine illegally and other such things."

"Do you know her?" asked Kristin derisively.

"I've never been inclined to become a monk or a priest," said Simon, turning red. "But I know that I have never acted unjustly toward a maiden or another man's wife. Don't you realize that it's not the conduct of an honorable man to allow you to go out at night in such company?"

"Erlend did not seduce me," said Kristin, blushing and indignant. "And he has promised me nothing. I set my heart on him though he did nothing to tempt me. I loved him above all men from the first moment I saw him."

Simon sat there, playing with his dagger, tossing it from one hand to the other.

"These are strange words to be hearing from one's betrothed," he said. "This does not bode well for us now, Kristin."

Kristin took a deep breath. "You would be poorly served to take me for your wife, Simon."

"Almighty God knows that this seems to be so," said Simon Andressøn.

"Then I trust that you will support me," said Kristin, meek and timid, "so that Sir Andres and my father will retract this agreement between us?"

"Oh, is that what you think?" said Simon. He was silent for a moment. "God only knows whether you truly understand what you're saying."

"I do," Kristin told him. "I know that the law is such that no one can force a maiden into a marriage against her will; then she can bring her case before the *ting*."

"I think it's before the bishop," said Simon, smiling harshly. "But I've never had any reason to look into what the law says about such matters. And don't think you'll have any need to do so either. You know I won't demand that you keep your promise if you're so strongly opposed to it. But don't you realize . . . it's been two years since our betrothal was agreed upon, and you've never said a word against it until now, when everything is being prepared for the betrothal banquet and the wedding. Have you thought about what it will mean if you step forward and ask for the bond to be broken, Kristin?"

"You wouldn't want me now, anyway," said Kristin.

"Yes, I would," replied Simon curtly. "If you think otherwise, you had better think again."

"Erlend Nikulaussøn and I have promised ourselves on our Christian faith," she said, trembling, "that if we cannot be joined in marriage, then neither of us will ever take a husband or a wife."

Simon was silent for a long time. Then he said wearily, "Then I don't understand what you meant, Kristin, when you said that he had neither seduced you nor promised you anything. He has lured you away from the counsel of all your kinsmen. Have you thought about what kind of husband you'll have if you marry a man who took another man's wife as his mistress? And now he wants to take as his wife another man's betrothed."

Kristin swallowed her tears, whispering in a thick voice, "You're saying this to hurt me."

"Do you think I want to hurt you?" asked Simon softly.

"This is not how things would have been if you . . . ," Kristin said hesitantly. "You were never asked, either, Simon. It was your father and mine who decided on this marriage. It would have been different if you had chosen me yourself."

Simon drove his dagger into the bench so that it stood upright. After a moment he pulled it out and tried to slip it back into its scabbard. But it refused to go in because the tip was bent. Then he went back to fumbling with it, tossing it from one hand to the other.

"You know very well . . . ," he said, his voice low and shaking. "You know that you would be lying if you tried to pretend that I didn't . . . You know quite well what I wanted to talk to you about, many times, but you received me in such a way that I wouldn't have been a man if I had mentioned it afterward, not if they tried to draw it out of me with burning tongs.

"At first I thought it was the dead boy. I thought I should give you some time . . . you didn't know me. . . . I thought it would be harmful to you, such a short time after. Now I see that you didn't need long to forget . . . and now . . . now . . . now . . ."

"No," said Kristin quietly. "I understand, Simon. I can't expect you to be my friend any longer."

"Friend!" Simon gave an odd little laugh. "Are you in need of my friendship now?"

Kristin blushed.

"You're a man now," she said softly. "And old enough. You can decide on your own marriage."

Simon gave her a sharp look. Then he laughed as he had before.

"I see. You want me to say that I'm the one who . . . I should take the blame for this breach of promise?

"If it's true that you are set in your decision—if you dare and are determined to press your case—then I will do it," he said softly. "To my family back home and before all your kinsmen—except one. You will have to tell your father the truth, such as it is. If you wish, I will take your message to him and make it as easy for you as I can. But Lavrans Bjørgulfsøn must know that I would never go against a promise that I have made to him."

Kristin gripped the edge of the bench with both hands; this affected her more strongly than everything else Simon Darre had said. Pale and frightened, she glanced up at him.

Simon stood up.

"We must go in now," he said. "I think we're both freezing, and the sister is waiting for us with the key. I'll give you a week to think things over. I have some business here in town. I'll come back to talk to you before I leave, but I doubt you'll want to see me before then."

SO THAT WAS FINALLY SETTLED, Kristin told herself. But she felt exhausted, drained, and sick with yearning for Erlend's arms.

She lay awake most of the night, and she decided to do what she had never before dared—she would send a message to Erlend. It wasn't easy to find someone who could carry out this errand for her. The lay sisters never went out alone, and she couldn't think of anyone she knew who would do it. The men who did the farm work were older and seldom came near the nuns' residence except to speak with the abbess. So Olav was the only one. He was a half-grown boy who worked in the gardens. He had been Fru Groa's foster son ever since he was found one morning as a newborn infant on the steps of the church. People said his mother was one of the lay sisters. She was supposed to become a nun, but after she had sat in the dark cell for six months—for gross disobedience, it was said, and that was after the child was found—she was given lay-sister garb, and since then she had worked in the farmyard. During the past months Kristin had often thought about Sister Ingrid's fate, but she had never had the chance to talk to her. It was risky to count on Olav; he was only a child, and Fru Groa and all the nuns talked to him and teased him whenever they saw him. But Kristin thought she had very little left to lose. And a couple of days later, when Olav was about to go into town one morning, Kristin asked him to take her message out to Akersnes, telling Erlend to find some excuse so they could meet alone.

That same afternoon Ulv, Erlend's own servant, appeared at the speaking gate. He said he was Aasmund Bjørgulfsøn's man and had been sent by his master to ask whether Aasmund's niece might come into town for a while, because he didn't have time to come up to Nonneseter himself. Kristin thought this would never work; but when Sister Potentia asked her whether she knew the messenger, she said yes. So she went with Ulv over to Brynhild Fluga's house.

Erlend was waiting for her in the loft. He was nervous and tense, and Kristin realized at once that he was again afraid of the one thing that he seemed to fear most.

She always felt a pang in her heart that he should be so terrified that she might be carrying a child, when they couldn't seem to stay away from each other. So anxious was she feeling that evening that she said as much to him, quite angrily. Erlend's face turned dark red; he lay his head on her shoulder.

"You're right," he said. "I should try to leave you alone, Kristin, and not keep testing your luck in this way. If you want me to . . ."

She threw her arms around him and laughed, but he clasped her tightly around the waist and pressed her down onto a bench; then he sat down on the other side of the table. When she reached her hand across to him, he impetuously kissed her palm.

"I've been trying harder than you have," he said fiercely. "If you only knew how important I think it is for both of us that we be married with full honor."

"Then you should not have taken me," said Kristin.

Erlend hid his face in his hands.

"No, I wish to God that I hadn't done you this wrong," he said.

"Neither one of us wishes that," said Kristin with a giddy laugh. "And as long as I can be reconciled and make peace in the end with my family and with God, then I won't grieve if I have to be wed wearing the wimple of a married woman. As long as I can be with you, I often think that I could even do without peace."

"You're going to bring honor back to my manor," said Erlend. "I'm not going to pull you down into my disgrace."

Kristin shook her head. Then she said, "You'll be glad to hear that I have spoken to Simon Andressøn—and he's not going to bind me to the agreements that were made for us before I met you."

Erlend was jubilant, and Kristin had to tell him everything, although she kept to herself the derogatory words that Simon had spoken about Erlend. But she did mention that he refused to let Lavrans think he was the one to blame.

"That's reasonable," said Erlend curtly. "They like each other, your father and Simon, don't they? Lavrans will like me less."

Kristin took these words to mean that Erlend understood she would still have a difficult path ahead of her before they had settled everything, and she was grateful for that. But he didn't return to this topic. He was overjoyed and said he had been afraid she wouldn't have the courage to speak to Simon.

"I can see that you're fond of him, in a way," he said.

"Does it matter to you," asked Kristin, "after all that you and I have been through, that I realize Simon is both a just and capable man?"

"If you had never met me," said Erlend, "you could have enjoyed good days with him, Kristin. Why do you laugh?"

"Oh, I'm thinking about something that Fru Aashild once said," replied Kristin. "I was only a child back then. But it was something about good days being granted to sensible people, but the grandest of days are enjoyed by those who dare to act unwisely."

"God bless Aunt Aashild for teaching you that," said Erlend, taking her onto his lap. "It's strange, Kristin, but I haven't noticed that you were ever afraid."

"Haven't you ever noticed?" she asked, pressing herself to him.

He set her on the edge of the bed and took off her shoes, but then he pulled her back over to the table.

"Oh no, Kristin—now things look bright for both of us. I wouldn't have acted toward you as I have," he said, stroking her hair over and over, "if it hadn't been for the fact that every time I saw you, I thought it was so unlikely that they would ever give me such a fine and beautiful wife. Sit down here and drink with me."

At that moment there was a pounding on the door, as if someone were striking it with the hilt of a sword.

"Open the door, Erlend Nikulaussøn, if you're in there!"

"It's Simon Darre," said Kristin softly.

"Open up, man, in the name of the Devil—if you *are* a man!" shouted Simon, striking the door again.

Erlend went over to the bed and took his sword down from the peg. He looked around in bewilderment. "There's no place here for you to hide—except in the bed . . ."

"It wouldn't make things any better if I did that," said Kristin. She had stood up and spoke quite calmly, but Erlend saw that she was trembling. "You'll have to open the door," she said in the same voice. Simon was hammering on the door again.

Erlend went over and drew back the bolt. Simon stepped inside, holding a drawn sword in his hand, but he stuck it back into its scabbard at once.

For a moment the three of them stood there without saying a word. Kristin was shaking, and yet in those first few moments she felt an oddly sweet excitement—deep inside her something rose up, sensing this fight between two men—and she exhaled slowly: here was the culmination to those endless months of silent waiting and longing and fear. She looked from one man to the other, their faces pale, their eyes shining; then her excitement collapsed into an unfathomable, freezing despair. There was more cold contempt than indignation or jealousy in Simon Darre's eyes, and she saw that Erlend, behind his obstinate expression, was burning with shame. It dawned on her how other men would judge him—he who had allowed her to come to him in such a place—and she realized that it was as if he had been struck in the face; she knew that he was burning to pull out his sword and fall upon Simon.

"Why have you come here, Simon?" she shouted loudly, sounding frightened.

Both men turned toward her.

"To take you home," said Simon. "You shouldn't be here."

"You no longer have any right to command Kristin Lavransdatter," said Erlend furiously. "She is mine now."

"No doubt she is," said Simon coarsely. "And what a lovely bridal house you've brought her to." He stood there for a moment, breathing hard. Then he regained control over his voice and continued calmly, "But as things stand right now, I'm still her betrothed—until her father can come to get her. And until then I intend to defend with both the point and the edge of my sword as much of her honor as can be protected—in the judgment of other people."

"You don't need to do that; I can do it myself." Erlend again turned as red as blood under Simon's gaze. "Do you think I would allow myself to be threatened by a whelp like you?" he bellowed, putting his hand on the hilt of his sword.

Simon put his hands behind his back.

"I'm not so timid that I'm afraid you'll think I'm afraid of you," he said in the same tone as before. "I shall fight you, Erlend Nikulaussøn, you can bet the Devil on that, if you do not ask Kristin's father for her hand within a reasonable time."

"I won't do it at your bidding, Simon Andressøn," said Erlend angrily; crimson washed over his face again.

"No, do it to right the wrong you have done to so young a wife," replied Simon, unperturbed. "That will be better for Kristin."

Kristin screamed shrilly, tormented by Erlend's pain. She stamped on the floor.

"Go now, Simon, go! What right do you have to meddle in our affairs?"

"I have already told you," replied Simon. "You'll have to put up with me until your father has released us from each other."

Kristin broke down completely.

"Go, go, I'll come right away. Jesus, why are you tormenting me like this, Simon? You can't think it's worth it for you to worry about my affairs."

"It's not for your sake I'm doing this," replied Simon. "Erlend, won't you tell her that she has to come with me?"

Erlend's face quivered. He touched her shoulder.

"You have to go now, Kristin. Simon Darre and I will talk about this some other time."

Kristin rose obediently. She fastened her cloak around her. Her shoes stood next to the bed; she remembered them, but didn't have the courage to put them on with Simon watching.

Outside the fog had descended again. Kristin rushed along with her head bowed and her hands clutching at her cloak. Her throat was bursting with suppressed sobs; wildly she wished that there was some place she could go to be alone, to weep and weep. The worst, the very worst she still had ahead of her. She had experienced something new that night, and now she was writhing from it—how it felt to see the man she had given herself to humiliated.

Simon was at her elbow as she dashed through the narrow alleys and across the streets and the open squares where the buildings had vanished; they could see nothing but the fog. Once, when she stumbled over something, he gripped her arm and stopped her from falling.

"Don't run so fast," he said. "People are staring at us. How you're trembling," he said in a gentler tone. Kristin was silent and kept walking.

She slipped on the muck of the road, she was soaking wet, and her feet were ice cold. The hose she wore were made of leather, but quite thin; she could feel them starting to split open, and the mud seeped in to her naked feet.

They reached the bridge across the convent creek and walked more slowly up the slope on the other side.

"Kristin," said Simon suddenly, "your father must never hear of this."

"How did you know that I was . . . there?" Kristin asked.

"I came to talk to you," replied Simon tersely. "Then I heard about the servant sent by your uncle. I knew that Aasmund was at Hadeland. The two of you aren't very good at inventing ruses. Did you hear what I just said?"

"Yes," replied Kristin. "I was the one who sent word to Erlend that we should meet at the Fluga house. I knew the woman."

"Then shame on you! But you couldn't have known what kind of woman she is—and he . . . Now listen," said Simon sternly. "If it *is* possible to conceal it, then you should conceal from Lavrans what you have thrown away. And if you cannot, then you must try to spare him the worst of the shame."

"You certainly show great concern for my father," said Kristin, trembling. She tried to speak defiantly, but her voice was about to break with tears.

Simon walked on a short distance. Then he stopped—she caught a glimpse of his face as they stood out there alone in the fog. She had never seen him look that way before.

"I've noticed it every time I've been out to visit your home," he said. "You, his women, have so little understanding of the kind of

man Lavrans is. Trond Gjesling says that he doesn't keep you all
in line. But why should Lavrans bother with such things when he
was born to rule over *men*? He had the makings of a *chieftain*, he
was someone men would have followed, gladly; but these are not
the times for such men. My father knew him at Baagahus. And so
it has ended with him living up there in the valley, almost like a
peasant. He was married off much too young; and your mother,
with that temperament of hers, was not the one to make it any
easier for him to lead such a life. It's true that he has many friends,
but do you think that any one of them can measure up to him?
His sons he was not allowed to keep; it was you daughters who
were to continue the lineage after him. Will he now have to endure
the day when he sees that one is without health and another is
without honor?"

Kristin clasped her hands to her heart. She felt that she had to
hold on to it to make herself as hard as she needed to be.

"Why are you telling me this?" she whispered after a moment.
"You neither want to possess me nor marry me anymore."

"That . . . I do not," said Simon uncertainly. "God help me,
Kristin. I remember you on that night in the loft at Finsbrekken.
But may the Devil take me alive if I ever trust a maiden by her
eyes again!

"Promise me this, that you will not see Erlend until your father
arrives," he said as they stood at the gate.

"I won't promise that," said Kristin.

"Then *he* will make me this promise," said Simon.

"I won't meet him," replied Kristin quickly.

"That poor little dog I once sent you," said Simon before they
parted. "You must let your sisters have him—they're so fond of
him—if you don't mind seeing him in the house, that is.

"I'm heading north tomorrow morning," he said, taking her
hand in farewell as the sister keeping the gate looked on.

Simon Darre walked down toward the town. He struck at the air
with his clenched fist as he walked, muttering in a low voice and
cursing at the mist. He swore to himself that he wasn't sorry about
her. Kristin was like something he had believed to be pure gold,
but when he saw it up close, it was merely brass and tin. White as

a snowflake, she had knelt and put her hand into the flame; that was a year ago. This year she was drinking wine with an excommunicated rogue in Fluga's loft. The Devil take it, no! It was because of Lavrans Bjørgulfsøn, who was sitting up there at Jørundgaard and believed . . . Never would it have occurred to Lavrans that they might betray him in this way. Now he would have to bring Lavrans the message himself and be an accomplice in lying to this man. That was why his heart was burning with grief and rage.

Kristin had not intended to keep her promise to Simon Darre, but she managed to exchange only a few words with Erlend, one evening up on the road.

She stood there holding his hand, strangely submissive, while he talked about what had happened up in Brynhild's loft the last time they had met. He would speak to Simon Andressøn some other time. "If we had fought up there, news of it would have spread all over town," said Erlend angrily. "He knew that quite well, that Simon."

Kristin could see how the incident had made him suffer. She had also been thinking about it constantly ever since. There was no escaping the fact that in this situation, Erlend was left with even less honor than she was. And she felt that now they were truly one flesh; she would have to answer for everything he did, even when she disliked his conduct, and she would feel it on her own hand when Erlend so much as scratched his skin.

Three weeks later Lavrans Bjørgulfsøn came to Oslo to get his daughter.

Kristin was both afraid and sick at heart when she went to the parlatory to meet her father. The first thing that struck her as she watched him conversing with Sister Potentia was that he didn't look the same as she remembered him. Perhaps he had not actually changed since they parted a year ago, but over the years she had always seen him as the young, vigorous, and handsome man she had been so proud to have as her father when she was small. Each winter and each summer that had passed up there at home had no doubt marked him and made him age, just as they had seen her develop into a grown-up young woman—but she had not noticed it. She hadn't noticed that his hair had paled in some spots and had acquired a rusty reddish sheen at his temples, the way blond hair goes gray. His cheeks had become dry and thin so that the muscles of his face extended like cords to his mouth; his youthful white and pink complexion had grown uniformly weather-beaten. His back was not bowed, and yet his shoulder blades curved in a different manner beneath his cape. His step was light and steady as he came toward her with his hand outstretched, but these were not the same limber, brisk movements of the past. All of these things had probably been present the year before, but Kristin simply hadn't noticed. Perhaps there was a slight touch of something else—a touch of dejection—that made her see these things now. She burst into tears.

Lavrans put his arm around her shoulder and held his hand to her cheek.

"Now, now, try to calm yourself, child," he said gently.

"Are you angry with me, Father?" she asked softly.

"Surely you must realize that I am," he replied, but he kept on caressing her cheek. "But you also know full well that you needn't be afraid of me," he said sadly. "No, you must calm down now, Kristin; aren't you ashamed to be acting this way?" She was crying so hard that she had to sit down on a bench. "We're not going to speak of these matters here where people are coming and going," he said, sitting down next to her and taking her hand. "Aren't you going to ask me about your mother? And your sisters?"

"What does Mother say about all this?" asked his daughter.

"Oh, you can imagine what she thinks—but we're not going to talk about that here," he said again. "Otherwise she's fine." And then he began to tell her all about everyone back home, until Kristin gradually grew calmer.

But she felt as if the tension only grew worse as her father refused to say anything about her breach of promise. He gave her money to distribute among the poor at the convent and gifts for the lay sisters; he himself gave generously to the convent and to the sisters, and no one at Nonneseter had any other thought than that Kristin was now going home to celebrate her betrothal and her marriage. They both ate the last meal at Fru Groa's table in the abbess's room, and the abbess gave Kristin the best report.

But all this finally came to an end. She said her last goodbyes to the sisters and her friends at the convent gate. Lavrans escorted her to her horse and lifted her into the saddle. It was so strange to be riding with her father and the men from Jørundgaard down to the bridge, along the road on which she had crept in the dark; it was odd to be riding so nobly and freely through the streets of Oslo. She thought about the magnificent wedding procession that Erlend had spoken of so often. Her heart grew heavy; it would have been easier if he had taken her with him. There was still a long time remaining for her to be one person in secret and another in public with other people. But then her gaze fell on her father's aging, somber face, and she tried to convince herself that Erlend was right after all.

There were other travelers at the hostel. In the evening they all ate together in a small room with an open hearth where there were only two beds. Lavrans and Kristin were to sleep there, for they were the foremost guests at the inn. The others left when it grew late, saying a friendly good night and then dispersing to find a place to sleep. Kristin thought about the fact that she was the one who had sneaked up to Brynhild Fluga's loft and allowed Erlend to take her in his arms. Sick with sorrow and the fear that she might never be his, she felt that she no longer belonged here, among these people.

Her father was sitting over on the bench, looking at her.

"We're not going to Skog this time?" Kristin asked, to break the silence.

"No," replied Lavrans. "I've had enough of listening to your uncle for a while—about why I don't use force against you," he explained when she looked at him.

"Yes, I would force you to keep your word," he said after a moment, "if only Simon hadn't said that he did not want an unwilling wife."

"*I* have never given Simon my word," said Kristin hastily. "You always said before that you would never force me into a marriage."

"It would not be force if I demanded that you keep to an agreement that has been known to everyone for such a long time," replied Lavrans. "For two winters people have called you betrothed, and you never said a word of protest or showed any unwillingness until the wedding day was set. If you want to hide behind the fact that the matter was postponed last year, so that you have never given Simon your promise, I would not call that honorable conduct."

Kristin stood there, gazing into the fire.

"I don't know which looks worse," her father continued. "People will either say that you have cast Simon out or that you have been abandoned. Sir Andres sent me a message . . ." Lavrans turned red as he said this. "He was angry with the boy and begged me to demand whatever penalties I might find reasonable. I had to tell him the truth—I don't know whether the alternative would have been any better—that if there were penalties to be paid, we were the ones to do so. We both share the shame."

"I can't see that the shame is so great," murmured Kristin. "Since Simon and I both agree."

"Agree!" Lavrans seized upon the word. "He didn't hide the fact that he was unhappy about it, but he said that after the two of you had talked he didn't think anything but misery would result if he demanded that you keep the agreement. But now you must tell me why you have made this decision."

"Didn't Simon say anything about it?" asked Kristin.

"He seemed to think," said her father, "that you had given your affections to another man. Now you must tell me how things stand, Kristin."

Kristin hesitated for a moment.

"God knows," she said quietly, "I realize that Simon would be good enough for me—more than that. But it's true that I have come to know another man, and then I realized that I would never have another joyous moment in my life if I had to live with Simon—not if he possessed all the gold in England. I would rather have the other man even if he owned no more than a single cow."

"You can't expect me to give you to a servant," said her father.

"He is my equal and more," replied Kristin. "He has enough of both possessions and land, but I simply meant that I would rather sleep with him on bare straw than with any other man in a silk bed."

Her father was silent for a moment.

"It's one thing, Kristin, that I would not force you to take a man you don't want—even though only God and Saint Olav know what you might have against the man I had promised you to. But it's another matter whether the man you have now set your heart on is the sort that I would allow you to marry. You're young and have little experience . . . and setting his sights on a maiden who is betrothed is not something a decent man would normally do."

"That's not something a person can help," said Kristin vehemently.

"Oh yes, he can. But this much you have to realize—that I will not offend the Dyfrin people by betrothing you again as soon as you turn your back on Simon—and least of all to a man who might seem more distinguished or who is richer. You must tell me who this man is," he said after a moment.

Kristin clasped her hands tight, breathing hard. Then she said hesitantly, "I can't do that, Father. Things are such that if I cannot have this man, then you can take me back to the convent and leave me there for good—then I don't think I can live any longer. But it wouldn't be right for me to tell you his name before I know whether he has as good intentions toward me as I do toward him. You . . . you mustn't force me to tell you who he is until . . . until it becomes clear whether he intends to ask you for my hand through his kinsmen."

Lavrans was silent for a long time. He could not be displeased that his daughter acted in this manner. At last he said, "Then let it be so. It's reasonable that you would prefer not to give his name, since you don't know his intentions."

After a moment he said, "You must go to bed now, Kristin." He came over to her and kissed her.

"You have caused much sorrow and anger with this notion of yours, my daughter, but you know that your welfare is what I have most at heart. God help me, I would feel the same no matter what you did. He and His gentle Mother will help us to turn this to the best. Go now and sleep well."

After he had gone to bed, Lavrans thought he heard the faint sound of sobbing from the other bed where his daughter lay, but he pretended to be asleep. He didn't have the heart to tell her that he now feared the old gossip about her and Arne and Bentein would be dug up again. But it weighed heavily on his mind that there was little he could do to prevent the child's good reputation from being sullied behind his back. And the worst thing was that he thought she might have brought this upon herself by her own thoughtlessness.

PART III

LAVRANS BJØRGULFSØN

CHAPTER 1

KRISTIN CAME HOME during the loveliest time of the spring. The Laag River raced in torrents around the farm and the fields; through the young leaves of the alder thickets the stream glittered and sparkled white with silver flashes. The glints of light seemed to have voices, singing along with the rush of the current; when dusk fell, the water seemed to flow with a more muted roar. The thunder of the river filled the air over Jørundgaard day and night, so that Kristin thought she could feel the very timbers of the walls quivering with the sound, like the sound box of a zither.

Thin tendrils of water shone on the mountain slopes, which were shrouded in a blue mist day after day. The heat steamed and trembled over the land; the spears of grain hid the soil in the fields almost completely, and the grass in the meadows grew deep and shimmered like silk when the wind blew across it. There was a sweet scent over the groves and hills, and as soon as the sun went down, a strong, fresh, sharp fragrance of sap and young plants streamed forth; the earth seemed to heave a great sigh, languorous and refreshed. Trembling, Kristin remembered how Erlend had released her from his embrace. Every night she lay down, sick with longing, and each morning she awoke, sweating and exhausted from her own dreams.

It seemed incomprehensible to her that everyone at home could avoid saying a word about the one thing that was in her thoughts. But week after week went by, and they were silent about her breach of promise to Simon and did not question what she had on her mind. Her father spent a great deal of time in the woods now that the spring plowing was done. He visited his tar-burners, and he took along his hawk and dogs and was gone for days. When he came home, he would speak to his daughter in just as friendly a manner as he always had; but he seemed to have so little to say to her, and he never asked her to come along when he went out riding.

Kristin had dreaded coming home to her mother's reproaches, but Ragnfrid didn't say a word, and to Kristin that felt even worse. For his ale feast on Saint Jon's Day each year, Lavrans Bjørgulfsøn distributed to the poor people of the village all the meat and food that was saved in the house during the last week of fasting. Those who lived closest to Jørundgaard usually came in person to receive the alms. Great hospitality was shown, and Lavrans and his guests and the entire household would gather around these poor folk, for some of them were old people who knew many sagas and ballads. Then they would sit in the hearth room and pass the time drinking ale and engaging in friendly conversation, and in the evening they would dance in the courtyard.

This year Saint Jon's Day was cold and overcast, but no one complained about it because the farmers of the valley were beginning to fear a drought. No rain had fallen since the Vigil of Saint Halvard, and there was so little snow on the mountains that in the past thirteen years people couldn't remember seeing the river so low at midsummer.

Lavrans and his guests were in a good mood when they went down to greet the poor folk in the hearth room. The people were sitting around the table eating milk porridge and drinking stout. Kristin went back and forth to the table, serving the old and the sick.

Lavrans greeted his guests and asked them if they were satisfied with the food. Then he went over to welcome a poor old peasant man who had been moved to Jørundgaard that very day. The man's name was Haakon, and he had been a soldier under old King Haakon and had taken part in the king's last expedition to Scotland. Now he was impoverished and nearly blind. People had offered to build a cottage for him, but he preferred to be taken from farm to farm, since he was received everywhere as an honored guest. He was unusually knowledgeable and had seen so much of the world.

Lavrans stood with his hand on his brother's shoulder; Aasmund Bjørgulfsøn had come to Jørundgaard as a guest. He too asked Haakon whether he was satisfied with the food.

"The ale is good, Lavrans Bjørgulfsøn," said Haakon. "But a slut must have made the porridge for us today. Overly bedded cooks make overly boiled porridge, as the saying goes, and this porridge is scorched."

"It's a shame for me to give you burned porridge," said Lavrans. "But I hope that the old saying isn't always true, because it was my daughter herself who made the porridge." He laughed and asked Kristin and Tordis to hurry and bring in the meat dishes.

Kristin dashed outside and over to the cookhouse. Her heart was pounding—she had caught a glimpse of her uncle's face when Haakon was talking about the cook and the porridge.

Late that evening she saw her father and uncle talking for a long time as they walked back and forth in the courtyard. She was dizzy with fear, and it was no better the next day when she noticed that her father was taciturn and morose. But he didn't say a word to her.

He said nothing after his brother left either. But Kristin noticed that he wasn't talking to Haakon as much as usual, and when their time was up for housing the old man, Lavrans didn't offer to keep him longer but let him move on to the next farm.

There were plenty of reasons for Lavrans Bjørgulfsøn to be unhappy and gloomy that summer, because there were signs it would be a bad harvest in the village. The landowners called a *ting* to discuss how they were going to face the coming winter. By late summer it was already clear to most people that they would have to slaughter their livestock or drive a large part of their cattle to market in the south in order to buy grain for people to eat in the winter. The year before had not been a good year for grain, so supplies of old grain were smaller than normal.

One morning in early autumn Ragnfrid went out with all three of her daughters to see to some linen she had spread out to bleach. Kristin praised her mother's weaving skill. Then Ragnfrid began stroking Ramborg's hair.

"This is for your wedding chest, little one."

"Mother," said Ulvhild, "will I have a chest too, if I go to a cloister?"

"You know that you'll have no smaller dowry than your

sisters," said Ragnfrid. "But you won't need the same kinds of things. And you know that you can stay with your father and me for as long as we live . . . if that's what you want."

"And by the time you go to the convent," said Kristin, her voice quavering, "it's possible, Ulvhild, that I will have been a nun for many years."

She glanced at her mother, but Ragnfrid was silent.

"If I could have married," said Ulvhild, "I would never have turned away from Simon. He was kind, and he was so sad when he said goodbye to all of us."

"You know your father has said we shouldn't talk about this," said Ragnfrid.

But Kristin said stubbornly, "Yes, I know he was sadder to part with all of you than with me."

Her mother said angrily, "He wouldn't have had much pride if he had shown you his sorrow. You didn't deal fairly with Simon Andressøn, my daughter. And yet he asked us not to threaten you or curse you."

"No, he probably thought he had cursed me so much that no one else needed to tell me how wretched I was," said Kristin in the same manner as before. "But I never noticed that Simon was particularly fond of me until he realized that I held another man dearer than I held him."

"Go on home," said Ragnfrid to the two younger ones. She sat down on a log lying on the ground and pulled Kristin down by her side. "You know very well," she began, "that it has always been thought more proper and honorable for a man not to speak too much of love to his betrothed—or to sit alone with her or show too much feeling."

"I'd be amazed," said Kristin, "if young people in love didn't forget themselves once in a while, instead of always keeping in mind what their elders regard as proper."

"Take care, Kristin," said her mother, "that you do keep it in mind." She was silent for a moment. "I think it's probably true that your father is afraid you have thrown your love away on a man to whom he is unwilling to give you."

"What did my uncle say?" asked Kristin after a moment.

"Nothing except that Erlend of Husaby has better lineage than reputation," her mother said. "Yes, he did ask Aasmund to put in a good word for him with Lavrans. Your father wasn't pleased when he heard about it."

But Kristin sat there beaming. Erlend had spoken to her uncle. And here she had been so miserable because he hadn't sent any word.

Then her mother spoke again. "Now, Aasmund did mention something about a rumor going around Oslo that this Erlend had been hanging around the streets near the convent and that you had gone out and talked to him by the fence."

"Is that so?" said Kristin.

"Aasmund advised us to accept this offer, you see," said Ragnfrid. "But then Lavrans grew angrier than I've ever seen him before. He said that a suitor who took such a path to his daughter would find him with his sword in hand. The manner in which we dealt with the Dyfrin people was dishonorable enough, but if Erlend had lured you into taking to the roads with him in the dark—and while you were living in a convent, at that—then Lavrans would take it as a sure sign that you would be better served to lose such a husband."

Kristin clenched her fists in her lap. The color came and went in her face. Her mother put her arm around her waist, but Kristin wrenched herself loose and screamed, beside herself with outrage, "Leave me be, Mother! Or maybe you'd like to feel whether I've grown thicker around the middle."

The next moment she was on her feet, holding her hand to her cheek. In confusion she stared down at her mother's furious face. No one had struck her since she was a child.

"Sit down," said Ragnfrid. "Sit down," she repeated so that her daughter obeyed. The mother sat in silence for a moment. When she spoke, her voice was unsteady.

"I've always known, Kristin, that you've never been very fond of me. I thought it might be because you didn't think I loved you enough—not the way your father loves you. I let it pass. I thought that when the time came for you to have children yourself, then you would realize . . .

"Even when I was nursing you, whenever Lavrans came near, you would always let go of my breast and reach out to him and laugh so the milk ran out of your mouth. Lavrans thought it was funny, and God knows I didn't begrudge him that. I didn't begrudge you either that your father would play and laugh whenever he saw you. I felt so sorry for you, poor little thing, because I couldn't help weeping all the time. I worried more about losing you than I rejoiced at having you. But God and the Virgin Mary know that I loved you no less than Lavrans did."

Tears ran down over Ragnfrid's cheeks, but her face was quite calm and her voice was too.

"God knows that I never resented him or you because of the affection you shared. I thought that I had not given him much happiness during the years we had lived together, and I was glad that he had you. And I also thought that if only my father Ivar had treated me that way . . ."

"There are many things, Kristin, that a mother should teach her daughter to watch out for. I didn't think it was necessary with you, since you've been your father's companion all these years; you ought to know what is proper and right. What you just mentioned—do you think I would believe that you would cause Lavrans such sorrow?

"I just want to say that I wish you would find a husband you could love. But then you must behave sensibly. Don't let Lavrans get the idea that you have chosen a troublemaker or someone who doesn't respect the peace and honor of women. For he would never give you to such a man—not even if it were a matter of protecting you from public shame. Then Lavrans would rather let steel be the judge between him and the man who had ruined your life."

And with that her mother rose and left her.

CHAPTER 2

ON SAINT BARTHOLOMEW'S DAY, the twenty-fourth of August, the grandson of blessed King Haakon was acclaimed at the Hauga *ting*. Among the men who were sent from northern Gudbrandsdal was Lavrans Bjørgulfsøn. He had been one of the king's men since his youth, but in all those years he had seldom spent any time with the king's retainers, and he had never tried to use for his own benefit the good name he had won in the campaign against Duke Eirik. He was not very keen on going to the *ting* of acclamation either, but he couldn't avoid it. The tribunal officials from Norddal had also been given the task of attempting to buy grain in the south and send it by ship to Raumsdal.

The people in the villages were despondent and worried about the approaching winter. The peasants also thought it a bad sign that yet another child was to be king of Norway. Old people remembered the time when King Magnus died and his sons were children.

Sira Eirik said, "*Vae terrae, ubi puer rex est.* In plain Norwegian it means: there's no peace at night for the rats on the farm when the cat is young."

Ragnfrid Ivarsdatter managed the farm while her husband was away, and both she and Kristin were glad to have their minds and hands full of cares and work. Everyone in the village was struggling to gather moss in the mountains and to cut bark because there was so little hay and almost no straw, and even the leaves that were collected after midsummer were yellow and withered. On Holy Cross Day, when Sira Eirik carried the crucifix across the fields, there were many in the procession who wept and loudly entreated God to have mercy on men and beasts.

* * *

One week after Holy Cross Day, Lavrans Bjørgulfsøn came home from the *ting*.

It was long past everyone's bedtime, but Ragnfrid was still sitting in her weaving room. She had so much to do these days that she often worked into the night at her weaving and sewing. And Ragnfrid always felt so happy in that building. It was thought to be the oldest one on the farm; they called it the women's house, and people said it had stood there since heathen times. Kristin and the maid named Astrid were with Ragnfrid, spinning wool next to the open hearth.

They had been sitting there, sleepy and silent, for a while when they heard the hoofbeats of a single horse; a man came riding at great speed into the wet courtyard. Astrid went to the entryway to look outside. She returned at once, followed by Lavrans Bjørgulfsøn.

Both his wife and daughter saw at once that he was quite drunk. He staggered and grabbed hold of the smoke vent pole as Ragnfrid removed his soaking wet cape and hat and unfastened his scabbard belt.

"What have you done with Halvdan and Kolbein?" she asked apprehensively. "Did you leave them behind along the road?"

"No, I left them behind at Loptsgaard," he said, laughing a bit. "I had such an urge to come home. I couldn't rest before I did. They went to bed down there, but I took Guldsvein and raced homeward.

"Go and find me some food, Astrid," he said to the maid. "Bring it over here so you won't have to walk so far in the rain. But be quick; I haven't eaten since early this morning."

"Didn't you have any food at Loptsgaard?" asked his wife in surprise.

Lavrans sat down on a bench and rocked back and forth, chuckling.

"There was food enough, but I didn't feel like eating while I was there. I drank with Sigurd for a while, but then I thought I might just as well come home at once instead of waiting till morning."

Astrid brought ale and food; she also brought dry shoes for her master.

Lavrans fumbled as he tried to unfasten his spurs but he kept lurching forward.

"Come over here, Kristin," he said, "and help your father. I know you'll do it with a loving heart—yes, a loving heart—today at least."

Kristin obeyed and knelt down. Then he put his hands on either side of her head and tilted her face up.

"You know very well, my daughter, that I want only what is best for you. I wouldn't cause you sorrow unless I saw that I was saving you from many sorrows later on. You're still so young, Kristin. You only turned seventeen this year, three days after Saint Halvard's Day. You're seventeen . . ."

Kristin had finished her task. Somewhat pale, she got up and sat down on her stool by the hearth again.

The intoxication seemed to wear off to some extent as Lavrans ate. He answered questions from his wife and the servant girl about the *ting*. Yes, it had been magnificent. They had bought grain and flour and malt, some in Oslo and some in Tunsberg. They were imported goods—could have been better, but could have been worse too. Yes, he had met many kinsmen and acquaintances and brought greetings from them all. He simply sat there, the answers dripping from him.

"I talked to Sir Andres Gudmundsøn," he said when Astrid had gone. "Simon has celebrated his betrothal to the young widow at Manvik. The wedding will be at Dyfrin on Saint Andreas's Day. The boy made the decision himself this time. I tried to avoid Sir Andres in Tunsberg, but he sought me out. He wanted to tell me that he was absolutely certain that Simon saw Fru Halfrid for the first time around midsummer this year. He was afraid I'd think that Simon was planning on this wealthy marriage when he broke off with us." Lavrans sat for a moment, laughing mirthlessly. "You see, this honorable man was terribly afraid that we'd think something like that of his son."

Kristin sighed with relief. She thought that this was what her father was so upset about. Maybe he had been hoping all along that it would still take place—the marriage between Simon Andressøn and herself. At first she had been afraid that he had inquired about her behavior down south in Oslo.

She stood up and said goodnight. Then her father told her to stay a while.

"I have some other news," said Lavrans. "I might have kept it from you, Kristin, but it's better that you hear it. Here it is: That man you have set your heart on, you must try to forget."

Kristin had been standing with her arms at her sides and her head bowed. Now she raised her head and looked into her father's face. Her lips moved, but she couldn't manage a single audible word.

Lavrans turned away from his daughter's gaze; he threw out his hand.

"You know I wouldn't be against it if I sincerely believed that it would be to your benefit," he said.

"What news have you heard on this journey, Father?" asked Kristin, her voice steady.

"Erlend Nikulaussøn and his kinsman Sir Munan Baardsøn came to me in Tunsberg," replied Lavrans. "Sir Munan asked me for your hand on Erlend's behalf, and I told him no."

Kristin stood in silence for a moment, breathing heavily.

"Why won't you give me to Erlend Nikulaussøn?" she asked.

"I don't know how much you know about this man you want for your husband," said Lavrans. "If you don't know the reason yourself, it won't be pleasant for you to hear it from my lips."

"Is it because he was excommunicated and outlawed?" asked Kristin in the same tone as before.

"Do you know what it was that caused King Haakon to drive his close kinsman from his court? And do you know that he was banned by the Church in the end because he defied the archbishop's decree? And that he did not leave the country alone?"

"Yes," said Kristin. Her voice grew uncertain. "I know too that he was eighteen years old when he met her—his mistress."

"That's how old I was when I was married," said Lavrans. "When I was young, we reckoned that from a man's eighteenth birthday he could answer for himself and be responsible for his own welfare and that of others."

Kristin stood in silence.

"You called her his mistress, that woman he has lived with for ten years and who has borne him children," said Lavrans after a moment. "I would regret the day I sent my daughter off with a husband who had lived openly with a mistress for years on end before he married. But you know it was more than merely living in sin."

"You weren't so harsh to judge Fru Aashild and Herr Bjørn," said Kristin quietly.

"Yet I cannot say I would willingly join families with them," replied Lavrans.

"Father," said Kristin, "have you and Mother been so without sin all your lives that you dare judge Erlend so harshly?"

"God knows," replied Lavrans sternly, "that I judge no man to be a greater sinner than I am myself. But one cannot expect me to give my daughter to any man who wishes to ask for her, just because we all need God's mercy."

"You know that's not what I meant," said Kristin hotly. "Father, Mother, you were both young once. Don't you remember that it's not easy to guard yourself against the sin that love provokes?"

Lavrans turned blood-red.

"No," he said curtly.

"Then you don't know what you're doing," screamed Kristin in despair, "if you separate Erlend Nikulaussøn and me!"

Lavrans sat down on the bench again.

"You're only seventeen years old, Kristin," he continued. "It might be that the two of you are more fond of each other than I thought. But he's not so young a man that he shouldn't have realized . . . If he were a good man, then he wouldn't have approached such a young, immature child as you with words of love. He seems to have considered it trivial that you were promised to someone else.

"But I will not betroth my daughter to a man who has two children with another man's true wife. Don't you realize that he has children?

"You're too young to understand that such an injustice breeds endless quarrels and strife among kinsmen. The man cannot abandon his own offspring; neither can he claim them. It will be difficult for him to find a way to present his son in society, or to marry off his daughter to anyone other than a servant boy or a smallholder. And his children would not be made of flesh and blood if they didn't despise you and your children. . . .

"Don't you see, Kristin? Sins like this . . . God may forgive such sins more readily than many others, but they damage a lineage so severely that it can never be redeemed. I was thinking about Bjørn and Aashild myself. There stood that Munan, her son. He was dripping with gold and he sits on the King's council. He and his brothers control the inheritance from their mother, and yet he hasn't visited Aashild in her poverty in all these years. Yes, this was the man that your friend chose as his spokesman.

"No, I say, no! You shall never be part of that family as long as my head is above ground."

Kristin covered her face with her hands and burst into tears. "Then I'll pray to God night and day, night and day, to take me away from here if you won't change your mind!"

"It's useless to discuss this any more tonight," said her father, aggrieved. "You may not believe it, but I must watch over you in such a way that I can answer for the consequences. Go to bed now, child."

He held out his hand to her, but she refused to acknowledge it and went sobbing out of the room.

The parents sat for a moment in silence.

Then Lavrans said to his wife, "Would you mind bringing some ale over here? No, bring some wine. I'm tired."

Ragnfrid did as he asked. When she returned with the tall goblet, her husband was sitting with his face in his hands. He looked up, and then stroked his hands over the wimple covering her head and down along her arms.

"Poor thing, now you've gotten wet. Drink a toast to me, Ragnfrid."

She placed the goblet to her lips.

"No, drink *with* me," said Lavrans vehemently, pulling his wife down onto his lap. Reluctantly she yielded to him.

Lavrans said, "You'll stand behind me in this matter, won't you, my wife? It will be best for Kristin if she realizes from the very start that she must put this man out of her mind."

"It will be hard for the child," said Ragnfrid.

"Yes, I know that," replied Lavrans.

They sat in silence for a while, and then Ragnfrid asked, "What does he look like, this Erlend of Husaby?"

"Oh," said Lavrans, hesitating, "he's a handsome fellow—in a way. But he doesn't look as if he were much good for anything but seducing women."

They were silent again for a while, and then Lavrans went on, "He has handled the great inheritance he received from Sir Niku-laus in such a way that it is much reduced. I haven't struggled and striven to protect my children for a son-in-law like that."

Ragnfrid paced the floor nervously.

Lavrans went on, "I was most displeased by the fact that he tried to bribe Kolbein with silver—he was supposed to carry a secret letter from Erlend to Kristin."

"Did you look at the letter?" asked Ragnfrid.

"No, I didn't want to," said Lavrans crossly. "I tossed it back to Sir Munan and told him what I thought of such behavior. He had put his seal on it too; I don't know what to make of such childish pranks. Sir Munan showed me the seal—said it was King Skule's privy seal that Erlend had inherited from his father. He thought I ought to realize that it's a great honor that they would ask for my daughter. But I don't think that Sir Munan would have presented this matter on Erlend's behalf with such great warmth if he hadn't realized that, with this man, the power and honor of the Husaby lineage—won in the days of Sir Nikulaus and Sir Baard—are now in decline. Erlend can no longer expect to make the kind of marriage that was his birthright."

Ragnfrid stopped in front of her husband.

"I don't know whether you're right about this matter or not, my husband. First I ought to mention that, in these times, many a man on the great estates has had to settle for less power and honor than his father before him. You know quite well yourself that it's not as easy for a man to gain wealth, whether from the land or through commerce, as it was before."

"I know, I know," interrupted her husband impatiently. "All the more reason to handle with caution what one *has* inherited."

But his wife continued. "There is also this: It doesn't seem to me that Kristin would be an unequal match for Erlend. In Sweden your lineage is among the best; your grandfather and your father bore the title of knight in this country. My distant ancestors were barons, son after father for many hundreds of years down to Ivar the Old; my father and my grandfather were sheriffs of the county. It's true that neither you nor Trond has acquired a title or land from the Crown. But I think it could be said that things are no different for Erlend Nikulaussøn than for the two of you."

"It's not the same thing," said Lavrans vehemently. "Power and a knight's title lay just within reach for Erlend, and he turned his back on them for the sake of whoring. But I see now that you're against me too. Maybe you think, like Aasmund and Trond, that it's an honor for me that these noblemen want my daughter to be one of their kinswomen."

"I told you," said Ragnfrid rather heatedly, "that I don't think you need to be so offended and afraid that Erlend's kinsmen will think they're condescending in this matter. But don't you realize one thing above all else? That gentle, obedient child had the courage to stand up to us and reject Simon Darre. Haven't you noticed that Kristin has not been herself since she came back from Oslo? Don't you see that she's walking around as if she had just stepped out from the spell of the mountain? Don't you realize that she loves this man so much that if you don't give in, a great misfortune may befall us?"

"What do you mean by that?" asked Lavrans, looking up sharply.

"Many a man greets his son-in-law and does not know it," said Ragnfrid.

Her husband seemed to stiffen; he slowly turned white in the face.

"And you are her mother!" he said hoarsely. "Have you . . . have you seen . . . such certain signs . . . that you dare accuse your own daughter of this?"

"No, no," said Ragnfrid quickly. "I didn't mean what you think. But no one can know what may have happened or is going to happen. Her only thought is that she loves this man. That much I've seen. She may show us someday that she loves him more than her honor—or her life!"

Lavrans leaped up.

"Have you taken leave of your senses? How can you think such things of our good, beautiful child? Nothing much can have happened to her there, with the nuns. I know she's no milkmaid who gives up her virtue behind a fence. You must realize that she can't have seen this man or spoken to him more than a few times. She'll get over him. It's probably just the whim of a young maiden. God knows it hurts me dearly to see her grieving so, but you know that this *has* to pass with time!

"Life, you say, and honor. Here at home on my own farm I can surely protect my own daughter. And I don't believe any maiden of good family and with an honorable and Christian upbringing would part so easily with her honor, or her life. No, this is the kind of thing people write ballads about. I think when a man or a maiden is tempted to do something like that, they make up a ballad about it, which helps them, but they refrain from actually doing it. . . .

"Even you," he said, stopping in front of his wife. "There was another man you would rather have had, back when the two of us were married. What kind of situation do you think you'd have been in if your father had let you make up your own mind?"

Now it was Ragnfrid's turn to grow pale as death.

"Jesus and Maria! Who told you . . ."

"Sigurd of Loptsgaard said something about it, right after we moved here to the valley," said Lavrans. "But give me an answer to my question. Do you think you would have been happier if Ivar had given you to that man?"

His wife stood with her head bowed low.

"That man," she said almost inaudibly, "didn't want *me*." A shudder seemed to pass through her body; she struck at the air with a clenched fist.

Then her husband gently placed his hands on her shoulders.

"Is *that* it?" he said, overcome, and a profound and sorrowful amazement filled his voice. "Is *that* it? For all these years . . . have you been harboring sorrow for *him*, Ragnfrid?"

She was shaking, but she did not answer.

"Ragnfrid?" he said in the same tone of voice. "But after Bjørgulf died . . . and when you . . . when you wanted me to be toward you—in a way that I couldn't . . . Were you thinking about the other man then?" he whispered, frightened and confused and tormented.

"How can you think such things?" she whispered, on the verge of tears.

Lavrans leaned his forehead against his wife's and turned his head gently from side to side.

"I don't know. You're so strange, everything you said tonight . . . I was afraid, Ragnfrid. I don't understand women very well."

Ragnfrid smiled wanly and put her arms around his neck.

"God knows, Lavrans . . . I begged you because I loved you more than is good for a human soul. And I hated the other man so much that I knew it made the Devil happy."

"I have loved you, dear wife, with all my heart," said Lavrans tenderly, kissing her. "Do you know that? I thought we were so happy together—weren't we, Ragnfrid?"

"You are the best husband," she said with a little sob, pressing herself against him.

Ardently he embraced her.

"Tonight I want to sleep with you, Ragnfrid. And if you would be toward me the way you were in the old days, then I wouldn't be . . . such a fool."

His wife stiffened in his arms and pulled away a little.

"It's fasting time," she said quietly, her voice strangely hard.

"So it is." Her husband chuckled. "You and I, Ragnfrid, we have observed all the fast days and have tried to live by God's commandments in all things. And now it almost seems to me . . . that we might have been happier if we had had more to regret."

"Don't talk that way," implored his wife in despair, holding his temples in her gaunt hands. "You know that I don't want you to do anything except what you think is right."

He pulled her to him once more. He gasped aloud as he said, "God help her. God help us all, my Ragnfrid.

"I'm tired," he said, releasing her. "You should go to bed now too, shouldn't you?"

He stood by the door, waiting as she put out the fire in the hearth, blew out the little iron lamp by the loom, and pinched the wick. Together they walked through the rain over to the main house.

Lavrans already had his foot on the stairs up to the loft when he turned back to his wife, who was still standing in the door to the entryway. He pulled her fervently to him one last time and kissed her in the darkness. Then he made the sign of the cross over his wife's face and went upstairs.

Ragnfrid threw off her clothes and crept into bed. She lay still for a while, listening to her husband's footsteps overhead in the loft room; then the bed creaked up there and silence fell. Ragnfrid crossed her thin arms over her withered breasts. Yes, God help her. What kind of woman was she? What kind of mother was she? She would soon be old. And yet she was just the same. She no longer begged the way she had when they were young, when she had threatened and raged against this man who closed himself off, shy and modest, when she grew ardent—who turned cold when she wanted to give him more than his husband's right. That's the way things were, and that's how she had gotten with child, time after time—humiliated, furious with shame because she couldn't be content with his lukewarm, married man's love. Then, when she was pregnant and in need of kindness and tenderness, he had had so much to give. Whenever she was sick or tormented, her husband's tireless, gentle concern for her fell like dew on her hot soul. He willingly took on all her troubles and bore them, but there was something of his own that he refused to share. She had loved her children so much that it felt as though her heart were cut out of her each time she lost one of them. God, God, what kind of woman was she, who in the midst of her suffering was capable of tasting that drop of sweetness when he took on her sorrow and laid it close to his own?

Kristin. She would gladly have walked through fire for her daughter; they wouldn't believe it, neither Lavrans nor the child, but it was true. And yet she felt an anger toward her that was close to hatred right now. It was to forget his own sorrow over the child's sorrow that Lavrans had wished tonight that he could have given in to his wife.

Ragnfrid didn't dare get up, for she didn't know whether Kristin might be lying awake over in the other bed. But she got soundlessly to her knees, and with her forehead leaning against the footboard of the bed, she tried to pray—for her daughter, for her husband, and for herself. As her body gradually grew stiff with the cold, she set out once more on one of her familiar night journeys, trying to break a path to a peaceful home for her heart.

CHAPTER 3

HAUGEN LAY HIGH up on the slope on the west side of the valley. On this moonlit night the whole world was white. Wave after wave of white mountains arched beneath the bluish, washed-out sky with few stars. Even the shadows cast across the snowy surfaces by rounded summits and crests seemed strangely light and airy, for the moon was sailing so high.

Down toward the valley the forest, laden white with snow and frost, stood enclosing the white slopes around the farms with intricate patterns of fences and buildings. But at the very bottom of the valley the shadows thickened into darkness.

Fru Aashild came out of the cowshed, pulled the door shut behind her, and paused for a moment in the snow. The whole world was white, and yet it was still more than three weeks until the beginning of Advent. The cold of Saint Clement's Day would herald the real arrival of winter. Well, it was all part of a bad harvest year.

The old woman sighed heavily, standing outdoors in the desolation. Winter again, and cold and loneliness. Then she picked up the milk pail and the lantern and walked toward the house, gazing around once more.

Four black spots emerged from the forest halfway down the slope. Four men on horseback. There was the flash of a spear point in the moonlight. They were making their way across with difficulty. No one had come here since the snowfall. Were they heading this way?

Four armed men. It was unlikely that anyone with a legitimate reason for visiting her would travel in such company. She thought about the chest containing Bjørn's and her valuables. Should she hide in the outbuilding?

She looked out across the wintry landscape and wilderness

around her. Then she went into the house. The two old dogs that had been lying in front of the fireplace beat their tails against the floorboards. Bjørn had taken the younger dogs along with him to the mountains.

She blew at the coals in the hearth and laid on some wood. She filled the iron pot with snow and hung it over the fire. She strained some milk into a wooden cask and carried it to the storeroom near the entryway.

Aashild took off her filthy, undyed homespun dress that stank of sweat and the cowshed and put on a dark blue one. She exchanged the rough muslin kerchief for a white linen wimple which she draped around her head and throat. She took off her fleecy leather boots and put on silver-buckled shoes.

Then she set about putting the room in order. She smoothed out the pillows and furs on the bed where Bjørn had been sleeping during the day, wiped off the long table, and straightened the cushions on the benches.

Fru Aashild was standing in front of the fireplace, stirring the evening porridge, when the dogs gave warning. She heard the horses in the yard, the men coming into the gallery, and a spear striking the door. Aashild lifted the pot from the fire, straightened her dress, and, with the dogs at her side, stepped forward and opened the door.

Out in the moonlit courtyard three young men were holding four frost-covered horses. The man standing in the gallery shouted joyfully, "Aunt Aashild, is that you opening the door yourself? Then I must say 'Ben trouvé!' "

"Nephew—is that you? Then I must say the same! Come inside while I show your men to the stable."

"Are you alone on the farm?" asked Erlend. He followed along as she showed the men where to go.

"Yes, Herr Bjørn and his man went out with the sleigh. They were going to see about bringing back some supplies we have stored on the mountain," said Fru Aashild. "And I have no servant girl," she added, laughing.

Soon afterward the four young men were seated on the outer bench with their backs against the table, watching the old woman quietly bustling about and putting out food for them. She spread a cloth on the table and set down a single lighted candle; she brought butter, cheese, a bear thigh, and a tall stack of fine, thin pieces of flatbread. She brought ale and mead from the cellar beneath the room, and then she served up the porridge in a beautiful wooden trencher and invited them to sit down and begin.

"It's not much for you young fellows," she said with a laugh. "I'll have to cook another pot of porridge. Tomorrow you'll have better fare—but I close up the cookhouse in the winter except when I'm baking or brewing. There are only a few of us here on the farm, and I'm starting to get old, my kinsman."

Erlend laughed and shook his head. He noticed that his men showed the old woman more courtesy and respect than he had ever seen them show before.

"You're a strange woman, Aunt. Mother was ten years younger than you, but the last time we visited, she looked older than you do tonight."

"Yes, youth fled quickly enough from Magnhild," said Fru Aashild softly. "Where are you coming from now?" she asked after a while.

"I've been spending some time on a farm up north in Lesja," said Erlend. "I've rented lodgings there. I don't know whether you can guess why I've come here to these parts."

"You mean whether I know that you've asked for the hand of Lavrans Bjørgulfsøn's daughter here in the south, at Jørundgaard?" asked Fru Aashild.

"Yes," said Erlend. "I asked for her in proper and honorable fashion, and Lavrans Bjørgulfsøn stubbornly said no. Since Kristin and I refuse to let anything part us, I know of no other way than to take her away by force. I have . . . I've had a scout here in the village, and I know that her mother is supposed to be at Sundbu until some time after Saint Clement's Day and that Lavrans is out at the headland with the other men to bring in the winter provisions for Sil."

Fru Aashild sat in silence for a moment.

"You'd better give up that idea, Erlend," she said. "I don't think the maiden would follow you willingly, and you wouldn't use force, would you?"

"Oh yes she will. We've talked about this many times. She's begged me many times to carry her away."

"Did Kristin . . . !" said Fru Aashild. Then she laughed. "That's no reason for you to count on the maiden coming with you when you show up to take her at her word."

"Oh yes it is," said Erlend. "And now I was thinking, Aunt, that you should send an invitation to Jørundgaard for Kristin to come and visit you—for a week or so while her parents are away. Then we could reach Hamar before anyone notices that she's gone," he explained.

Fru Aashild replied, still laughing a little, "Did you also think about what we should say—Herr Bjørn and I—when Lavrans comes to call us to account for his daughter?"

"Yes," said Erlend. "We were four armed men, and the maiden was willing."

"I won't help you with this," said his aunt sternly. "Lavrans has been a faithful friend to us for many years. He and his wife are honorable people, and I won't participate in betraying them or shaming her. Leave the maiden in peace, Erlend. It's also about time that your kinsmen heard of other exploits from you than that you were slipping in and out of the country with stolen women."

"We need to talk alone, Aunt," said Erlend abruptly.

Fru Aashild took a candle, went into the storeroom, and shut the door behind them. She sat down on a cask of flour; Erlend stood with his hands stuck in his belt looking down at her.

"You can also tell Lavrans Bjørgulfsøn that Sira Jon in Gerdarud married us before we continued on to stay with Duchess Ingebjørg Haakonsdatter in Sweden."

"I see," said Fru Aashild. "Do you know whether the duchess will receive you when you arrive there?"

"I spoke with her in Tunsberg," said Erlend. "She greeted me as her dear kinsman and thanked me for offering her my service, either here or in Sweden. And Munan has promised to give me letters to her."

"Then you know," said Fru Aashild, "that even if you can find a priest to marry you, Kristin will relinquish all right to property and inheritance from her father. And her children will not be legitimate heirs. It's uncertain whether she will be considered your wife."

"Maybe not here in this country. That's also why I want to head for Sweden. Her forefather, Laurentius Lagmand, was never married to the maiden Bengta in any other way; they never received her brother's blessing. And yet she was considered his wife."

"There were no children," said Fru Aashild. "Do you think my sons would keep their hands off their inheritance from you if Kristin were left a widow with children and there was any doubt that they were born legitimate?"

"You do Munan an injustice," replied Erlend. "I know little of your other children. You have no reason to be kind to them, that I know. But Munan has always been my loyal kinsman. He would like to see me married; he spoke with Lavrans on my behalf. Otherwise, by law, I can sue for the inheritance and the good name of whatever children we may have."

"With that you will brand their mother as your mistress," said Fru Aashild. "But I don't think that meek priest, Jon Helgesøn, would dare risk trouble with his bishop in order to marry you against the law."

"I confessed to him this summer," said Erlend, his voice muted. "He promised then to marry us if all other means were exhausted."

"I see," replied Fru Aashild. "Then you have taken a grave sin upon yourself, Erlend. Kristin was happy at home with her father and mother. A good marriage with a handsome and honorable man of good family was arranged for her."

"Kristin told me herself," said Erlend, "that you said she and I might suit each other well. And that Simon Andressøn was no fit husband for her."

"Oh, never mind what I said or didn't say," snapped his aunt. "I've said so much in my time. I don't think you could have had your way with Kristin so easily. You couldn't have met very often. And I wouldn't think she was easy to win over, that maiden."

"We met in Oslo," said Erlend. "Afterward she was staying with her uncle in Gerdarud. She came out to the woods to meet me." He looked down and said quite softly, "I had her alone to myself out there."

Fru Aashild sprang up. Erlend bowed his head even lower.

"And after that . . . was she friends with you?" asked his aunt in disbelief.

"Yes." Erlend's smile was wan and quivering. "We were friends after that. And she didn't resist very strongly; but she is without blame. That was when she wanted me to take her away; she didn't want to go back to her kinsmen."

"But you refused?"

"Yes, I wanted to attempt to win her as my wife with her father's consent."

"Was this long ago?" asked Fru Aashild.

"It was a year ago, on Saint Lavrans's Day," replied Erlend.

"You haven't made much haste to ask for her hand," said his aunt.

"She wasn't free of her previous betrothal," said Erlend.

"And since then you haven't come too close to her?" asked Aashild.

"We made arrangements so that we could meet several times." Once again that quavering smile flitted across his face. "At a place in town."

"In God's name," said Fru Aashild. "I'll help the two of you as much as I can. I see that it will be much too painful for Kristin to stay here with her parents with something like this on her conscience. There's nothing else, is there?" she asked.

"Not that I know of," said Erlend curtly.

After a pause, Fru Aashild asked, "Have you thought about the fact that Kristin has friends and kinsmen all along this valley?"

"We must travel in secrecy as best we can," said Erlend. "That's why it's important for us to get away quickly, so we can put some distance behind us before her father comes home. You have to lend us your sleigh, Aunt."

Aashild shrugged her shoulders. "Then there's her uncle at Skog. What if he hears you're celebrating a wedding with his brother's daughter in Gerdarud?"

"Aasmund has spoken with Lavrans on my behalf," said Erlend. "He can't be an accomplice, that's true, but he'll probably look the other way. We'll go to the priest at night and keep on traveling by night. I imagine that Aasmund will probably tell Lavrans after-

ward that it's improper for a God-fearing man like him to part us
once we've been married by a priest. Rather, he ought to give
us his blessing so that we will be legally married. You must tell
Lavrans the same thing. He can state his own conditions for a
reconciliation with us and demand whatever penalties he deems
reasonable."

"I don't think Lavrans Bjørgulfsøn will be easy to advise in this
matter," said Fru Aashild. "God and Saint Olav know that I do
not like this business, nephew. But I realize that this is your last
recourse if you are to repair the harm you have done to Kristin.
Tomorrow I will ride to Jørundgaard myself if you'll lend me one
of your men, and I can get Ingrid to the north to look after my
livestock."

Fru Aashild arrived at Jørundgaard the following evening just as
the moonlight broke away from the last glow of the day. She saw
how pale and hollow-cheeked Kristin had become when the girl
came out to the courtyard to receive her guest.

Fru Aashild sat next to the hearth and played with the two
younger sisters. Secretly she watched Kristin with searching eyes as
the maiden set the table. She was thin and silent. She had always
been quiet, but it was a different kind of silence that had come
over her now. Fru Aashild could imagine all the tension and stubborn defiance that lay behind it.

"You've probably heard," said Kristin, coming over to her,
"about what happened here this fall?"

"Yes, that my sister's son has asked for your hand?"

"Do you remember," said Kristin, "that you once said he and
I might suit each other well? Except that he was much too rich
and of too good a family for me?"

"I hear that Lavrans is of another mind," said Aashild dryly.
There was a sparkle in Kristin's eye, and she smiled a little. She'll
do, thought Fru Aashild. As little as she liked it, she would oblige
Erlend and give him the help he had asked for.

Kristin made up her parents' bed for the guest, and Fru Aashild
asked the young woman to sleep with her. After they lay down
and the main room was quiet, Fru Aashild explained her errand.

Her heart grew strangely heavy when she saw that this child did not seem to give a thought to the sorrow she would cause her parents. Yet I lived in sorrow and torment with Baard for more than twenty years, thought Aashild. But that's probably the way it is for all of us. Kristin didn't even seem to have noticed how Ulvhild's health had declined that autumn. Aashild thought it unlikely that Kristin would see her little sister alive again. But she said nothing of this. The longer Kristin could hold on to this wild joy and keep up her courage, the better it would be for her.

Kristin got up, and in the darkness she collected her jewelry in a small box, which she brought over to the bed.

Then Fru Aashild said to her, "It still seems to me, Kristin, a better idea for Erlend to ride over here when your father comes home, admit openly that he has done you a great wrong, and place his case in Lavrans's hands."

"Then I think Father would kill Erlend," said Kristin.

"Lavrans wouldn't do that if Erlend refused to draw his sword against his father-in-law," replied Aashild.

"I don't want Erlend to be humiliated like that," said Kristin. "And I don't want Father to know that Erlend touched me before he asked for my hand with honor and respect."

"Do you think Lavrans will be less angry when he hears that you've fled the farm with him?" asked Aashild. "And do you think it will be any easier for him to bear? According to the law you'll be nothing more than Erlend's mistress as long as you live with him without your father's consent."

"This is a different matter," said Kristin, "since he tried to win me as his wife but could not. I will not be considered his mistress."

Fru Aashild was silent. She thought about having to meet Lavrans Bjørgulfsøn when he returned home and found out that his daughter had stolen away.

Then Kristin said, "I see that you think me a bad daughter, Fru Aashild. But ever since Father came back from the *ting*, every day here at home has been torture for him as well as for me. It's best for everyone if this matter is finally settled."

They set off from Jørundgaard early the next day and reached Haugen at a little past the hour of midafternoon prayers. Erlend

met them in the courtyard, and Kristin threw herself into his arms
without regard for Erlend's manservant, who had accompanied Fru
Aashild and herself. Inside the house she greeted Bjørn Gunnarsøn
and then Erlend's two other men as if she knew them well. Fru
Aashild could see no sign that she was either shy or afraid. And
later, when they were sitting at the table and Erlend presented his
plan, Kristin joined in and suggested what road they should take.
She said they should ride from Haugen the following night so late
that they would arrive at the gorge as the moon went down, then
travel in darkness through Sil until they had passed Loptsgaard.
From there they should go along the Otta River to the bridge, and
then on the west side of the Otta and Laag by back roads as far
as the horses could carry them. They would rest during the day at
one of the spring huts there on the slopes, she said, "for as far as
the law of the Holledis *ting* reaches, we might run into people who
know me."

"Have you thought about fodder for the horses?" asked Fru
Aashild. "You can't take feed from people's spring huts in a year
like this—if there's any there at all—and you know no one has
any to sell here in the valley this year."

"I've thought of that," said Kristin. "You must lend us fodder
and provisions for three days. That's also the reason why we
shouldn't travel in a large group. Erlend will have to send Jon back
to Husaby. In Trøndelag it's been a better year, and it should be
possible to get some supplies over the mountain before Christmas.
There are some poor people south of the village that I'd like you
to give some alms to, from Erlend and me, Fru Aashild."

Bjørn uttered a strangely mirthless guffaw. Fru Aashild shook
her head.

But the manservant Ulv lifted his sharp, swarthy face and looked
at Kristin with a particularly sly smile. "There's never anything left
over at Husaby, Kristin Lavransdatter, neither in a good year nor
a bad one. But maybe things will be different when you manage
the household. From your speech it sounds like you're the wife
Erlend needs."

Kristin nodded calmly at the man and continued hastily. They
would have to keep away from the main road as much as possible.
And it didn't seem advisable for them to travel via Hamar. Erlend

objected that that was where Munan was waiting—there was the matter of the letter for the duchess.

"Ulv will have to leave us at Fagaberg and ride to Sir Munan while we head west toward Lake Mjøsa and ride across country and by back roads via Hadeland down to Hakedal. From there a desolate road goes south to Margretadal; I've heard my uncle speak of it. It's not advisable for us to ride through Raumarike while the great wedding is taking place at Dyfrin," she said with a laugh.

Erlend came over and put his arm around her shoulders, and she leaned back against him, not caring about all the people who were sitting there watching.

Fru Aashild said acidly, "Anyone might think you had eloped before."

And Herr Bjørn guffawed again.

A little later Fru Aashild stood up to go to the cookhouse and prepare some food. She had started the fire out there because Erlend's men would be sleeping in the cookhouse that night. She asked Kristin to come along, "because I want to be able to swear to Lavrans Bjørgulfsøn that the two of you were never alone for a single minute in my house," she said crossly.

Kristin laughed and went out with Aashild. Erlend at once came sauntering after them, pulled up a three-legged stool to the hearth and sat down. He kept getting in the women's way. He grabbed Kristin every time she came near him as she bustled and flew around. Finally he pulled her down onto his knee.

"It's probably true what Ulv said, that you're the wife I need."

"Oh yes," said Aashild, both laughing and annoyed, "she will certainly serve you well. She's the one risking everything in this venture; you're not risking much."

"That's true," said Erlend, "but I've shown my willingness to go to her along the proper paths. Don't be so angry, Aunt Aashild."

"I have every right to be angry," she said. "No sooner do you get your affairs in order than you put yourself in a position where you have to run away from everything with a woman."

"You must remember, Aunt," said Erlend, "that it has always been true that it's not the worst men who get themselves into trouble for the sake of a woman. That's what all the sagas say."

"Oh, God help us," said Aashild. Her face grew soft and young. "I've heard that speech before, Erlend." She took his head in her hands and ruffled his hair.

At that moment Ulv Haldorsøn tore open the door and shut it at once behind him.

"A guest has arrived at the farm, Erlend—the one person you would least want to see, I think."

"Is it Lavrans Bjørgulfsøn?" asked Erlend, jumping up.

"Unfortunately not," said the man. "It's Eline Ormsdatter."

The door was opened from the outside; the woman who entered shoved Ulv aside and stepped into the light. Kristin looked over at Erlend. At first he seemed to wither and collapse; then he straightened up, his face dark red.

"Where the Devil did you come from? What do you want here?"

Fru Aashild stepped forward and said, "Come with us up to the house, Eline Ormsdatter. We have enough courtesy on this farm that we don't receive our guests in the cookhouse."

"I don't expect Erlend's kin to greet me as a guest, Fru Aashild," said the woman. "You asked where I came from? I come from Husaby, as you well know. I bring you greetings from Orm and Margret; they are well."

Erlend didn't reply.

"When I heard that you had asked Gissur Arnfinsøn to raise money for you, and that you were heading south again," she went on, "I thought you would probably visit your kinsmen in Gudbrandsdal this time. I knew that you had made inquiries about the daughter of their neighbor."

She looked at Kristin for the first time and met the girl's eyes. Kristin was very pale, but she gazed at the other woman with a calm and searching expression.

Kristin was as calm as a rock. From the moment she heard who had arrived, she realized that it was the thought of Eline Ormsdatter that she had been constantly fleeing from, that she had tried to drown it out with defiance and restlessness and impatience. The whole time she had been striving not to think about whether Erlend had freed himself completely from his former mistress. Now she had been overtaken, and it was futile to fight it anymore. But she did not try to avoid it.

She saw that Eline Ormsdatter was beautiful. She was no longer young, but she was lovely, and at one time she must have been radiantly beautiful. She had let her hood fall back; her forehead was round and smooth, her cheekbones jutted out slightly—but it was still easy to see that once she had been quite striking. Her wimple covered only the back of her head; as she spoke, Eline tucked the shiny gold, wavy hair in front under the cloth. Kristin had never seen a woman with such big eyes; they were dark brown, round, and hard, but beneath the narrow, coal-black eyebrows and the long eyelashes her eyes were strangely beautiful next to her golden hair. Her skin and lips were chapped from the ride in the cold, but this did not detract from her appearance; she was much too beautiful for that. The heavy traveling clothes enshrouded her figure, but she wore them and carried herself as only a woman can who bears the most confident pride in the splendor of her own body. She was not quite as tall as Kristin, but she had such a bearing that she seemed taller than the slim, small-boned girl.

"Has she been with you at Husaby the whole time?" Kristin asked quietly.

"I haven't been at Husaby," said Erlend brusquely, his face flushing again. "I've been at Hestnæs for most of the summer."

"Here is the news I wanted to bring you, Erlend," said Eline. "You no longer need to seek lodgings with your kinsmen and test their hospitality while I keep house for you. This autumn I became a widow."

Erlend stood motionless.

"I wasn't the one who asked you to come to Husaby to keep house last year," he said with difficulty.

"I heard that everything was going downhill there," said Eline. "I still had enough good feelings toward you from the old days, Erlend, that I thought I should look out for your well-being—though God knows you haven't treated me or our children very kindly."

"I've done what I could for the children," said Erlend, "and you know full well that it was for their sake that I allowed you to stay at Husaby. You can't say that you did either them or me any good," he added, smiling spitefully. "Gissur could manage quite well without your help."

"Yes, you've always trusted Gissur," said Eline, laughing softly. "But the fact is, Erlend—now I am free. If you wish, you can keep the promise you once gave me."

Erlend was silent.

"Do you remember," said Eline, "the night I gave birth to your son? You promised then that you would marry me when Sigurd died."

Erlend pushed back his hair, wet with sweat.

"Yes, I remember," he said.

"Will you keep your word now?" asked Eline.

"No," said Erlend.

Eline Ormsdatter looked over at Kristin, smiled slightly, and nodded. Then she turned back to Erlend.

"That was ten years ago, Eline," he said. "Since that day we have lived together year in and year out like two people condemned to Hell."

"That's not entirely true," she said with the same smile.

"It's been years since there was anything else," said Erlend, exhausted. "It wouldn't help the children. And you know . . . you know that I can hardly stand to be in the same room with you anymore," he almost screamed.

"I didn't notice that when you were home this summer," said Eline with a telling smile. "We weren't enemies then. Not all the time."

"If you think that meant we were friends, go ahead and think so," said Erlend wearily.

"Are you just going to stand here?" said Fru Aashild. She ladled some porridge into two large wooden trenchers and handed one of them to Kristin. The girl took it. "Take it over to the house. Here, Ulv, take the other one. Put them on the table; we must have supper no matter how things stand."

Kristin and the servant went out with the dishes of food. Fru Aashild said to the others, "Come along, you two; it does no good for you to stand here barking at each other."

"It's best for Eline and me to talk this out with each other now," said Erlend.

Fru Aashild said no more and left.

Over in the house Kristin put the food on the table and brought up ale from the cellar. She sat down on the outer bench, erect as a candlestick, her face calm, but she did not eat. Bjørn and Erlend's men didn't have much appetite either. Only Bjørn's man and the servant who had come with Eline ate anything. Fru Aashild sat down and ate a little porridge. No one said a word.

Finally Eline Ormsdatter came in alone. Fru Aashild offered her a place between Kristin and herself; Eline sat down and ate something. Every once in a while the trace of a secret smile flitted across her face, and she would glance at Kristin.

After a while Fru Aashild went out to the cookhouse.

The fire had almost gone out. Erlend was sitting on the three-legged stool near the hearth, huddled up with his head on his arms. Fru Aashild went over and put her hand on his shoulder. "God forgive you, Erlend, for the way you have handled things."

Erlend looked up. His face was tear-streaked with misery.

"She's with child," he said and closed his eyes.

Fru Aashild's face flamed up; she gripped his shoulder hard. "Whose is it?" she asked bluntly and with contempt.

"Well, it isn't mine," said Erlend dully. "But you probably won't believe me. No one will. . . ." He collapsed once more.

Fru Aashild sat down in front of him at the edge of the hearth.

"You must try to pull yourself together, Erlend. It's not so easy to believe you in this matter. Do you swear that it's not yours?"

Erlend lifted his haggard face. "As truly as I need God's mercy. As truly as I hope that . . . that God has comforted Mother in Heaven for all that she had to endure down here. I have *not* touched Eline since the first time I saw Kristin!" He shouted so that Fru Aashild had to hush him.

"Then I don't see that this is such a misfortune. You must find out who the father is and pay him to marry her."

"I think it's Gissur Arnfinsøn, my foreman at Husaby," said Erlend wearily. "We talked about it last fall—and since then too.

Sigurd's death has been expected for some time. Gissur was willing to marry her when she became a widow if I would give her a sufficient dowry."

"I see," said Fru Aashild.

Erlend went on. "She swears that she won't have him. She will name me as the father. If I swear that I'm not . . . do you think anyone will believe that I'm not swearing falsely?"

"You'll have to dissuade her," said Fru Aashild. "There's no other way out. You must go home with her to Husaby tomorrow. And then you must stand firm and arrange this marriage between your foreman and Eline."

"You're right," said Erlend. Then he bent forward and sobbed aloud.

"Don't you see, Aunt . . . What do you think Kristin will believe?"

That night Erlend slept in the cookhouse with the servants. In the house Kristin slept with Fru Aashild in her bed, and Eline Ormsdatter slept in the other one. Bjørn went out to sleep in the stable.

The next morning Kristin followed Fru Aashild out to the cowshed. While Fru Aashild went to the cookhouse to make breakfast, Kristin carried the milk up to the house.

A candle was burning on the table. Eline was dressed and sitting on the edge of the bed. Kristin greeted her quietly, got out a basin, and strained the milk.

"Would you give me some milk?" asked Eline. Kristin took a wooden ladle and handed it to the woman. She drank greedily and looked over the rim at Kristin.

"So you're Kristin Lavransdatter, the one who has robbed me of Erlend's affections," she said, handing the ladle back.

"You're the one who should know whether there were any affections to rob," replied the young maiden.

Eline bit her lip. "What will you do," she said, "if Erlend grows tired of you and one day offers to marry you to his servant? Would you obey Erlend in that too?"

Kristin didn't answer.

Then the other woman laughed and said, "You obey him in everything, I imagine. What do you think, Kristin—shall we throw the dice for our man, we two mistresses of Erlend Nikulaussøn?" When she received no reply, she laughed again and said, "Are you so simple-minded that you don't deny you're a kept woman?"

"To you I don't feel like lying," said Kristin.

"It wouldn't do you much good anyway," replied Eline in the same tone of voice. "I know that boy. I can imagine that he probably rushed at you like a black grouse the second time you were together. And it's too bad for you, pretty child that you are."

Kristin's cheeks grew pale. Sick with loathing she said quietly, "I don't want to talk to you."

"Do you think he'll treat you any better than he did me?" Eline continued.

Then Kristin replied sharply, "I won't complain about Erlend, no matter what he does. I was the one who took the wrong path, and I won't moan and feel sorry for myself even if it leads me out over the scree."

Eline was silent for a moment. Then she said, flushed and uncertain, "I was a maiden too, when he took me, Kristin—even though I had been the old man's wife for seven years. But you probably can't understand what a wretched life that was."

Kristin started to tremble violently. Eline gazed at her. Then she took a little horn out of her traveling box which stood at her side on the step of the bed.

She broke the seal and said quietly, "You are young and I am old, Kristin. I know it's useless for me to fight against you—now it's your turn. Will you drink with me, Kristin?"

Kristin didn't move. Then the other woman put the horn to her lips. Kristin noticed that she did not drink.

Eline said, "You might at least do me the honor of drinking to me—and promise that you won't be a harsh stepmother to my children."

Kristin took the horn. At that moment Erlend opened the door. He stood there, looking from one woman to the other.

"What's this?" he asked.

Then Kristin replied, and her voice was shrill and wild. "We're drinking to each other, your two mistresses."

He grabbed her wrist and snatched away the horn. "Be quiet," he said harshly. "You shall not drink with her."

"Why not?" said Kristin in the same voice as before. "She was just as pure as I was when you seduced her."

"She's said that so often that she believes it herself," replied Erlend. "Do you remember when you made me go to Sigurd with that lie, Eline, and he produced witnesses that he had caught you with another man?"

Pale with disgust, Kristin turned away. Eline's face had flushed dark red. Then she said spitefully, "Even so, that girl isn't going to turn into a leper if she drinks with me."

Furious, Erlend turned toward Eline—and then his face suddenly grew rigid and the man gasped in horror.

"Jesus!" he said almost inaudibly. He grabbed Eline by the arm.

"Then drink to *her*," he said, his voice harsh and quavering. "Drink first, and then she'll drink with you."

Eline wrenched herself away with a gasp. She fled backward across the room, the man after her.

"Drink," he said. He pulled his dagger out of his belt and followed her with it in his hand. "Taste the drink you've made for Kristin." He grabbed Eline by the arm, dragged her over to the table, and forced her to bend toward the horn.

Eline screamed once and hid her face in her arm.

Erlend released her and stood there shaking.

"It was a hell with Sigurd," shrieked Eline. "You . . . you promised—but you've treated me even worse, Erlend!"

Then Kristin stepped forward and grabbed the horn. "One of us must drink—you can't keep both of us."

Erlend took the horn from her and flung her across the room so she fell to the floor over by Fru Aashild's bed. He forced the drink to Eline Ormsdatter's mouth. Standing with one knee on the bench next to her and his hand on her head, he tried to force her to drink.

She fumbled under his arm, snatched the dagger from the table, and stabbed at the man. The blow didn't seem to cut much but his clothes. Then she turned the point on herself, and immediately fell sideways into his arms.

Kristin got up and came over to them. Erlend was holding Eline; her head hung back over his arm. The death rattle came almost at once; she had blood in her throat and it was running out of her mouth. She spat out a great quantity and said, "I had intended . . . that drink . . . for you . . . for all the times . . . you betrayed me."

"Go get Aunt Aashild," said Erlend in a low voice. Kristin stood motionless.

"She's dying," said Erlend.

"Then she'll fare better than we will," replied Kristin. Erlend looked at her, and the despair in his eyes softened her. She left the room.

"What is it?" asked Fru Aashild when Kristin called her away from the cookhouse.

"We've killed Eline Ormsdatter," said Kristin. "She's dying."

Fru Aashild set off at a run. But Eline breathed her last as she stepped through the door.

Fru Aashild had laid out the dead woman on the bench; she wiped the blood from her face and covered it with a linen cloth. Erlend stood leaning against the wall behind the body.

"Do you realize," said Fru Aashild, "that this was the worst thing that could have happened?"

She had put branches and kindling into the fireplace; now she placed the horn in the middle and blew on it till it flared up.

"Can you trust your men?" she asked.

"Ulv and Haftor, I think I can. I don't know Jon very well, or the man who came with Eline."

"You realize," said Fru Aashild, "that if it comes out that you and Kristin were here together, and that you were alone with Eline when she died, then you might as well have let Kristin drink Eline's brew. And if there's any talk of poison, people will remember what I have been accused of in the past. Did she have any kinsmen or friends?"

"No," said Erlend in a subdued voice. "She had no one but me."

"Even so," said Fru Aashild, "it'll be difficult to cover this up and remove the body without the deepest suspicion falling on you."

"She must be buried in consecrated ground," said Erlend, "if it costs me Husaby to do it. What do you say, Kristin?"

Kristin nodded.

Fru Aashild sat in silence. The more she thought about it, the more impossible it seemed to find a solution. In the cookhouse sat four men; could Erlend bribe all of them to keep quiet? Could any of them, could Eline's man, be paid to leave the country? That would always be risky. And at Jørundgaard they knew that Kristin had been here. If Lavrans found out about it, she couldn't imagine what he might do. They would have to take the body away. The mountain road to the west was unthinkable now; there was the road to Raumsdal or across the mountain to Nidaros or south down the valley. And if the truth came out, it would never be believed—even if it were accepted.

"I have to discuss this with Bjørn," she said, standing up and going out.

Bjørn Gunnarsøn listened to his wife's account without changing expression and without taking his eyes off Erlend.

"Bjørn," said Aashild desperately, "someone has to swear that he saw her lay hands on herself."

The life slowly darkened in Bjørn's eyes; he looked at his wife, and his mouth twisted into a crooked smile.

"You mean that someone should be me?"

Fru Aashild clasped her hands and raised them toward him. "Bjørn, you know what it means for these two. . . ."

"And you think it's all over for me anyway?" he asked slowly. "Or do you think there's enough left of the man I once was that I'll dare to swear falsely to save this boy from going under? I, who was dragged under myself . . . all those years ago. Dragged under, I say," he repeated.

"You say this because I'm old now," whispered Aashild.

Kristin burst into sobs that cut through the room. Rigid and silent, she had been sitting in the corner near Aashild's bed. Now she began to weep out loud. It was as if Fru Aashild's voice had torn open her heart. This voice, heavy with memories of the sweetness of love, seemed to make Kristin fully realize for the first time what the love between her and Erlend had been. The memory of burning, passionate happiness washed over everything else, washed away the cruel despairing hatred from the night before. She felt only her love and her will to survive.

All three of them looked at her. Then Herr Bjørn went over, put his hand under her chin, and gazed down at her. "Kristin, do you say that she did it herself?"

"Every word you've heard is true," said Kristin firmly. "We threatened her until she did it."

"She had planned a worse fate for Kristin," said Aashild.

Herr Bjørn let go of the girl. He went over to the body, lifted it onto the bed where Eline had slept the night before, and laid it close to the wall with the blankets pulled over it.

"You must send Jon and the man you don't know back to Husaby with the message that Eline will accompany you to the south. Have them ride off around noon. Tell them that the women are asleep in here; they'll have to eat in the cookhouse. Then speak to Ulv and Haftor. Has she threatened to do this before? Can you bring witnesses forward if anyone asks about this?"

"Everyone who has been at Husaby during the last years we lived together," said Erlend wearily, "can testify that she threatened to take her own life—and sometimes mine too—whenever I talked about leaving her."

Bjørn laughed harshly. "I thought so. Tonight we'll dress her in traveling clothes and put her in the sleigh. You'll have to sit next to her—"

Erlend swayed where he stood. "I can't do that."

"God only knows how much of a man there will be left of *you* when you take stock of yourself twenty years from now," said Bjørn. "Do you think you can drive the sleigh, then? I'll sit next to her. We'll have to travel by night and on back roads until we reach Fron. In this cold no one will know how long she's been dead. We'll drive to the monks' hostel at Roaldstad. There you and I will testify that the two of you came to words in the back of the sleigh. It's well attested that you haven't wanted to live with her since the ban was lifted from you and that you have asked for the hand of a maiden who is your equal. Ulv and Haftor must keep their distance during the whole journey so that they can swear, if necessary, that she was alive the last time they saw her. You can get them to do that, can't you? At the monks' hostel you can have her placed in a casket; and then you must negotiate with the priests for peace in the grave for her and peace of the soul for yourself.

"I know it's not pleasant, but you haven't handled matters so that it could be pleasant. Don't stand there like a child bride who's about to swoon away. God help you, my boy—I suppose you've never tried feeling the edge of a knife at your throat, have you?"

A biting wind was coming down off the mountain. Snow was blowing, fine and silvery, from the drifts up toward the moon-blue sky as the men prepared to set off.

Two horses were hitched up, one in front of the other. Erlend sat in the front of the sleigh. Kristin went over to him.

"This time, Erlend, you must take the trouble to send me word about how the journey goes and where you end up."

He squeezed her hand so hard she thought the blood would burst from her fingernails.

"Do you still dare stand by me, Kristin?"

"Yes, I still do," she said, and after a moment, "We both bear the blame for this deed. I urged you on because I wanted her dead."

Fru Aashild and Kristin stood and watched them go. The sleigh dipped down and rose up over the drifts. It vanished in a hollow, to appear farther down on a white meadow. But then the men passed into the shadow of a slope and disappeared for good.

The two women were sitting in front of the fireplace, their backs to the empty bed; Fru Aashild had taken out the bedclothes and straw. They both knew that it was standing there empty, gaping at them.

"Do you want us to sleep in the cookhouse tonight?" Fru Aashild asked.

"It makes no difference where we sleep," said Kristin.

Fru Aashild went outside to look at the weather.

"No, it doesn't matter whether a storm blows in or a thaw comes; they won't get far before the truth comes out," said Kristin.

"It always blows here at Haugen," replied Fru Aashild. "There's no sign of a break in the weather."

Then they sat in silence again.

"You mustn't forget what fate she had intended for the two of you," said Fru Aashild.

Kristin said softly, "I keep thinking that in her place I might have wanted to do the same."

"You would never have wanted to cause another person to become a leper," said Fru Aashild staunchly.

"Do you remember, Aunt, you once told me that it's a good thing when you don't dare do something if you don't think it's right. But it's not good when you think something's not right because you don't dare do it."

"You didn't dare because it was a sin," said Fru Aashild.

"No, I don't think so," said Kristin. "I've done many things that I thought I would never dare do because they were sins. But I didn't realize then that the consequence of sin is that you have to trample on other people."

"Erlend wanted to mend his ways long before he met you," replied Aashild vehemently. "It was over between those two."

"I know that," said Kristin, "but she probably never had reason to believe that Erlend's plans were so firm that she wouldn't be able to change them."

"Kristin," pleaded Fru Aashild fearfully, "you won't give up Erlend now, will you? The two of you can't be saved unless you save each other."

"That's hardly what a priest would say," said Kristin, smiling coldly. "But I know that I won't let go of Erlend—even if I have to trample on my own father."

Fru Aashild stood up.

"We might as well keep ourselves busy instead of sitting here like this," she said. "It would probably be useless for us to try to go to bed."

She brought the butter churn from the storeroom, carried in some basins of milk, and filled it up; then she took up her position to churn.

"Let me do that," begged Kristin. "I have a younger back."

They worked without talking. Kristin stood near the storeroom door and churned, and Aashild carded wool over by the hearth. Not until Kristin had strained out the churn and was forming the butter did she suddenly say, "Aunt Aashild—aren't you ever afraid of the day when you have to face God's judgment?"

Fru Aashild stood up and went over to stand in front of Kristin in the light.

"Perhaps I'll have the courage to ask the one who created me, such as I am, whether He will have mercy on me when the time comes. For I have never asked for His mercy when I went against His commandments. And I have never asked God or man to return one *penning* of the fines I've had to pay here in my earthly home."

A moment later she said quietly, "Munan, my eldest son, was twenty years old. Back then he wasn't the way I know him to be now. They weren't like that then, those children of mine . . ."

Kristin replied softly, "And yet you've had Herr Bjørn by your side every day and every night all these years."

"Yes," said Aashild, "that I have."

A little later Kristin was done with forming the butter. Then Fru Aashild said that they ought to try lying down for a while.

In the dark bed she put her arm around Kristin's shoulder and pulled the girl's head toward her. And it wasn't long before she could hear by her even and quiet breathing that Kristin was asleep.

THE FROST HUNG ON. In every stable of the village the starving animals lowed and complained, suffering from the cold. But the people were already rationing the fodder as best they could.

There was not much visiting done during the Christmas season that year; everyone was staying at home.

At Christmas the cold grew worse; each day felt colder than the one before. People could hardly remember such a harsh winter. And while no more snow fell, even up in the mountains, the snow that had fallen on Saint Clement's Day froze as hard as stone. The sun shone in a clear sky, now that the days were growing lighter. At night the northern lights flickered and sputtered above the mountain ridges to the north; they flickered over half the sky, but they didn't bring a change in the weather. Once in a while it would cloud over, sprinkling a little dry snow, but then the clear skies and biting cold would return. The Laag murmured and gurgled lazily beneath the bridges of ice.

Each morning Kristin would think that now she could stand it no longer; that she wouldn't be able to make it through the day, because each day felt like a duel between her father and herself. And was it right for them to be so at odds with each other right now, when every living thing, every person and beast in the valleys, was enduring a common trial? But when evening came she had made it through after all.

It was not that her father was unfriendly. They never spoke of what lay between them, but Kristin could feel that in everything he left unsaid he was steadfastly determined to stand by his refusal.

And she burned with longing for his affection. Her anguish was even greater because she knew how much else her father had to bear; and if things had been as they were before, he would have talked to her about his concerns. It's true that at Jørundgaard they were better prepared than most other places, but even here they felt the effects of the bad year, every day and every hour. In the winter Lavrans usually spent time breaking and training his foals, but this year, during the autumn, he had sold all of them in the south. His daughter missed hearing his voice out in the courtyard and watching him tussle with the lanky, shaggy two-year-old horses in the game that he loved so much. The storerooms, barns, and bins on the farm had not been emptied after the harvest of the previous year, but many people came to Jørundgaard asking for help, either as a purchase or a gift, and no one asked in vain.

Late one evening a very old man, dressed in furs, arrived on skis. Lavrans spoke to him out in the courtyard, and Halvdan took food to him in the hearth room. No one on the farm who had seen him knew who he was, but it was assumed that he was one of the people who lived in the mountains; perhaps Lavrans had run into him out there. But Kristin's father didn't speak of the visit, nor did Halvdan.

Then one evening a man arrived with whom Lavrans Bjørgulfsøn had had a score to settle for many years. Lavrans went out to the storeroom with him. But when he returned to the house, he said, "Everyone wants me to help them. And yet here on my farm you're all against me. Even you, wife," he said angrily to Ragnfrid.

Then Ragnfrid lashed out at Kristin.

"Do you hear what your father is saying to me? I'm not against you, Lavrans. You know full well, Kristin, what happened south of here at Roaldstad late in the fall, when he traveled through the valley in the company of that other whoremonger, his kinsman from Haugen—she took her own life, that unfortunate woman he had enticed away from all her kinsmen."

Her face rigid, Kristin replied harshly, "I see that you blame him as much for the years when he was striving to get out of sin as for those when he was living in it."

"Jesus Maria," cried Ragnfrid, clasping her hands together. "Look what's become of you! Won't even this make you change your mind?"

"No," said Kristin. "I haven't changed my mind."

Then Lavrans looked up from the bench where he was sitting with Ulvhild.

"Nor have I, Kristin," he said quietly.

But Kristin knew in her heart that in some way she had changed —if not her decision, then her outlook. She had received word of the progress of that ill-fated journey. It had gone easier than anyone could have expected. Whether it was because the cold had settled in his wound or for some other reason, the knife injury which Erlend had received in his chest had become infected. He lay ill at the hostel in Roaldstad for a long time, and Herr Bjørn tended to him during those days. But because Erlend had been wounded, it was easier to explain everything else and to make others believe them.

When he was able to continue, he transported the dead woman in a coffin all the way to Oslo. There, with Sira Jon's intervention, he found a gravesite for her in the cemetery of Nikolaus Church, which lay in ruins. Then he had confessed to the Bishop of Oslo himself, who had enjoined him to travel to the Shrine of the Holy Blood in Schwerin. So now he had left the country.

There was no place to which *she* could make a pilgrimage to seek redemption. Her lot was to stay here, to wait and worry and try to endure her opposition to her parents. A strange, cold winter light fell over all her memories of her meetings with Erlend. She thought about his ardor—in love and in sorrow—and it occurred to her that if she had been able to seize on all things with equal abruptness and plunge ahead at once, then afterward they might seem of less consequence and easier to bear. Sometimes she thought that Erlend might give her up. She had always had a slight fear that it could become too difficult for them, and he would lose heart. But she would not give him up—not unless he released her from all promises.

And so the winter wore on. And Kristin could no longer fool herself; she had to admit that now the most difficult trial awaited all of them, for Ulvhild did not have long to live. And in the midst of her bitter sorrow over her sister, Kristin realized with horror that her own soul had been led astray and was corrupted by sin.

For as she witnessed the dying child and her parents' unspeakable grief, she thought of only one thing: if Ulvhild dies, how will I be able to endure facing my father without throwing myself down before him, to confess everything and to beg him to forgive me and to do with me what he will.

The Lenten fast was upon them. People were slaughtering the small animals they had hoped to save before the livestock perished on its own. And people were falling ill from living on fish and the scant and wretched portions of grain. Sira Eirik released the entire village from the ban against consuming milk. But no one had even a drop of milk.

Ulvhild was confined to bed. She slept alone in the sisters' bed, and someone watched over her every night. Sometimes Kristin and her father would both sit with her. On one such night Lavrans said to his daughter, "Do you remember what Brother Edvin said about Ulvhild's fate? I thought at the time that maybe this was what he meant. But I put it out of my mind."

During those nights he would occasionally talk about one thing or another from the time when the children were small. Kristin would sit there, pale and miserable, understanding that behind his words, her father was pleading with her.

One day Lavrans had gone out with Kolbein to seek out a bear's lair in the mountain forest to the north. They returned home with a female bear on a sled, and Lavrans was carrying a little bear cub, still alive, inside his tunic. Ulvhild smiled a little when he showed it to her. But Ragnfrid said that this was no time to take in that kind of animal, and what was he going to do with it now?

"I'm going to fatten it up and then tie it to the bedchamber of my maidens," said Lavrans, laughing harshly.

But they couldn't find the kind of rich milk that the bear cub needed, and so several days later Lavrans killed it.

The sun had grown so strong that occasionally, in the middle of the day, the eaves would begin to drip. The titmice clung to the timbered walls and hopped around on the sunny side; the pecking of their beaks resounded as they looked for flies asleep in the gaps between the wood. Out across the meadows the snow gleamed, hard and shiny like silver.

Finally one evening clouds began to gather in front of the moon. In the morning they woke up at Jørundgaard to a whirl of snow that blocked their view in all directions.

On that day it became clear that Ulvhild was going to die.

The entire household had gathered inside, and Sira Eirik had come. Many candles were burning in the room. Early that evening, Ulvhild passed on, calmly and peacefully, in her mother's arms.

Ragnfrid bore it better than anyone could have expected. The parents sat together, both of them weeping softly. Everyone in the room was crying. When Kristin went over to her father, he put his arm around her shoulders. He noticed how she was trembling and shaking, and then he pulled her close. But it seemed to her that he must have felt as if she had been snatched farther away from him than her dead little sister in the bed.

She didn't know how she had managed to endure. She hardly remembered why she was enduring, but, lethargic and mute with pain, she managed to stay on her feet and did not collapse.

Then a couple of planks were pulled up in the floor in front of the altar of Saint Thomas, and a grave was dug in the rock-hard earth underneath for Ulvhild Lavransdatter.

It snowed heavily and silently for all those days the child lay on the straw bier; it was snowing as she was laid in the earth; and it continued to snow, almost without stop, for an entire month.

For those who were waiting for the redemption of spring, it seemed as if it would never come. The days grew long and bright, and the valley lay in a haze of thawing snow while the sun shone. But frost was still in the air, and the heat had no power. At night it froze hard; great cracking sounds came from the ice, a rumbling issued from the mountains, and the wolves howled and the foxes yipped all the way down in the village, as if it were midwinter. People scraped off bark for the livestock, but they were perishing by the dozens in their stalls. No one knew when it would end.

Kristin went out on such a day, when the water was trickling in the furrows of the road and the snow glistened like silver across the fields. Facing the sun, the snowdrifts had become hollowed out so that the delicate ice lattice of the crusted snow broke with the gentle ring of silver when she pressed her foot against it. But wherever there was the slightest shadow, the air was sharp with frost and the snow was hard.

She walked up toward the church. She didn't know why she was going there, but she felt drawn to it. Her father was there. Several farmers—guild brothers—were holding a meeting in the gallery, that much she knew.

Up on the hill she met the group of farmers as they were leaving. Sira Eirik was with them. The men were all on foot, walking in a dark, fur-wrapped cluster, nodding and talking to each other; they returned her greeting in a surly manner as she passed.

Kristin thought to herself that it had been a long time since everyone in the village had been her friend. Everyone no doubt knew that she was a bad daughter. Perhaps they knew even more about her. Now they probably all thought that there must have been some truth to the old gossip about her and Arne and Bentein. Perhaps she was in terrible disrepute. She lifted her chin and walked on toward the church.

The door stood ajar. It was cold inside the church, and yet a certain warmth streamed toward her from this dim brown room, with the tall columns soaring upward, lifting the darkness toward the crossbeams of the roof. There were no lit candles on the altars, but a little sunshine came in through the open door, casting a faint light on the paintings and vessels.

Up near the Saint Thomas altar she saw her father on his knees with his head resting on his folded hands, which were clutching his cap against his chest.

Shy and dispirited, Kristin tiptoed out and stood on the gallery. Framed by the arch of two small pillars, which she held on to, she saw Jørundgaard lying below, and beyond her home the pale blue haze over the valley. In the sun the river glinted white with water and ice all through the village. But the alder thicket along its bank was golden brown with blossoms, the spruce forest was spring-green even up by the church, and tiny birds chittered and chirped and trilled in the grove nearby. Oh yes, she had heard birdsong like that every evening after the sun set.

And now she felt the longing that she thought had been wrung out of her, the longing in her body and in her blood; it began to stir now, feeble and faint, as if it were waking up from a winter's hibernation.

Lavrans Bjørgulfsøn came outside and closed the church door behind him. He went over and stood near his daughter, looking out from the next arch. She noticed how the winter had ravaged her father. She didn't think that she could bring this up now, but it tumbled out of her all the same.

"Is it true what Mother said the other day, that you told her . . . if it had been Arne Gyrdsøn, then you would have relented?"

"Yes," said Lavrans without looking at her.

"You never said that while Arne was alive," replied Kristin.

"It was never discussed. I could see that the boy was fond of you, but he said nothing . . . and he was young . . . and I never noticed that you thought of him in that way. You couldn't expect me to *offer* my daughter to a man who owned no property." He smiled fleetingly. "But I was fond of the boy," he said softly. "And if I had seen that you were pining with love for him . . ."

They remained standing there, staring straight ahead. Kristin sensed her father looking at her. She struggled to keep her expression calm, but she could feel how pale she was. Then her father came over to her, put both arms around her, and hugged her tight. He tilted her head back, looked into his daughter's face, and then hid it against his shoulder.

"Jesus Christus, little Kristin, are you so unhappy?"

"I think I'm going to die from it, Father," she said against his chest.

She burst into tears. But she was crying because she had felt in his caress and seen in his eyes that now he was so worn out with anguish that he could no longer hold on to his opposition. She had won.

In the middle of the night she woke up when her father touched her shoulder in the dark.

"Get up," he said quietly. "Do you hear it?"

Then she heard the singing at the corners of the house—the

deep, full tone of the moisture-laden south wind. Water was streaming off the roof, and the rain whispered as it fell on soft, melting snow.

Kristin threw on a dress and followed her father to the outer door. Together they stood and looked out into the bright May night. Warm wind and rain swept toward them. The sky was a heap of tangled, surging rain clouds; there was a seething from the woods, a whistling between the buildings. And up on the mountains they heard the hollow rumble of snow sliding down.

Kristin reached for her father's hand and held it. He had called her and wanted to show her this. It was the kind of thing he would have done in the past, before things changed between them. And now he was doing it again.

When they went back inside to lie down, Lavrans said, "The stranger who was here this week carried a letter to me from Sir Munan Baardsøn. He intends to come here this summer to visit his mother, and he asked whether he might seek me out and speak with me."

"How will you answer him, my father?" she whispered.

"I can't tell you that now," replied Lavrans. "But I will speak to him, and then I must act in such a way that I can answer for myself before God, my daughter."

Kristin crawled into bed beside Ramborg, and Lavrans went over and lay down next to his sleeping wife. He lay there, thinking that if the flood waters rose high and suddenly, then few farms in the village would be as vulnerable as Jørundgaard. There was supposed to be a prophecy about it—that one day the river would take the farm.

CHAPTER 5

SPRING ARRIVED ABRUPTLY. Several days after the frost broke, the village lay brown and black beneath the torrents of rain. Water rushed down the mountain slopes, and the river swelled and lay like a leaden-gray lake at the bottom of the valley, with small flooded groves at the edge of the water and a sly, gurgling furrow of current. At Jørundgaard the water reached far into the fields. And yet everywhere the damage was much less than people had feared.

The spring farm work was late that year, and everyone sowed their sparse seeds with prayers to God that He might spare them from the night frost until harvest time. And it looked as if He would heed their prayers and lighten their burden a little. June came with favorable weather, the summer was good, and everyone began to hope that in time the traces of the bad year would be erased.

The hay harvesting was over when one evening four men came riding toward Jørundgaard. Two gentlemen and their two servants: Sir Munan Baardsøn and Sir Baard Petersøn of Hestnes.

Ragnfrid and Lavrans ordered the table to be set in the high loft and beds to be made up in the loft above the storehouse. But Lavrans asked the gentlemen to wait to set forth their purpose until the following day, after they had rested from their journey.

Sir Munan did most of the talking during the meal, directing much of the conversation toward Kristin, speaking to her as if they were well acquainted. She noticed that her father was not pleased by this. Sir Munan was thickset, with a ruddy face—an ugly and garrulous man with a rather foolish manner. People called him Munan the Stump or Munan the Prancer. But in spite of the impression he made, Fru Aashild's son was still a sensible and capable man who had been the Crown's envoy in several matters and who doubtless had some influence on those who counseled the governance of the kingdom. He lived on his mother's ancestral property in the Skogheim district. He was quite wealthy and he had made a rich marriage. Fru Katrin, his wife, was peculiarly ugly and she seldom opened her mouth, but her husband always spoke of her as if she were the wisest of women. In jest people called Fru Katrin the "resourceful woman with the lovely voice." They seemed to get on well together and treated each other with affection, even though Sir Munan was notorious for his wayward behavior, both before and after his marriage.

Sir Baard Petersøn was a handsome and stately old man, although he was rather portly and heavy of limb. His hair and beard were somewhat faded now, but there was still as much gold in them as there was white. Ever since the death of King Magnus Haakonsøn he had lived quietly, managing his vast properties at Nordmøre. He was a widower after the death of his second wife, and he had many children, who were all said to be handsome, well-mannered, and well-to-do.

The following day Lavrans and his guests went up to the loft to talk. Lavrans asked his wife to join them, but she refused.

"This must lie solely in your hands," said Ragnfrid. "You know that it would be the greatest sorrow for our daughter if this matter could not be resolved, but I see that there is much to be said against this marriage."

Sir Munan presented a letter from Erlend Nikulaussøn. Erlend proposed that Lavrans should decide on all of the conditions if he would agree to the betrothal of his daughter Kristin. Erlend himself was willing to have his properties appraised and his income examined by impartial men, and to offer Kristin such betrothal and wedding gifts that she would own a third of his possessions, in addition to whatever she brought to the marriage herself, and all inheritances that she might acquire from her kinsmen if she should become a widow with no children surviving the father. Furthermore, he offered to allow Kristin to manage with full authority her part of the property, both that which she brought into the marriage and that which she was given by him. But if Lavrans preferred

other conditions for the division of property, then Erlend would
be willing to hear his views and to act accordingly. There was only
one condition to which Kristin's kinsmen would have to bind
themselves: if they acquired guardianship over any children that he
and she might have, they must never try to revoke the gifts that he
had given to his children by Eline Ormsdatter. They must recognize
as valid the claim that these properties had been separated from
his possessions before he entered into the marriage with Kristin
Lavransdatter. Finally, Erlend offered to hold the wedding with all
appropriate splendor at his manor at Husaby.

It was then Lavrans's turn to speak, and he said, "This is a
handsome offer. I see that it is your kinsman's fervent desire to
come to an agreement with me. I also realize that he has asked
you, Sir Munan, for a second time to come on such an errand to
me—a man of no great import outside this village—and a gentleman such as you, Sir Baard, to take the trouble to make this journey on his behalf. But now I must tell you in regard to Erlend's
offer that my daughter has not been raised to manage properties
and riches herself, and I have always intended to give her to a man
in whose hands I could confidently place the maiden's welfare. I
don't know whether Kristin is capable of handling such responsibility or not, but I hardly think that she would thrive by doing so.
She is placid and compliant in temperament. One of the reasons
that I bore in mind when I opposed the marriage was this: that
Erlend has shown a certain imprudence in several areas. Had she
been a domineering, bold, and headstrong woman, then the situation would have been quite different."

Sir Munan burst out laughing and said, "My dear Lavrans, are
you complaining that the maiden is not headstrong enough?"

And Sir Baard said with a little smile, "It seems to me that your
daughter has demonstrated that she is not lacking in will. For two
years she has stood by Erlend, in spite of your wishes."

Lavrans said, "I know that quite well, and yet I know what I'm
talking about. It has been hard for her during the time she has
defied me, and she won't be happy with a husband for long unless
he can rule her."

"The Devil take me," said Sir Munan. "Then your daughter
must be quite unlike all the women I have known, for I've never

found a single one who didn't prefer to rule over both herself and her husband."

Lavrans shrugged his shoulders and didn't reply.

Then Baard Petersøn said, "I can imagine, Lavrans Bjørgulfsøn, that now you are even less in favor of this marriage between your daughter and my foster son since the woman he was with came to such an end. But you should know that it has now come to light that the wretched woman had let herself be seduced by another man, the foreman of Erlend's farm at Husaby. Erlend knew about this when he journeyed with her through the valley; he had offered to provide her with a proper dowry if the man would marry her."

"Are you sure this is true?" asked Lavrans. "And yet I don't know whether it makes the situation any better. It must be bitter for a woman of good family to arrive on the arm of the landowner, only to leave with the farm hand."

Munan Baardsøn put in, "I see, Lavrans Bjørgulfsøn, that your strongest objection to my cousin is that he has had this unfortunate trouble with Sigurd Saksulvsøn's wife. And it's true that it was ill advised. But in the name of God, man, you must remember—there he was, a young boy in the same house with a young and beautiful wife, and she had a cold and useless old husband, and the nights last half the year up there. I don't think much else could have been expected, unless Erlend had actually been a holy man. It can't be denied that Erlend has never had any monk flesh in him, but I don't imagine that your lovely young daughter would be grateful if you gave her to a monk. It's true that Erlend conducted himself foolishly, and even worse later on. But this matter must finally be considered closed. We, his kinsmen, have striven to help set the boy on his feet again. The woman is dead, and Erlend has done everything within his power for her body and soul. The Bishop of Oslo himself has redeemed him from his sin, and now he has come home, cleansed by the Holy Blood in Schwerin. Do you intend to be harsher than the Bishop of Oslo and the archbishop or whoever it is down there who presides over the precious blood?

"My dear Lavrans, it's true that pure living is an admirable thing, but it's hardly within the powers of a grown man unless he is particularly blessed by God. By Saint Olav—you should keep in mind that the holy king himself was not given that blessing until the end of his life on earth. It was evidently God's will that he should first produce the capable boy-king Magnus, who repelled the heathens' invasion of the north. King Olav did not have that son by his queen, and yet he sits among the highest of saints in Heaven. Yes, I can see that you think this improper talk . . ."

Sir Baard interrupted, "Lavrans Bjørgulfsøn, I didn't like this matter any better than you when Erlend first came to me and said that he had set his heart on a maiden who was betrothed. But I have since realized that there is such a strong love between these two young people, it would be a great sin to separate their affections. Erlend was with me at the Christmas feast that King Haakon held for his men. That's where they met, and as soon as they saw each other, your daughter fainted and lay as if dead for a long time—and I could see that my foster son would rather lose his own life than lose her."

Lavrans sat in silence for a moment before he replied.

"Yes, that sort of thing sounds so beautiful when we hear it in a courtly tale from the southern lands. But we are not in Bretland,[1] and surely you would demand more of a man you intend to take as a son-in-law than that he had made your daughter swoon with love before everyone's eyes."

The other two didn't speak, and then Lavrans continued, "I think, good sirs, that if Erlend Nikulaussøn had not so greatly diminished both his property and his reputation, then you would not be sitting here, asking so earnestly for a man of my circumstances to give my daughter to him. But I won't have it said about Kristin that she was honored by coming to Husaby through marriage to a man belonging to this country's best lineage—after that man had disgraced himself so badly that he could neither expect a better match nor maintain his family's distinction."

He stood up abruptly and paced back and forth across the floor.

But Sir Munan jumped up. "No, Lavrans, if you're going to talk about bringing shame upon oneself, then by God you should know that you're being much too proud—"

Sir Baard cut him off. He went over to Lavrans and said, "And proud you are, Lavrans. You're like those landowners in the past we've heard about, who refused to accept titles from the kings because their sense of pride could not tolerate hearing people say that they owed anything to anyone but themselves. I must tell you that if Erlend had possessed all the honor and wealth that the boy was born with, I would still not consider it disparaging to myself when I asked a man of good lineage and good circumstances to give his daughter to my foster son, if I could see that it would break the hearts of these two young people to be kept apart. Especially," he said softly, placing his hand on the other man's shoulder, "if things were such that it was best for the health of both their souls if they were allowed to marry."

Lavrans shook off Baard's hand. His face grew stony and cold. "I don't know what you mean, sir."

The two men looked at each other for a moment. Then Sir Baard said, "I mean that Erlend has told me that they have sworn themselves to each other with the most solemn of oaths. Perhaps you think you have the authority to release your child, since she has sworn without your consent. But you cannot release Erlend. And I can't see that there is anything standing in the way except your pride—and your abhorrence of sin. But in this it seems to me that you wish to be harsher than God Himself, Lavrans Bjørgulfsøn!"

Lavrans answered somewhat uncertainly, "You may be right in what you say, Sir Baard. But I have mainly opposed this marriage because Erlend seemed to me an unreliable man to whom I would not want to entrust my daughter."

"I think I can vouch for my foster son now," said Baard in a subdued tone of voice. "He loves Kristin so much that if you give her to him, I am convinced he will conduct himself in such a manner that you will have no cause to complain of your son-in-law."

Lavrans didn't reply at once.

Then Sir Baard said imploringly, holding out his hand, "In God's name, Lavrans Bjørgulfsøn, give your consent!"

Lavrans gave his hand to Sir Baard. "In God's name."

Ragnfrid and Kristin were called to the loft, and Lavrans told them of his decision. Sir Baard graciously greeted the two women. Sir Munan shook Ragnfrid's hand and spoke courteously to her, but he greeted Kristin in the foreign manner with kisses, and he took his time about it. Kristin noticed that her father was looking at her as he did this.

"How do you like your new kinsman, Sir Munan?" he asked with derision when he was alone with her for a moment that evening.

Kristin gave her father an imploring look. Then he stroked her face several times and said nothing more.

When Sir Baard and Sir Munan had gone to bed, the latter said, "What wouldn't I give to see the face of this Lavrans Bjørgulfsøn if he ever learned the truth about his precious daughter. Here you and I had to beg on our knees for Erlend to win a woman as his wife whom he has had with him up at Brynhild's inn so many times."

"You keep quiet about that," replied Sir Baard bitterly. "It was the worst thing Erlend could have done when he enticed the child to such a place. And never let Lavrans get word of this; it will be best for everyone if those two can be friends."

It was agreed that the betrothal celebration would be held that same autumn. Lavrans said that he could not offer a grand banquet because the previous year had been so bad in the valley; but he would, on the other hand, host the wedding and hold it at Jørundgaard with all appropriate splendor. He mentioned again the bad year as his reason for demanding that the betrothal period should last a year.

CHAPTER 6

THE BETROTHAL CELEBRATION was postponed for various reasons. It didn't take place until the New Year, but Lavrans agreed that the wedding needn't be delayed because of that. It would be held immediately following Michaelmas, as had been originally agreed.

So Kristin continued to live at Jørundgaard as Erlend's properly acknowledged betrothed. Along with her mother she went over the dowry that had been assembled for her and strove to add even more to the piles of bed linen and clothing, for Lavrans wanted nothing to be spared now that he had given his daughter to the master of Husaby.

Kristin was surprised that she didn't feel happier. But in spite of all the activity, there was no real joy at Jørundgaard.

Her parents missed Ulvhild deeply—she knew thàt. But she also realized that this was not the only reason they were so silent and somber. They were kind to her, but when they spoke of her betrothed, she could see that they had to force themselves to do so. And they did it to please her and to be kind; they did not do it out of any desire to speak of Erlend themselves. They were not any happier about the husband she had chosen now that they had come to know the man. Erlend was also silent and reserved during the brief time he was at Jørundgaard for the betrothal celebration—and it could not have been any other way, thought Kristin. He knew that her father had only reluctantly given his consent.

Even she and Erlend had hardly exchanged more than a few words alone. And it had been awkward and strange for them to sit together in full view of everyone; they had had little to talk about because they had shared so many secrets. A slight fear began to stir inside her—faint and dim, but always present—that perhaps, in some way, it might be difficult for them when they were finally married, because they had been too close to each other in the beginning and then had been separated for far too long.

But she tried to push this thought aside. Erlend was supposed to stay with them at Jørundgaard during Whitsuntide. He had asked Lavrans and Ragnfrid whether they would have any objections if he came to visit, and Lavrans had hesitated a moment but then replied that he would welcome his son-in-law, Erlend could be assured of that.

During Whitsuntide they would be able to take walks together, and they would talk as they had in the old days; then it would surely go away, this shadow that had come between them during the long separation, when they had each struggled and borne everything alone.

At Easter Simon Andressøn and his wife were at Formo. Kristin saw them in church. Simon's wife was standing quite close to her.

She must be much older than he is, thought Kristin—almost thirty. Fru Halfrid was short and delicate and thin, but she had an unusually lovely face. Even the pale brown color of her hair, which billowed from under her wimple, seemed so gentle, and her eyes were full of gentleness too; they were large and gray with a sprinkling of tiny glints of gold. Every line of her face was fine and pure; but her complexion was a pale gray, and when she opened her mouth, it was apparent that she did not have good teeth. She didn't look strong, and she was also said to be sickly. Kristin had heard that she had already miscarried several times. She wondered how Simon felt about this wife.

The people from Jørundgaard and from Formo had greeted each other across the church hill several times, though they had not spoken. But on the third day Simon came to church without his wife. Then he came over to Lavrans, and they talked together for a while. Kristin heard them mention Ulvhild. Afterward he spoke to Ragnfrid. Ramborg, who was with her mother, said quite loudly, "I remember you. I know who you are."

Simon lifted up the child and swung her around. "It was nice of you not to forget me, Ramborg." Kristin he greeted only from a short distance away. And her parents didn't mention the meeting again.

But Kristin thought a great deal about it. It had been strange to see Simon Darre as a married man. So many things from the past came alive once more: she remembered her own blind and submissive love for Erlend back then. Now it was somehow different. She wondered whether Simon had told his wife how the two of them had parted. But she knew that he wouldn't have done that, "for my father's sake," she thought with derision. She felt so oddly destitute to be still unmarried and living at home with her parents. But they were betrothed; Simon could see that they had forced their will through. Whatever else Erlend might have done, he had remained faithful to *her*, and she had been neither reckless nor frivolous.

One evening in early spring Ragnfrid wanted to send a message south to Old Gunhild, the widow who sewed fur pelts. The evening was so beautiful that Kristin asked if she could go. In the end she was given permission because all the men were busy.

It was after sunset, and a fine white frosty mist rose up toward the golden-green sky. With every hoofbeat Kristin heard the brittle sound of evening ice as it shattered and then dispersed with a rattling sound. But in the twilight, from the thickets along the road, came a jubilant birdsong, soft and full of spring.

Kristin rode briskly down the road without thinking about much of anything, simply feeling how good it was to be outside alone. She rode with her gaze fixed on the new moon, which was about to sink behind the mountain ridge on the other side of the valley. She almost fell off her horse when the animal abruptly swerved to the side and then reared up.

She saw a dark body curled up at the edge of the road. At first she was afraid. The dire fear of meeting someone alone out on the road never left her. But she thought it might be a wanderer who had fallen ill, so when she had regained control of her horse, she turned around and rode back as she called out, "Is anyone there?"

The bundle stirred a bit and a voice said, "I think it must be you, Kristin Lavransdatter."

"Brother Edvin?" she asked softly. She almost thought it was a phantom or some kind of deviltry that was trying to fool her. But she went over to him, and it was the old man after all, but he couldn't get up without help.

"My dear Father, are you out here wandering at this time of year?" she asked in astonishment.

"Praise be to God for sending you this way tonight," said the monk. Kristin noticed that he was shivering all over. "I was on my way north to visit you, but I could go no farther tonight. I almost thought it was God's will that I should lie here and die on the roads where I've roamed and slept all my life. But I would have liked to receive absolution and the last rites. And I wanted to see you again, my daughter."

Kristin helped the monk up onto her horse and then led it by the bridle as she supported him. In between his protests that she was getting her feet wet in the icy slush, he moaned softly in pain.

He told her that he had been at Eyabu since Christmas; some wealthy farmers in the village had promised during the bad year to furnish their church with new adornments. But his work had gone slowly; he had been ill during the winter. There was something wrong with his stomach that made him vomit blood, and he couldn't tolerate food. He didn't think he had long to live, so he was headed home to his cloister; he wanted to die there, among his brothers. But he had set his mind on coming north through the valley one last time, and so he had accompanied the monk from Hamar when he traveled north to become the new resident priest at the pilgrim hostel in Roaldstad. From Fron he had gone on alone.

"I heard that you were betrothed," he said, "to that man. . . . And then I had such a yearning to see you. I felt so anguished that our meeting in the church at the cloister should be our last. It's been weighing so heavy on my heart, Kristin, that you had strayed from the path of peace."

Kristin kissed the monk's hand and said, "I don't understand, Father, what I have done to deserve your willingness to show me such great love."

The monk replied quietly, "I have often thought, Kristin, that if it had been possible for us to meet more often, you might have become my spiritual daughter."

"Do you mean you would have guided me so that I turned my

heart to the convent life?" asked Kristin. After a pause she went on. "Sira Eirik impressed on me that if I couldn't win my father's consent to marry Erlend, then I would have to enter a holy sister-hood and do penance for my sins."

"I have often prayed that you might have a yearning for the convent life," said Brother Edvin, "but not since you told me what you know. I wish that you could have come to God with your wreath, Kristin."

When they reached Jørundgaard, Brother Edvin had to be carried inside and put to bed. They put him in the old winter house, in the hearth room, and made him as comfortable as they could. He was very ill, and Sira Eirik came and tended to him with medica-ments for his body and soul. But the priest said that the old man was suffering from cancer, and that he didn't have long to live. Brother Edvin himself thought that when he had regained some of his strength he would head south again and try to make it back to his cloister. Sira Eirik told the others that he didn't believe this was likely.

Everyone at Jørundgaard felt that great peace and joy had come to them with the monk. People went in and out of the hearth room all day long, and it was never difficult to find someone willing to keep vigil over the sick man at night. They flocked around him, as many as could find the time to sit and listen when Sira Eirik came and read to the dying man from the holy books; and they talked with Brother Edvin about spiritual matters. And even though much of what he said was vague and obscure, as was his manner of speaking, the people seemed to draw strength and comfort for their souls, because everyone could see that Brother Edvin was filled with his love for God.

But the monk also wanted to hear about everything else; he asked for news from the villages and wanted Lavrans to tell him about the bad year. Some people had seized upon evil counsel in that time of adversity and had sought out the sort of help that Christian men must shun. A short way into the mountains west of the valley, there was a place with great white stones that were shaped like the secret parts of human beings, and some men had fallen to sacrificing boars and cats before this monstrosity. Sira

Eirik had then taken several of the most pious and brave of the farmers out there one night, and they had smashed the stones flat. Lavrans had gone along and could testify that they were completely smeared with blood, and there were bones and the like lying all around. Up in Heidal people had apparently made an old woman sit outside on a buried stone and recite ancient incantations on three Thursday nights in a row.

One night Kristin was sitting alone with Brother Edvin.

Around midnight he woke up and seemed to be suffering great pain. Then he asked Kristin to read to him from the book about the miracles of the Virgin Mary, which Sira Eirik had lent to him.

Kristin wasn't used to reading aloud, but she sat down on the step of the bed and put the candle next to her. She placed the book on her knees and read as best she could.

After a while she noticed that the sick man was lying in bed with his teeth clamped tight, and he had clenched his emaciated hands into fists from the pain.

"You're suffering badly, dear Father," said Kristin with dismay.

"It seems that way to me now. But I know it's because God has made me into a child again, and is tossing me up and down.

"I remember a time when I was small—I was four winters old—and I ran away from home and headed into the forest. I got lost and was out there for many days and nights. My mother was with the people who found me, and when she lifted me up into her arms, I remember that she bit me on the back of the neck. I thought it was because she was angry with me, but later I understood otherwise.

"Now I'm longing for home, away from this forest. It is written: 'Forsake all things and follow me.' But there has been far too much here in this world that I didn't have the heart to forsake."

"You, Father?" said Kristin. "I've always heard everyone say that you were a model of pure living and poverty and humility."

The monk chuckled.

"Ah, young child, you probably think there's nothing else that entices in the world save sensual pleasure and wealth and power. I must tell you that these are small things that are found along the side of the road—but I, I have loved the roads themselves. It was not the small things of the world that I loved but the entire world. God in His mercy allowed me to love Sister Poverty and Sister Celibacy even in my youth, and that was why I thought that with these lay sisters I could walk in safety. And so I have wandered and roamed, wishing that I could travel all the roads of the world. And my heart and my thoughts have wandered and roamed too— I fear that I have often gone astray in my thoughts about the darkest of things. But now that's over, little Kristin. Now I want to go back to my home and put aside all my own thoughts and listen to the clear words of the guardian about what I should believe, and think about my sins and about God's mercy."

A little while later he fell asleep. Kristin sat down near the hearth and tended the fire. But toward morning, when she was also about to doze off, Brother Edvin suddenly said to her from the bed, "I'm glad, Kristin, that this matter between Erlend Nikulaussøn and you has come to a good end."

Then Kristin burst into tears.

"We have done so much wrong to come this far. And worst of all is this gnawing at my heart that I have caused my father such great sorrow. He's not happy about this either. And yet he doesn't know . . . if he knew everything, then he would surely withdraw all his affection from me."

"Kristin," said Brother Edvin gently, "don't you understand, child, that this is why you must never tell him, and why you must not cause him any more sorrow? Because he would never demand penance from you. Nothing you do could ever change your father's heart toward you."

A few days later Brother Edvin was feeling so much better that he wanted to head south. Since he had set his heart on this, Lavrans had a kind of stretcher made that was hung between two horses, and in this manner he carried the sick man as far south as Lidstad. There Brother Edvin was given new horses and a new escort, and in this way he was taken as far as Hamar. There he died in the monastery of the Dominican brothers and was buried in their church. Later the barefoot friars demanded that the body be delivered to them, because many people in the villages considered him a holy man and called him Saint Even. The farmers in the outlying districts and valleys as far north as Nidaros prayed to him. And thus there was a long dispute between the two cloisters over his body.

Kristin didn't hear of this until much later. But she grieved deeply when she parted with the monk. It seemed to her that he alone knew her whole life—he had known the foolish child that she had been under her father's care, and he had known of her secret life with Erlend. So he was like a clasp, she thought, which bound everything she had loved to all that now filled her heart. She was now quite cut off from the person she had been—the time when she was a maiden.

CHAPTER 7

AS SHE TESTED the lukewarm brew in the vats, Ragnfrid said, "I think it's cool enough that we can put in the yeast."

Kristin had been sitting inside the brewhouse door, spinning, while she waited for the liquid to cool. She set the spindle on the doorstep, unwrapped the blanket from around the bucket with the dissolved yeast, and measured out a portion.

"Shut the door first," said her mother, "so there won't be any draft. You're acting as if you're asleep, Kristin," she added, annoyed.

Kristin slowly poured the yeast into the brewing vats as Ragnfrid stirred.

Geirhild Drivsdatter invoked the name of Hatt, but it was Odin who came and helped her with the brewing; in return he demanded what was between her and the vat. This was a saga that Lavrans had once told Kristin when she was little.

What was between her and the vat . . . Kristin felt ill and dizzy from the heat and the sweet, spicy steam in the dark, close brewhouse.

Out in the courtyard Ramborg was dancing in a circle with a group of children and singing:

The eagle sits in the highest hall
flexing his golden claw . . .

Kristin followed her mother out to the little entryway, which was filled with empty ale kegs and all kinds of implements. From there a door led out to a strip of ground between the back wall of the brewhouse and the fence surrounding the barley field. A swarm of pigs jostled each other, biting and squealing as they fought over the tepid, discarded mash.

261

Kristin shaded her eyes with her hand from the glaring noonday sun. Her mother glanced at the scuffling pigs and said, "We won't be able to get by with fewer than eighteen reindeer."

"Do you think we'll need so many?" asked her daughter, distracted.

"Yes, we must serve game with the pork each day," replied her mother. "And we'll only have enough fowl and hare to serve the guests in the high loft. You must remember that close to two hundred people will be coming here, with their servants and children, and the poor must be fed as well. And even though you and Erlend will leave on the fifth day, some of the guests will no doubt stay on for the rest of the week—at least.

"Stay here and tend to the ale, Kristin," said Ragnfrid. "I have to go and cook dinner for your father and the haymakers."

Kristin went to get her spinning and then sat down in the back doorway. She tucked the distaff with the wool under her arm, but her hands sank into her lap, holding the spindle.

Beyond the fence the tips of the barley glinted like silver and silk in the sun. Above the rush of the river, she heard now and then the sound of the scythes in the meadows out on the islet; occasionally the iron would strike against stone. Her father and the servants were working hard to put the worst of the mowing season behind them. There was so much to do for her wedding.

The smell of the tepid mash and the rank breath of the pigs . . . she suddenly felt nauseated again. And the noontime heat made her so faint and weak. White-faced, her spine rigid, she sat there waiting for the sensation to pass; she didn't want to be sick again.

She had never felt this way before. It would do no good for her to try to console herself with the thought that it wasn't yet certain—that she might be mistaken. What was between her and the vat . . .

Eighteen reindeer. Close to two hundred wedding guests. People would have something to laugh about then, when they heard that all the commotion was for the sake of a pregnant woman who had to be married off in time.

Oh no! She tossed aside her spinning and leaped to her feet.

With her forehead pressed against the wall of the brewhouse she vomited into the thicket of nettles that grew in abundance there. Brown caterpillars were swarming over the nettles; the sight of them made her feel even sicker.

Kristin rubbed her temples, wet with sweat. Oh no, surely that was enough.

They were going to be married on the second Sunday after Michaelmas, and then their wedding would be celebrated for five days. That was more than two months away. By then her mother and the other women of the village would be able to see it. They were always so wise about such matters; they could always tell when a woman was with child months before Kristin could see how they knew. Poor thing, she has grown so pale. . . . Impatiently Kristin rubbed her hands against her cheeks, for she could feel that they were wan and bloodless.

In the past she had so often thought that this was bound to happen one day. And she had not been terribly afraid of it. But it wouldn't have been the same back then, when they could not and would not be allowed to marry in the proper fashion. It was considered . . . yes, it was thought to be shameful in many ways, and a sin too. But if it was a matter of two young people who *refused* to be forced from each other, that was something everyone would remember, and they would speak of the two with compassion. *She* would not have been ashamed. But when it happened to those who were betrothed, then everyone merely laughed and teased them mercilessly. She realized herself that it was laughable. Here they were brewing ale and making wine, slaughtering and baking and cooking for a wedding that would be talked about far and wide—and she, the bride, felt ill at the mere smell of food and crept behind the outbuildings, in a cold sweat, to throw up.

Erlend. She clenched her teeth in anger. He should have spared her this. She had not been willing. He should have remembered how it had been before, when everything had been uncertain for her, when she had had nothing to hold on to except his love; then she had always, always gladly yielded to his wishes. He should have left her alone this time, when she tried to refuse because she thought it improper for them to steal something in secret after her father had placed their hands together in the sight of all their kins-

men. But he had taken her, partly by force, but with laughter and
with caresses too, so she had been unable to show him that she
was serious in her refusal.

Kristin went inside to tend to the ale, and then came back and
stood leaning over the fence. The grain swayed faintly, glinting in
the light breeze. She couldn't remember ever seeing the crops so
dense and lush as this year. She caught a glimpse of the river
in the distance, and she heard her father's voice shouting; she
couldn't distinguish his words, but the workers out on the islet
were laughing.

What if she went to her father and told him? It would be better
to forgo all this trouble, to marry her to Erlend quietly, without a
church wedding and grand feast—now that it was a matter of her
acquiring a wife's name before it became apparent to everyone that
she was already carrying Erlend's child.

Erlend would be ridiculed too, just as much as she would be,
or more. He was not a young boy, after all. But he was the one
who wanted this wedding, he wanted to see her as a bride wearing
silk and velvet and a high golden crown; he wanted *that*, but he
also wanted to possess her during all those sweet, secret hours. She
had acquiesced to everything. She would continue to do as he
wanted in this matter too.

And in the end, no doubt, he would realize that no one could
have both. He who had talked of the great Christmas celebration
he would hold at Husaby during the first year she was his wife on
the manor—then he would show all his kinsmen and friends and
the people of the villages far and wide what a beautiful wife he
had won. Kristin smiled spitefully. Christmas this year would
hardly be a fitting occasion for that.

It would happen around Saint Gregor's Day. Her thoughts
seemed to swirl in her head whenever she told herself that sometime close to Saint Gregor's Day she would give birth to a child.
She was a little frightened by it too; she remembered her mother's
shrill screams, which had rung out over the farm for two days
when Ulvhild had come into the world. Over at Ulvsvold two
young women had died, one after the other, in childbirth; and
Sigurd of Loptsgaard's first two wives had died too. And her own
grandmother, for whom she was named.

But fear was not what she felt most. These past years, when she realized again that she was still not pregnant, she had thought that perhaps this was to be their punishment, hers and Erlend's—that she would continue to be barren. They would wait and wait in vain for what they had feared before; they would hope so futilely, just as they had feared so needlessly. Until at last they would realize that one day they would be carried out from his ancestral estate and vanish. His brother was a priest, after all, and the children that Erlend already had could never inherit from him. Munan the Stump and his sons would come in and take their place, and Erlend would be erased from the lineage.

She pressed her hand hard against her womb. It was there—between her and the fence, between her and the vat. Between her and the whole world—Erlend's legitimate son. She had tried everything she had heard Fru Aashild once speak of, with blood from her right and left arm. She was carrying a son, whatever fate he might bring her. She remembered her brothers who had died and her parents' sorrowful faces whenever they mentioned them; she remembered all those times when she had seen them in despair over Ulvhild, and the night she died. And she thought about all the sorrow she herself had caused them, and about her father's care-worn face. And yet this was not the end of the grief she would bring to her father and mother.

And yet, and yet. Kristin rested her head on her arm lying along the fence; the other hand she kept pressed against her womb. Even if this brought her new sorrows, even if it caused her own death, she would still rather die giving Erlend a son than have them both die someday, with the buildings standing empty and with the grain in their fields swaying for strangers.

Someone came into the front room. The ale! thought Kristin. I should have looked at it long ago. She straightened up—and then Erlend stooped as he came out of the doorway and stepped forward into the sunlight, beaming with joy.

"So this is where you are," he said. "And you don't even take a step to meet me?" he asked. He came over and embraced her.

"Beloved, have you come to visit?" she asked, astonished.

He must have just dismounted from his horse; he still had his cape over his shoulders and his sword at his side. He was un-

shaven, filthy, and covered with dust. He was wearing a red surcoat, which draped from the neckline and was slit up the sides
almost to his arms. As they went through the brewhouse and across
the courtyard, his clothes fluttered around him so that his thighs
were visible clear up to his waist. It was odd; she had never noticed
before that he walked slightly crooked. Before she had only seen
that he had long, slender legs and narrow ankles and small, well-
shaped feet.

Erlend had brought a full escort along with him: five men and
four spare horses. He told Ragnfrid that he had come to get Kristin's household goods. Wouldn't it be a comfort for her to find her
things at Husaby when she arrived? And since the wedding was to
take place so late in the fall, it might be more difficult to transport
everything then. And wouldn't it be more likely to suffer damage
from sea water on the ship? The abbot at Nidarholm had offered
to send everything now with the Laurentius cloister's ship; they
expected to set sail from Veøy around Assumption Day. That was
why he had come to convey her things through Raumsdal to the
headland.

He sat in the doorway to the cookhouse and drank ale and
talked while Ragnfrid and Kristin plucked the wild ducks that Lavrans had brought home the day before. The mother and daughter
were alone at home; the women servants were all out in the meadows, raking. He looked so happy; he was so pleased with himself
for coming on such a sensible errand.

Her mother left, and Kristin tended to the birds on the spit.
Through the open door she caught a glimpse of Erlend's men lying
in the shade across the courtyard, passing the basin of ale among
them. He sat on the stoop, chatting and laughing. The sun shone
brightly on his bare, soot-black hair; she noticed that there were
several gray streaks in it. Well, he would soon be thirty-two, after
all, but he acted like a brash young man. She knew that she
wouldn't tell him about her trouble; there would be time enough
for that when he realized it himself. A good-humored tenderness
coursed through her heart, over the hard little anger that lay at the
bottom, like a glittering river over stones.

She loved him more than anything; it filled her heart, even
though she always saw and remembered everything else. How out

of place this courtier seemed amidst the busy farm work, wearing his elegant red surcoat, silver spurs on his feet, and a belt studded with gold. She also noticed that her father didn't come up to the farm, even though her mother had sent Ramborg down to the river with word of the guest who had arrived.

Erlend came over to Kristin and put his hands on her shoulders. "Can you believe it?" he said, his face radiant. "Doesn't it seem strange to you—that all these preparations are being made for *our* wedding?"

Kristin gave him a kiss and pushed him aside. She poured fat over the birds and told him not to get in her way. No, she wouldn't tell him.

Lavrans didn't come up to the farm until the haymakers did, around suppertime. He wasn't dressed much differently from the workmen, in an undyed, knee-length homespun tunic and ankle-length leggings of the same fabric. He was barefoot and carried his scythe over his shoulder. The only thing that distinguished his attire from that of the servants was a shoulder collar of leather for the hawk that was perched on his left shoulder. He was holding Ramborg's hand.

Lavrans greeted his son-in-law heartily enough and asked his forgiveness for not coming earlier. They had to push as hard as they could to get the farm work done because he had to make a journey into town between the haying season and the harvest. But when Erlend presented the reason for his visit at the supper table, Lavrans became quite cross.

It was impossible for him to do without any of his wagons or horses right now. Erlend replied that he had brought along four extra horses himself. Lavrans thought there would be at least three cartloads. Besides, the maiden would have to keep all her clothing at Jørundgaard. And the bed linen that Kristin would be taking with her would be needed at the farm during the wedding for all the guests they would have to house.

"Never mind," said Erlend. Surely they would find a way to transport everything in the fall. But he had been so pleased, and he thought it sounded so sensible, when the abbot had suggested that Kristin's things might travel with the monastery's ship. The

abbot had reminded him of their kinship. "That's something
they're all remembering now," said Erlend with a smile. His
father-in-law's disapproval did not seem to affect him in the least.

And so it was decided that Erlend should borrow a wagon and
take a cartload of those things that Kristin would need most when
she arrived at her new home.

The next day they were busy with the packing. Ragnfrid thought
that both the large and the small looms could be sent along now;
she wouldn't have time to weave anything else before the wedding.
The mother and daughter cut off the weaving that was on the
loom. It was an undyed homespun fabric, but of the finest and
softest wool, with tufts of black wool woven in to form a pattern.
Kristin and her mother rolled up the cloth and placed it in a leather
bag. Kristin thought it would be good for swaddling clothes, and
it would be pretty with red or blue ribbons around it.

The sewing chest that Arne had once made for her could also
go along. Kristin took from her box all the things that Erlend had
given her over time. She showed her mother the blue velvet cape
with the red pattern that she was going to wear in the bridal procession. Her mother turned it this way and that, feeling the fabric
and the fur lining.

"This is a most costly cloak," said Ragnfrid. "When did Erlend
give this to you?"

"He gave it to me while I was at Nonneseter," her daughter
told her.

Kristin's bridal chest, which her mother had been adding to ever
since she was little, was repacked. It was carved in panels, and on
each there was a leaping deer or a bird sitting amidst the foliage.
Ragnfrid placed Kristin's bridal gown in one of her own chests. It
was not quite done; they had been sewing on it all winter long. It
was made of scarlet silk and cut in such a fashion that it would fit
snugly to her body. Kristin thought that now it would be much
too tight across her breasts.

Toward evening the load was all packed and tied under the wagon's cover. Erlend would leave early the next morning.

He stood with Kristin, leaning over the farm gate, looking
north, where the bluish-black smudge of a storm cloud filled the

valley. Thunder rumbled from the mountains, but to the south the meadows and the river lay in dazzling yellow sunlight.

"Do you remember the storm on that day in the forest near Gerdarud?" he asked softly, playing with her fingers.

Kristin nodded and tried to smile. The air was so heavy and sultry; her head was aching and she was sweating with every breath she took.

Lavrans came over to them at the gate and talked about the weather. It seldom did any harm down here in the village, but God only knew whether it would bring trouble to the cattle and horses up in the mountains.

It was as black as night up behind the church on the hill. A flash of lightning revealed a group of horses, crowding together restlessly, on the meadow outside the church gate. Lavrans didn't think they belonged there in the valley—the horses were more likely from Dovre and had been wandering in the mountains up beneath Jetta. He shouted over the thunder that he had a mind to go up and see to them, to find out whether there were any of his among them.

A terrible bolt of lightning ripped through the darkness up there. Thunder crashed and roared so they could hear nothing else. The horses raced across the grass beneath the ridge. All three of them crossed themselves.

Then more lightning flashed; the sky seemed about to split in half, and a tremendous snow-white bolt of lightning hurtled down toward them. All three were thrown against each other; they stood there with their eyes closed, blinded, and noticed a smell like scorched stone—and then the crash of thunder exploded in their ears.

"Saint Olav, help us," murmured Lavrans.

"Look at the birch, look at the birch!" cried Erlend. The huge birch out in the field seemed to wobble, and then a heavy limb broke off and dropped to the ground, leaving a long gash in the trunk.

"I think it's burning. Jesus Christus! The church roof is on fire!" shouted Lavrans.

They stood there and stared. No . . . yes, it was! Red flames were flickering out of the shingles beneath the ridge turret.

Both men set off running, back across the farmyard. Lavrans

tore open all the doors to the buildings, yelling to those inside. Everyone came rushing out.

"Bring axes, bring axes—the felling axes," he shouted. "And the pickaxes!" He raced over to the stables. A moment later he reemerged, leading Guldsvein by his mane. He leaped up onto the unsaddled horse and tore off toward the north. He had the big broadaxe in his hand. Erlend rode right behind him, and all the other men followed. Some were on horseback, but others couldn't control the frightened animals and gave up and set off running. Behind them came Ragnfrid and the women of the farm with basins and buckets.

No one seemed to notice the storm any longer. In the flash of the lightning they saw people come streaming from the buildings farther down in the village. Sira Eirik was already running up the hill, followed by his servants. Horse hooves thundered across the bridge below, and several farm hands raced past. They all turned their pale, terrified faces toward the burning church.

A light wind was blowing from the southeast. The fire was firmly entrenched in the north wall; on the west side the entrance was already blocked. But it had not yet seized the south side or the apse.

Kristin and the women from Jørundgaard entered the churchyard south of the church, at a place where the gate had collapsed.

The tremendous red blaze lit up the grove north of the church and the area where posts had been erected for tying up the horses. No one could approach the spot because of the heat. Only the cross stood there, bathed in the glow of the flames. It looked as if it were alive and moving.

Through the roaring and seething of the fire they could hear the crash of axes against the staves of the south wall. There were men on the gallery, slashing and chopping, while others tried to tear down the gallery itself. Someone shouted to the women from Jørundgaard that Lavrans and a few other men had followed Sira Eirik into the church. They had to break an opening in the wall— little tongues of fire were playing here and there among the shingles on the roof. If the wind changed or died down altogether, the flames would engulf the whole church.

Any thought of extinguishing the blaze was futile; there was no

time to form a chain down to the river, but at Ragnfrid's command, the women took up positions and passed water from the
small creek running along the road to the west; at least there was
a little water to throw on the south wall and on the men who were
toiling there. Many of the women were sobbing as they worked,
out of fear and anguish for those who had gone inside the burning
building, and out of sorrow for their church.

Kristin stood at the very front of the line of women, throwing
the water from the buckets. She stared breathlessly at the church,
where they had both gone inside, her father and Erlend.

The posts of the gallery had been torn down and lay in a heap
of wood amid pieces of shingle from the gallery's roof. The men
were chopping at the stave wall with all their might; a whole group
had lifted up a timber and was using it as a battering ram.

Erlend and one of his men came out of the small south door of
the choir; they were carrying between them the large chest from
the sacristy, the chest that Eirik usually sat on when he heard confession. Erlend and the servant tipped the chest out into the
churchyard.

Kristin didn't hear what he shouted; he ran back, up onto the
gallery again. He was as lithe as a cat as he dashed along. He had
thrown off his outer garments and was dressed only in his shirt,
pants, and hose.

The others took up his cry—the sacristy and choir were burning.
No one could go from the nave up to the south door anymore; the
fire was now blocking both exits. A couple of staves in the wall
had been splintered, and Erlend had picked up a fire axe and was
slashing and hacking at the wreckage of the staves. They had
smashed a hole in the side of the church, while other people were
shouting for them to watch out—the roof might collapse and bury
them all inside the church. The shingled roof was now burning
briskly on this side too, and the heat was becoming unbearable.

Erlend leaped through the hole and helped to bring Sira Eirik
out. The priest had his robes full of holy vessels from the altars.

A young boy followed with his hand over his face and the tall
processional cross held out in front of him. Lavrans came next. He
had closed his eyes against the smoke, staggering under the heavy
crucifix he held in his arms; it was much taller than he was.

People ran forward and helped them move down to the churchyard. Sira Eirik stumbled, fell to his knees, and the altar vessels
rolled across the slope. The silver dove opened, and the Host fell
out. The priest picked it up, brushed it off, and kissed it as he
sobbed loudly. He kissed the gilded man's head which had stood
above the altar with a scrap of Saint Olav's hair and nails inside.

Lavrans Bjørgulfsøn was still standing there, holding the crucifix. His arm lay across the arms of the cross, and he was leaning
his head on the shoulder of Christ. It looked as if the Savior were
bending his beautiful, sad face toward the man to console him.

The roof had begun to collapse bit by bit on the north side of
the church. A blazing roof beam shot out and struck the great bell
in the low tower near the churchyard gate. The bell rang with a
deep, mournful tone, which faded into a long moan, drowned out
by the roar of the fire.

No one had paid any attention to the weather during all the
tumult. The whole event had not taken much time, but no one was
aware of that either. Now the thunder and lightning were far away,
to the south of the valley. The rain, which had been falling for a
while, was now coming down harder, and the wind had ceased.

But suddenly it was as if a sail of flames had been hoisted up
from the foundation. In a flash, and with a shriek, the fire engulfed
the church from one end to the other.

Everyone dashed away from the consuming heat. Erlend was
suddenly at Kristin's side and urging her down the hill. His body
reeked with the stench of the fire; she pulled away a handful of
singed hair when she stroked his head and face.

They couldn't hear each other's voices above the roaring of the
flames. But she saw that his eyebrows had been scorched right off,
he had burns on his face, and his shirt was burned in places too.
He laughed as he pulled her along after the others.

Everyone followed behind the weeping old priest and Lavrans
Bjørgulfsøn, carrying the crucifix.

At the edge of the churchyard, Lavrans leaned the cross against
a tree, and then sank down onto the wreckage of the gate. Sira
Eirik was already sitting there; he stretched out his arms toward
the burning church.

"Farewell, farewell, Olav's church. God bless you, my Olav's church. God bless you for every hour I have spent inside you, singing and saying the mass. Olav's church, good night, good night."

Everyone from the parish wept loudly along with him. The rain was pouring down on the people, huddled together, but no one thought of leaving. It didn't look as if the rain were damping the heat in the charred timbers; fiery pieces of wood and smoldering shingles were flying everywhere. A moment later the ridge turret fell into the blaze with a shower of sparks rising up behind it.

Lavrans sat with one hand covering his face; his other arm lay across his lap, and Kristin saw that his sleeve was bloody from the shoulder all the way down. Blood was running along his fingers. She went over and touched his arm.

"I don't think it's serious. Something fell on my shoulder," he said, looking up. He was so pale that even his lips were white. "Ulvhild," he whispered with anguish as he gazed at the inferno.

Sira Eirik heard him and placed a hand on his shoulder.

"It will not wake your child, Lavrans. She will sleep just as soundly with the fire burning over her resting place," he said. "She has not lost the home of her soul, as the rest of us have this evening."

Kristin hid her face against Erlend's chest. She stood there, feeling his arms around her. Then she heard her father ask for his wife.

Someone said that out of terror a woman had started having labor pains; they had carried her down to the parsonage, and Ragnfrid had gone along.

Kristin was suddenly reminded of what she had completely forgotten ever since they realized that the church was on fire: she shouldn't have looked at it. There was a man south of the village who had a red splotch covering half his face. They said he was born that way because his mother had looked at a fire while she was carrying him. Dear Holy Virgin Mary, she prayed in silence, don't let my unborn child be harmed by this.

The next day a village *ting* was to be convened on the church hillside. The people would decide on how to rebuild the church.

Kristin sought out Sira Eirik up at Romundgaard before he left for the *ting*. She asked the priest whether he thought she should take this as an omen. Perhaps it was God's will that she should tell her father she was unworthy to stand beneath the bridal crown, and that it would be more fitting for her to be married to Erlend Nikulaussøn without a wedding feast.

But Sira Eirik flew into a rage, his eyes flashing with fury.

"Do you think God cares so much about the way you sluts surrender and throw yourselves away that He would burn down a beautiful and honorable church for your sake? Rid yourself of your pride and do not cause your mother and Lavrans a sorrow from which they would scarcely recover. If you do not wear the crown with honor on your wedding day, it will be bad enough for you; but you and Erlend are in even greater need of this sacrament as you are joined together. Everyone has his sins to answer for; no doubt that is why this misfortune has been brought upon us all. Try to better your life, and help us to rebuild this church, both you and Erlend."

Kristin thought to herself that she had not yet told him of the latest thing that had befallen her—but she decided to let it be.

She went to the *ting* with the men. Lavrans attended with his arm in a sling, and Erlend had numerous burns on his face. He looked so ghastly, but he only laughed. None of the wounds was serious, and he said that he hoped they wouldn't disfigure him on his wedding day. He stood up after Lavrans and promised to give to the church four marks of silver, and to the village, on behalf of his betrothed and with Lavrans's consent, a section of Kristin's property worth one mark in land tax.

Erlend had to stay at Jørundgaard for a week because of his wounds. Kristin saw that Lavrans seemed to like his son-in-law better after the night of the fire; the men now seemed to be quite good friends. Then she thought that perhaps her father might be so pleased with Erlend Nikulaussøn that he would be more forbearing and not take it as hard as she had feared when one day he realized that they had sinned against him.

CHAPTER 8

THAT YEAR was an unusually good one in all the valleys of the north. The hay was abundant, and it was all safely harvested. Everyone returned home from the mountain pastures with fattened livestock and great quantities of butter and cheese—and they had been mercifully free of predators that year. The grain stood so high that few people could remember ever seeing it look so fine. The crops ripened well and were bounteous, and the weather was the best it could be. Between Saint Bartholomew's Day and the Feast of the Birth of Mary, during the time when frosty nights were most likely, it rained a little and the weather was warm and overcast, but after that the harvest month proceeded with sunshine and wind and mild, hazy nights. By the week after Michaelmas, most of the grain had been brought in throughout the valley.

At Jørundgaard they were toiling and preparing for the great wedding. For the past two months Kristin had been so busy from morning to night, every single day, that she had had little time to worry about anything but her work. She could see that her breasts had grown heavier, and that her small pink nipples had turned brown and were as tender as wounds every morning when she had to get out of bed in the cold. But the pain passed as soon as she warmed up from her work, and then she thought only of what she had to do before nightfall. Sometimes when she straightened up to stretch out her back and paused to rest for a moment, she would notice that what she was carrying in her womb was growing heavy. But she was still just as slender and trim in appearance. She smoothed her hands over her long, fine hips. No, she didn't want to worry about it now. At times she would suddenly think, with a prickling sense of longing, that in a month or two she would be able to feel life inside her. By that time she would be at Husaby.

Maybe Erlend would be pleased. She closed her eyes and bit down on her betrothal ring—she saw Erlend's face, pale with emotion, when he stood up in the high loft and spoke the betrothal vows in a loud, clear voice:

"As God is my witness, along with these men who stand before me, I, Erlend Nikulaussøn, promise myself to Kristin Lavransdatter in accordance with the laws of God and men, on such conditions as have been presented to these witnesses who stand here with us. That I shall possess you as my wife, and you shall possess me as your husband as long as we both shall live, that we shall live together in matrimony with all such communion as God's laws and the laws of the land acknowledge."

She was running errands across the courtyard, going from building to building, and she stopped for a moment. The mountain ash was full of berries this year; it would be a snowy winter. And the sun was shining over the pale fields, where the sheaves of grain stood piled on poles. If only the weather would hold until the wedding.

Lavrans held firm to his intention that his daughter should be married in a church. It was therefore decided that this would take place in the chapel at Sundbu. On Saturday the bridal procession would ride over the mountains to Vaage. They would stay the night at Sundbu and the neighboring farms, and then ride back on Sunday after the wedding mass. On the same evening, after vespers, when the Sabbath was over, the wedding would be celebrated and Lavrans would give his daughter away to Erlend. And after midnight the bride and groom would be escorted to bed.[1]

On Friday, in the afternoon, Kristin was standing on the gallery of the high loft, watching the travelers who came riding from the north, past the burned church on the hill. It was Erlend with all his groomsmen. She strained to distinguish him from the others. They were not allowed to see each other; no man could see her until she was led out in the morning, wearing her bridal clothes.

At the place where the road turned toward Jørundgaard, several women pulled away from the group. The men continued on toward Laugarbru, where they would spend the night.

Kristin went downstairs to welcome the guests. She felt so tired after her bath, and her scalp ached terribly; her mother had rinsed her hair in a strong lye solution to give it a bright sheen for the next day.

Fru Aashild Gautesdatter slipped down from her saddle into Lavrans's arms. How lissome and young she keeps herself, thought Kristin. Her daughter-in-law Katrin, Sir Munan's wife, almost looked older than she did; she was tall and stout, her eyes and skin colorless. It's strange, thought Kristin, that she's ugly and he's unfaithful, and yet people say that they get on well together. Two of Sir Baard Petersøn's daughters had also come, one of them married, the other not. They were neither ugly nor beautiful; they looked trustworthy and kind, but seemed quite reserved with strangers. Lavrans thanked them courteously for their willingness to honor this wedding and for making the long journey so late in the fall.

"Erlend was raised by our father when he was a boy," said the older sister, and she stepped forward to greet Kristin.

Then two young men came trotting briskly into the courtyard. They leaped from their horses and ran laughing toward Kristin, who dashed into the house and hid. They were Trond Gjesling's young sons, handsome and promising boys. They brought with them the bridal crown from Sundbu in a chest. Trond and his wife wouldn't come to Jørundgaard until Sunday after the mass.

Kristin had fled to the hearth room, and Fru Aashild had followed. She placed her hands on Kristin's shoulders and pulled her face down to her own for a kiss.

"I'm glad that I shall see this day," said Fru Aashild.

She noticed as she held Kristin's hands how gaunt they had become. She saw that the bride had also grown thin, but her bosom was full. All the lines of her face had become leaner and more delicate than before; in the shadow of her thick, damp hair her temples seemed slightly hollowed. Her cheeks were no longer round, and her fresh complexion had faded. But Kristin's eyes had grown much larger and darker.

Fru Aashild kissed her again.

"I see you've had much to struggle with, Kristin," she said. "I'll

give you something to drink tonight so you'll be rested and fresh
in the morning."

Kristin's lips began to quiver.

"Hush," said Fru Aashild, patting her hand. "I'm looking forward to dressing you in your finery—no one will ever see a lovelier
bride than you shall be tomorrow."

Lavrans rode over to Laugarbru to dine with his guests who were
staying there.

The men could not praise the food enough; a better Friday supper could not be had even in the richest cloister. There was rye-
flour porridge, boiled beans, and white bread. And the fish that
was served was trout, both salted and fresh, and long strips of
dried halibut.

Gradually, as they helped themselves to the ale, the men became
more and more boisterous and their teasing of the bridegroom became more and more vulgar. All of Erlend's groomsmen were
much younger than he was; his own peers and friends had all become married men long ago. Now the men joked about the fact
that he was so old and would lie in the bridal bed for the first
time. Some of Erlend's older kinsmen, who were still rather sober,
were afraid that with each new word uttered the talk might shift
to subjects that would be better left untouched. Sir Baard of Hestnæs kept an eye on Lavrans. He was drinking heavily, but it didn't
look as if the ale was making him any happier as he sat there in
the high seat; his face grew more and more tense as his gaze grew
stonier. But Erlend, who was sitting to the right of his father-in-
law, parried the teasing merrily and laughed a good deal; his face
was red and his eyes sparkled.

Suddenly Lavrans bellowed, "That wagon, son-in-law—while I
think of it, what did you do with the wagon that you borrowed
from me this past summer?"

"Wagon?" said Erlend.

"Don't you remember that you borrowed a wagon from me last
summer? God knows it was a good wagon. I'll probably never see
a better one, because I was here myself when it was built on this
farm. You promised and you swore, as I can testify before God.

And my house servants can verify that you promised you would bring it back to me, but you haven't kept your word."

Some of the guests shouted that this was nothing to talk about right now, but Lavrans pounded on the table and swore that he would find out what Erlend had done with his wagon.

"Oh, it's probably still at the farm on the headland, where we took the boat out to Veøy," said Erlend indifferently. "I didn't think it was so important. You see, Father-in-law, it was a long and arduous journey with the cartload through the valleys, so by the time we reached the fjord, none of my men had a mind to travel the whole way back with the wagon and then over the mountains north to Nidaros. So I thought it could wait for the time being. . . ."

"No, may the Devil seize me right here where I'm sitting if I've ever heard the likes of this," Lavrans interrupted him. "What kind of people do you employ in your household? Is it you or your men who decide where they will or will not go?"

Erlend shrugged his shoulders.

"It's true that many things have not been as they should be in my home. The wagon will be sent back south to you when Kristin and I journey that way. My dear Father-in-law," he said with a smile, putting out his hand, "you must know that now everything will be different, and I will be too, now that Kristin will be coming home as my wife. The matter of the wagon was unfortunate. But I promise you, this will be the last time you shall have reason to complain about me."

"Dear Lavrans," said Baard Petersøn, "reconcile yourself with him over this paltry matter. . . ."

"A paltry matter or a great one . . ." began Lavrans. But then he stopped himself and shook hands with Erlend.

Soon afterward he left, and the guests at Laugarbru went to find their beds for the night.

On Saturday before noon the women and maidens were busy in the old loft. Some were making up the bridal bed, while others were helping the bride to finish dressing.

Ragnfrid had chosen this building for the bridal house because it was the smallest of the lofts—they could house many more guests in the new loft over the storeroom—and it was the bedchamber they had used themselves in the summertime, when Kristin was small, before Lavrans had built the high loft house, where they now lived both summer and winter. But the old storehouse was undoubtedly also the loveliest building on the farm, ever since Lavrans had had it rebuilt; it had been in a state of disrepair when they moved to Jørundgaard. It was now decorated with the most beautiful carvings both inside and out, and the loft was not large, so it was easier to adorn it with tapestries and weavings and pelts.

The bridal bed had been made ready with silk-covered pillows, and lovely blankets had been hung all around as draperies; over the furs and woolen blankets had been spread an embroidered silk coverlet. Ragnfrid and several women were hanging tapestries up on the timbered walls and placing cushions on the benches.

Kristin was sitting in an armchair that had been carried up to the loft. She was wearing her scarlet bridal gown. Large brooches held it together at her breast and closed the yellow silk shift at the neck; golden armbands gleamed on the yellow silk sleeves. A gilded silver belt had been wrapped three times around her waist, and around her neck and on her bosom lay necklace upon necklace— and on top of them all lay her father's old gold chain with the large reliquary cross. Her hands, which lay in her lap, were heavy with rings.

Fru Aashild was standing behind her chair, brushing out Kristin's thick, golden-brown hair.

"Tomorrow you will wear it loose for the last time," she said with a smile, winding around Kristin's head the red and green silk cords that would support the crown. Then the women gathered around the bride.

Ragnfrid and Gyrid of Skog brought over from the table the great bridal crown of the Gjesling family. It was completely gilded; the tips alternated between crosses and cloverleaves, and the circlet was set with rock crystals.

They pressed it down onto the bride's head. Ragnfrid was pale, and her hands shook as she did this.

Kristin slowly rose to her feet. Jesus, how heavy it was to bear

all that silver and gold. Then Fru Aashild took her by the hand
and led her forward to a large water basin, while the bridesmaids
threw open the door to let in the sun and brighten up the loft.

"Look at yourself now, Kristin," said Fru Aashild, and Kristin
bent over the basin. She saw her own face rise up, white, from the
water; it came so close that she could see the golden crown above.
So many light and dark shadows played all around her reflec-
tion—there was something she was just about to remember—and
suddenly she felt as if she would faint away. She gripped the edge
of the basin. Then Fru Aashild placed her hand on top of hers and
dug in her nails so hard that Kristin came to her senses.

The sound of *lur* horns² came from the bridge. People shouted
from the courtyard that now the bridegroom had arrived with his
entourage. The women led Kristin out onto the gallery.

The courtyard was swarming with horses, magnificently bridled,
and people in festive dress; everything glittered and gleamed in the
sun. Kristin stared past everything, out toward the valley. Her village lay bright and still beneath a thin, hazy-blue mist, and out of
the mist towered the mountains, gray with scree and black with
forests, and the sun poured its light down into the basin of the
valley from a cloudless sky.

She hadn't noticed it before, but all the leaves had fallen from
the trees, and the groves shone silver-gray and naked. Only the
alder thicket along the river still had a little faded green in the
crowns of the trees, and a few birches held on to some pale yellow
leaves at the very tips of their branches. But the trees were almost
bare, except the mountain ash, which was still shining with
brownish-red foliage surrounding the blood-red berries. In the still,
warm day the acrid smell of autumn rose up from the ash-colored
blanket of fallen leaves spread all around.

If not for the mountain ash trees, it might have been springtime—except for the silence, because it was autumn-quiet, so quiet.
Every time the *lur* horns ceased, no sound was heard from the
village but the clinking of bells from the fallow and harvested fields
where the cattle were grazing.

The river was small and low, and it flowed so quietly; it was
nothing more than tiny currents trickling between the sandbars and
the heavy shoals of white stones worn smooth. No streams rushed

down the slopes; it had been such a dry autumn. There were glints of moisture all over the fields, but it was only the dampness that always seeped up from the earth in the fall, no matter how hot the day or how clear the sky.

The throng of people down in the courtyard parted to make way for the bridegroom's entourage. The young groomsmen rode forward. There was a ripple of excitement among the women on the gallery.

Fru Aashild was standing next to the bride.

"Be strong now, Kristin," she said. "It won't be long before you are safely under the wimple of a married woman."

Kristin nodded helplessly. She could feel how terribly pale her face was.

"I'm much too pale a bride," she murmured.

"You are the loveliest bride," replied Aashild. "And there's Erlend—it would be hard to find a more handsome pair than the two of you."

Erlend rode forward beneath the gallery. He leaped from his horse, agile and unhampered by the heavy drapery of his clothing. Kristin thought he was so handsome that her whole body ached.

He was dressed in dark attire: a silk surcoat, pale brown interwoven with a black-and-white pattern, ankle-length and slit at the sides. Around his waist he wore a gold-studded belt and on his left hip a sword with gold on the hilt and scabbard. Over his shoulders hung a heavy, dark-blue velvet cape, and on his black hair he wore a black French silk cap which was shirred like wings at the sides and ended in two long streamers, one of which was draped across his chest from his left shoulder and then thrown back over the other.

Erlend greeted his bride, went over to her horse, and stood there with his hand on the saddlebow as Lavrans climbed the stairs. Kristin felt so odd and dizzy faced with all this splendor; her father seemed a stranger in the formal green velvet surcoat that reached to his ankles. But her mother's face was ashen white beneath the wimple she wore with her red silk dress. Ragnfrid came over and placed the cloak around her daughter.

Then Lavrans took the bride's hand and led her down to Erlend, who lifted her up onto her horse and then mounted his own. They sat there, side by side, in front of the bridal loft as the procession began to pass through the farm gates: first the priests, Sira Eirik and Sira Tormod from Ulvsvold, and a Brother of the Cross from Hamar who was a friend of Lavrans. Next came the groomsmen' and the maidens, two by two. And then it was time for Erlend and Kristin to ride forward. After them followed the bride's parents, kinsmen, friends, and guests in long lines, riding between the fences out to the village road. A long stretch of the road was strewn with clusters of mountain ash berries, spruce boughs, and the last white chamomile blossoms of the autumn. People stood along the road as the procession passed, greeting it with cheers.

On Sunday just after sundown the mounted procession returned to Jørundgaard. Through the first patches of twilight the bonfires shone red from the courtyard of the bridal farm. Musicians and fiddlers sang and played their drums and fiddles as the group rode toward the warm red glow.

Kristin was about to collapse when Erlend lifted her down from her horse in front of the gallery to the high loft.

"I was so cold crossing the mountain," she whispered. "I'm so tired." She stood still for a moment; when she climbed the stairway to the loft, she swayed on every step.

Up in the high loft the frozen wedding guests soon had the warmth restored to their bodies. It was hot from all the candles burning in the room, steaming hot food was served, and wine and mead and strong ale were passed around. The din of voices and the sounds of people eating droned in Kristin's ears.

She sat there, unable to get warm. Her cheeks began to burn after a while, but her feet refused to thaw out and shivers of cold ran down her spine. All the heavy gold forced her to lean forward as she sat in the high seat at Erlend's side.

Every time the bridegroom drank a toast to her, she had to look at the red blotches and patches that were so evident on his face now that he was warming up after the ride in the cold air. They were the marks of the burns from that summer.

A terrible fear had come over her the evening before, while they were at dinner at Sundbu, when she felt the vacant stare of Bjørn Gunnarsøn on her and Erlend—eyes that did not blink and did not waver. They had dressed Herr Bjørn in knight's clothing; he looked like a dead man who had been conjured back to life.

That night she shared a bed with Fru Aashild, who was the bridegroom's closest kinswoman.

"What's the matter with you, Kristin?" asked Fru Aashild a little impatiently. "You must be strong now and not so despondent."

"I'm thinking about all the people we have hurt so that we could live to see this day," said Kristin, shivering.

"It wasn't easy for you two either," said Fru Aashild. "Not for Erlend. And I imagine it's been even harder for you."

"I'm thinking about those helpless children of his," said the bride in the same tone as before. "I wonder whether they know that their father is celebrating his wedding today. . . ."

"Think about your own child," said Fru Aashild. "Be glad that you're celebrating your wedding with the one who is the father."

Kristin lay still for a while, helplessly dizzy. It was so pleasant to hear it mentioned—what had occupied her mind every single day for three months or more, though she hadn't been able to breathe a word about it to a living soul. But this helped her for only a moment.

"I'm thinking about the woman who had to pay with her life because she loved Erlend," she whispered, trembling.

"You may have to pay with your own life before you're half a year older," said Fru Aashild harshly. "Be happy while you can.

"What should I say to you, Kristin?" the old woman continued, in despair. "Have you lost all your courage? The time will come soon enough when the two of you will have to pay for everything that you've taken—have no fear of that."

But Kristin felt as if one landslide after another were ravaging her soul; everything was being torn down that she had built up since that terrifying day at Haugen. During those first days she had simply thought, wildly and blindly, that she had to hold out, she had to hold out one day at a time. And she *had* held out until things became easier—quite easy, in the end, when she had cast off all thoughts except one: that now their wedding would take place at last, Erlend's wedding at last.

She and Erlend knelt together during the wedding mass, but it was all like a hallucination: the candles, the paintings, the shining vessels, the priests dressed in linen albs and long chasubles. All those people who had known her in the past seemed like dream images as they stood there filling the church in their unfamiliar festive garb. But Herr Bjørn was leaning against a pillar and looking at them with his dead eyes, and she thought that the other dead one must have come back with him, in his arms.

She tried to look up at the painting of Saint Olav—he stood there, pink and white and handsome, leaning on his axe, treading his own sinful human form underfoot—but Herr Bjørn drew her eyes. And next to him she saw Eline Ormsdatter's dead countenance; she was looking at them with indifference. They had trampled over her in order to get here, and she did not begrudge them that.

She had risen up and cast off all the stones that Kristin had striven so hard to place over the dead. Erlend's squandered youth, his honor and well-being, the good graces of his friends, the health of his soul—the dead woman shook them all off. "He wanted me and I wanted him, you wanted him and he wanted you," said Eline. "I had to pay, and he must pay, and you must pay when your time comes. When the sin is consummated it will give birth to death."

Kristin felt that she was kneeling with Erlend on a cold stone. He knelt with the red, singed patches on his pale face. She knelt beneath the heavy bridal crown and felt the crushing, oppressive weight in her womb—the burden of sin she was carrying. She had played and romped with her sin, measuring it out as if in a child's game. Holy Virgin—soon it would be time for it to lie fully formed before her, looking at her with living eyes, revealing to her the brands of her sin, the hideous deformity of sin, striking hatefully with misshapen hands at his mother's breast. After she had borne her child, after she had seen the marks of sin on him and loved him the way she had loved her sin, then the game would be played to the end.

Kristin thought: What if she screamed now so that her voice pierced through the song and the deep, droning male voices and reverberated out over the crowd? Would she then be rid of Eline's face? Would life appear in the dead man's eyes? But she clenched her teeth together.

Holy King Olav, I call to you. Among all those in Heaven, I beg you for help, for I know that you loved God's righteousness above all else. I beseech you to protect the innocent one who is in my womb. Turn God's anger away from the innocent, turn it toward me. Amen, in the precious name of the Lord.

"My children are innocent," said Eline, "yet there is no room for them in a land where Christian people live. Your child was conceived out of wedlock just as my children were. You can no more demand justice for your child in the land you have stràyed from than I could demand it for mine."

Holy Olav, I beg for mercy nevertheless, I beg for compassion for my son. Take him under your protection, then I will carry him to your church in my bare feet. I will bring my golden crown to you and place it on your altar, if you will help me. Amen.

Her face was as rigid as stone, she was trying so hard to keep herself calm, but her body trembled and shuddered as she knelt there and was married to Erlend.

And now Kristin sat beside him in the high seat at home and sensed everything around her as a mere illusion in the delirium of fever.

There were musicians playing on harps and fiddles in the high loft; singing and music came from the room below and from out in the courtyard. A reddish glow from the fire outside was visible whenever servants came through the door, carrying things back and forth.

Everyone stood up around the table; she stood between her father and Erlend. Her father announced in a loud voice that now he had given his daughter Kristin to Erlend Nikulaussøn as his wife. Erlend thanked his father-in-law and all the good people who had gathered to honor him and his wife.

Then they told Kristin to sit down, and Erlend placed his wedding gifts in her lap. Sira Eirik and Sir Munan Baardsøn unrolled documents and read off a list of their property. The groomsmen stood by with spears in hand, pounding the shafts on the floor now and then during the reading and whenever gifts or moneybags were placed on the table.

The tabletops and trestles were removed. Erlend led her out onto the floor and they danced. Kristin thought: Our bridesmaids and groomsmen are much too young for us. Everyone who grew up with us has moved away from this region; how can it be that we have come back here?

"You seem so strange, Kristin," whispered Erlend as they danced. "I'm afraid for you, Kristin. Aren't you happy?"

They went from building to building and greeted their guests. All the rooms were filled with many candles, and people were drinking and singing and dancing everywhere. Kristin felt as though everything was so unfamiliar at home, and she had lost all sense of time; the hours and the images flowed around each other, oddly disconnected.

The autumn night was mild. There were fiddlers in the courtyard too, and people dancing around the bonfire. They shouted that the bride and groom must also do them the honor, so Kristin danced with Erlend in the cold, dew-laden courtyard. That seemed to wake her up a little and her head felt clearer.

Out in the darkness a light band of fog hovered over the rushing river. The mountains stood pitch black against the star-strewn sky.

Erlend led her away from the dance and crushed her to him in the darkness beneath an overhanging gallery.

"I haven't even told you that you're beautiful, so beautiful and so lovely. Your cheeks are as red as flames." He pressed his cheek against hers as he spoke. "Kristin, what's the matter?"

"I'm just so tired, so tired," she whispered in reply.

"Soon we'll go in and sleep," said the bridegroom, looking up at the sky. The Milky Way had swung around and was stretching almost due north and south. "Do you know we've never spent a whole night together except that one time when I slept with you in your bedchamber at Skog?"

Some time later Sira Eirik shouted across the courtyard that now it was Monday, and then the women came to lead the bride to bed. Kristin was so tired that she hardly had the energy to resist, as she was supposed to do for the sake of propriety. She let herself be led out of the loft by Fru Aashild and Gyrid of Skog. The groomsmen stood at the foot of the stairs with burning tapers and drawn swords; they formed a circle around the group of women and escorted Kristin across the courtyard, up to the old loft.

The women removed her wedding finery, piece by piece, and laid it aside. Kristin noticed that at the foot of the bed was draped the violet-blue velvet dress that she would wear the next day, and on top of it lay a long, finely pleated, snow-white linen cloth. This was the wimple that married women wore and that Erlend had brought for her; tomorrow she would bind up her hair in a bun and fasten the cloth over it. It looked so fresh and cool and reassuring.

Finally she stood before the bridal bed, in her bare feet, bare-armed, dressed only in the ankle-length, golden-yellow silk shift. They had placed the crown on her head again; the bridegroom would take it off when the two of them were alone.

Ragnfrid placed her hands on her daughter's shoulders and kissed her cheek; the mother's face and hands were strangely cold, but she felt sobs bursting deep inside her breast. Then she threw back the covers of the bed and invited the bride to sit down. Kristin obeyed and leaned back on the silk pillows propped up against the headboard; she had to tilt her head slightly forward because of the crown. Fru Aashild pulled the covers up to Kristin's waist, placed the bride's hands on top of the silk coverlet, and arranged her shining hair, spreading it out over her breast and her slender, naked arms.

Then the men led the bridegroom into the loft. Munan Baardsøn removed Erlend's gold belt and sword; when he hung it up on the wall above the bed, he whispered something to the bride. Kristin didn't understand what he said, but she did her best to smile.

The groomsmen unlaced Erlend's silk clothing and lifted the long, heavy garment over his head. He sat down in the high-backed armchair, and they helped him take off his spurs and boots.

Only once did the bride dare to look up and meet his eyes.

Then everyone wished the couple good night. The wedding guests left the loft. Last to leave was Lavrans Bjørgulfsøn, who closed the door to the bridal chamber.

Erlend stood up and tore off his underclothes and threw them onto the bench. He stood before the bed, took the crown and silk ribbons from Kristin's hair, and placed them over on the table. Then he came back and climbed into bed. And kneeling beside her on the bed, he took her head in his hands, pressing it to his hot, naked chest as he kissed her forehead all along the red band that the crown had made.

She threw her arms around him and sobbed loudly. Sweet and wild, she felt that now it would all be chased away—the terror, the ghostly visions—now, at last, it was just the two of them again. He raised her face for a moment, looked down at her, and stroked her face and her body with his hand, strangely quick and rough, as if he were tearing away a covering.

"Forget," he begged in an ardent whisper, "forget everything, my Kristin—everything except that you're my wife, and I'm your husband."

With his hand he put out the last flame and threw himself down next to her in the dark; he was sobbing too.

"I never believed, never in all these years, that we would live to see this day."

Outside in the courtyard the noise died out, little by little. Weary from the ride earlier in the day and bleary with drink, the guests wandered around a while longer for the sake of propriety, but more and more of them began to slip away to find the places where they would sleep.

Ragnfrid escorted the most honored guests to their beds and bade them good night. Her husband, who should have been helping her with this, was nowhere to be found.

Small groups of youths, mostly servants, were the only ones remaining in the dark courtyard when she finally slipped away to find her husband and take him along to bed. She had noticed that Lavrans had grown exceedingly drunk as the evening wore on.

At last she stumbled upon him as she was walking stealthily outside the farmyard, looking for him. He was lying face down in the grass behind the bathhouse.

Fumbling in the dark, she recognized him—yes, it was him. She thought he was sleeping, and she touched his shoulder, trying to pull him up from the ice-cold ground. But he wasn't asleep—at least not completely.

"What do you want?" he asked, his voice groggy.

"You can't stay here," said his wife. She held on to him, for he was reeling as he stood there. With her other hand she brushed off his velvet clothes. "It's time for us to go to bed too, husband." She put her hand under his arm and led the staggering man up toward the farm. They walked along behind the farmyard buildings.

"*You* didn't look up, Ragnfrid, when you sat in the bridal bed wearing the crown," he said in the same voice. "Our daughter was less modest than you were; her eyes were not shy as she looked at her bridegroom."

"She has waited for him for three and a half years," said the mother quietly. "After that I think she would dare to look up."

"No, the Devil take me if they've waited!" shouted the father, and his wife hushed him, alarmed.

They were standing in the narrow lane between the back of the latrine and the fence. Lavrans slammed his fist against the lower timber of the outhouse.

"I put you here to suffer ridicule and shame, you timber. I put you here so the muck would devour you. I put you here as punishment because you struck down my pretty little maiden. I should have put you above the door of my loft and honored and thanked you with decorative carvings because you saved her from shame and from sorrow—for you caused my Ulvhild to die an innocent child."

He spun around, staggered against the fence, and collapsed against it with his head resting on his arms as he sobbed uncontrollably, with long deep moans in between.

His wife put her arms around his shoulders.

"Lavrans, Lavrans." But she could not console him. "Husband."

"Oh, I never, never, never should have given her to that man. God help me—I knew it all along—he has crushed her youth and her fair honor. I refused to believe it, no, I could not believe such a thing of Kristin. But I knew it all the same. Even so, she is too good for that weak boy, who has shamed both her and himself. I shouldn't have given her to him, even if he had seduced her ten times, so that now he can squander more of her life and happiness."

"What else was there to do?" said Ragnfrid in resignation. "You could see for yourself that she was already his."

"Yes, but I didn't need to make such a great fuss to give Erlend what he had already taken himself," said Lavrans. "It's a fine husband she has won, my Kristin." He yanked at the fence. Then he wept some more. Ragnfrid thought he had grown a bit more sober, but now the drink took the upper hand again.

As drunk as he was and as overcome with despair, she didn't think she could take him up to the hearth room where they were supposed to sleep—it was filled with guests. She looked around. Nearby was a small barn where they kept the best hay for the horses during the spring farm work. She walked over and peered inside; no one was there. Then she led her husband inside and shut the door behind them.

Ragnfrid piled the hay up all around and then placed their capes over both of them. Lavrans continued to weep off and on, and occasionally he would say something, but it was so confused that she couldn't understand him. After a while she lifted his head into her lap.

"My dear husband, since they feel such love for each other, maybe everything will turn out better than we expect. . . ."

Lavrans, who now seemed more clearheaded, replied, gasping, "Don't you see? He now has complete power over her; this man who could never restrain himself. She will find it difficult to oppose anything that her husband wishes—and if she is forced to do so one day, then it will torment her bitterly, that gentle child of mine.

"I don't understand any longer why God has given me so many great sorrows. I have striven faithfully to do His will. Why did He take our children from us, Ragnfrid, one after the other? First our sons, then little Ulvhild, and now I have given the one I love most dearly, without honor, to an unreliable and imprudent man. Now we have only the little one left. And it seems to me unwise to rejoice over Ramborg until I see how things may go for her."

Ragnfrid was shaking like a leaf. Then she touched her husband's shoulder.

"Lie down," she begged him. "Let's go to sleep." And with his head in his wife's arms Lavrans lay quietly for a while, sighing now and then, until finally he fell asleep.

It was still pitch dark in the barn when Ragnfrid stirred; she was surprised she had slept at all. She put out her hand. Lavrans was sitting up with his hands clasped around his knees.

"Are you already awake?" she asked, astonished. "Are you cold?"

"No," he replied, his voice hoarse, "but I can't sleep anymore."

"Is it Kristin you're thinking about?" asked Ragnfrid. "It may turn out better than we think, Lavrans," she told him again.

"Yes, that's what I'm thinking about," said her husband. "Well, well. Maiden or wife, at least she lay in the bridal bed with the one she had given her love to. Neither you nor I did that, my poor Ragnfrid."

His wife gave a deep, hollow moan. She threw herself down next to him in the hay. Lavrans placed his hand on her shoulder.

"But I *could* not," he said with fervor and anguish. "No, I *could* not . . . act toward you the way you wanted me to—back when we were young. I'm not the kind of man . . ."

After a moment Ragnfrid murmured, in tears, "We have lived well together all the same, Lavrans—all these years."

"So I too have believed," he replied gloomily.

His thoughts were tumbling and racing through his mind. That one naked glance which the groom and bride had cast at each other, the two young faces blushing with red flames—he thought it so brazen. It had stung him that she was his daughter. But he kept on seeing those eyes, and he struggled wildly and blindly against tearing away the veil from something in his own heart which he had never wanted to acknowledge—there he had concealed a part of himself from his own wife when she had searched for it.

He had not been able to, he interrupted himself harshly. In the name of the Devil, he had been married off as a young boy; he had not chosen her himself. She was older than he was. He had not desired her. He had not wanted to learn this from her—how to love. He still grew hot with shame at the thought of it—that

she had wanted him to love her when he had not wanted that kind
of love from her. That she had offered him everything that he had
never asked for.

He had been a good husband to her; he believed that himself.
He had shown her all the respect he could, given her full authority,
asked her advice about everything, been faithful to her; and they
had had six children. He had simply wanted to live with her without her always trying to seize what was in his heart—and what he
refused to reveal.

He had never loved anyone. What about Ingunn, Karl's wife at
Bru? Lavrans blushed in the darkness. He had always visited them
when he traveled through the valley. He had probably never spoken to the woman alone even *once*. But whenever he saw her—if
he merely thought of her—he felt something like that first smell of
the earth in the spring, right after the snow had gone. Now he
realized: it could have happened to him too . . . he could have
loved someone too.

But he had been married so young, and he had grown wary.
Then he found that he thrived best out in the wilderness—up on
the mountain plateaus, where every living creature demands wide-
open space, with room enough to flee. Wary, they watch every
stranger that tries to sneak up on them.

Once a year the animals of the forest and in the mountains
would forget their wariness. Then they would rush at their females.
But he had been given his as a gift. And she had offered him everything for which he had never wooed her.

But the young ones in the nest . . . they had been the little warm
spot in his desolation, the most profound and sweetest pleasure of
his life. Those small blonde girls' heads beneath his hand . . .

Married off—that was what had happened to him, practically
unconsulted. Friends . . . he had many, and he had none. War . . .
it had been a joy, but there was no more war; his armor was
hanging up in the loft, seldom used. He had become a farmer. But
he had had daughters; everything he had done in his life became
dear to him because he had done it to provide for those tender
young lives that he held in his hands. He remembered Kristin's tiny
two-year-old body on his shoulder, her flaxen soft hair against his

cheek. Her little hands holding on to his belt while she pressed her hard, round forehead against his shoulder blades when he went riding with her sitting behind him on the horse.

And now she had those ardent eyes, and she had won the man she wanted. She was sitting up there in the dim light, leaning against the silk pillows of the bed. In the glow of the candle she was all golden—golden crown and golden shift and golden hair spread over her naked golden arms. Her eyes were no longer shy.

The father moaned with shame.

And yet it seemed that his heart had burst with blood—for what he had never had. And for his wife, here at his side, to whom he had been unable to give himself.

Sick with compassion, he reached for Ragnfrid's hand in the dark.

"Yes, I thought we lived well together," he said. "I thought you were grieving for our children. And I thought you had a melancholy heart. I never thought that it might be because I wasn't a good husband to you."

Ragnfrid was trembling feverishly.

"You have always been a good husband, Lavrans."

"Hm . . ." Lavrans sat with his chin resting on his knees. "And yet you might have done better if you had been married as our daughter was today."

Ragnfrid sprang up, uttering a low, piercing cry. "You know! How did you find out? How long have you known?"

"I don't know what you're talking about," said Lavrans after a moment, his voice strangely dispirited.

"I'm talking about the fact that I wasn't a maiden when I became your wife," replied Ragnfrid, and her voice was clear and resounding with despair.

After a moment Lavrans said, in the same voice as before, "I never knew of this until now."

Ragnfrid lay down in the hay, shaking with sobs. When the spell had passed she raised her head. A faint gray light was beginning to seep in through the holes in the wall. She could dimly see her husband as he sat there with his hands clasped around his knees, as motionless as if he were made of stone.

"Lavrans—speak to me," she whimpered.

"What do you want me to say?" he asked, not moving.

"Oh, I don't know. You should curse me—strike me . . ."

"It's a little late for that now," replied her husband; there was the shadow of a scornful smile in his voice.

Ragnfrid wept again. "No, I didn't think I was deceiving you, so deceived and betrayed did I feel myself. No one spared me. They brought you . . . I saw you only three times before we were married. I thought you were only a boy, so pink and white . . . so young and childish."

"That I was," said Lavrans, and his voice seemed to acquire more resonance. "And that's why I would have thought that you, who were a woman, you would have been more afraid of . . . of deceiving someone who was so young that he didn't realize . . ."

"I began to think that way later on," said Ragnfrid, weeping. "After I came to know you. Soon the time came when I would have given my soul twenty times over if I could have been without blame toward you."

Lavrans sat silent and motionless.

Then his wife continued, "You're not going to ask me anything?"

"What good would that do now? It was the man who . . . we met his funeral procession at Feginsbrekka, when we were carrying Ulvhild to Nidaros."

"Yes," said Ragnfrid. "We had to step off the road, into the meadow. I watched them carry his bier past, with priests and monks and armed men. I heard that he had been granted a good death—reconciled with God. As we stood there with Ulvhild's litter between us I prayed that my sin and my sorrow might be placed at his feet on that last day."

"Yes, no doubt you did," said Lavrans, and there was that same shadow of scorn in his quiet voice.

"You don't know everything," said Ragnfrid, cold with despair. "Do you remember when he came out to visit us at Skog that first winter after we were married?"

"Yes," said her husband.

"When Bjørgulf was struggling with death . . . Oh, no one had spared me. He was drunk when he did it to me—later he said that he had never loved me, he didn't want me, he told me to forget

about it. My father didn't know about it; he didn't deceive you—
you must never believe that. But Trond . . . my brother and I were
the dearest of friends back then, and I complained to him. He tried
to threaten the man into marrying me—but he was only a boy, so
he lost the fight. Later he advised me not to speak of it and to
take you. . . ."

She sat in silence for a moment.

"When he came out to Skog . . . a year had passed, and I didn't
think much about it anymore. But he came to visit. He said that
he regretted what he had done, that he would have taken me then
if I hadn't been married, that he was fond of me. So he said. God
must judge whether he spoke the truth. After he left . . . I didn't
dare go out on the fjord; I didn't dare because of the sin, not with
the child. And by then I had . . . by then I had begun to love you
so!" She uttered a cry, as if in the wildest torment. Her husband
turned his head toward her.

"When Bjørgulf was born," Ragnfrid went on, "oh, I thought
I loved him more than my own life. When he lay there, struggling
with death, I thought: If he perishes, I will perish too. But I did
not ask God to spare the boy's life."

Lavrans sat for a long time before he asked, his voice heavy and
dead, "Was it because I wasn't his father?"

"I didn't know whether you were or not," said Ragnfrid, stif-
fening.

For a long time both of them sat there, as still as death.

Then the husband said fervently, "In the name of Jesus, Ragnfrid, why are you telling me this—now?"

"Oh, I don't know." She wrung her hands so hard that her
knuckles cracked. "So that you can take vengeance on me. Chase
me away from your manor . . ."

"Do you think that would help me?" His voice was shaking
with scorn. "What about our daughters?" he said quietly. "Kristin,
and the little one?"

Ragnfrid said nothing for a moment.

"I remember how you judged Erlend Nikulaussøn," she murmured. "So how will you judge me?"

A long icy shiver rippled through the man's body, releasing
some of his stiffness.

"You have now . . . we have now lived together . . . for almost twenty-seven years. It's not the same thing as with a man who's a stranger. I can see that you have suffered the greatest anguish."

Ragnfrid collapsed into sobs at his words. She tried to reach out for his hand. He didn't move, but sat as still as a dead man. Then she wept louder and louder, but her husband sat motionless, staring at the gray light around the door. Finally she lay there as if all her tears had run out. Then he gave her arm a fleeting caress. And she began to cry again.

"Do you remember," she said in between her sobs, "that man who once visited us while we were at Skog? The one who knew the old ballads? Do you remember the one about a dead man who had come back from the land of torment and told his son the legend of what he had seen? He said that a great clamor was heard from the depths of Hell, and unfaithful wives ground up earth for their husbands' food. Bloody were the stones that they turned, bloody hung their hearts from their breasts . . ."

Lavrans said nothing.

"For all these years I have thought of those words," said Ragnfrid. "Each day I felt as if my heart were bleeding, for I felt as if I were grinding up earth for your food."

Lavrans didn't know why he answered the way he did. His chest felt empty and hollow, like a man whose heart and lungs had been ripped out through his back. But he placed his hand, heavy and weary, on his wife's head and said, "Earth has to be ground up, my Ragnfrid, before the food can grow."

When she tried to take his hand to kiss it, he pulled it abruptly away. Then he looked down at his wife, took her hand, placed it on his knee, and leaned his cold, rigid face against it. And in this manner they sat there together, without moving and without speaking another word.

EXPLANATORY NOTES

References Used

Blangstrup, Chr., ed. *Salmonsens Konversations Leksikon*. 2nd ed. Copenhagen: J. H. Schultz Forlagsboghandel, 1928.

Knudsen, Trygve, and Alf Sommerfelt, eds. *Norsk Riksmåls Ordbok*. Oslo: Det Norske Akademi for Sprog og Litteratur og Kunnskapsforlaget, 1983.

Mørkhagen, Sverre. *Kristins Verden: Om norsk middelalder på Kristin Lavransdatters tid*. Oslo: J. W. Cappelens Forlag, 1995.

Pulsiano, Phillip, ed. *Medieval Scandinavia: An Encyclopedia*. New York: Garland Publishing Co., 1993.

PART I

Chapter 1

1. *Nidaros*: One of five episcopal seats in Norway during the Middle Ages; now the city of Trondheim. The cathedral in Nidaros housed the famous shrine of Saint Olav and was the destination of thousands of pilgrims every year, particularly during the Feast of Saint Olav in late July. The main road between Oslo and Nidaros passed through Gudbrandsdal, the valley where most of Undset's novel takes place.
2. *vigil nights*: Festive celebrations, called "vigils," were held on the night before many religious holidays.
3. *courtyard*: The multiple buildings of Norwegian farms were laid out around two courtyards: an "inner" courtyard surrounded by the various living quarters, storehouses, and cookhouse; and next to it an "outer" courtyard (or farmyard) surrounded by the stables, cowshed, barn, and other outbuildings. All of the buildings were constructed of wood, and most consisted of a single room that served a specific function on the farm. None of the buildings was more than two stories high. Many had an external gallery (a type of balcony) and stairway along one side. Lofts built above the storerooms were used as bedchambers for both family members and guests. At Jørundgaard, the high loft in the main house was the finest room on the manor

and the one used for feasts and celebrations. Hearth fires in the center of the room (or corner fireplaces on the finer estates) provided the only heat in the living quarters.

4. *his daughter*: Christianity was introduced in Norway in the 11th century, but it wasn't until 1270 that celibacy for priests became part of Norwegian Church law. Even then, it was not strictly enforced, particularly in the countryside.

5. *village*: Unlike villages in the rest of Europe, rural villages in medieval Norway consisted of little more than hamletlike clusters of several large farm-estates, each surrounded by smaller leaseholdings. A settlement of at least three farms constituted a village. Many of them also included a small parish church. Norwegian villages were situated in remote valleys, separated from other settlements by rugged mountains.

6. *river sprite*: In medieval Norway a clear demarcation was made between inside and outside, between the protective circle of human habitation and the dark forces of the wilderness beyond. People believed that the forests and mountains were populated by many types of supernatural beings, which were both unpredictable and menacing.

7. *tar-burners*: Men who produced wood tar, a distilled liquid used for caulking and for preserving wood and rope.

8. *hawk hunters*: Hawks rather than falcons were generally used for hunting in Norway, due to the mountainous, forested terrain. Hawks follow the prey from behind and have an astonishing ability to steer around trees and bushes.

9. *lefse*: A thin pancake of rolled-out dough, folded and served with butter.

Chapter 2

1. *allodial property*: Land held in absolute ownership, without obligation or service to any feudal overlord. In Norway this was an ancient institution in which a man's inherited allodial rights depended on proof that the land had been possessed continuously by his family or kin group for at least four generations. If there was no male heir, the land could be passed down to a female family member.

2. *canons' house*: Canon was an ecclesiastical title for a member of a group of priests who served in a cathedral and who were usually expected to live a communal life.

3. *Minorite*: A widespread order of friars founded by Saint Francis of Assisi in 1223. The monastic movement in Norway began at Selje, outside Bergen, where a Benedictine monastery was dedicated to Saint Alban in the early 12th century. Cistercians later settled on Hovedø,

an island in the Oslo fjord. During the 13th century mendicant orders of Dominican and Franciscan monks established cloisters in the Norwegian bishoprics and trading centers.

4. *windowpane*: The introduction of Christianity brought the art of making stained-glass windows to Scandinavia. Most 14th-century Norwegian manors and farmhouses, however, did not have windows of any kind. Light came into the room from the smoke vent in the roof and from the doorway. In some cases small openings might be cut in the wall and then covered either with horn or with a translucent membrane, usually made from a cow's stomach.

5. *Selje men*: According to legend, Sunniva (a Christian princess of Irish blood) found it necessary to flee England in the 10th century along with her entourage. They sought refuge on the Norwegian island of Selje and took up residence in the caves, where a rock slide eventually buried them. Rumors of a strange light over the island brought the authorities to investigate, and the body of Sunniva was discovered, completely unmarked.

Chapter 3

1. *Saint Olav*: During his reign from 1015 to 1030, King Olav Haraldssøn firmly established Christianity in Norway. Churches were built, priests were appointed, and Nidaros regained its stature as a spiritual center after years of neglect. The king also unified the country under a single monarchy by driving out the noblemen pretenders who had risen up against him. When King Olav died a hero's death in battle, rumors began to circulate that he was a holy man and that miracles had occurred at his grave in Nidaros. Pilgrims began streaming to the cathedral, and the cult of Saint Olav grew rapidly. Olav churches and altars were built throughout Norway, and cloisters were dedicated to the holy man. Although never officially canonized, Olav became the most popular of Norwegian saints and was recognized as the patron saint of the country.

2. *medical things*: The parish priest was often the only one in an isolated settlement who could offer some type of medical skill, based on what he had been taught of the principles of monastic medicine from southern Europe. Otherwise the community had to rely on local people with special knowledge of traditional remedies and curative herbs.

Chapter 4

1. *King Sverre*: Sverre Sigurdssøn asserted his right to the Norwegian throne in 1177 by ousting King Magnus Erlingssøn with the help of

302EXPLANATORY NOTES

the "Birch-Leg" party (see chapter 7, note 2). King Sverre's reign, which lasted until 1202, was marked by a continuous struggle to maintain his right to succession. This period of strife was just the beginning of years of civil war in Norway.
2. *high seat*: The place of honor at the dining table, reserved for the male head of the family or an honored guest. The high seat was in the middle of the table, on the side against the wall.

Chapter 5

1. *ting*: A meeting of free, adult men (women rarely attended) which took place at regular intervals to discuss matters of concern to a particular community. On the local level, the *ting* might consider such issues as pasture rights, fencing, bridge and road construction, taxes, and the maintenance of the local warship. A regional *ting*, attended by chieftains or appointed deputies, would address such issues as defense and legal jurisdiction. The regional *ting* also functioned as a court, although its authority diminished as the power of the king grew. In addition to its regular meetings, a *ting* could be called for a specific purpose, such as the acclamation of a new king.

Chapter 7

1. *prebendary*: A clergyman who received a stipend provided by a special endowment or derived from the revenues of his cathedral or church.
2. *"Birch-Leg" followers*: A political group formed in 1174 in southeastern Norway during the conflict over the rightful successor to the throne. They gained their name from the birchbark they tied to their feet because many were too poor to own shoes. The Birch-Legs supported Sverre in his successful bid to become king in 1177, and many of them were later rewarded by being allowed to marry into distinguished families and enter the higher circles of society.

PART II

Chapter 1

1. *corrodians*: People who donated land or property to a cloister in exchange for a pension or allowance (called a corrody), which permitted the holder to retire into the cloister as a boarder. Some corrodians took their meals at the cloister but lived outside unless they were ill. They were often clothed by the cloister as well.

Chapter 2

1. *townyard*: A plot of land in an urban area where several wooden buildings, each serving a specific function, were clustered around a central courtyard. A townyard might have one or more owners, or it could be subdivided into tenements or other types of property.
2. *ørtug*: A coin equal in value to one-third of an *øre* or 10 *penninger*. One *øre* was equal to one-eighth of a *mark*.
3. *silver spurs*: Golden spurs, not silver, were a sign of knighthood.

Chapter 4

1. *campaign*: The support of war campaigns initiated by the king was based on a defense system which divided Norway first into counties and then into parishes. Each county was required to supply and equip a warship, and each parish had to provide a member of the ship's crew. In addition, taxes were levied to finance the campaigns. Wealthy landowners, who had both horses and weapons needed for the war, were required to do military service and were thus exempted from these taxes.
2. *Duke Eirik's devastating incursion*: Duke Eirik Magnussön of Sweden attempted to extend his power by attacking Oslo in 1308 and again in 1310. Both incursions were repelled, but after the second one the Norwegian king launched a retaliatory campaign, which was a great drain on the country's resources.

Chapter 5

1. *against the orders of the bishop*: Duke Haakon Magnussøn provided land for a Franciscan monastery to be built in Oslo, but bitter opposition from the bishop led to a prohibition against the building project. The monks, however, were not subject to the bishop's authority and proceeded with their plans. The bishop then refused them permission to preach in his dioceses, which rankled the Franciscans but did not stop them. Infuriated, the local ecclesiastical officials finally ordered armed men to attack and destroy the building site. The friars complained to the Pope, who interceded on their behalf in 1291, and the monastery in Oslo was finally built.

PART III

Chapter 5

1. *Bretland*: Old Norwegian name for Wales.

Chapter 8

1. *escorted to bed*: A pre-Christian wedding ritual, still prevalent in medieval times, which required that six people witness the couple openly going to bed; only then would the marriage be considered legally binding.

2. *lur horn*: A trumpetlike wind instrument without a mouthpiece, made from a hollow piece of wood wrapped with bark.

LIST OF HOLY DAYS

Saint Gregor's Day	March 12
Holy Cross Day	May 3
Saint Halvard's Day	May 15
Saint Jon's Day	June 24
Saint Margareta's Day	July 20
Saint Olav's Day	July 29
Saint Lavrans's Day	August 10
Assumption Day	August 15
Saint Bartholomew's Day	August 24
Feast of the Birth of Mary	September 8
Holy Cross Day	September 14
Michaelmas	September 29
Saint Clement's Day	November 23
Saint Andreas's Day	November 30
Whitsunday	First Sunday after Easter
Advent	December *(varies annually)*
Lent	Winter *(varies annually)*

FOR THE BEST IN CLASSICS, LOOK FOR THE

"No other novelist has bodied forth the medieval world with such richness and fullness."
— *The New York Herald Tribune*

Norway's most beloved author, Sigrid Undset won the Nobel Prize for Literature in 1928. These exquisite and definitive translations of Undset's medieval epic *Kristin Lavransdatter* are by award-winning translator Tiina Nunnally.

KRISTIN LAVRANSDATTER I: THE WREATH
Set in fourteenth-century Norway, the first volume introduces a strong-willed heroine who has long captivated contemporary readers. With her headstrong pursuit of her own happiness, Kristin becomes a woman who not only loves with power and passion but intrepidly confronts her sexuality. *ISBN 0-14-118041-2*

KRISTIN LAVRANSDATTER II: THE WIFE
The Wife explores Kristin's tumultuous married life with Erlend Nikulaussøn. His single-minded determination to become an influential political figure forces Kristin to take over management of his estate, Husaby, while raising their seven sons. *ISBN 0-14-118128-1*

KRISTIN LAVRANSDATTER III: THE CROSS
The final volume of the trilogy finds Kristin returning with Erlend to her childhood home and increasingly worried about her sons' prospects. *The Cross* chronicles the trials and losses Kristin must bear and stresses Undset's belief that the spiritual world has primacy over the material one. *ISBN 0-14-118235-0*

**Back in print, Undset's extraordinary
first medieval novel, originally published in 1909.**

GUNNAR'S DAUGHTER
This dramatic tale of a female avenger takes place in Norway and Iceland at the beginning of the eleventh century, during the violent Saga Age. The beautiful, spoiled Vidgis Gunnarsdatter, raped by the man she had wanted to love, must reconstruct her life and restore her family's honor. *ISBN 0-14-118020-X*